RACHEL CAINE

ASH AND QUILL

THE GREAT LIBRARY

BERKLEY

NEW YORK

BERKLEY
An imprint of Penguin Random House LLC
375 Hudson Street, New York, New York 10014

Copyright © 2017 by Rachel Caine LLC
Readers Guide copyright © 2017 by Penguin Random House LLC
Excerpt from *Smoke and Iron* copyright © 2018 by Rachel Caine LLC

ISBN 9780451473158

The Library of Congress has cataloged the hardcover edition of this title as follows:

Names: Caine, Rachel, author.
Title: Ash and quill/Rachel Caine.
Description: First Edition. | New York: Berkley, 2017. | Series: The Great Library; 3
Identifiers: LCCN 2016058978 (print) | LCCN 2017004422 (ebook) |
ISBN 9780451472410 (hardback) | ISBN 9780698180833 (ebook)
Subjects: LCSH: Libraries—Fiction. | Alexandrian Library—Fiction. |
GSAFD: Alternative histories (Fiction) | Dystopias.
Classification: LCC PS3603.O557 A93 2017 (print) | LCC PS3603.O557 (ebook) |
DDC 813/.6—dc23
LC record available at https://lccn.loc.gov/2016058978

Berkley hardcover edition / July 2017
Berkley trade paperback edition / June 2018

Printed in the United States of America
1 3 5 7 9 10 8 6 4 2

Cover art and design by Katie Anderson
Cover photograph of library by Joop van Meer

To all those who face change without fear. Go forward.
To the ever-transforming glory of the public library,
without which we would all be diminished.
No one with a book is ever alone, even in the darkest moments.
We are all book lovers.
And we all chase the Great Library of Alexandria, one book at a time.

ACKNOWLEDGMENTS

It would be impossible to thank everybody who encouraged and helped this story along, but I must especially thank Anne Sowards, who saw a better book than the one I imagined, and encouraged me to chase it.

But *special* thanks go to my fantastic volunteer beta readers: Zahdia, Fauzia, Zaheerah, Mona, and Sajda.

Whatever mistakes I've made are all mine. Whatever shines is theirs.

ASH AND QUILL

EPHEMERA

Text of a letter from the Archivist Magister, head of
the Great Library of Alexandria, to the commander
of the High Garda of the Great Library. Not indexed in
the Codex. Restricted viewing.

The Welsh army has broken treaty with the Library and shamelessly looted the valuable books located in our daughter library in London. St. Paul's Serapeum was a monument and sacred space of knowledge for hundreds of years, and now they claim it for their own.

We excused the destruction of our Oxford Serapeum as an accident of war. But this? This is too much. The Welsh king has gone too far and must be shown his mistake.

The king of Wales and England must make immediate reparation for our losses or face the consequences. There are stirrings of rebellion against us on every front, and we must contain and control kingdoms and countries that refuse our authority.

I will allow no further disobedience, whether that comes from foreign kings or our own Scholars.

The penalty for traitors is death.

Handwritten addendum to the Artifex Magnus by the Archivist

I care little for provincial kingdoms and their spats, but London is the last place our troubling band of Scholar-traitors was spotted . . . and near St. Paul's, too. I know the Welsh have no love for us, but under threat of total war with the High Garda, they'll hand them over. If they're still alive.

Handwritten reply from the Artifex Magnus

They were seen inside St. Paul's by one of the last librarians to flee, so we know that they were, at least, alive then. Whether they escaped in the confusion or are in a mass grave dug by the Welsh remains to be seen. I wouldn't assume them dead. Christopher Wolfe should have been dead years ago, and none of us has managed to put him in the ground yet.

In regard to your earlier request, I must regretfully recommend that Gregory be appointed to the position of Obscurist Magnus. I know he's a vile creature, but the only other candidate is Eskander. I had him dragged out of his self-imposed prison to be shown to me, so I could ensure, on your behalf, that he's still alive and well. Still a lot of fight left in him, no doubt about that, but as he swore so long ago, he's saying nothing. Not a word. He decided decades ago to make himself useless to us, and I think he's succeeded all too well. Don't pin your hopes on him.

He did write a note for you. I took the liberty of reading it, and I'll just say that he'd like you dead. I suppose he blames you for Keria Morning's death, the way his son does. I suppose neither of them is particularly wrong, come to that.

Don't worry about your rogue Scholars. We've put a high price on their heads. Their own families will be tempted to sell them soon enough.

EPHEMERA

Text of a paper letter from the Burner leader of London to Willinger Beck, head of the Burner city of Philadelphia. Destroyed upon receipt.

I send you a gift out of the ashes of London: four full Scholars of the Library—a gloriously decorated High Garda captain and two of his soldiers, and . . . best of all . . . an Obscurist! Not a half-wild hedge witch, but a real, Iron Tower—trained Obscurist with power even I've never seen.

Not only that—they come bearing their own gifts. It's said that the Scholars have some secret that might well destroy the Great Library's power forever. I suppose it's up to you to find a way to coax that out of them.

Strength and courage, my brother.

CHAPTER ONE

Books burned so easily.

Paper tanned in the fluttering heat, then sparked sullen red at the edges. Flames left fragile curls of ash. Leather bindings smoked and shriveled and blackened, just like burning flesh.

Jess Brightwell watched the fire climb the pyramid of books and willed himself not to flinch as each layer caught. His brain raced with involuntary calculations. *One hundred books in five layers.* The burning bottom layer: *forty-four gone.* The second level held another thirty-two, and it was already billowing dull smoke. The next had eighteen more volumes, then five on top of that. The pyramid was capped by one lone book that sat tantalizingly ready for the grabbing. Easy to save as the flames climbed the stack, consuming layer after layer and burning something inside him blacker and colder.

If I could just save one . . .

But he couldn't save anything. Even himself, at the moment.

Jess's head hurt fiercely in the glare of the sun. Everything was still a blur. He remembered the chaos of London as the Welsh army descended on it, a battle even he had never imagined the English would lose; he remembered the mesmerizing sight of the dome of St. Paul's catching fire above them as librarians struggled to save what they could.

He remembered his father and brother, when it counted, turning their backs on him and running.

Most of all, he remembered being forced into the Translation Chamber, and the sickening ripping sensation of being destroyed and created again far, far from London . . . here in the Burner-held city of Philadelphia.

Sent to the rebellious colonies of *America*.

Jess and his friends hadn't been granted any time to recover; they'd been dragged, still sick and weak, to what must have once been a sports stadium; in better times, maybe it had been filled with cheering crowds. Now it was half ruined, melted into a misshapen lump on one side of the concrete stands, and instead of a grassy field in the middle there were bare ground and a funeral pyre of books.

Jess couldn't take his eyes off of them as they burned, because he was thinking, sickly, *We're next.*

"Jess," said Scholar Christopher Wolfe, who was on his knees next to him in the dirt. "They're not original books. They're Blanks." That was true. But Jess didn't miss the tremors running through the man, either. The shine in Wolfe's dark eyes was made of pure, unholy rage. He was right: Blanks were just empty paper and bindings provided by the Great Library of Alexandria, vessels to hold words copied on command from originals kept safe within the Library's archives. These were empty symbols that were burning. In any Library territory, they'd be cheaply and easily replaced, and nothing would be lost at all.

But seeing them destroyed still hurt. He'd been raised to love books, for all that his family had smuggled them, sold them, and profited from them.

Words were sacred things, and this was a particularly awful kind of heresy.

As he watched, the last book shivered in the rising heat, as if it might break free and escape the fire. But then the edges crisped, paper smoked, and it was gone in rising curls of ash.

Scholar Khalila Seif knelt on his left side, as straight and quiet as a statue. She looked perfectly calm; she had her hands resting lightly on her thighs, her head high and her hijab fluttering lightly at the edges in the hot breeze. Beneath the black silk Scholar's outer robe she wore a still-clean dress, only a little muddy and ashen at the hem from their progress through London. Next to Khalila, Glain Wathen looked as if she were only momentarily frozen in the act of rising—a lithe warrior, all vibrating tension. Beyond her was Thomas Schreiber, then Morgan Hault, then—last and least, in Jess's thoughts—Dario Santiago. Outcast, even among their little band of exiles.

To Jess's right was Scholar Wolfe and, beyond him, Captain Santi. That was the entire roll call of their party of prisoners, and not a single useful weapon among them. They'd not had time to make a plan. Jess couldn't imagine that any of them had much worthwhile to say just now.

There was an audience in the crumbling stands: the good citizens of Philadelphia. A ragged, patchwork crowd of hard men and women and children who'd survived starvation, deprivation of all sorts, and constant attacks. They had no pity for the pampered servants of the Great Library.

What would Wolfe tell them if he had the chance? That the Great Library was still a great and precious thing, something to be saved, not destroyed? That the cancer that had rotted it from within could still be healed? They'd never believe it. Jess took in a deep breath and choked on the stench of burning books. *Imaginary Wolfe*, he thought, *gave crap speeches.*

A man dressed in a fine-cut suit of black wool stepped up to block Jess's view of the pyre. He was a tall, bespectacled fellow, full of the confidence of a man of property; he could have, by appearance, been a banker or a lawyer in a more normal sort of place. The smoke that rose black against the pale blue morning sky seemed to billow right from the crown of his head. His collar-length hair was the same gray as the ash.

Willinger Beck. Elected leader of the Burners of Philadelphia—and, by extension, all Burners everywhere, since this place was the symbol of their fanatical movement. The head fanatic in a movement composed entirely of fanatics.

He studied their faces without making any comment at all. He must have enjoyed what he saw.

"Very impressive waste of resources," Scholar Wolfe said. His tone was sour, and completely bracing to Jess. *Wolfe sounds the same, no matter what.* "Is this a prelude to setting us on fire next?"

"Don't be ridiculous," Beck said. "Surely our learned guests understand the power of a symbol."

"This is barbaric," Khalila said from Jess's other side. "A criminal waste."

"My dear Scholar, we handwrite our own books here. On paper we rescue by picking apart the Library's Blanks and destroying their alchemical bindings. You speak of us as barbaric? Do you know whose symbols you wear? *You will not take that tone with us.*" At the end of it, his friendly voice sharpened into an edge.

Jess said, "Talk to her that way again and I'll snap your kneecaps."

His hands were not bound. He was free to move; they all were. Which meant they could, as a group, do serious damage before they were taken down by the Burner guards stationed behind them.

In theory, anyway. He knew the guard directly behind him held a gun barrel trained on the back of his neck, precisely where it could blow a hole that would instantly end his life.

But he'd gotten Beck's attention, and his stare. *Good.*

"Here now," Beck said, back to mild and reproving. "We should be friends, after all; we share a common sense that the Great Library of Alexandria has become a destructive parasite. It's no longer some great, untouchable icon. There's no need for anger between us."

"I'm not familiar with American customs," said Captain Santi, on the other side of Wolfe. He sounded pleasant and calm. Jess sincerely doubted he was either. "Is this how you treat your friends?"

"Considering you alone put three of my men in the infirmary on your arrival, even in your weakened state? Yes," Beck said. "Captain Santi, we really do resist the Library, just as I am told you do. So should we all. The Library grants people pitiful drops of knowledge while it hoards up oceans for itself. Surely you, too, must see the way it manipulates the world to its own gain." He nodded at the black robe that Wolfe wore. "The common man calls you Scholars by another name: *Stormcrows*. That black robe isn't a sign of your scholarship anymore, and it isn't an object of reverence. It's a sign of the chaos and destruction you bring down in your wake."

"No," Wolfe said. "It still stands for what it's always stood for: that I will die to preserve the knowledge of this world. I may hate the Archivist, I may want him and his brand of greed and cruelty gone, but I still hold to the ideals. The robe is a symbol of that." He paused, and his tone took on silky, dark contempt. "You, of all people, understand the power of a symbol."

"Oh, I do," Beck said. "Take the robe off."

Wolfe's chin went up, just a fraction. He was staring straight at Beck. His graying hair whipped in the hot breeze from the pyre, and still he didn't blink as he said, simply, "No."

"Last chance, Scholar Wolfe. If you repudiate the Library now, it will all go better for you. The Library certainly doesn't stand by you."

"No."

Beck nodded to someone behind them, and Jess, from the corner of his eye, saw the flash of a knife being drawn. He tried to turn, but a hand fell hard on his shoulder, and the gun barrel pressed close enough to bruise the base of his skull.

He was already too late for any kind of rescue.

One of Beck's guards grabbed Wolfe's black robe by the sleeve and sliced the silk all the way to the neck—left sleeve, then right, efficient and ruthlessly precise cuts. With the flourish of a cheap street magician, the man tore the robe from Wolfe to leave him kneeling in plain, dark street clothes. He held the mangled fabric up above his head. A breeze heated by burning books caught the silk and fluttered it out like a ragged banner.

Wolfe's expression never changed, but next to him, Niccolo Santi let out a purely murderous growl and came half up from his knees before the guard behind him slammed a heavy metal club into the back of his head. The blow crashed Santi back down. He looked dazed but still dangerous.

The man who'd taken Wolfe's robe paraded it around, as proud as a strutting rooster, and from the stands applause and cheers swelled. It nearly covered up the muttering roar of burning books. Beck ignored that and pointed to Khalila. "Now her." Another guard stepped up to the young woman, but before he could use his knife, Khalila held up both hands. The gesture looked like an order, not a surrender, and it stopped the guard in his tracks.

"I will stand up now," Khalila said. "I will not resist."

The guard looked uncertainly at Beck, who raised his eyebrows and nodded.

Jess watched her tensely from the corner of his eye as she stood in a smooth, calm motion, and from her other side, he saw Glain doing the same, openly ready to fight if Khalila gave a sign she needed help.

But Khalila lifted her hands in a graceful, unhurried way to unfasten the catch that held the black silk robe closed at her throat. She slipped the robe off her shoulders and caught it as it fluttered down, then folded it with precise movements into a neat, smooth square.

Then she took a step forward and held the folded silk out, one hand supporting it, the other on top, like a queen presenting a gift to a subject. In one calculated move, she had taken Willinger Beck's symbol away and made it her own. Jess felt a fierce surge of savage joy at the look on Beck's face. He'd just been bested by a girl a quarter of his age, and the taste seemed bitter.

But he wasn't taking that without hitting back, and Jess saw that an instant before Beck grabbed the folded robe and flung it into the pyre of burning books. Petty contempt, but it struck Jess like a gut punch. He saw a shiver run through Khalila, too . . . just the barest flinch. Like Wolfe, she lifted her chin. Defiant.

"Only cowards are so afraid of a scrap of cloth," she said, clear enough to carry to the stands. There was a shimmer in her eyes: anger, not tears. "We may not agree with the Archivist; we may want to see him gone and better Scholars take his place. But we still stand for knowledge. You stand for *nothing*."

Beck looked past her and gave a bare, terse nod to a guard, and in the next instant, Khalila was seized, yanked back, and forced to her knees. She almost fell, toppling toward Jess. He instinctively put out a hand to help her, and her fingers twined with his.

That was the instant he understood what she was *really* about. Removing her robe hadn't been just defiance; it was distraction. Concealed between her fingers, she held a single metal hairpin—one she'd plucked from under her hijab.

She knew that in Jess's hands, a hairpin was as good a weapon as any.

A vast, cooling sense of relief washed through his chest, and he exchanged a swift glance with her as he slipped the pin between his own fingers. *She's right. Sooner or later, there'll be locks to open. If we live so long.*

He let go of her and hid the metal inside his shirtsleeve. He'd need to find a better hiding place for it, but that would do for now.

Beck ignored them. He was busy throwing Wolfe's robe to the flames. Farther down the line, they had taken Thomas's robe, and Dario's. Four robes flung onto the pyre, one by one, while the crowd roared approval. Jess expected the silk to burn fast, but instead the robes smoked, smoldered, shriveled in, and finally turned to gray and began to powder at the edges. Hardly any drama to it at all, which must have been disappointing for Beck's purposes. A stench of burning hair joined the meaty reek of crisping leather bindings, and for a moment, Jess had the vision again of a body burning in those flames.

One of their bodies.

"Now we may start fresh," Beck said after the silk was nothing but a tangle of ashes. "You are no longer part of the Library. In time, you'll come to see that we are your brothers and sisters."

"If you want to convince us of that, let us stand up," Santi said, and Jess could hear the ragged edge in his voice. A trickle of bright red blood ran down the sharp plane of his cheekbone from his hairline, but his eyes were clear and intensely focused on Beck. "Let us up and see how *fraternal* we can be."

"In time," Beck said. "In due time, Captain."

Jess swallowed and tasted ashes. *Fraternal.* He didn't want to believe that he and his friends—for whom this had started as personal loyalty, personal risk, and nothing they'd deliberately planned—had anything in common with Burners. He loathed them, even though they wanted books to be free and owned by anyone who wanted them. He'd grown up a book smuggler, so by definition he believed in that same ideal.

But he didn't believe in indiscriminate murder, either, and the Burners had been known to incinerate the guilty and the innocent alike, just to make their point.

The Great Library, for all its shining history and high ideals, had just as rotten a heart; it might even be worse. The Archivist Magister might love books just as he did, but that evil old man loved power far more. He and the Curia were part of a system that had turned toxic hundreds of years ago, when a long-dead Archivist had chosen to destroy an invention, and a Scholar, to keep his firm hold on power. Every Archivist since had chosen the same dark road. Maybe now they couldn't see any other way.

But there had to be a way. The Library was too precious to let it fall without trying to save what was good at its heart. And if it was just the eight of them who'd fight to save it . . . then that was a start.

Saving anything didn't seem very likely. He was on his knees in a ruined arena in a Burner-held city, with nothing but a hairpin. Still, to a criminal like him? A hairpin was enough.

"I'll ask you now," Beck said, raising his voice to be heard in the stands. The echoes came back cold. "Will you swear to join our city?

To work for the ruin of the Great Library that keeps its foot on our necks, and the necks of every man, woman, and child on this earth? To do what must be done to prove our cause?"

He was walking down the line. He stopped in front of Dario Santiago.

Jess forgot to take in the next breath, because if there was a weak link in their chain, Beck had put his finger directly on it. Dario would do what was good for Dario. Without fail. None of them expected anything else at this point.

Dario looked tired. He'd suffered some burns—so had Jess—in London, and his normal cocky grace was gone. He looked beaten.

So it came as a shock when he got to his feet to face Beck and said, very clearly, in as strong a voice as Jess could remember from him, "Really? Do I look like a witless Burner? Don't insult me with the question." He followed it up with something in Spanish so fast Jess missed the meaning, but from scattered laughter in the stands, it must have been cutting.

Beck's expression didn't change. He took a step onward. Morgan Hault was next, and just like Dario, she stood up. Not especially tall, not especially strong. Her hair blew wild around her face, and if she was frightened, she didn't show it as she said, "No." A clear, firm, unshakeable denial.

They held Thomas down on his knees, probably worrying that he'd do real damage if they let him get up. He gave his answer with a sweet, broad smile. "Of course not." He almost seemed amused.

Glain definitely wasn't, and since she was held down as well, she contented herself with a rude gesture and a long string of Welsh syllables. Jess knew the gist of it well enough: *screw off.* Very Glain.

Khalila got up, too. Like Thomas, she was smiling. "I absolutely will not agree," she said. "Foolish of you to even ask."

Jess stayed down. No choice, really, since the guard behind him whispered, "Stand up and I'll splatter you all over the ground." But Beck barely paused to hear his clipped *no* before moving on to Wolfe.

Wolfe had been still and calm the whole time, but it was a brittle kind of stillness. His answer came, sharp: "Never."

Next to him, Santi bared his teeth in a savage grin. "So say we all."

Beck stared at them for such a long, silent moment that Jess started to sweat; that pyre was still hot, and Beck looked like a man who liked to make an example. But he finally shook his head and beckoned a woman of African descent who looked every bit as competent and dangerous as Glain. The woman moved like a trained soldier, though she wore no uniform, only a plain-spun shirt and trousers with heavy boots.

"Very well. Lock them up—"

"There's the good Burner welcome I was waiting for," Wolfe said sourly.

"—and see that they are well treated," Beck continued. But he glanced at Wolfe, and behind the artifice of good humor, there was something far darker. He was the leader of a city that was fighting a war, and worse than that, he was a true believer. A fanatic who didn't hesitate to kill, maim, and destroy in his attempts to make the world in his own image. "But search them thoroughly. I want no mistakes."

Jess's fingers tightened over the fragile metal pin he'd embedded in the fabric of his shirtsleeve. He'd need to find a good hiding place. Quickly.

By the time he was allowed up off his knees, he found his legs were steady, and his stomach, too. At least this horrible bit of theater had given them all time to recover from the shock of Translation and start to put their brains to use.

Philadelphia was going to be, in its own way, as dangerous a place as London, Rome, or Alexandria. It was impossible to know yet what the Burners wanted from them, or what they'd have to do to survive.

But that didn't matter. The idea of going behind bars actually cheered him up.

After all, prisons—like locks—were made to be broken.

The guards weren't stupid, which was too bad; they separated the party out, two by two, and shoved them into barred cells inside a long, low building made of heavy stone. Cramped ceilings and rudimentary toilets, but it was far from the worst Jess had ever seen. Didn't even smell particularly bad. Maybe crime was low in Burnertown.

But, more important, the locks on the cells were large, crude, and old.

By a little subtle maneuvering that his friends managed without *seeming* to manage it, everyone sorted out nicely in ordered pairs: Wolfe and Santi, Glain and Khalila, Thomas and Jess. Dario and Morgan each managed their own private cells, which made Jess a little jealous. But only a little, because he needed to stay close to Thomas. The German had only just escaped from one prison. He might need help adjusting to yet another one.

"Search them thoroughly. You don't have to be gentle about it," the tall woman—Beck's captain, Jess thought—said, and exited without waiting to see it done. She left behind three men to do the job, which did seem adequate with the cell doors shut and locked.

"Right," said one of the men—the squad leader, Jess thought—who had a dramatic scar on one cheek: a melted look, courtesy of Greek fire. He didn't seem particularly nice and, after considering the pickings, unlocked the cell that Glain and Khalila shared first. "You. Tall one. Step out."

That was, of course, Glain. She likely looked to be the bigger threat, though appearances *might* have been deceptive, depending on the situation. Glain shrugged, stepped out, and put her hands flat on the far stone wall of the hallway. Her quick glance at Wolfe asked the silent question: *Are we cooperating?* Jess couldn't see the reply from where he stood—there was a wall between his cell and the next, where Wolfe and Santi were held—but he saw her relax, so the answer must have been *yes.*

Glain took having a guard's hands on her with the same indifference she gave most issues of modesty. Beyond saying, "You missed a spot. Bad form," to the man searching her, she gave him no trouble.

"Right. Back in. You, in the veil. Come out."

"It's not a veil," Khalila said as she moved into the center hallway. "It's called a hijab. Or a scarf, if you like."

The guard surveyed her uncertainly from head to toe. He was clearly not familiar with the traditional clothing that Khalila favored; Glain in battered trousers hadn't bothered him, but the volume of that dress did. "Against the wall," he said. Khalila obligingly leaned, and though she clearly didn't like being touched, especially so freely, she said nothing as the man searched her. "All right. Turn around."

She did, and started back to her cell. He put out a hand to stop her. "No. Scarf comes off."

"It is against my religion. Does no one follow the Prophet here, peace and blessings be upon him? Here. I've removed the pins from my hair," Khalila said, and extended her hand to surrender a palmful of them. "I have nothing else hidden beneath it. I swear that."

"I don't trust your oath, *Scholar*," the man said, and without any warning, he stepped behind her, grabbed a handful of the fabric of her hijab and yanked. Khalila's head snapped back as the scarf was dragged off, and she let out a small cry of dismay and shock as she grabbed for the fabric. He shoved her hard against the bars of the cell with his hand on the back of her neck. "Stay still!"

"Hey! Hands off!" Jess shouted as a sudden ball of fury ignited inside him like Greek fire and he grabbed the bars and rattled them. Dario swore to knife the man in his sleep.

Khalila didn't make another sound.

The guard pulled the scarf loose from where it sagged around Khalila's neck, and a riot of smooth, basalt black hair cascaded over her shoulders. He crumpled the fabric in his hand and stuck it in his belt. "Better," he said to her. "No special treatment around here for you or whatever god you follow, *Scholar*. Best you learn that quickly."

Khalila turned whip fast to grab the man's wrist and extended and twisted his whole arm. She continued the spin and pressed her palm hard into the back of his elbow, reversing it to the breaking point, and held him there as he cried out. He shifted to try to take the strain off the joint, and she pressed harder. This time, she got a shrill cry. His knees buckled.

The other guards moved forward, and Glain glided out to get in their way. Khalila acknowledged that with a quick flick of a glance but kept her attention on the man she had in the painful, joint-cracking hold.

"Don't make me break it," she said. "Never do that again. *Never*. It's insulting and disrespectful. Do you understand?"

"Let go!" he panted. Khalila took her head scarf from his belt and shoved him away. He got his balance and lowered his chin, and Jess saw him reach for a knife at his belt.

Glain, without a word, turned immediately and landed a swift, strong uppercut that jerked the guard's head up and rolled his eyes back to the whites. Her distraction gave the other two guards an opening, of course, and one grabbed Glain and pushed her back against the wall. He slammed a fist straight into her guts. She grinned with bare, wet teeth. "Weak sauce, Burner," she almost purred. "Have another go."

He followed up with a second punch, harder. Useless, and Jess knew it; Glain had made a lot of money in the High Garda barracks with this trick. As long as she had time to tense her abdominal muscles, he wouldn't do her damage, and she'd never let on that it hurt. A bloody savage kind of game, but it suited Glain to the ground.

"Enough," the last guard said, and shoved his friend back when he prepared to punch Glain again. "You, get back in the cell and there'll be no more trouble," he told Khalila. "I won't touch you if you don't force me to it. All right? You can keep the scarf. No need for any more of this."

Khalila nodded. "Thank you," she said. "You might want to check on your friend. I think he might need a Medica." She stepped over the man Glain had put down as she slid the scarf back over her head and began to tuck it into shape.

"You too, soldier. Get back in," the third guard said to Glain, and stood out of her way. She hadn't stopped smiling—it was a frighteningly feral thing—and walked without a care in the world into the cell. She managed to step on the fallen guard as she did so. He didn't even groan.

"I appreciate the help." Khalila held up her palm; Glain casually slapped it.

"Oh, I did it for the fun," she said, and, with a flourish Jess rather enjoyed, swung the cell door closed once she was inside. It reminded him of Khalila removing her Scholar's robe before it could be taken. "Well? Are you planning to lock it, *y twpsyn?*" He didn't know the Welsh term, but he assumed it wasn't flattering.

The guard who'd punched Glain stepped up to turn the key. "Next time," he said to Glain.

"Precious, next time I won't just stand there," she replied. "And after that, I'll send flowers."

Jess laughed. "You know, Glain, there was a time when I didn't like you. I was very stupid."

Glain gave him that half-wild grin. "Shut up. You still are."

The guards were a lot more careful, and they chose Morgan next; while they focused on her, Jess leaned against the bars with his arms folded to wait his turn. That conveniently put his right hand close enough to extract the precious metal hairpin from his sleeve and tease a long loose strand from the fraying cloth. The resulting thread wasn't as long as he would have preferred, but he was low on options. He tied the string one-handed onto the pin, made a running loop on the other end, and raised his hand to cover a cough as the guards finished with Morgan and locked her door. He pushed the loop over a back tooth and swallowed, and for a perilous second he was afraid the pin would catch in his throat before it slid through to dangle at the end of the string, halfway down his gullet.

It wasn't comfortable.

"Now you," the guard said, and unlocked the door to their cell. "Big one. No resistance or I swear, we'll put you down for good." He pulled a gun this time and leveled it on Thomas as the big young man stepped out. "Face the wall. Hands up and flat on the stone. No sudden moves."

Thomas seemed perfectly content to be searched, which was a relief to everyone; since his rescue from the Library's secret prison, his reactions had an unpredictable quality that put Jess on edge at moments like this. But he stayed docile, was pronounced clear, and was sent back into the cell without trouble.

Jess's turn went fast, but not fast enough; he'd never been as good at this magic trick as his brother Brendan, and sweat broke out on his brow as he fought the urge to gag the string and hairpin up again. He could maddeningly, constantly feel the foreign object in his throat, bouncing against tender parts, and even the fastest sweep of the guard's hands felt like eternity. It was important not to panic. He'd seen smugglers choke on swallowed keys.

"All right," the guard said, and shoved him back into the cell. "Next. You. Spaniard."

Jess sat and slowed his breathing and pulse as best he could while the search went on. His stomach roiled and rebelled, but he somehow kept it from destroying him. Dario's search began and ended. The third guard had come around by then, muttering drunkenly about revenge, and was sent on his way to see a Medica.

Even Wolfe and Santi submitted without trouble, as if they knew how important it was to get the guards out quickly.

The outer door finally shut behind the departing guards with a metallic clang, and Jess closed his eyes as he listened for the sound of keys. He heard them. So, he had individual cell locks to contend with and an outer door to get through as well. And one small hairpin to his name.

"They're gone," Thomas told him, and Jess opened his eyes. "You've turned the color of spoiled milk. Are you sick?"

Jess held up a finger to signal him to wait and then reached into his mouth to take hold of the slippery piece of string. *Relax,* he told himself, and gave it a steady pull. He couldn't hold back the half-retching cough as the pin slid free of his throat, but the temporary nausea was a small price to pay for the triumph of holding that pin up for Thomas to inspect. "Old street magician's trick," Jess told him, and pulled the looped string off his tooth. "Swallow it down, vomit it up. Preferably without vomit."

"That," Thomas said with real admiration, "is *disgusting*."

"Agreed." Jess wiped the hairpin off and carefully bent it flat, then began to work the center until it snapped into two halves. "So many useful things you learn running with a bad set."

"So I'm learning," Dario said from across the way. "What good will that do?"

"Lockpicks."

"So? You unlock our cells. We're still trapped in Philadelphia."

"Then I won't unlock yours."

"I take it back, dear English!"

Jess ignored him as he bent one of the halves into a tension wrench and the other into the beginnings of a pick. Thomas leaned forward to watch him work. "Do you need help?" he asked, and Jess shook his head. "Dario is right, you know. Opening a lock isn't escape."

"It's one step toward it, and Dario's never right."

"You know I can hear you," Dario said. "Because you're talking out loud."

"Why do you think I said it?" Jess used the fulcrum of a cell bar to put a bend into the pick, then knelt at the door to try out the feel. It required adjustments, which he made patiently, bit by bit, testing the lock and learning its peculiarities.

"Khalila, are you all right?" Dario asked. His voice had shifted, gone warm and quiet. "I'm sorry for what he did to you. That was vile."

"I'm all right," she said. She couldn't see Dario from her side. Walls between them. "No damage done. You all stood with me. That matters more." Her voice was steady, but Jess could see her face. She was still shaken, and angry.

"Well," he said, because he couldn't think of anything other than the obvious truth, "we're all family here, aren't we? It's what family does."

She took in a quick breath and let it out slowly. "Yes," she said, "I suppose we are. And that means a great deal."

Jess went back to work on the lock. "Mind you, if I claim you as family, that's a huge step up for me, and probably several ones down for you," he said. "I never said it, but . . . sorry about my father letting us down, everyone. He's always been rubbish as a parent. I just thought he was a better businessman than to let Burners get the better of him in a deal." *And sell me out in the process,* he thought, but didn't say. It still hurt.

"That wasn't your fault," Morgan said. "My father tried to kill me, in case you've forgotten. Yours is the soul of family warmth next to him." She sat down on the bunk in her cell and pulled her feet up to sit cross-legged. "Oh, all right, I suppose I'll claim the lot of you as my kin, too."

"Try not to sound so enthusiastic about it," Glain said. "And, no offense, but I have a great father and mother and a lot of excellent brothers, so I'll be keeping them. Still, you make all right friends— I'll give you that."

Khalila sighed and stretched. "Our time is going to pass very slowly if the only entertainment is listening to you all insult one another, and they won't give us books."

"I can recite a few books," Thomas said. "If you're bored already." He began sonorously droning some desert-dry text about gear ratios he'd committed to memory while the others begged him to stop, and Jess muttered under his breath and felt the lock's stubborn, stiff mechanism and the unnerving fragility of his picks. *Come on,* he begged them. *Work.* He could feel the tension in the pick now and slipped the wrench in place for leverage. Hairpins weren't the ideal material for this, given the weight of the lock, and his fingertips told him the metal was bending under the strain. *Needs better angles.* He suppressed a groan and slipped the lockpicks free, studying the damage done, then began working carefully to put a sharper bend in the pick. Slipped them in place again, and suddenly, it felt as if the whole mechanism was laid out before him, brilliant white lines shining in his mind's eye. A subtle shift here, pressure there . . .

With a sudden harsh click, the pick caught, held, and turned.

Thomas sat up straight, breaking off his recitation, as Jess pushed on the door. It slowly swung open.

"Mother of God," Dario breathed, and rushed to his own cell door to wrap his hands around the bars. "Well, come on, you beautiful criminal! Let us out!"

"Changed your tune, didn't you?" Santi said. "Jess. That's enough."

"Yes, sir." It was tempting to step out into the hall, *very* tempting to go try his luck on the outer door's lock, but he knew Santi was right. He grabbed the loose door and swung it closed, held it there with his boot jammed through the bars while he plied the pick again to refasten it. That was easier.

"No, no, no!" Dario hammered the heel of his hand on the bars, a racket Jess could have well done without. "You fool, what are you doing?"

"He's biding his time, which you'll also do, *quietly*," Santi said. "We need time to recover and regain our strength. We need to win their trust, scout the city, and make a decent plan of escape. That's going to take time, and some measure of trust from our captors. We earn none making a useless attempt now."

Dario must have known that was true, but his frustration was sharp enough to cut the air, and he hit the bars one last time and flung himself onto his bunk. No arguments, though. Not even Dario was foolish enough to rush out without a plan.

Santi made it sound easy, Jess thought, but it wouldn't be. None of it. And he had the unpleasant thought that after escape, *if* they made it out of this city, then they were still in America, far from help.

Still, having the small length of metal in his hand, and a bit of control, quieted the storm inside his head from a hurricane to a grumble of thunder. The thunder was muttering, *It's useless; the metal won't last; the picks will break. What then?*

Out of nowhere, he remembered something his father had told him when he was just a child. *When all the world is a lock, boy, you don't make a key. You become a key.*

Brightwell wisdom. Sharp, unsentimental, and right now, something that settled the last of his worry. For the time being.

EPHEMERA

Text from the volume *Liber de Potentia*, addressing the dangers of unregulated Obscurists. For full reading only by the Curia and Archivist Magister. Certain sections available to the Medica division.

. . . *the toxic effect of the overuse of Obscurist abilities. This is most clearly and dreadfully illustrated by the case of French Obscurist Gilles de Rais. While trained in the Iron Tower, he left of his own accord to return to his family lands (n.b., for this reason we recommend no further releases, even for compassionate reasons, be allowed from the Iron Tower). He then used his great talents not in the service of the Library, as he was sworn to do, but in raising up a French warrior to do battle against the English for purely partisan reasons.*

De Rais used his God-granted quintessence to reckless and extravagant excess in keeping Jeanne d'Arc alive and well protected; while there is no doubt the woman was a born fighter who would have done the High Garda great credit had she been drawn to its service, his constant use of power to strengthen her armor and heal her wounds took the inevitable toll upon them both.

De Rais's power increased, as is typical for an Obscurist allowed to hone his skills without restriction, but as Aristotle himself observed, that which comes in contact with contaminants is never again clean. His healings began well enough, but as the rot inside him took hold, his touch brought madness, fevers, and, ultimately, the downfall of his own sworn champion.

Retreating to his castle, he swore to resurrect the fallen Jeanne. Corrupted from within, and maddened with it, he enacted a resulting horror within those walls that is a thing of terrible legend. That he was eventually purged by fire by his own people can only be seen as justice.

His case is, therefore, a stark warning to those who believe that Obscurists may be left on their own to manage their power and duties unchecked. Inside the Iron Tower, Obscurists use their powers in a careful and constructed way; the very metal of the Tower itself acts to limit their ability. To this end, and with the dark example of Gilles de Rais before us, we must recommend that all Obscurists be forever confined to the Iron Tower, save for specific missions that lead them beyond its protection, and on those rare occasions, that they be carefully watched. Should any signs of danger emerge, the Obscurist must be immediately and decisively prevented from any further use of power until natural healing, if possible, might occur.

While contamination may be reversed in early stages, it nevertheless poses a grave threat not only to the Obscurist who carries it but also to all those nearby.

Power holds always the hidden edge of threat.

CHAPTER TWO

In the morning, well before sunrise, Jess woke and started a systematic inventory of the cell, down to the stones, mortar, and bars.

Thomas overflowed his narrow bunk, hands folded on his chest, and his breathing seemed even and calm, but in the dim light seeping through the high window, Jess saw he wasn't asleep. Thomas's blue eyes were open, staring at the ceiling—but not a blank stare. His mind was all too active.

"What are you thinking?" Jess asked quietly as he stood on his bunk and pulled at the iron bars on the cell window. He kept it to a neutral question, because it was likely that the other young man's thoughts were on the past. These cells were cleaner than the Library's, and thus far refreshingly free of torture devices, but the similarities still chilled. He couldn't imagine what being imprisoned dredged up for Thomas, who'd endured months in that hell.

Thomas let two slow breaths pass in and out before he said, "I imagine they'll try to take Morgan first."

That was far from what he'd been expecting, and Jess swung down to the floor with an almost noiseless hop. "Why do you say that?"

"The Burners may hate the Library, but they're not stupid—at least, not this nest of them. They've resisted for more than a hundred years, and turned the American colonies into boiling pots of trouble on all fronts for the Library. Beck will fully understand the advantages of having a pet Obscurist. She could help them in their terrorist operations, repair their Translation Chamber, create their own Codex . . . They could build their own splinter version of the Great Library here in Philadelphia, but under their own control. They have original books, I imagine. What they need is an Obscurist. The rest of us . . ." Thomas shrugged. "We're only a bonus."

A new voice said, "We must use skills to our advantage." That was Khalila, who perched on the edge of her cot near her cell's door. "Our knowledge is our value. We have to make them see that."

"Did you not hear the part where they're likely to take Morgan by force?"

"Morgan is right here, and quite tired of being talked about as if she's some delicate treasure," Morgan said. "I'm in the least danger of all of you; Thomas just eloquently pointed that out."

"Is *nobody* asleep?" Jess asked in exasperation.

It drew a dry laugh from Dario's cell, though the Spaniard didn't bother to rise at all. "Have you tried finding a comfortable position on these devil's excuses for beds? Khalila's right. Work with the Burners, or escape. Those are our choices."

"There is no working with them," Scholar Wolfe said. Jess couldn't see him; he was on the other side of the stone wall to Jess's left. "There is *appearing* to work with them, and that is a means to a greater end than just survival. We need to have a goal of escaping not the cells, not the building, but the city. Even after, we must have a plan for what comes next. Make no move without knowing at least three ahead."

"I have a plan. Build my mechanical printer," Thomas said. "Use it to break the Library's hold on knowledge. That is a good plan."

"That isn't a plan, my poor engineer. That is a goal," Dario said. "A plan is steps we take to achieve the goal. You know, the boring part of being clever."

"I know how to build my part," Thomas replied. "Which is more than I can say of you, Dario."

"Gentlemen, didn't we agree we are family?" Khalila said.

"I argue with my family," Dario said. "But yes, desert flower. I will do better."

"Agreed," Thomas said. "I apologize. I'm sure Dario has some skill I'm not aware of."

Khalila almost laughed. "Then let's proceed. Beck isn't stupid, or overly fanatical, or he wouldn't have survived as their leader this long. So . . ."

"So we offer him something he won't find in the books he confiscated from us," Jess said. "As Thomas said. The press."

Dario made a rude noise. "Stupid idea. Once he has the plans, he has no need of us."

"You forget, he's got no need of us *now*," Wolfe said. His tone was as heavy and sharp as a guillotine blade. "The only one of us he actually needs is Morgan. The rest of us are—as Thomas so correctly put it—bonuses. He has to want us alive."

Thomas still hadn't moved from his deathlike stillness on the bunk. His gaze hadn't varied from the shadowed ceiling. "Then I don't give him the plans. I build the press first and prove to him it works," he said. "And Jess builds it with me. Along with Morgan, that gives us three Beck can't kill, and it buys us time."

"He'll accept that for you. Jess is just another pair of hands."

"I hate to say it, but Beck does need me," Jess said. "Not for my brilliant mind so much as his own survival. Have you looked around this so-called town? It isn't staying alive on its own merits; the buildings are half ruins, the people all but starved."

"A hundred years of unrelenting siege will do that," Santi said.

"And they don't survive on whatever meager crops they raise in here. At least, not completely."

Santi's voice turned contemplative. "I see your point. This town survives on smugglers getting them extra food and supplies."

"Exactly. And those smugglers will have ties that lead back to my family, one way or another. I'm more valuable for what I represent, once Beck knows who I am. I'm worth better terms and more supplies. Or the reverse, because if he kills me, he loses his flow of supplies."

"Nice for you," Dario said. "That last bit is particularly good. I mean, better chance of us escaping in the chaos, of course, if you want to volunteer as sacrificial goat."

Jess replied silently. With a gesture.

"Getting beyond these walls will be a much greater challenge," said Santi. "The walls have been standing for a hundred years—treated by an Obscurist, most likely, to withstand Greek fire and other, more conventional bombardment. Plus, there are no fewer than four full High Garda companies stationed around the walls of Philadelphia, and they're constantly on watch. My own company—" His voice broke a bit, as if he'd only just remembered that they'd abandoned everything to save Thomas, including his position as a High Garda captain, and so, his soldiers. "My own company spent a year here some time ago."

"About that," Dario said. "I'd have thought the impressive armed High Garda could defeat a few hundred Burners inside a half-ruined city in less than a week, never mind a hundred years."

"Standing orders from two Archivists back," Santi answered. "The American colonies have always been a powder keg of dissent. Burning Philadelphia could set the whole continent ablaze. Containment is the policy, with occasional bombardments."

"And I assume you had run-ins with smugglers."

"Of course. We caught hundreds of amateurs. Most were fanatics caught trying to fling supplies over the walls."

"Any of them ever use one of your ballistae?" Jess asked.

"What?"

"To throw supplies. I would have. Could get a lot over in a couple of quick tosses."

"Thank God you were not advising them." Santi sounded amused at that one. "Jess—I'm all for using your family's reputation, but don't push Beck too far. He might kill you just to make the point that he doesn't need your father's goodwill. He has an ego."

"You sound as if you know him," Jess said.

"I should—we study him. He's survived here, head of a desperate group trapped like rats, and he's kept order by being equal parts clever and ruthless. His math is very cold: he doesn't keep anyone alive, wasting resources, who doesn't gain him something."

Khalila said, "Scholar Wolfe, Dario and I can interpret the books we brought from the Black Archives; I know Master Beck was quite excited about those. Most of the books are in dead and obscure languages I doubt anyone else in Philadelphia can decipher. That might give us some protection, at least for a time."

"That still leaves Glain and Santi," Wolfe said. "And I'm not giving them up."

Glain groaned sleepily and said, "Would you all just *shut up* and let me rest? We're High Garda. We'll survive. Chatter when the sun's up, you wretches."

"Do you want us to sing to you?" Dario asked.

"I swear to my gods and yours, Dario. *Shut. Up.*"

After that, it went quiet again. Some of them, Jess sensed, did go back to sleep. Not him. Not Thomas. Jess went back to a fingertip search of the cell, mind as white as a snowfield. His father had taught him how to look for hidden panels and triggers doing this, but the same principle served for anything you were looking to discover. It just took patience and focus.

From time to time, he glanced up at Thomas. The other young man hadn't closed his eyes. He looked . . . dead. But Jess had no doubt that the mind inside that skull was whirring at top speed.

Jess finally paused his search. He'd covered most of the cell, and his back was on fire, his fingertips raw from scraping them over stone. He sat down on the floor to lean against his friend's cot. "You all right?" He whispered it softly enough that it wouldn't wake Thomas if he were asleep.

But he wasn't at all surprised to get a reply.

"To be truthful, I'm glad you're here, Jess." He didn't say the rest, but Jess could guess. Being trapped in a cell again, even surrounded by friends, wasn't good for him. Thomas had endured torment in that dark hell underneath Rome; he'd survived unimaginable things, and it had taken a toll. Jess wanted to ask, but he knew better; there was a gulf between what they *could* say and what they *would* say. Best to keep things simple. Thomas was fragile, raw inside and out, and the ugly truth of it was they needed him strong if they were going to survive Philadelphia.

Thomas said, "Would you stay there while I sleep a little?"

Jess looked over his shoulder and saw that Thomas's gaze had shifted to him. Neither of them looked away, and Jess finally said, "I'll stand watch."

It was, he thought, exactly what Thomas needed, and with a sigh, the big German closed his eyes and let himself finally drift away.

Jess fell asleep, too, despite the hard stones under his behind, and the chill. He dreamed he was a guard at a gate, and the gate was on fire, and he knew, he *knew*, that what waited beyond it was something terrible and monstrous and impossible to defeat. But that he'd have to fight it anyway. The hopelessness of it overwhelmed him.

He woke with a start when he heard voices, the dream still vivid and vibrating in his muscles. The sun was well up, and the sky a cloudy teal blue beyond the window bars. No one had arrived to wake them, Jess realized, and there was nothing to eat. His stomach was growling. He also had an urgent need for the toilet. Bucket. Well, he'd made do with worse, and he rose and made use of the thing.

"Wathen, what in Heron's name are you doing?" That was Wolfe's sharp, annoyed voice, and Jess buttoned up and angled a look over at the cell Glain shared with Khalila. Glain was, bafflingly enough, doing a handstand in the middle of her cell. Perfect balance, as steady as a rock. "Practicing to become Philadelphia's court jester?"

Glain put her legs down in a smooth, perfectly coordinated move that Jess could in no way have duplicated, stood up straight, and stretched. "It feels good," she said. "Blood to the brain. Helps me think."

"Did you see anything useful from that position?" Dario asked.

"Did you, from lying on your oh-so-uncomfortable mattress, lazybones?"

The young man shrugged, which was a feat considering he was casually leaning a shoulder against the bars *and* had his arms crossed. "What do you want me to say? It's a cell. There's nothing in here."

"Dario, you're hopeless," Wolfe said. "Jess. Tell him how he's wrong."

"Strip the netting under the mattresses. Braid it together, tie it to the window bars, and twist. The torque will unseat at least one of the bars pretty easily. You can use it for a tool, sharpen it up as a weapon . . ."

"The mattresses are flammable enough to make a decent amount of smoke," Morgan added. "We'd need to be careful to keep it to a distraction. The air circulation isn't very good. Easy to breathe in too much if it gets thick."

Khalila held up her head scarf and unfolded it with a snap of her hand. "If I weight the two ends with pieces of stone, this makes a perfectly good weapon."

Dario said, "Fine. You're all much better at dirty fighting and jail survival than I am. But as the Scholar so wisely said, we need to think three moves ahead. Let's assume that we're out of the cells, we've saved our lives from the Burners, we've found a way out of the city. What then? I think we need a way to communicate with whatever allies we have left out there. I don't suppose you've got that answer tucked up your sleeve."

Jess said, "If they're getting supplies, they must have a smuggling tunnel."

"Explain," Wolfe said sharply. "Because I'm not allowing you to run blindly out into unknown territory. We must—"

"They're coming," Santi interrupted him.

Jess heard footsteps then, and the scrape of the lock turning to the outer door, and was on his feet and at the bars so quickly he might have been spring-loaded. Thomas, by contrast, didn't even move a muscle from where he sat on the edge of his cot—though it was an icy calm that Jess thought hard-won.

The door gaped open, and three men came in—different ones this time, but with a brawny look that said they were ready for trouble. Khalila, across the way, unhurriedly tied her scarf in place and tucked the edges in to hold it. How she could stay so perfectly clean in these conditions, Jess had no idea, but she wouldn't have looked out of place in her own Library office, despite all they'd been through. Made him feel somewhat better.

Morgan, on the other hand, looked more like he felt—pale, tired, her hair tangled and badly in need of combing. He wanted to do that for her, run his fingers gently through that riot of silk and curls. Had they come for her? He was afraid that Thomas had been right—Morgan's abilities were a valuable, vanishingly rare resource that the Burners would lock a collar around as sure as the Library had done.

But they didn't stop at Morgan's cell, which was a temporary relief that vanished as they stopped at Jess and Thomas's barred door and pointed at Thomas. "You there. Come with us." The clipped tone of the guard's accent made the command sound that much more unfriendly. He had pale skin and straw blond hair cropped to a shimmer around his skull, and he'd been in more than one fight; noses didn't get that distorted from just one punch.

Jess was caught wrong-footed, and it took him a second to realize what it might mean. He turned to look at Thomas, and one glance at the other young man's set face was enough.

"He's not going anywhere alone," Jess said.

"Back up, boy."

"Never happen. You want him, you take us both."

The guard laughed. "You mean go through you? Not a problem."

Jess was afraid that assessment was correct. He could fight; his High Garda training had made him efficient, fast, and deadly, and he was confident he could make them bleed. But there were three of them, and he couldn't count on Thomas, who wavered between sudden bursts of violence and crippling fear at the strangest of times. Thomas would probably fight for others. Jess wasn't sure he'd fight to save himself.

Jess was afraid, but it was a fear he was familiar with, after all the High Garda drills and the horror he'd already survived. An old friend, this kind of fear. Almost a strength.

"If you make us put you down, you'll go hard," the Burner said. He grinned and revealed an array of jagged teeth as battered and broken as his nose. "Your choice."

"Gentlemen," Santi said, from the next cell over, and leaned against the bars of the cell he shared with Wolfe. His tone was charming, which meant he was ready to do awful things. "If you want answers, come and get someone who has command rank."

"Oh, we'll get to you," the man said. He smacked a heavy wooden club in his palm and moved down to look in at Santi. "We'll ask real loud, if you keep it up, *booklover.*"

"It's funny you think that's an insult. Whereas, I'd rather talk about the misshapen state of your face. Just how many fights did you lose? I think a much greater number than those you won. Are you sure you brought enough friends?"

The man slammed his club against the bars of Santi's cell, which was a mistake; instead of moving back, Santi must have been ready, and he wrapped his fingers around the club and yanked the man's whole arm inside his cell. The man yelped in pain. Jess couldn't see much, but he heard the clatter of the club as it fell, and Santi must have retrieved it first, because he slammed it against the cell bars, which rang like a struck bell.

All three of the men on the other side flinched.

"*Now* we can talk," Santi said.

It almost worked, but unfortunately, the tough in charge was smarter than Jess gave him credit for . . . and he backed off, drew a large, crudely forged gun, and pointed it not at Santi, but square at Jess. "Throw it out, Captain," he said. "Now. We don't need all of you; you know that."

The man cocked the weapon as he spoke. Jess forced a smile. "It's a bluff, Captain," he said. He'd gone cold inside, but he wasn't about to show it. His family had trained him first and well to fight like a cornered rat when there wasn't anywhere to run. "He's not going to shoot. His master would have his hide."

"Oh, I don't think so. We can afford to lose one or two. Especially those of you wearing Library uniforms. No worth in your hides except to toss you over the wall at our enemies."

Jess watched the man's finger whiten on the trigger—and then quickly pull away as the club Santi had been holding hit the floor, bounced, and rolled to bump against the man's boot. "All right," Santi said. "Pax."

"Smart choice." The tough lowered the hammer on the pistol— not Library issue, an American-produced slug-throwing device that undoubtedly would have blown a gruesomely large hole straight through Jess's chest—and put it in a leather holster at his side. "Now, let's start over. You. The big one. Like I said, you're coming with us."

Jess opened his mouth, but Thomas put a hand on his shoulder and moved him—not unkindly, but firmly—out of the way as he stepped up. He silently turned his back to the bars, which puzzled Jess until he realized it was to allow the men to reach in and snap ratcheted metal shackles around his wrists. He'd obviously been through this process before, many times, while in Library custody.

Thomas nodded to Jess, blue eyes clear and calm. "I'll be fine," he said, which was a rotten lie.

Jess tried to think of something to say, and as the key turned, the door opened, and Thomas stepped out, he finally did. "Thomas. *In bocca al lupo.*" It was the phrase that the High Garda used to wish one another luck traveling through the Translation portals, a process that was painful and terrifying and dangerous in equal measure, and it seemed right now. *In the mouth of the wolf.*

"*Crepi il lupo,*" Thomas responded as Jess's cell was locked tight, and then he was gone, prodded down the hall and to the outer door and away. *Kill the wolf.*

It slammed and locked behind him.

Jess let out a deeply felt English expletive and knelt to examine the lock as he dug the picks out of their hiding place, deep in the cotton ticking of his mattress.

"Jess?" Wolfe was watching him with a frown. "Don't."

"I'm not leaving him on his own!"

Wolfe made a sound that managed to be completely disgusted. "You'll be shot two steps out the door. Think. I know you're somewhat capable. Thomas has survived far worse than they'll ever do to him here, and he knows his business. He's going to sell Willinger Beck the idea of the press. He's safe enough right now. Beck doesn't want blood."

"Unlike me," Santi said. "I'm not averse to spilling some."

"Nic."

"Jess is right. We need to keep an eye on Thomas."

"We *wait*," Wolfe said again. "I've waited in worse places."

He had. Wolfe had suffered everything Thomas had in Library prisons . . . and for far longer. If anyone had things to fear, it was Christopher Wolfe, who was, at the best of times, bitterly fragile. It took some familiarity to see it; he was masterful at putting on a front. But everyone had a breaking point. Wolfe had passed his, shattered, and somehow painfully patchworked himself back together.

"We wait," Wolfe said. It sounded firm enough, but there was a hollow sound to his voice. "Until we know more. That's all we can do."

The wait passed in grueling silence, but Wolfe was right. In a little over three hours, which Jess torturously calculated by the movement of the shadow of the bars on the cell floor, the men were back unlocking Jess's cell door. "You," the ugly one said. "Come on. You're wanted."

"Seen the reward posters, have you?" he said, and managed a cocky grin, mostly for Morgan's benefit, because she was watching him with a worried frown. "Back soon," he told her, and she nodded.

"In bocca al lupo," she murmured, and the others repeated it, like a prayer. That nearly knocked the grin off him. Nearly.

"Crepi il lupo," he said. "Morgan. If I don't come back—"

"Walk," his guard said, and planted a hand in the center of his back to shove him onward. He stumbled, twisted his knee, and fell hard with his hands grasping the bars of Morgan's cell. "Oh, for the love of God—get up, you clumsy fool!"

Jess hadn't had a chance to throw a signal, but that didn't matter. Morgan's quick fingers retrieved the lockpicks he'd been holding out stuck between two knuckles, and her touch skimmed light as breath over his skin. That almost stole his breath, and he looked up into her face.

Into a quick, broken smile.

He'd wanted her to have them, in case he didn't come back, and she understood that without a word being said. He wanted to say a great deal more to her and was parting his lips to try when he was yanked upright again, and his head slammed hard into unyielding iron to teach him better balance. It didn't have that effect. His knees went weak, and he nearly fell again, this time not on purpose. While he was down, they added manacles to his wrists.

"Hey, scrubber." He looked up at the sound of Dario Santiago's voice and saw the Spaniard staring at him through the bars of the next cell. Dario didn't look like the pampered, arrogant dandy anymore; he looked like a pirate, with an evil gleam in those dark eyes. "Don't embarrass us. Come back alive. Fetch Thomas while you're at it, eh?"

He transferred the look to the guard dragging on Jess's wrists. "You, Burner, feel free to not come back at all. I see you again, friend . . ." He made a lazy little throat-cutting gesture.

"Lovely," Wolfe said sourly from the far end of the hall. "Leave it to you to make new friends, Santiago." He raised his voice a little. "Brightwell. He's right. Bring yourselves back safe."

Dear God. *Wolfe is worried about us? We are in real trouble.*

A hand shoved hard between his shoulder blades pushed Jess on, and the outer door gaped wide on a square of sunlight so bright it seemed like running face-first into a solid object. It dazed for a few seconds, then comforted as the guards locked up the door behind him and marched him away.

Pay attention, he told himself, and blinked his prison-adapted eyes back into focus. The building, which so far was devoted solely to their care, was a long, low, unprepossessing block set to one side of a wide public square full of grass and spreading trees that had the shimmering early colors of fall. The arena where they'd been forced to watch books burn lay on his right, and directly in front, on the other side of the park, rose a four-story building of gray stone and French blue accents, all gingerbreaded with thin windows and arches like raised eyebrows. A single tall tower rose at the back of it, topped with a statue: Benjamin Franklin, who'd been a Scholar in the Library, and then left it for the Burners later in life. Patron saint of the city, so they said. They'd destroyed the old statue of William Penn to elevate their own hero.

Saint Franklin was doing a crap job of it. The town—village, really—of Philadelphia was half in ruins. The city hall in front of Jess was the only building of any size; the rest of the place was cottages and shops that looked cobbled together, and rightly so, because the Library's ballista bombs regularly shattered entire blocks, and with the city starved for resources by the permanent encampments around it, new building materials must have been hard to come by. So the remaining buildings were made of a dangerous hodgepodge of scrap metal, mismatched brick and stone, and patched lumber that managed to have a style all its own. *I might not like them, but they're survivors,* Jess had to admit. A hundred years they'd held out, against forces that had made short work of taking over entire countries.

Philadelphia was the defiant, rebellious example the Burners held up to the world. But Jess had a strong suspicion that it was less the Burners' valiant efforts than the Library's own agenda that kept the place alive. The decision had been made long ago to contain them inside their walls and wait them out. The Archivist had many other considerations, and destroying this place must have been lowest on his list.

The citizens of the town were as individual as the buildings, and their clothing as patchworked, heavily used, and durable. He saw tribal people walking the streets, shoulder to shoulder with fellows of European, African, and Asian descent. Odd, how varied the makeup of the place was, and how well they all seemed to get along. Common enemies, he supposed. And for Burners, this place had to be as much a draw as Alexandria was for would-be Scholars. He'd fully expected Alexandria to be a richly varied city. Somehow, he hadn't expected the same of the Burners.

The air smelled faintly of ashes coming from the stadium, with the whip of chill on a breeze that rattled leaves. *I wonder what they do for heating,* Jess thought. Winters must be brutal. Philadelphia survived on raw pride.

Raw pride and smugglers. The place had to survive on smugglers bringing in food, fuel, weapons, materials. Slipping past the High Garda would be difficult, but difficult was meat and drink to people like his clan, who'd been thumbing their noses at the Library for longer than the family tree had been kept. And the Brightwells had cousins everywhere—by kind, if not by kin. Someone who smuggled into Philadelphia would have at least a passing amount of loyalty to his family. Had to have.

The question would be who to trust, and how far. Right now, Jess didn't trust anyone except his own friends and fellows.

"Where are we going?" he asked the guard, though he was fairly sure he already knew. "Is Thomas all right?"

That didn't even get a look, and that made nerves prick painfully along his back. Thomas had *better* be in fine shape and good spirits, or someone—Willinger Beck, by preference—was going to pay for it in blood.

The walls that towered around Philadelphia looked as patchwork as its buildings, but *something* must be extraordinary about them; the Library had Greek fire and other terrible weapons of war, and it would take an Obscurist's reinforcements to build something to stand firm against the constant assault. The Burners must have had at least one once, and a gifted one at that. *Thomas is right,* Jess thought. *They'll take Morgan because they need her. So much she could do for them.* Let them try. She was brighter than he was and had run from capture for most of her life. She hadn't allowed the Library to keep her long. The Burners wouldn't have any better luck.

"Move it," his guard grumbled, and shoved him between the shoulder blades. Jess kept his balance and shot the man a humorless grin.

"I can run," he said. "If you want to make it a footrace."

For answer, the guard put a hand on his gun.

"Understandable that you'd say no. Truthfully, you're in no shape to run against my old, sainted grandmother."

"Shut up, booklover."

It was still funny to hear that as an insult.

Jess set himself to memorizing everything within view—the position of trees, buildings, streets. He'd need to get a closer look at the walls to find any hidden doors. There had to be doors known only to the smugglers and the city's guards. Jess didn't think they'd remain hidden for long if a decent thief—and he was a quite good one—got a chance to take a dedicated look around.

They marched him straight to city hall, the only remaining building of any elegance. It wasn't immune to the war; he could see places where the granite had been melted and deformed, where walls had been smashed and cobbled back together. But it held a kind of rigid, gritty nobility, especially today, with a clear, breakable blue sky arching over it. The tower, impossibly enough, was still intact. A remnant of a better time.

"So what's behind this?" Jess asked. "Come on. It isn't like I can't find out for myself with a look out a window."

"Fields," said one of them. Interesting. The people of Philadelphia grew enough, then, that they tried not to rely solely on the good graces of the smugglers. That was understandable.

It also made them more vulnerable, but Jess doubted they realized it.

Inside city hall, Jess marched into antique grandeur. This place had originally been built as a Serapeum of the Great Library, and it still had the Library's trademark elegance stamped on it in the tall pillars, the inlaid marble floor, and the dazzling design of the place.

What it *didn't* have were books. No shelves, no Codex, no statues of Scholars. The inlaid design in the center of the hall they passed had a far less intricate design than the rest of it, and he thought it had once been the Library's seal, broken up and redesigned by local craftsmen. The symbol that they walked over now was an open volume with flames leaping up from curling, burning pages. Sickeningly appropriate.

They climbed stairs, circling around to the third level and then down a long hall warmed with dark wood trim and old portraits of American notables. A large, well-done painting near the end depicted one of the battles that had raged for the city . . . a heroic army of Burners rebelling against the Library's troops while eerie green flames of Greek fire consumed trees and buildings around them. Chilling and thrilling at once.

He avoided looking too closely at the companion illustration of the victory, which showed books being piled on the steps of this building and set alight. It made him want to take a knife to it. Burning books for religion or politics was all the same to him: evil.

One of the guards knocked, a muffled voice said, "Enter," and the guards eased the heavy door open at the end of the hall. One of them pushed Jess forward, as if he needed the instruction, but they didn't follow him inside.

"Shut the door behind you; there's a draft," said the man who sat behind the desk: Willinger Beck, as smug and self-satisfied as ever. Jess obliged, more because he wanted to block the guards than from any desire to please this man.

He ignored Beck, because Thomas sat off to the side in a comfortably plush old chair that *almost* was large enough to seem proportional to his frame. Thomas looked up and met Jess's gaze and nodded slightly. *I'm all right.* Jess wasn't sure that was true, but he knew what his friend intended to convey. And truthfully, being out of the cell probably was better than whatever threats Beck had to hand in this place.

The office didn't look particularly intimidating. It did look self-congratulatory, compared to the ruined poverty of the rest of the town.

It was filled with gleaming wood, sleek, comfortable couches and chairs, and a desk large enough to double as a dining table for eight, except that it had papers piled atop it. There were shelves in this room, and books, too . . . every one an original, not a single Blank among them. Some had the gilt and flash of rare volumes; Jess recognized a few at a glance that he'd personally read, held, or run across London for his father. The majority, though, had the shabby, handmade look of local production.

What made Jess's stomach turn sour, though, were the books—almost a hundred of them—stacked near Thomas. He recognized those volumes, and the packs and bags that lay discarded in the corner that had held them. They were the books he and the others had rescued from Alexandria, from the Black Archives. Forbidden books, full of dangerous ideas and inventions and knowledge.

Thomas, he realized, was currently reading one of them.

"Ah," Beck said, and rose from his desk to come over to a chair near Thomas. "Come, sit. We have things to discuss, you and I."

"I'm fine here," Jess said. He wanted to stay on his feet and mobile. He'd already begun analyzing ways out of the room—the broad windows looked like the best exit. Chuck one of the handy, heavy sculptures through the glass, and oh, the possibilities. His main worry was in getting Thomas to follow him out. One thing at a time. *I could kill Beck on the way.*

"I said sit down," Beck said, and all the false good humor was gone now, which was an improvement. Jess responded by leaning against the wall, between two paintings he hadn't even glanced at, and crossing his arms. The silent standoff went on for almost half a minute before Beck pretended Jess hadn't just forced his hand, and turned to Thomas. "You said he would be cooperative."

"He will be," Thomas said, unruffled, "once you tell him why he's here."

Beck didn't like this, Jess realized. He didn't like that Thomas, despite all sense and appearances, held power right now. He certainly didn't like having to pretend to be civil. *Good,* Jess thought, imagining those books going up in ash toward the sky. "Well, this sounds interesting," Jess said. "Go on."

Thomas didn't, which forced Beck to say—growl, really, "He's told me that you together can build a machine to reproduce original books without the use of an Obscurist or a copyist. He says the job requires you both."

"That's true," Thomas said. "My first model was crude and unreliable. Jess designed many improvements to make the machine run correctly."

Thomas was getting very good at lying. *I'm having a bad influence,* Jess thought, and was rather proud of that. Beck glared at both of them, ending with Jess, who shrugged. "Think of it this way: use us, and you'll be able to undermine the Library in a way that counts for more than just destroying books."

"It's true," Thomas said. "How do you devalue a country's currency? Make more until it's worthless. Knowledge is the common currency of the Great Library. If you make books freely available with no restrictions, the Library has no power over you. Over anyone."

Beck's resting expression—dour—didn't change, and Jess found himself thinking the man might be either very stupid or very good at holding his cards close. Since he'd survived as Burner leader so long, it had to be the latter. Beck's fingers reached for a pen and twirled it as he sat back, staring at Jess—only at Jess—and thinking. "I see," he finally said. A gambit, that phrase, to buy time. "Most interesting."

Jess sighed. "Get to the point."

Beck didn't like being rushed. He wanted to appear deeply thoughtful about it, but in fact, Jess knew, he'd already made up his mind. So despite the glare, Beck said, "We have no opportunity to take any books you produce here beyond these walls. Unless you have some magical means of transporting them . . . your Obscurist, perhaps . . ."

Keep any mention of Morgan out of it, Jess thought, but he didn't know how to signal that to Thomas.

He didn't need to. "You miss our meaning," Thomas said without missing a beat. "What we offer eliminates the need for an Obscurist. We will build you a machine, and give you the plans to build more, out of simple components that can be made anywhere. Send those plans out, not books. Set up printing facilities in every corner of the world."

Beck didn't manage to conceal a greedy little spark this time, something that fired through his expression in an instant and disappeared, leaving him professionally disinterested. "I would have to see such a miracle in operation first."

"Naturally," Jess said. "And you will, provided you give us the tools and supplies to build it."

"And you will prepare written instructions for the building of this machine in return for what?"

"Freedom," Jess replied. "For us and all our friends."

That made Beck give a bitter little laugh. "I can't set my *own* people free outside these walls. What makes you believe I can promise you any such thing?"

"He means freedom here, in Philadelphia," Thomas said. He cut in so smoothly Jess couldn't tell if he'd anticipated the objection or just reacted fast. "No more locked cells. You feed us and allow us to live as we wish. Freely."

That made Beck laugh out loud, but it was fast and humorless and ended in "No." A flat slap of a word. "You must think I'm a mewling idiot. Let Scholars and soldiers loose here to sabotage and destroy our city? I'd be better off trading you to the High Garda!"

That was exactly what they *didn't* need to happen. Once the Great Library learned that Wolfe and his students had survived London and were trapped inside Philadelphia, Jess thought that would be a perfectly simple puzzle for the Archivist to solve: destroy the entire city. Kill them all in the process. Neat, and a dual benefit.

"Trading us to the High Garda wouldn't get you as much as trading with my family," Jess said, to head off the entire discussion. "I assume you know of my father. Callum Brightwell."

He saw the exact second when Willinger Beck's world shifted. The man's eyes widened, blinked. In that moment, he didn't look like a man who'd be good at any game that required a bluff. "Brightwell," he repeated, as if he couldn't quite believe it. *"Brightwell."* That last repetition was weighted by a heavy varnish of chagrin.

"I see you know of him," Jess said. "I assume you work with smugglers to stay alive. Might be a mistake to get on the wrong side of one of the most powerful families for a stupid, preventable reason."

Beck's face went still, but red spots formed and burned high in his cheeks. Still, he wasn't a rash sort. He thought it out. While he did, Jess glanced at Thomas, who had raised his eyebrows and now quickly lowered them again. Surprised? Worried? Hard to tell.

Beck gained control of his voice. It sounded smooth, but the tension underneath was as sharp as sharks. "I didn't recognize the connection. I'm familiar with your illustrious father, and your very impressive brother."

Of course you are, Jess thought. "My illustrious father and very impressive brother got sold down the river by your people in London," he said. "My father won't be in a good mood. And he won't look kindly on any further insults toward his family."

"I never heard that he had a son in Library uniform. I wonder, are you really still considered part of the family?"

That struck, and cut. Jess smiled to hide it. "Oh, Callum Bright-well knows full well I'm in this uniform. I can promise you, sending me to the Library was his plan." Both those things were true. They didn't quite add up to the sum of the parts, but Jess saw Beck reconsidering his stance.

Beck went for a cautious half measure and said, "He's always been fair to us. Sympathetic, even. I think I can count on him to be consistent in his dealings with us, whatever your . . . situation."

"My father values two things above all else: his business and his family. He considers the two the same. If you harm his son—or my friends—I can promise you that he'll take that personally."

Beck took his time thinking it over. He stood up, walked to the window, and looked out, clasping his hands behind his back; with the soft light on his face, he looked like a flattering portrait of a statesman. Jess wondered if he'd done it for the effect. "I must do what is the best for my people, of course. Alienating the Brightwells might not be in their interest."

"That's good sense," Jess said. He wasn't averse to praising people when they said the bloody obvious, so long as it was in his favor. "My recommendation is to let me write and explain."

Beck ignored that. He stared out for another long set of clock ticks and then turned to regard him and Thomas with a sudden smile on his face. Far too wide. Far too warm.

"No, I think that I will write to him. No doubt the fact you are in residence here will make him a stronger friend to Philadelphia. And of course, I welcome the construction of this machine you're talking about. We can discuss some small privileges for your friends while you do the work." He turned to Thomas then. "If that is acceptable to you, Scholar Schreiber?"

That speech, Jess thought, was a bit of a wonder. An implication of hostage taking; in the same breath, a promise of favors; and as an apple polish on the end, lauding Thomas with his rightfully earned title. A title the Burners normally used as a term of scorn.

"No," Thomas said. Not a diplomat, Thomas. Blunt, earnest, and to the point. "For the price of humbling your pride and giving us food and trust, you get a weapon that kills no one, destroys nothing, and yet undermines the tyranny you claim to resist. A life is worth more than a book; that is your motto. We can make that a *fact*, not mere words."

In the silence that followed Thomas's words—slow, deliberate, powerful words—Jess imagined he could feel the world changing around him. It was subtle, but it was *there*.

He could see by the look in Willinger Beck's eyes that the man felt it, too. But he hadn't survived this long, against these odds, by being gullible. "I will provide you with supplies to build your machine, and food for you two, and you two *only*," Beck said. "Rations are dear here. The others need to earn their bread with useful work, and while I agree to leave the prison doors unlocked, there is no such thing as freedom of movement for any of you; you will go guarded, or you do not go anywhere. *If* your machine proves all that you promise, then you may earn additional rights. Not before."

Jess locked gazes with Thomas, and Thomas gave a rolling shrug. A very German sort of move, and it made Jess feel a slow burn of satisfaction. *This could work.* He nodded to Thomas.

"Acceptable," the other young man said. Looking at him, Jess could suddenly see the Scholar he'd one day become—sure, centered, deliberate and calm, and sharply intelligent. A great man, if they survived this. "I will make you a list of what we need."

Beck laughed. It sounded barren. "You may make all the lists you like, my boy. We have what we have, and you will make do, as we all must. I will write to your father, Brightwell. If there is something you need that can't be crafted here, we'll send to him for it. He might feel inclined to gift us with it, if he knows his son's life is at risk with the rest of us."

Maybe. Jess's brother Liam had died dangling from a noose in London and was buried in an unmarked grave as a nameless book smuggler. *Da could have saved him.* Da hadn't bothered, because getting caught was, in his world, a mortal sin.

Jess was caught, too. The trick was letting Beck think he wasn't.

It seemed the agreement had been reached, and Jess allowed his shoulders to relax just a little . . . and a little too soon, because Beck suddenly said, "One more thing. You're aware that Captain Santi once commanded troops outside these walls?"

"Did he?" Jess asked. And shrugged. He wasn't about to answer that. He'd hoped that Beck didn't know the identities of the many, many High Garda captains who'd camped out there in the dark.

"He is to sit with my guard captain, Indira, and map out for her everything he knows of the Library camps. Troop strengths, placement of tents, routines. *Everything.*"

He's not going to do that. Jess knew it instantly. Santi might turn his back on the Library, but betray other High Garda? Never.

The next instant, he thought, *But he might like the chance to lie his head off about it, though.* And so he let a second pass before he said, without any change of tone or expression, "I'll pass along your request."

"It wasn't a request."

Jess stared back without saying anything. There was something about Beck that reminded him, strongly, of his father. It wasn't a happy comparison, and he had no issue at all waiting the man out. He knew his father got impatient when faced with silence.

And sure enough, so did Beck. "I'll expect his attendance in the morning," Beck said. "Tell him to report to Indira. If he isn't there at dawn, he'll be dragged along in chains."

"Everyone except us will be with you here tomorrow," Thomas said. "The Scholars and Morgan will begin to translate these books. And that earns the bread we take from you, yes?"

"Your soldier girl—Wathen, is it? Wathen is of no use to me," Beck began, and Thomas cut him right off.

"Squad Leader Glain Wathen is Scholar Seif's personal guard. She stays with her. Protocol."

That was a truly *excellent* lie, and Jess had to admire it; he'd simultaneously made Khalila mysteriously important and given Glain status, too. Beck might have some information, but surely not enough. They only had to work around his preconceptions.

Beck let out an offended little huff and tugged his jacket down. "Protocol!"

"Consider that it's for your own protection," Jess said. "One of your men insulted Scholar Seif, and she's not in a forgiving mood."

"If Seif is so touchy, she can stay in her cell!"

Thomas suddenly clapped shut the book he had open in his hand. It was a shockingly loud sound, and he got to his feet in the startled silence. "She is properly addressed as Scholar Seif, and if you want your books translated, you need her above all the others," he said. "Your man laid hands on her. Don't ever do it again."

"Oh, threats now? You must fancy yourself dangerous," Beck said.

Jess raised his eyebrows and looked at Thomas. "Do we?"

"Occasionally," Thomas said gravely.

For the first time, Beck lost his temper. He slammed both hands down on his desk, sending papers scattering. "This is not a matter for your amusement, you spoiled children! You think it's easy to keep my people safe, fed, housed, and warmed with the Library bombing our city with regularity? Now, shut up and appreciate my forbearance, or you might not enjoy quite such special treatment in the future!"

Jess opened his mouth to reply but shut it when Thomas shook his head. *Best to let him have this,* he realized. *We have what we need.*

Thomas bowed, the picture of calm. He made it seem easy. "Thank you," he said.

"Just get out!"

Thomas inclined his head meekly, and when Beck's office door opened, they followed the tall guard woman down the hall. More guards fell in behind.

"You're called Indira," Jess said. The woman glanced at him. Barely. "You're in charge?"

"As far as you're concerned," she said. Nothing else. Jess tried smiling, but he was aware he gave off a more criminal air next to Thomas's pleasant farm-boy charm. She remained distinctly uncharmed. He gave it up and concentrated instead on noting everything about the building they passed through, and everything he could see outside.

They were on the steps when the first alarms began to sound. It was a terrible wailing sound, coming from all around them. Outside the walls. It rose and fell like the cries of the damned, and even though Jess knew what it was, he felt a sick, falling sensation in his stomach. He had to resist an overwhelming urge to cover his ears.

"What is that?" Thomas's shout near his ear was only just barely audible, and he heard the rattle of panic in it.

"High Garda warning signal," Jess shouted back. "Bombardment."

He'd been exposed to it in training sessions, but he'd never expected to hear it this close; it sounded like an ancient, eerie thing, like the screaming of gods, and it was meant to warn the citizens of a city that hell was coming down.

And the Philadelphians, he saw, were used to it. No one even covered their ears, except a few small children.

Indira grabbed Jess's arm in a manacle grip and towed him along at a fast walk. It was the same fast but calm pace of all the other people he could see on the streets. As she pulled Thomas and him, and their guard escort, off toward the right, he saw that a steady stream of traffic was already moving in that direction, toward a doorway. Jess nearly pulled away. Buildings, in a Greek fire attack, couldn't protect you; they caught fire, burned around you, trapped you screaming.

Indira sensed his hesitation and shouted, "Basement!"

Better. Not great, but better.

They'd just reached the steps that led down into darkness when the sirens cut off with a last warning wail, and the silence that swirled felt heavy and full of dread.

"Wait!" Jess tried to turn back. "The others—"

Indira shoved him forward. "They must fend for themselves, and God defend them now. *Move!*"

"She's right," Thomas said. "We'll never reach them in time."

I'm fast, Jess wanted to argue, but what would he do if he made it? Was he fast enough to unlock all the doors, too? Morgan had his picks, but she might not know how to use them under pressure . . .

He still tried to turn back, but Thomas put a huge hand on the back of his neck and moved him on, down the stairs, and there was nothing he could do.

By the time Jess found leverage to break the hold, they were down the stairs, and above, three strong men lifted a massive hinged door and bolted it in place. That, at least, was smart; a door that opened upward might end up buried by debris. This way, at least they could dig their way out, after, if necessary.

They're alone out there. Locked up.

Jess turned on Thomas. He would have shouted at him, but he saw the other young man's face. The tears in his eyes. It silenced him.

"We couldn't have made it there in time," Thomas said. "I'm sorry."

Jess no longer wanted to yell, but he couldn't bring himself to agree, either. He just turned away.

Inside, the place was lit by flickering candles and oil lamps and was crowded with long wooden benches that wouldn't have been out of place in a pub. Rows of Philadelphia citizens sat in silence, eyes turned up at the blank ceiling.

"Sit," Indira said, and pushed him down with a firm hand on his shoulder. She crowded in next to him on the bench, with Thomas on the other side and her two men blocking the stairs, though it didn't seem likely anyone would try to rush for the exit. "Quiet."

Jess took in the sharp smell of sweat and the rapid, ragged sound of breathing. Everyone stared upward.

Then the world above shuddered with impact, like a giant's foot crushing down.

Dust sifted from the ceiling, and Jess ducked and coughed out the taste of it. A murmur went through those sitting near him—an old gray-haired European man clutching a carved wooden pipe, a slender native woman with beads braided in patterns in her long black hair, two small African children who held each other's hands. Frightened but desperately silent.

The people in the bunker clung to their benches as another Library bomb fell, as the cellar ceiling trembled, as Philadelphia ignited above them. Jess thought of the mismatched scraps of timber and brick, stone and metal, that made up homes and stores. What wasn't burning would be shaken apart. And yet, as he looked around, he didn't see despair.

He saw determination.

Tomorrow, maybe even within the hour, they'd be scavenging the wreckage and building anew. Jess didn't like the Burners. Didn't agree with them in many critical ways. But he knew courage when he saw it. It would have been so much easier if he could see them as just enemies, instead of . . . people.

It took only a few minutes, and then the shuddering barrage stopped. Jess smelled the Greek fire . . . it was impossible not to recognize the sharp, sweetish reek of it. It was warm in the bunker but not, he thought, hot enough for the fire to be raging right above them. They waited. A child fussed and was quieted, but no one spoke.

They all relaxed when they heard a sudden, loud thumping on the overhead cellar door.

"All clear," Indira said, and as if they'd all been released from some spell, people around them stood and took in deep breaths. No one seemed relieved. Three muscular guards unbolted the door and eased it back on a latch, to allow the public to exit in slow, shuffling steps.

Jess followed, and came out into hell. Philadelphia was a confusion of broken ruins, flames, smoke, and screams.

Part of the city hall had been hit and was a luminously green inferno; a team of people pulling a long wagon thundered past; then two clambered up to work a hand crank as the others unrolled a long hose and trained it on the blaze. The foam that vomited out smothered the flames as water couldn't; Greek fire was notorious for that, an oily compound that splashed and clung and ignited on its own, and nothing but thick powders or foams could starve it. Once those flames were doused, it was obvious that they'd lost at least a quarter of the building—though not the end where Jess had been meeting with Beck. If the Library had been aiming to kill the Burner leader, they'd missed their shot.

More buildings on the street vomited black smoke—half a dozen ruined, and farther on, what seemed a residential block had half the houses lit by that haunted green. Some were just black, smoldering cinders and boards scattered in the street. People moved quickly, with a purpose, but he also saw the human damage—a woman weeping in the gutter, clutching a child. A man with a burned face staggering away into the smoke. A soldier hauling a body from rubble.

Until that moment, he'd pushed it away, but Jess felt panic hit him as he turned to look toward the prison, because one part of it was a mass of smoking, green-flickering debris.

"Thomas!" he shouted, and pelted away across the soft grass, under the hissing sway of trees. One was burning, and he had to dodge around an orange, ashy rain of flaming leaves. Smoke welled up to smudge the sky. He heard Thomas running behind him, and the shouts of Indira and her fellow guards, but he didn't wait. A few rescuers had already gathered at the prison, and a tall, brawny man with a wheelbarrow was shoveling thick powder into the flames to quell them.

The door into the prison had been blocked by a fall of thick, cracked concrete and stones. Jess reached for one and hauled it aside, even as his mind mapped out the prison on the other side for him. *That's the far corner, the cell Santi and Wolfe share. Across from Khalila and Glain.*

He didn't hear any shouting inside, and that made his guts curdle in dread. Greek fire smoke was toxic. Morgan had pointed out the poor ventilation inside.

They had to get the door open. *Quickly.* Jess didn't think to ask for help; he just fell to it, grabbing fallen stones.

Thomas joined him at the door, and together they hefted a staggeringly large chunk of concrete and rolled it out of the way. Jess's muscles burned with effort, and the sharp edges of stone slashed red gashes in his fingers, and when he breathed in he smelled that horrible reek of Greek fire. The smoke made him cough until he was spitting up black bile.

He and Thomas cleared the rest of the blockage, hauling the last away with desperate strength, and Indira shoved between them and fitted keys into the door's lock. It turned with a shriek of protesting metal, and Thomas shoved the door in with a scrape and shudder.

Jess plunged into a thick cloud of rank, drifting smoke. He coughed at the chemical stench as he shouted, "Morgan!" It was the first name that came to him. "Morgan!"

He almost ran into a cell door, which stood completely open and gaping.

"Here!" a voice called, and coughed. Metal banged on metal. "We're here!"

He almost tripped over them in the gloom. All of them were together—Khalila, Glain, Santi, Wolfe, Dario, Morgan—wedged together in the corner farthest from the smoke and flames, low to the ground to suck in the cleanest air. Jess grabbed Khalila and Morgan and hauled them up to their feet. "Go, the door's open!" he said. Glain stood and pulled Dario up with her. "Go!"

Jess reached down to pull Santi up, and Wolfe stopped him. The Scholar's face had gone ghostly pale, and his outstretched hand shook with urgency.

He was holding Santi against his chest in a protective, supportive embrace.

Jess crouched down. He pulled in his breath sharply when he saw the blackened edges on the captain's sleeve and the raw, red skin beneath, and looked at Wolfe, whose face in that moment was utterly unguarded . . . but only for an instant, before the bitter mask slipped back in place.

"Carefully," Wolfe said. "For the love of Heron, *careful*."

Jess took hold of Santi's unburned arm, and Wolfe supported the captain with both his arms around Santi's waist as they rose together. Jess moved carefully in on the burned side without touching what had to be incredibly painful injuries. Santi's breath came in short, ragged pants, and his face was the color of pale amber. Still conscious, and sick with it.

"Easy, Captain," Jess said, and guided him out of the cell. He tried to sound reassuring. "We'll get you help. Easy now."

Santi let out a tortured gasp, and his legs suddenly folded. The man's full weight crushed down on Jess's shoulder and Wolfe's, but between the two they kept him upright and moving through the choking, smoky fog and out into the cleaner air.

It felt like coming up out of a grave, even if that grave looked out on ruins.

Indira quickly took command and saw Santi settled on the grass while she sent one of her men running for a Medica—no, they called them *doctors* here, Jess remembered. Some of their doctors had Library training but rejected the authority of the Medica branch, and they certainly didn't have the facilities, or the supplies. *They probably heal with poultices and folk remedies,* he thought, and felt a sick roil in his stomach. *Santi could recover cleanly if we were on the other side of that wall.* But that didn't matter. Santi, and all of them, were stuck here for now, in a city that despised them and distrusted them, among fanatics who'd burn a book to make a point.

Santi took in a deep, slow breath and let it out. He still looked too pale, and he shivered convulsively. "I'm all right," he lied. "Chris. Don't look so angry."

"Do you expect me to look pleased?" Wolfe shot back, and though his expression was harsh, his fingers were undeniably gentle as he eased Santi's burned sleeve aside to get a better look at the damage. It looked worse without the cover: a handspan of skin burned away nearly through to the muscle, and where it wasn't gone, the remaining skin had a scorched, puckered look that didn't bode well. "Jess. Get that powder. *Get it now.*"

The sudden tension in his voice sent Jess to his feet without question, and he ran to the wheelbarrow, scooped up a double handful of the heavy powder that the Philadelphia man was using to kill the blaze inside the prison, and raced back.

Realization nearly made him falter, because *Santi's arm was still burning.* It was hard to see in daylight: little greenish flickers, but he could hear the sizzle as the Greek fire drew new breath in the open air. It would continue to burn, right down to the bone, if it wasn't smothered.

Jess dumped powder on it, spreading it thick, and ran back for another double handful. He used that, too, just in case, and couldn't imagine how that grit felt on raw, burned skin and exposed nerves. Santi didn't make a sound, though his shuddering was far worse now, and he looked seconds from passing out completely. Wolfe was holding him up in a reclining position, trying to keep the arm up and away from any more contamination.

They all waited tensely to see if the flames burned through the powder. A defeated wisp of smoke curled up instead, and Jess allowed himself a little jolt of relief. *It's out.*

Santi slowly shut his eyes, and now the remaining color bled out of his face. Wolfe looked nearly as bad as he stared at the arm, alert for any sign of the fire's return. When it didn't come, he glanced to Indira, who was crouched nearby, watching. "Knife," he demanded. "I need to cut the cloth away. There might be more soaked in."

She silently handed one over, and Wolfe sliced the fabric of Santi's uniform sleeve off, high up at the shoulder, to bare a strongly muscled biceps, old seamed scars, and farther down, the wholesale ruin of his forearm. It looked bad, Jess thought. Very bad.

Indira said, without any sign of emotion, "He's done for."

Wolfe's head snapped up, and he gripped the knife in a way that made the back of Jess's neck go cold and tight. There was pure murder in the man's eyes, and it was only the fact that he was cradling Santi against him that kept him from it.

"He isn't," Jess said. "The captain's been through worse. We need a Medica."

"Don't have Library Medica," she said. "We have a doctor."

"Where?"

She stood up in a smooth motion. "Give me the knife, Scholar. Now." Wolfe didn't move, and Indira drew the gun that hung heavy at her belt. *"Right now."*

Jess reached over and took the knife. He was nearly as surprised by it as Wolfe, but something had to be done to keep this from turning worse. He offered it to Indira, hilt first, but kept his fingers firmly gripping the flat of the blade when she started to pull it free. "Doctor," he insisted.

She sighed impatiently and said, "I'll take you."

She set off, and Jess, after a look exchanged with Wolfe, ran to catch up. He heard someone behind him and looked back to see that Morgan was following, too. She caught up and jogged along with him. Heat from the fires blew her hair in disorderly curls around her face. "I used the lockpicks," she blurted out. "When the Greek fire hit, all I could think was to get everyone out. But the pick broke on the outer door and I couldn't open it." Her voice trembled, and he felt her body shudder along with it. "I thought we'd die in there, Jess. Is Captain Santi—"

"He'll be all right," Jess said, which was a lie, but it seemed to help. "Wait. You broke my picks?"

"Don't. Don't try to make me laugh, Jess, I was terrified and you were *gone*."

"I know." He'd never wanted to kiss her so badly as he did in that moment, to put his hands on her face and look into those lovely eyes and make her feel safe again. But there was no time. "You saved their lives."

"Where are you going?"

"Indira's leading us to find a doctor for Santi. His arm looks—" Jess shook his head. "I don't know what kind of barbaric medicine they practice here. I hope it's enough."

"It has to be." She pulled in a breath, and when he shot a glance at her, he saw that the reality of the attack, the devastation around them, was starting to hit home. "My God. Santi warned us when he heard the sirens that we needed to get out. I did my best, Jess, I did, but—"

"You did as well as anyone could."

She just shook her head at that. "At least I might be able to help the doctor. Obscurists can sometimes add power to medicines, speed healing, prevent infection . . ."

He hated the thought of betraying her power to more people, making her more valuable to Beck and his Burners . . . but there was nothing else to do if they wanted to save Santi now.

They ran with Indira through the smoking wreckage of the Burner town, and he had no idea how to keep any of them safe anymore.

EPHEMERA

Text of a letter from Aurelian, emperor of the Roman
World, to Zenobia, queen of the East. Indexed in the
Codex.

*I command you to surrender upon the terms I propose, which are
these—your life shall be spared, so that you spend that life with your
friends, where I shall, with the advice of the august Senate of Rome, think
fit to place you. Your jewels, silver, gold, and precious things, you must
give up to the Roman treasury.*

Text of a letter in response from Zenobia, queen of the
East, to Aurelian Augustus. Indexed in the Codex.

*It is not by the pen but by the sword that the business of war is to be
transacted. You forget that my ancestor, the royal Cleopatra, chose death
rather than splendid slavery.*

Text of a notation from the Archivist Magister Zoran.
Indexed in the Codex.

*By all means, let these two giants clash. Zenobia, we have heard, has
a rare library of hoarded manuscripts, and Rome still hides their rarest and choicest works. Once both empires are on their knees, we will
broker peace, at a price.*
   I intend for the Great Library to become more than mere knowledge.
   I intend for it to use both pen and sword.

CHAPTER THREE

I ndira spotted the doctor from a distance away. "There," she said.
"The one in the long coat and hat." She immediately turned and
grabbed a passing man—one of hers, Jess assumed, though maybe Indira had the authority to press anyone into service she liked. "Take
them to the doctor. Watch them. If they try to escape, shoot them
down."

"Ma'am," the man said, and gave a rough salute. He was young,
only twenty at most, but the look in his eyes was ages older. Indira
strode off, shouting at a group pulling apart boards on a burning
building nearby. Saving what they could. Their new escort studied
Jess, then Morgan, and said, "You're the booklovers."

"Guilty," Morgan said. "Where's the doctor?"

"There." The young man pointed, and once he had, it was hard
to miss the man. The doctor was a tall American native, with long
hair tied in a square braid that trained down his back, and a wide-
brimmed hat trimmed with a broad red ribbon. The coat was a faded,
tattered patchwork of leather and cloth that somehow retained a hint
of a Medica's robe about it. Beanpole thin, as most Philadelphians

were, but he moved with smooth assurance as he parted a knot of people and knelt beside someone lying on the ground.

"Come on," Jess said, and he and Morgan ran forward. The circle of watchers had closed up, shoulder to shoulder, but he was well used to slipping in where he wasn't wanted. He hoped their guard wouldn't take Indira literally and start shooting, but if he did, at least they'd have cover.

Once he'd wormed through to clear space, Jess found himself standing at the feet of a fallen young woman who gasped for breath through lips as blue as the clear, enameled sky overhead. The doctor bent next to her, fingers on her wrist, then on her neck. He pressed his ear to her chest, then snapped his fingers without looking up. He pointed . . . directly at Jess. "In the bag there is a covered pot with a red cord. Get it."

The bag in question lay right at Jess's feet, and he bent down and sorted through the contents. Mismatched jars and pots, most chipped and carefully mended. *There's another thing they have to reuse,* Jess thought. *Things so common we throw them out in other parts of the world. Every scrap is precious here.*

The pot with the red cord—though red was a generous description; it was more gray with a hint of orange at the frayed edges—lay near the bottom. Jess took it and held it out for the doctor, who glanced up impatiently. "Well? Open it!"

When Jess did, the smell hit the back of his throat and clung there like an oily parasite, and he coughed and gagged and quickly shoved the pot in the doctor's direction. The man took it, sniffed without appearing to flinch at all, and then dabbed two fingers into the liquid mess before smearing it under the nose of the woman lying before him. She took in a gasp, then another and another. Each seemed deeper than the one before, and the bluish tint to her skin began to shift to something less dire. "Good," the doctor said, and thrust the pot back at Jess. "Put the cap on tight; no leaks or you'll be paying for it."

Jess nodded and recapped the vile mixture while holding his breath, but somehow, the stench still crawled deep into his nose and mouth before he could secure the top in place with the cord again. By the time he was done, the girl on the ground was sitting up, clinging to the doctor's hand but breathing well.

"You took in a good dose of fumes," he was telling her, "but keep the tincture on your upper lip and breathe it in until you don't feel liquid in your lungs. It'll burn your skin and leave a bright red patch, but that's better than death, isn't it? Go on, now. Help someone else when you feel strong enough."

"Doctor—," Jess began.

"Who are you?" The doctor climbed to his feet and assisted the girl up. He handed her off to two others waiting anxiously nearby. "What do you want?"

"We need you at the prison," Jess said. "We have someone seriously burned."

The doctor looked at him for the first time with real interest. "Ah. The prisoners. You're still wearing a Library uniform. Strange no one has killed you for that yet."

It was a casual enough observation, but it caught Jess short; he hadn't even thought about it, in the heat of his worry about Santi, but on a day when the Great Library forces were raining destruction and death down on Philadelphia, wearing his High Garda uniform might well deserve a beating from the townsfolk. "I'll worry about appropriate dress later," he said. "Are you coming?"

"I heal my own first. Anyone else? Anyone?" No one stepped forward to claim the doctor's attention, so he sighed and focused back on Jess. "Is your friend also wearing a High Garda uniform?"

"Yes," Jess said, and held the doctor's cool stare with an effort. "And you took a Medica oath to help any who ask."

"Years and many atrocities ago," the doctor said. "No one is holding me accountable to it."

"No one but the gods."

"Then I'm sure my afterlife will be interesting." The tall man reached out and snatched the bag from Jess's grasp—no mean feat, given Jess's High Garda–trained reflexes—and put it over one bony shoulder. "Well? Go on. If you have a patient for me, show me!"

"Yes, Med— I mean, Doctor."

"Dr. Askuwheteau. Go!"

Jess pushed back out of the crowd and looked for Morgan. She was standing with their guard, who'd clearly not been comfortable allowing both out of his sight, and seemed relieved to see Jess, with the tall man striding behind him. "Doctor," the guard greeted him. "One of the prisoners is injured."

"Burns, the boy said."

"Yes."

"Worth my time?"

The guard shrugged. "Not my call."

Askuwheteau struck out in a walk that forced the three of them to a run to keep up. No one stopped them. Chaos had turned to organization in the short time they'd been to find the doctor, and teams of workers were on every burning building, while others were already at work salvaging from smoking wreckage. Everyone moved with a purpose.

And, to Jess's relief, no one signaled to the doctor for help along the way.

As they hit the park, Askuwheteau lengthened his stride even more, moving at a speed that even Jess was hard-pressed to match, and despite his best efforts he was three steps behind when they arrived at the prison. He found Askuwheteau crouched down next to Santi and Wolfe.

He took one quick look at the wound and shook his head. He slipped his battered bag from his shoulder and, without a word, took Santi's arm and held it up for inspection in the smoky afternoon light. It was getting near on sunset, Jess realized.

"Are you trained?" Wolfe demanded. The Philadelphia doctor gave him a narrow look and ignored him to focus past Jess, on Morgan, who'd just arrived.

"You. Girl. Give me the pot with green and yellow strings from my bag," he said.

Morgan opened the bag and began rummaging in it. The doctor looked away, and then, as if he'd noticed something, returned his attention to her. He studied her closely, and his lips parted to say something.

Morgan beat him to it, without looking up from the sack. "Yes. And I can feel you have the talent, too. Not strong enough to send you to the Tower, but enough. Are you their only Obscurist?" Jess knew he looked a fool; he'd never asked if Obscurists could recognize each other. Never thought of it. Morgan saw his look as she glanced up. "The best Medica are often gifted, but not enough to be Obscurists," she said. "He's *almost* strong enough."

"Almost, yes. I worked with the Obscurists when I was young, developing Library medicines," the doctor said. "And yes, I am the only one with anything like Obscurist powers here. I've done what I could, but you are *much* stronger. You can increase the potency of what I've prepared. If you would, please. It might well save your friend."

She found the pot with green and yellow strings—though those were almost as colorless as the red cord had been—and opened it. She dipped her fingers inside and closed her eyes, and a faint shimmer of gold seemed to pass through her skin and into the pot. She handed it to the doctor, who sniffed and nodded, then took a soft brush from a kit at his belt and began painting the stuff onto Santi's burns. It *did* glow, Jess thought, a very faint, whispering shimmer.

"Excellent," Askuwheteau said. "Never work against the properties of nature unless you have time, and focus. You know that, I suppose. Start with a healing potion, and you can make it much stronger quite easily. Changing poison to a healing potion takes a great deal more time, talent, and energy." He paused to look at the balm he'd applied. It continued to glimmer. "You have a real gift, girl. Valuable. It's best you keep it hidden, or you'll find yourself serving the Iron Tower, locked in a collar."

"I escaped," she said. That earned her a set of raised eyebrows. Askuwheteau gestured for the bag, and she passed it over. "You won't tell Beck about me?"

"I expect he already knows. After all, the eight of you came here with two London Burners. They would have told him."

Askuwheteau was right, of course. Beck had to know, though he'd said little. Not yet.

Morgan said nothing, but her quick glance at Jess spoke volumes. Worry, but mixed with something else he couldn't identify as easily. *She's plotting something,* he thought, and the idea turned him cold. He didn't want Morgan risking herself.

"I can help you more," she told the doctor quietly. "At least, with Captain Santi. If you'll allow it."

Jess watched as she methodically strengthened the potency of every one of Dr. Askuwheteau's medicines. The doctor applied them, layer on layer. He was examining the rest of Santi's arm now. Santi, while Jess hadn't been watching, had slipped into the kind embrace of unconsciousness, so if there was pain from the doctor's manipulations, he wasn't feeling it.

"You're Library trained," Wolfe said. "But you left the service."

"My people have been living in and around this city since time began," Askuwheteau said. "These are our lands, and we were trapped when the Burners took over. They needed a doctor. I wouldn't be true to the Lenape if I did what I was told by the Library and turned my back on them, would I?"

Jess stayed silent and watched as the doctor applied another layer of salve. Wolfe studied Askuwheteau with angry intensity. Without looking up at him, Askuwheteau said, "You are a Scholar? You have a touch of gift, too."

"Not enough," Wolfe said.

The doctor's long fingers smoothed more cream over weeping, burned flesh. "Any power is enough to matter," he said. "Love and power both. Stay with him. He will need strength." He sat back, frowning, and studied the arm again. Jess had the sense he wasn't looking with regular human sight. Morgan often got that same gauzy, unfocused look. "All right. If we keep infection at bay, he may live. Will he have use of his arm?" Askuwheteau moved his shoulders in a peculiar kind of rolling shrug. "Perhaps. I will check him in the morning." He stoppered jars and bottles, slotted them back into his case, and stopped to give Morgan a nod. "Good work."

"Thank you. I'll do whatever I can for him tonight."

The doctor's eyebrows rose, then fell into a straight line as he took another long look at her. "Don't do as much as you think you can. Power is like fire," he said. "It will turn on you in an instant, if you fail to respect it. I've seen it happen. And you? If you burn, you'll burn fast."

She murmured thanks, and with that, he was off again, striding at a pace that made those in his way scramble to leave it. He might look like a patchwork scarecrow, but the doctor had a certain strange grace to him. Jess thought he wouldn't like to have to fight the man. He had no doubt that the healer could take him apart as easily as fix him.

Morgan moved to Santi's side and put her hand on his uninjured shoulder. "Scholar, if you'll allow it, I can try to speed the healing for him."

"Yes," Wolfe said. "The sooner he's back on his feet, the better we can plan our exit from this wretched place." That sounded businesslike, but there was fear and grief in the man's face—there, and gone. Wolfe transferred his focus to Jess. "Thank you." A simple thing, but Wolfe rarely was civil, much less grateful, and Jess knew by that just how terrified he'd been of losing Niccolo Santi. "Now. Fetch Schreiber. I want to hear everything."

Thomas relayed the news—Jess and Thomas, tasked with building the press; the rest, working to catalog the Black Books. Santi was in no shape now to endure any questioning, and Beck couldn't possibly think it a ruse; Indira herself had seen the damage the Greek fire had done. So that was, Jess thought, one danger avoided, even if it led Santi deep into another.

"A decent bargain," Wolfe said. "Serving as his translators and interpreters of the work gives us the chance to . . . obscure some of the more dangerously useful bits of information."

Jess frowned at that. "Censorship," he said. "So now we're taking on the role of Archivist?"

"Would you prefer to hand Willinger Beck an arsenal of inventions even the Great Library thought too deadly?"

Put that way, Jess thought, there wasn't much he could muster in the way of an objection. But he didn't like it. He wondered if this was how it had started, all those ages ago, when some Scholar had earnestly advised an Archivist that a discovery was just too advanced, would cause too much damage. Who'd put the first of the books in the Black Archives? The records were all ashes now; they'd never know. But it worried him, how easy it was to slip down that path for reasons that seemed logical at the time.

It apparently didn't worry anyone else. Wolfe and Thomas had moved on to discussing the rest of the deal with Beck. "We'll still be guarded," Thomas said. "But not locked in. And we'll be fed, such as they have to offer. Which, I gather, isn't very much."

Wolfe nodded his satisfaction. "I'll talk to the guards, but there's not likely to be rations tonight. The city's bound to save its own first. We'll ask tomorrow." At the mention of food, Jess's stomach let out an unhappy growl, and he wondered when it was he'd last managed to eat. Seemed a long time ago, and too little to matter.

Khalila, Dario, and Glain, who'd been watching from the periphery, came back, one after the other. Khalila bent down and touched Scholar Wolfe's shoulder. "Sir? How is he?"

"Sleeping," Wolfe said. "Their doctor is competent. I hope it'll be enough."

"The guards say the smoke's out of the building and the fires are all doused," Dario said. "They also say we'd be better off staying in there, never mind the draft. Didn't say so, but the townsfolk left with houses and buildings in ruins might make our evening rough if we try to take up beds in the shelters. We'd best not press our luck."

"Captain Santi will rest better inside," Thomas said, and stepped forward. "Let me, sir."

Wolfe didn't react for a few seconds, and then he nodded and stood up. Thomas scooped Santi up in his arms, careful of the salve-smeared burned arm. He didn't seem bothered by the man's weight in the least, and they all followed as he carried Santi's unconscious body through the narrow door into their prison. Morgan darted ahead to look over the cells and finally pointed to Dario's. Dario, to his credit, didn't even protest. "This one's best; it'll be the warmest," she said, and Thomas eased the man down on the mattress. "Thank you, Thomas. I'll take care of him now."

Thomas had positioned Santi with his head toward the wall so that his wounded arm lay straight and still, and now Morgan sank down on her knees next to the bed, studying the injury; Jess had the sense she was looking at something far different from what he could see, and her fingers spread out in a precise pattern to hover above his wounds. She let out a breath, closed her eyes, and went still.

Wolfe stood in the corner of the cell, all his focus on Santi's quiet face.

"Nothing more we can do here," Thomas said softly, and Jess nodded. "Best we take stock of what Beck's given us to work with in this workshop of his. The sooner we know, the better we can plan."

It was oddly hard to leave, though there was plainly nothing to do; Jess's gaze lingered on Morgan's face—fixed, tranquil, oddly tense beneath all that. Whatever she was doing, though, he knew it would take a toll. He could almost see the power, energy, quintessence— whatever one wanted to call it—pouring out of her, into Captain Santi's injured flesh. He remembered Askuwheteau's caution to her and wondered what price she was going to pay. Whatever it was, she wouldn't turn back.

In that way, he and Morgan were exactly alike.

The workshop was nothing but a junk heap.

The tools and materials that Philadelphia had to hand were, at best, a disaster. Broken bits of metal scavenged from wreckage, scrap bricks and broken stones, leather that had been rebraided and oiled to within an inch of its very ancient life. Rope was in short supply, and what they had, they kept carefully stored in barrels.

The wood—and there was not a lot of it—consisted mostly of scraps that showed hard use. A few precious new boards that must have been cut from trees inside the town walls lay in a neat, shallow stack. Miraculous that there were any trees standing at all, Jess thought, between desperate inhabitants and Library bombardments. Beck must have been brutal in his punishments for cutting them down.

"This is not so bad," Thomas said with forced good cheer as they looked over the disappointing lot. "I've done more with less. Does that forge work?"

"It does, but there's not much fuel," the guard who'd accompanied them said. "We can't use wood. There's some coal. Not much. We can bring you some Blanks to burn."

Jess shuddered at the thought. "Any Greek fire jugs that landed and didn't explode?" The guard frowned. "We just need a drop or two a day. Add some to a little supply of coal, you have a superheated forge that can stay hot for hours. It can burn rocks, if necessary."

"You can keep charge of what we don't use," Thomas quickly said. "I understand you would not want to give us unlimited access."

"You're dead right. And if Master Beck approves it, you'll keep your mouths well shut about it. Greek fire in Library hands? The people would tear you all apart."

He was right. The Library had been a constant, faceless enemy to the Burners for more than a century. It was a minor miracle he and his friends were all still alive now, since they were the breathing, vulnerable examples of it. Given the slightest hint of betrayal, the people of Philadelphia would turn on them fast.

"We're here to give you a great weapon against the Library,"

Thomas said. "Destroying us would be killing your own chance to win."

"I'm not listening. Master Beck can think what he likes." The guard glared at both of them with open, naked hatred now. "But if I'd had my way, we'd have roasted the lot of you on top of the books, and thrown your skulls over the wall for your friends to mourn."

Thomas exchanged a look with Jess. "You understand that we're under a sentence of death, to the Library? Killing us *helps the Archivist*. Not your own people."

Jess said, "He's telling you the truth. We're enemies of the Archivist Magister, and we're going to find a way to bring him down."

"You. Your little band of children."

"You're at most three years older. How long have you been fighting? All your life, I think."

"I hate the *Library*, not the Archivist. Take him away, and you still have the same corrupt system. It will breed another just like him."

"He's not wrong. We have a great deal to repair to ensure another tyrant doesn't rise," Thomas said to Jess, and then turned back to the guard. "What is your name?"

"Diwell." It came out reluctantly, as if giving up his name meant forming a long-term relationship he didn't want.

"Diwell, five hundred years ago, the Great Library went down a dark path. But it still shines a light. Weaker now, but putting it out plunges us all into darkness together."

"Don't give me your recruiting speech."

"All right," Jess said. "Beck wants us to build a machine for him. How do we do that, if we can't forge parts? We need the Greek fire, or we need a lot of fuel. His choice which he gives us."

Diwell glared, but he nodded. "I'll run it by Indira. What else?"

"Wax," Thomas said. "For casting parts. It doesn't matter if it's already been used."

"Candles are in short supply. Like wood and every other damned thing here."

"We'll make you new candles from the melt when we're done with it. The loss won't be so much, we promise," Thomas said, and rubbed his hands together. "Mr. Diwell, please, take your ease. My friend and I will need to go through everything stored here. It will be a very long evening, and I promise we will do nothing more interesting than talking and writing things down."

Thomas's face had taken on a healthy color in the lamplight. It wasn't, Jess thought, just that they were out of the cells and relatively free; a workshop, however poor, was his real home, and he looked forward to surveying the tools and supplies and making do with what little they were given. Thomas loved a challenge.

Thomas's careful inventory took most of the night. Diwell tried his best to stay alert, but dozed, eventually, as Jess and Thomas created a list of all that the storehouse could offer. Some of it had nothing to do with the press at all, of course, but all of it could, in one way or another, come in handy. Once that was done, they used charcoal to sketch out plans on the stone wall of the workshop.

By the time they finished their plans, they were both as dirty handed as chimney sweeps, and when Thomas put the last touches on the sketch, they both stepped back to admire it by the flickering light of a single, smoky lamp that had the stench of many-times-fried bacon fat. "Not bad," Jess said. "Not a patch as good as we could do with decent materials, but—"

"But this will do," Thomas agreed. "We don't even need to wait on more supplies. It'll take both of us, and hard, sweaty work, but it can be done, yes?"

"Yeah," Jess agreed. "There should be enough wood in here to make the frame, though I can't say how long this rotten stuff will hold together under strain. Then we just need to make springs, plates, and gears. Paper could be a problem. I imagine it's as dear as wood around here."

"Why? They're burning Blanks," Thomas said. "We take some and cut the pages out."

He was right, and it was a far better fate for the Blanks than being set on fire just to inspire Burner fanaticism. "I'll get some from Beck," Jess said, and surprised himself with a skull-cracking yawn. It was no longer just late; the night had advanced toward morning, and Jess realized he was well past exhausted. He cast a glance at Diwell, who was slumped in a corner near the door. Too far away to hear, and too deep asleep to care. He lowered his voice anyway, to just above a whisper. "Thomas? Are you sure this will work?"

"The press? Yes," Thomas said. "And the Ray of Apollo? There are certain things we'll need to complete that. Glass to make mirrors, and so forth."

"And if it doesn't work?"

"Then we die here," he said. "And, Jess? I won't survive in a cage."

In a cold flash of memory, Jess saw Thomas as he'd been not so very long ago—half-starved, bruised, shaking, with a matted head of hair and beard that made him look decades older. He looked better now, but by no means the old Thomas Schreiber. That boy had never known despair. The bleak shadow in Thomas's eyes now said he would never again know a day without it. *Thomas can't go back in a cage. Neither can Wolfe.* The elder Scholar had borne it in silence, but that silence had been heavy, and telling, and Jess had heard him cry out in nightmares before.

"How much time will we need?" Jess asked him.

"That . . . I'm not sure," Thomas said. "The press is only a few days. But the Ray of Apollo . . . well. A full day for the mirrors, but that must be done without anyone questioning our work, so two days, and we must be careful. I will consult Khalila with the calculations of focus. A week, at least, before we can be ready, and then we must find a power source."

"That's my job, then." He was overtaken by another yawn, and Thomas's smile broadened.

"Enough for tonight," his big friend said, and took a dampened cloth to the meticulous charcoal drawings they'd made on the walls. Jess sucked in a breath to protest, but Thomas shook his head. "I've got them memorized. We can't leave them up for anyone to see."

Once the wall was clean again, Jess walked over and nudged Diwell's chair with one foot, bringing the guard instantly back to startled wakefulness, with one hand on his gun. "We're finished for now."

Diwell muttered something that probably wasn't kind, or complimentary, and led them back to the prison.

N o way of knowing how late it was, but the moon was down. It felt like the world was spinning fast toward morning. Jess looked into Dario's old cell as they passed. Captain Santi was still asleep on one bunk, and on the opposite, he recognized the brown curls of Morgan's hair, though she slept facing the wall.

Wolfe, wrapped in one thin blanket, came awake the instant he felt their presence, and reached for a loose, jagged rock that was lying near to hand. He relaxed when he made out their faces in the dimness. He slipped the blanket away and climbed to his feet to meet them in the narrow hallway. "You took your good time," he said. "Can you do it?"

"The press, yes. And possibly something more that could be a valuable help to getting us past these walls."

Wolfe took that in and mulled it in silence for a few seconds before he said, "No unnecessary risks. Understand?"

"Yes," Thomas said. "But everything is risk. You know that, sir. How is the captain?"

"Resting. The doctor's not half the idiot I would have assumed." From Wolfe, that was high praise. "Morgan's been tending to him, as much as she can. If she weren't, he'd certainly lose the arm. He still could."

It was the studied calm in the way he said it that hurt. Jess cast a quick look at Santi, then away. Nothing more to be done for him. "How much is it hurting her?"

For a long moment, Wolfe didn't answer; maybe he didn't think Jess was ready to hear it. But finally, he said, "The power that the Obscurists possess comes from their life force, their quintessence. As they use it to transform and shift the nature of other organic and inorganic things, it becomes . . . affected by what it transforms. Think of it as water. Dip a dirty cloth in it, the cloth comes out clean, but the pollution remains." Wolfe finally shifted his gaze to meet Jess's stare. Jess wished he hadn't. "Obscurists in the Iron Tower have time-tested ways to manage their work. They create scripts and formulae and touchstones—filters, so that the corruption doesn't touch them directly. But using the quintessence daily . . . It's dangerous. There's a reason people have always feared witches. And there's a reason we never call Obscurists magicians."

"Because they aren't?" Thomas asked. "They have an ability, the same as gifted engineers."

"Engineers' gifts don't destroy them from within. An Obscurist without controls, without barriers . . ." Wolfe shook his head. "Nothing stops them. And that's dangerous. *She's* dangerous. She's learning too much, too fast, and no one to hold her back."

Jess swallowed. He didn't like the sound of that, but it had the ring of truth. "And what do we do about that?"

"Nothing," Wolfe said grimly. "Because we need her. And every single bit of power she can provide, if we're to survive this and find a way out. I'm sorry about that, but you and I are alike: we'll do what must be done. Even if it means letting those we care for put themselves in danger."

Wolfe's gaze slipped back to Santi as he said it, and Jess knew he was thinking of all the times Santi had stepped into the path of harm for him. And would, for as long as he could stand, or crawl.

I'm not like you, Jess thought. But he knew he was, really. He'd learned to be practical too young.

Thomas said, "And everyone else is all right?"

"Well enough. Are you hungry?"

"Starving," Jess said. His stomach cramped and growled like a wild beast.

"Glain stole us a small supply of food. It's not enough, but I expect no one in this town gets more, except Willinger Beck." Wolfe nodded to two empty bunks in their cell. "Eat quickly, and sleep while you can. It's very late." He went back to his uncomfortable bed on the cold floor beside Santi, wrapped himself up, and was asleep again—at least, apparently—within minutes.

Thomas had already found a handful of cheese and a small slice of bread that sat out on a small shelf near the unlit furnace, and was making an effort not to take more than his share, though he was twice the size of the rest of them. Jess wolfed down a smaller portion of the hard crusts and soft cheese; it tasted like a promise of heaven, but just a taste. He wanted a dozen more mouthfuls and had to convince himself to leave the rest for the others, who must not have gotten anything yet. Nothing but cold water to wash it down, but by the time he'd drunk his fill, Thomas was already in his bunk and halfway to dreams.

Jess took the other bed and blew out the lantern, and was dreamlessly unconscious before the afterimage of the burning wick died.

He woke up with a metallic, filthy taste in his mouth—the aftermath of the Greek fire's toxic smoke—with the glow of early sunlight spilling into the cell. Dario Santiago was looming over him, hands on his hips as he nudged the bunk with one knee. "Come on, scrubber. Up. It's a bright new day."

Jess raised himself onto his elbows and looked around. He could tell by the stiffness in his spine that he hadn't moved much in the night, and he certainly hadn't been on guard, though he ought to have been. Khalila was up and bustling around, tucking her hair under the scarf and giving him a distracted smile as she took one of the small, broken pieces of dry cheese from the shelf. Glain was doing another handstand and then rolled into a rapid flurry of push-ups before she got to her feet.

But when Jess looked at the cell across the way, he saw two empty bunks. Santi was gone, and Morgan, too. Wolfe's blanket lay discarded on the floor.

Jess sat up and fixed his stare on Dario. "Where are they?"

Dario's normally cocky expression shifted a little into something . . . less. "The captain woke up in some distress. They moved him into that Medica's house this morning."

"Some distress? What does that mean?" Jess demanded as he swung his legs over the side of the bunk and sat up. Dario shook his head and looked away. It was rare to see him struck without words, and it didn't offer comfort. "Did Morgan go with them?"

"She said not to wake you."

Because she damned well knew I'd go with her, and I might try to stop her from killing herself, Jess thought, and for a moment he felt a surge of sick dread so real that it froze him in place. He finally cleared his throat and said, "So you kindly waited here to rub my face in it?"

"No," Dario said. "Thomas left for the workshop, and he told me to give this to you." He reached inside his jacket and took out a thin, ragged scrap of cloth. It stank of dried sweat—torn, Jess guessed, from the bottom of Thomas's shirt. There were words written on it in tiny, precise letters that had smudged just a little. Jess held the cloth closer to the light to read them.

"Where does he think I'm going to get this?" he asked. "Not from Beck. He'll want to know too much about what it's for."

"He said you're resourceful," Dario said. "He's not wrong."

Down the way, Glain stretched like a particularly large and dangerous cat, and went to join Khalila. The two of them left without a word, which left Dario and Jess alone. Somehow, Jess thought, Dario had asked for that solitude.

"All right," Jess said, and reached for his boots. "What?"

Dario seated himself on Thomas's bunk. "You and I, in Santi's absence, are what passes for strategists in our little company, wouldn't you agree?"

"I don't agree with much you say," Jess said. "But I suppose."

"While Santi is—indisposed, it's our job to think ahead," Dario said. "Not just to tomorrow. Not to next week. Not to escape. We need to think beyond."

"Beyond to what?"

"That," Dario said, "is why you're the inferior chess player. What say you take a walk with me?"

"We're not that friendly, in case you've forgotten."

"Relax, scrubber, I'm not suddenly thirsty for your company. But I thought a stroll near the wall . . ."

That got Jess's firm attention. "Meaning?"

Dario's voice had gone very quiet, even though the room was deserted. "Meaning, I struck up an acquaintance with two disreputable characters late last night who wanted to place bets on the fastest of three roaches. I won, by the way, quite nicely. One of them was one of Beck's guards, and they have access to some strong—not *good*, mind you—liquor. He was well into it when he told me they'd posted extra men at the eastern wall. I don't expect he'll remember much of any of that conversation today."

Jess's mind raced. Extra guards on a wall meant they expected something—either someone trying to go out or someone coming in. The Library wasn't likely to give advance notice of tunneling in, though they'd been most polite about the bombardment. So that meant . . .

Jess pulled his boots on. "Let's take a walk, like friends."

"I thought you'd see it my way," Dario said, and they went up and out the door.

"Don't let it go to your head."

"If we find this tunnel," Dario said as they walked—oh so casually— on a street of ruined buildings near the wall, "then what comes next?" No one was watching them. Crews of Philadelphians were up to their knees in rubble, sorting out bricks, metal, broken bits of wood that could be reused. Grimly repairing anything that could be saved.

"Finding a way to follow it without anyone here knowing. Scouting the exit. Figuring out a diversion to get us a chance to use it. Finding a way to cover our escape from the High Garda camped outside. Communicating with someone who can see us safely out of here and out of America." Jess listed it off without even thinking about it. Dario nodded soberly at the end of it.

"As I said, you're not a very good chess player," Dario said. "You think too small." Usually, that would have come with a snide grin, or at the very least, a smarmy tone, but it sounded . . . contemplative. "Skip those things. They are important, yes, but the question is, what is your endgame?"

"Staying alive."

"*Winning,*" Dario said. "And how do you win?"

"Me? Not you?"

Dario drew in a deep breath and let it out in a sigh. "We both know my ambitions are different from yours. You want to change the world. I just want to have what I want. Whatever that is." He shrugged. "You've got aspirations. So tell me what you want to achieve."

"All right," Jess said. "Winning means defeating the Archivist. Making us all safe again."

"And, of course, changing the mission and direction of the oldest, largest, most powerful institution on earth."

"If you want to put it that way." Jess was silent for a while. The walk felt good, the sunshine, the slight breeze. The stretch of his legs. "You win in chess by capturing the king. So we remove the Archivist Magister."

"The king, yes." Dario clasped his hands behind his back as they walked. "You take a king by two methods: brute force or subtle attack. Brute force is beyond us, at least as I see it. So to win, we have to plan an attack he can't see coming. In chess, you don't play your opponent. You make your opponent play *you*. You draw him out. You make him watch one piece while another moves."

"And why are we talking about bloody chess?"

Dario stopped in his tracks, turned, and faced Jess head-on. Suddenly, his friend looked like a man twice their age. A statesman, burdened with responsibility. "Because Wolfe is an honest man. So is Santi. In their hearts, they are loyal, and they are not good liars. Khalila and Thomas are the same. Pure, down to their souls. You and I, and Morgan—we're different. We understand the need for expedience. For deception. And when we need to be, the three of us can be ruthless. Wouldn't you agree?"

Jess watched him for a moment, thinking, and then nodded. Dario turned and began walking again, and Jess joined him. It felt different now. It felt much more serious. "And Glain?"

"Glain is loyal, and also ruthless. I don't know. I give it even odds she would support or oppose us. So I leave her aside for now."

"You're talking about planning something that even our own friends don't know about," Jess said. "Something the others wouldn't support."

"Yes."

"And you have a plan?"

"No," Dario said. "I have a goal. *You* will have a plan. I know you well enough to know that given time, you will understand what needs to be done. I only wanted to say it, so you'll look for it. But it needs to be something no one else can see coming. If Wolfe and Santi see it, then so will the Archivist. They're all trained the same. I'm a disreputable black sheep. You are a thief and a criminal. Morgan has spent her life running from the Library. You see the difference?"

"We're the difference," Jess said.

"Yes. And that will cost us. Victory always costs." Dario cleared his throat and said, in a very different tone, "Oh look. We've picked up a new friend."

Another of Beck's guards—not Diwell, this time, but someone older—had joined them at a distance. Watching. Jess hadn't really expected anything less. They'd only gone a quarter of the way around the outer wall, and already he could sense that trouble was coming.

They'd been careful to keep a good distance away from the wall itself; there were Philadelphia guards posted at strategically effective distances, so that one was never out of sight of the others on either side. Jess had observed the guards along the western side yesterday, and Dario was right: security had been tightened all along this eastern wall. Here, near the center, there were four guards in attendance, all close together. They seemed less than relaxed, and when they spotted Jess and Dario walking parallel to them, one of them—the largest, Jess noticed—came stalking out to meet them.

Jess stopped. Dario did, too, and they both turned to face up to the newcomer. He was a Native American, like Askuwheteau; he wore his hair in a stiff, short brush down the center of his skull. Broad across the shoulders and chest, with the build of a born wrestler. And he had scars—burns, mostly. Almost everyone in Philadelphia had burns.

"Leave," he said flatly. "You can't walk here."

"Beck said we have freedom to move around the town," Jess said.

"Not here. Go."

Their guard caught up to them, red-faced. "I'll move them on," he said, and turned a raw, furious look on Jess and Dario. "When you're told to go, don't argue!"

"We didn't argue," Dario said. "We're looking for a dealer in glass. We were told to look near the wall around here."

"*Glass?*" their guard said, and then his face slid into a twisting sneer. "You need mirrors to look at your pretty faces?"

"Well, yes, personal grooming is a virtue," Dario said, without so much as a flicker, "but I understand that's a foreign concept here. *Is* there a glass vendor?"

The native guard, who was looking at them with eyes that Jess thought were almost on the verge of catching fire, said, "Sev sells broken glass." He jerked his chin toward a row of partially demolished buildings a street farther on. "Maybe we'll feed it to you for dinner."

"Thank you," Dario said, "but I'm trying to cut down." It was *just* enough of a pun that Jess had to control a laugh. Sometimes— very occasionally—Dario was good for that. But there was nothing casual about the tense set of the Spaniard's muscles. He *looked* relaxed, but he was ready for a fight, just as Jess was. They didn't even have to exchange a look to be in agreement. "We'll move on, then. Jess? If you're ready?"

"I'm ready," he said, and together, they turned and headed off. His shoulder blades itched, waiting to feel any hint of movement behind, but when he glanced back, the native soldier had gone back to take up his post against the wall.

However, their trailing guard had decided to greatly close the gap. Inconvenient, and it kept Jess from talking to Dario until they were in the next street and the rattle of a passing cart—drawn by a single, exhausted horse, the poor creature—loaded with scavenged materials provided enough noise to cover it. Jess spoke fast, and to the point. "Couldn't see the tunnel, but look there." He pointed quickly toward a weathered, half-burned old tree that grew in the no-man's-land between the wall and the street. "See the mark?"

"No," Dario whispered back, and then the cart was past them, and they had to go quiet again. It wasn't until they were inside the cramped, reeking confines of the shop—a generous word for it; Jess thought *repur-*

posed privy might have been a better one—and looking at sad piles of broken glass sorted by color on the warped floor that they had another chance to talk. The place held no attraction for their guard; he stayed outside, in the fresher air. There weren't any other ways out. "What mark?"

"Two parallel lines and a circle," Jess said. "Means a tunnel controlled by the Comprehensive." Dario gave him a blank glance. "Group of smugglers."

"Run by your family?"

"No. Rivals. It's a problem." Jess crouched and looked at the clear glass pile. The largest pieces were the size of his hand, but those were rare. Most were just barely better than slivers.

He stood up and gestured at the tiny woman who stood half asleep at the back of the shop. "How much?"

"For what?"

"All of this. The clear."

She blinked. "In exchange for what fortune?"

Jess looked at Dario. Steadily. Until the Spaniard sighed and produced a very fine money pouch. A fat one. "You're taking my roach-racing winnings, you know."

"Why do you think I brought you along, for pleasant company?"

"Ass." Dario handed over the pouch, and when the woman opened it, she gave an audible gasp and clutched it to her chest. She pushed a threadbare bag across with her foot.

"Take it," she said. "Go."

"Everybody wants us gone," Dario said, and picked up the bag and thrust it toward Jess. "You get the glass splinters. I paid."

Dario was right. It wasn't fun, handling the broken glass, but Jess took the cuts and jabs in stride. He'd had worse, and would again. Once he was done, he lifted the heavy, crunching bag and tried to think how best to carry it without giving his back a scratching it would never forget.

The woman held out a second, thicker bag. "Free," she said, and smiled just a little. "It's easy to get hurt, you know."

Her arm was in the light from the door, and he saw the scars then, old and new layered into gnarled patterns. Her fingers looked raw. It was like looking at a map of pain, and he had to shake his head. "No," he said. "I can bear a few more scars. You keep that."

Once they were outside, he carefully put the bag over his shoulder and winced at the immediate sharp bites . . . but it was bearable. Dario said nothing, just shook his head. "You're an idiot," he said. "You should have taken it."

"You gave her all your money. She probably wouldn't have asked for half that much."

Dario shrugged, eloquently. "Philadelphian notes. Worthless. Let her have the use of it."

Truth was, Jess thought, that money could have bought Dario meat, bad liquor, all manner of indulgences. But Dario didn't like to be thought of as anything like kind.

So Jess just said, "Let's go find the rest of Thomas's shopping list."

EPHEMERA

Text of a work from the Black Archives, untitled, credited to Heron of Alexandria. Not indexed in the Codex.

I have written before on the curvature of metals, and the reflections of light that may be done with such. The simplest use is a mirror, which reflects light upon the viewer. But light may also be concentrated in a series of highly polished mirrors, sending it from one surface to another to another, until the light is so bright and it becomes a solid thing, like a beam of fire. I have achieved this effect upon three occasions. With one, I used mirrors the size of shields, and was able to set alight a distant tree, which burned as if Zeus himself had cast down lightning upon it. In the second case, I used a finely polished set of jewels loaned to me by the gracious hand of Pharaoh, and the result was much stronger, and much smaller in width. Upon the third attempt, I seated these highly polished gems within an array of holders, precisely set to amplify the light, and contained it within a tube of brass. This attempt, shown before Pharaoh, melted through seven feet of thick, hardened iron, to the awe and terror of his court.

It is the power of Apollo contained within mortal hands, and by the order of Pharaoh, I have been ordered not to continue these experiments, for the gods will not share such wonders without punishment.

The will of Pharaoh is ever wise.

CHAPTER FOUR

Working with Thomas was like being a student playing next to a master pianist. Not that Jess didn't have aptitude; he was good at whittling parts from spare scraps of wood to Thomas's specifications, and then transferring those models to a hot wax impression, ready for casting. Thomas measured and cut what little good, solid wood they'd been given, and spent his time at the forge, melting scrap metal and casting the gears.

When he wasn't sweating in front of the forge, Thomas had a strange way of staring at the empty space in the middle of the workroom, walking around and around it as if he were examining an actual machine that stood there.

Jess finally left off carving to stare at him. "You really can see it, can't you?" he asked.

"Yes, of course. It's right there." Thomas raised his eyebrows and pointed to the plans they'd sketched again, in charcoal, on the wall. Jess shook his head.

"Yes, I can see the *plans*. But you see the whole thing already built, don't you? All the way around?"

"Of course," Thomas said. "You don't? How else do you create something that doesn't exist?"

Jess tried creating that machine in his imagination, but the sketch—though he understood it—remained stubbornly as flat as the charcoal on the wall. "I don't think I'm meant for a gold band," he said, and grinned. "And I think you always were, Scholar Schreiber."

Thomas turned and looked at him. "I'm not really a Scholar."

"Didn't anyone tell you? Wolfe commissioned you. Lifetime appointment, gold band and all. When they told us you were dead, you were entered on the rolls as an honor. There was a ceremony. They put your name in hieroglyphs on the Scholar Steps." It had been, Jess thought, a somber and emotional afternoon; just six of them together on the vast Serapeum steps while an Egyptian priest intoned a prayer for the dead. Morgan had been gone in the Iron Tower, and Thomas . . . Thomas had been screaming in a cell underneath the streets of Rome.

"I didn't think—" Thomas broke off. "I—don't know what to feel. The Library did try to kill me. But—"

"But it's the only thing you ever wanted," Jess finished when Thomas didn't. "It's complicated." What he didn't say was maybe it was worse that Thomas had been granted that dream, given how things stood now. Chances were, Thomas would never wear the gold band he so richly deserved.

Thomas shook his head and—incredibly, to Jess—smiled. "It's fine, Jess. An honor. And it's not all I want. I want to *build*. And we are going to do that, right now. Yes?"

"Yes."

Thomas walked over and studied the gear. "Almost right."

"Almost?"

"Smoother here, yes?" Somehow, getting a correction from Thomas didn't make Jess feel foolish; he nodded and took up a file to fix the problem. "It's late. Are you tired?"

"Do you have any idea what High Garda training is like? They run you until you forget how to *be* tired. No, I'm fine. How much have we done?"

"We are a third complete, I think. Though we need to make extras of several of these gears. I'm not confident they'll take the stress even from the test. They must last for a few passes."

Jess put the finishing touches on the wooden model before handing it over. Thomas walked to the empty space, held out the wooden gear in a precise location, and cocked his head as he stared. It was the eeriest thing, Jess thought; he could actually see Thomas thinking. The power radiating out of that head seemed to fill the space around them with energy. Maybe Thomas had been right in his observation that geniuses and Obscurists had something in common.

"This is good," Thomas said, and tossed the gear back to him with a sudden flash of a grin. "Twenty more to go, yes?"

"I hate you." Jess put the tools down and stretched. His hands ached, and so did his back; his eyes burned from focusing in the dim light. "Maybe we should stop for the night after all."

"I knew the High Garda had no real stamina," Thomas said as he scrubbed the plans from the wall. "I'll bank the coals in the forge. A drop of Greek fire will bring it up in the morning." He nodded toward the guard—Diwell again—who dozed in the corner. By which Jess knew he meant, *Distract him.* So as Thomas carefully, quietly hefted the flimsy bag full of broken glass, Jess moved over to a large pile of scrap metal that he'd taken care to build up to tottering heights all day, and on Thomas's cue, he shoved the whole thing over.

The noisy racket of metal clanging together drowned out the tinkling sounds of the glass being poured into a thick stone bowl, and Thomas quickly picked it up and shoved it into the forge, then banged the door closed. Diwell came upright, tripped, and had his gun out and aimed at Jess and Thomas within a respectable few seconds, though he was smart enough not to fire. Thomas had managed to throw the empty bag into the forge, and all trace of it was already gone.

"What the *hell* do you think you're doing?" Diwell barked. Thomas slowly held up his hands. They were nearly black with soot and charcoal and, here and there, reddened with burns. He never seemed to mind the wounds he took when working.

"Just an accident," Thomas said. "We are banking the fire for the night. We will be leaving now." When Diwell finally put his weapon away, Thomas raked coals forward and added a layer of new ones behind, then a single drop of green liquid. The fire blazed up with a hiss, then subsided. Burning hot but steady.

The glass would slowly, surely melt overnight and be ready for the morning.

"Hurry up," Diwell growled near the door. "I've missed my meal because of you."

He was out the door and locking it behind them, and as he fiddled with the padlock it allowed Jess and Thomas to stride on ahead a bit. Jess said, "Do you think this is going to work?" He didn't mean the press they were building; he knew that would.

Thomas met his gaze squarely and said, "The Ray of Apollo? God preserve us if it doesn't. Did you get the power source?"

"As it happens, yes." Jess reached into his trouser pocket, took out a small wooden box, and watched as Thomas slid it open. Inside, a little mechanical bird turned its head, hopped to its metal feet, and began to sing in a clear, warbling tone. Thomas reached down and touched a particular spot on the tail feathers, and the bird froze in midsong. Disabled. "Morgan won't be happy you're destroying it. She treasures it, you know. She carried it with her into the Iron Tower, and out again. Khalila got it from the bag in Beck's office. Which, by the way, reminds me: I should look into wearing full skirts. Seems like they hide a wealth of tricky behavior."

"I'd be delighted to see you try."

"I'll bet Dario would be."

"So now we have our power source," Thomas said, and closed the box. He slipped it into his vest. "We make our mirrors. And then, we will nearly be ready."

Jess didn't share the optimism. He knew it was in Thomas's nature; he knew Thomas needed it right now to see his way through the nights spent in a room with bars, in a city that was a trap. But he couldn't share it.

In his experience, optimism got people killed.

One of Khalila's requests had been put in place by the time they were back in the prison; she'd asked for privacy walls, and Beck—probably as a bitter little joke—had ordered pieces of paper glued across the bars of their cells. The paper, Jess immediately recognized, had been torn from Blanks. A little sting in the tail of his gift. But it was a little better, Jess had to admit. More of a sense of safety, even if it was an illusion.

It put a tiny scar on Jess's heart when he saw Dario, of all people, escort Morgan into the prison that evening and extravagantly bow her into her private cell. The two of them were spending days together in a comfortable sitting room in Willinger Beck's office, where the most dangerous thing either would do was to collect a paper cut. He also knew that it gave Dario time to talk with Morgan, to propose to her the same thing he'd discussed with Jess: *deception.*

He just hoped that Dario wasn't playing him false, along with everyone else. And he hoped that if Dario was, Morgan would refuse to go along with it.

But he didn't know. He'd lost that ability, in the hot glare of jealousy that he wasn't the one walking with her, smiling at her.

Dario said something to her, and she laughed and shook her head. It was a free sort of sound, that laugh, which was strange because they were anything but free here in Philadelphia. Then again, Morgan's talent, her mind, and her body had all been the Library's property. By contrast, this might seem like real freedom to her.

Morgan's gaze skimmed across and snagged on Jess's, and he saw the laughter die away. *Don't stop laughing,* he wanted to tell her. *I like it when you laugh. I just wish it was me.*

But the smile that melted onto her lips was better, richer, deeper. It meant more, because it was meant only for him. And unlike the laughter, it lingered.

She held out her hand to him, and it felt right to take it. Just for a moment. She looked down at their twined hands and winced as she noticed his fingers. "What have you been doing? Your hands—"

"Glass cuts," he said. "Look, not even bleeding anymore. I'm fine. How—" He wanted to ask, *How are you?* because he was worried by the dark shadows beneath her eyes, the slight tremble in her hands. But he said, "How is Santi?"

"I haven't been there, but we're told he's better," she said. "Scholar Wolfe sent me away once he was moved to the doctor's house. Beck demanded me at city hall."

"Why?" Jess asked.

"He wanted me to reactivate the Translation Chamber. They'd walled it up over a hundred years ago, the day they took the city. The floor was covered in giant spikes. If we'd entered there, when we left

London—" Jess winced, imagining them dropping into such a place . . . sealed, and full of deadly traps. When the Burners had kidnapped them and forced her to make the journey, she'd chosen the park outside city hall; it had been the largest space, the easiest to find. "He wanted it functioning, for use with his smugglers."

Jess lowered his voice. "Could you do it?" Because that might be exactly what they needed. But she shook her head.

"No chance. Translation Chambers work because they're places rich in quintessence—and they're rich because they're used, over and over. Because people pour energy out inside them. But a hundred years of disuse has stripped it bare. There's nothing left. I'm sorry, Jess." She'd been thinking the same, that she could lie to Beck and hold that escape route in reserve. But if it was dead, that left only the smugglers' tunnel and the desperate, last-ditch idea of the Ray of Apollo. Jess didn't much like the chances of either one.

Khalila came in soon after, with Glain, and she beamed when she saw Jess and Thomas. "It makes me glad to see you both at the end of the day," she said. "Sweaty and dirty as you are. I think we all worry, having you apart from us." Her smile slipped away, and she washed her hands and face in the cold-water bucket by the door. "If only Santi and Wolfe were here to meet us, too." She'd found time, Jess saw, to change to a clean dress—unbleached linen, something that Dario had found for her, no doubt. Neat, as always. "I'm not sure I trust the work of this provincial Medica . . ."

"I think the doctor is doing his best," Morgan said. Jess moved past them to plunge his hands into the cold water and used the sand provided next to it to scrub the charcoal from his skin. The cuts, he had to admit, looked bad. And they stung. "And the captain is strong. A few days of rest will let him heal."

"If he doesn't take another turn for the worse," Dario said. When they all glared at him, he held his hands up. "We were all thinking it."

"I wasn't," Glain said, and shoved past him. "And I'm not. The captain's going to be fine."

"What if he isn't?" Thomas asked. The question fell into a sudden, and very dark, silence. "What happens to Wolfe?"

"We look out for him," Khalila said. "As he'd do for any one of us. But Captain Santi will be fine. That might be only my love of him speaking, but it's what I must believe."

She'd be the only one to admit it, but they all loved the captain, Jess thought; Santi brought out all the best parts of Wolfe. Without him . . . Jess could only think of the term Beck had used. *Stormcrow.* Without Santi, Wolfe would be more that than ever.

They were all silent for a moment. Not even Dario found anything stupid or inconsequential to say. Jess, without thinking about it, put his arm around Morgan, and she leaned against him, a lovely burst of warmth.

"Progress?" Jess asked quietly, and Khalila seemed relieved to have something else to think about.

"Find me a pen and paper," she said. "I took time in Beck's office today to study a city map."

"What map? You never moved from your chair!" Glain said. "I sat across from you the whole time, and it was easily the most boring day of my life!"

Khalila slowly smiled at her. "The map was hidden in plain sight," she said. "Framed. On the wall above your head."

Glain froze, thinking back, and Jess saw the exact moment she remembered. She looked well kicked, but Jess didn't blame her at all. He'd been in that office. He didn't remember a map, either.

"It looked like another of their damned Burner paintings," Glain said. "Mostly in orange. They like things the color of flames."

"It's not detailed, but it clearly shows fields behind city hall, the walls, the streets. A primitive style, and not by any real mapmaker. But it gives a good idea," Khalila said. "Paper?"

For answer, Dario plucked a sheet fastened to the inside of his cell—the paper wall—and handed it over. "I'll make ink." He walked over to the very small pile of coal near the furnace that sat by the door—designed, Jess thought, to barely keep them alive in colder weather—and took one piece. With efficient motions, he used his boot heel to pound it into bits, grinding it fine, then used another paper sheet stripped from his cell to wrap into a cone, and scraped the black powder in. Added some drops of water and stirred, measuring and adding carefully, until he had a little pool of black, watery ink in the cone. It wicked steadily into the paper, but he presented the cone to Khalila, and a small stick he found just at the door. She accepted both with a dimpled smile and an appreciative flash in her eyes, and set to work.

"I don't have colors," she said as she carefully crosshatched lines across certain of the buildings, "so I am using patterns. This one, I believe, shows the location of shelters, like the ones they use for bomb attacks." She used diagonal lines for the next, fewer landmarks. "These, I don't know. We should take a look at them. Storehouses, perhaps? They might contain something useful."

"Brilliant," Jess said. "Dario and I located a smugglers' tunnel marked here—" He hovered a finger over the part of the wall they'd strolled past earlier. "They've put more guards on it, which could mean that they're getting ready to receive goods through it." A thought suddenly struck him, and he tried to think how his father would have conducted such a business, if he'd sat in that city hall office instead of Willinger Beck. *He'd be much, much cleverer than that.* "Or they just want us to think that. If Beck is smart, he'd have increased the guards just to draw our attention to it. Make us commit to an attempt at using it. That gives him an excuse to draw us out."

"Or it could be genuine," Dario said, "and Master Beck is just a provincial warlord who doesn't think like you do."

"I've talked to him," Jess said. "I wouldn't trust anything he does."

"And if we tried to use it—"

"We'd end up captured, back in these cells without our comforts, and one or two of us roasted on a spit for our troubles," Glain broke in. "Jess is right. Take our time. Note the obvious. Look harder."

Dario sighed. "I like the obvious. It's easier."

Khalila was still drawing. She colored two last squares in solid black. Jess leaned forward. Both were close to the wall, one at the far eastern end, one at the far western. They mirrored each other. "And these?" he asked.

"I don't know. But something. They were marked with red on his map."

Glain said, "The western one is a barracks room. I haven't managed to scout the eastern one yet. It's at the end of the fields behind city hall. Too exposed. It looks like it could be a barn, though I've seen few enough farm animals. Possibly some kind of storage."

"Don't risk it when they're too alert," Thomas said, and Glain glanced at him and gave him a smile that was only half-mocking.

"Do you think I'm afraid of risk, Thomas? Have you met me?"

"If you want the guards distracted, I can help with that," Morgan said. Jess didn't know what she meant until she brushed fingers over the back of his hand, and he felt a wave of weariness break over him. It didn't feel unnatural, just the accumulation of days and weeks of the terror and stress they'd been under, and before he could stop himself, he felt a yawn coming on. He clenched his jaw and suppressed it, and sent her a disbelieving look. She gave him a sweetly crooked smile. "We're all tired. Even the guards. Hardly takes more than a brush of fingers to make them less alert. Glain, let me know when you need the distraction." She brushed fingers over his skin again, and he felt the weariness lift like a cloud blowing away.

He felt chilled by it, not heartened. *Is she getting stronger?* Askuwheteau's warning, Wolfe's predictions . . . none of it felt good. "Morgan," he said, and took her hand. Skin to skin. He didn't think she was using any of her quintessence on him now, but if she was, he wasn't certain he'd be able to tell. He bent his head closer to hers and whispered, "You need to be careful. Slow down."

She pulled back in surprise, and her eyes found his. She didn't ask what he meant, and he supposed she already knew. "Would *you?*" she asked him. "If you knew you could help? I know you, Jess. You'd run until your heart burst in your chest if you felt it would save the rest of us. How can you ask me to do less?"

"Because—" He wanted to say something, but this wasn't the time. Wasn't the place. "Because we'll need all your skill at some point. Don't waste it on small things. Promise me."

Her jaw set in a way he was coming to know well, a look he was certain her tutors in the Iron Tower had learned to their regret.

Khalila blew gently on the map to dry it, and then carefully rolled it up and looked around. "Jess," she said. "Where can I hide it . . . ?"

He went into his cell and took a small piece of metal from his pocket. It was about the size of a coin, with filed protrusions on all sides; he'd spent half an hour crafting it in the workshop, between making wooden models of gears. It was the sort of concealable tool that all smugglers and thieves used, and he plied it to loosen the screws of his bed and slip one of the rails loose. It was hollow. He put the map inside and screwed it together again.

"Why do you get to guard it, scrubber?" Dario asked, frowning. "Who made you Archivist?"

"If it's discovered, he will be the one blamed," Thomas said. "He's protecting you. And all of us."

"No," Jess said. "I'm just the one with the clever little screwdriver." But Thomas was, of course, correct. Jess was the one with the precious Brightwell immunity. Best any trouble fall on him, because Glain was right: Burners would be looking for an excuse to call them traitors, and make examples.

At least he had a better chance of staying alive, in that case.

"So what now?" Morgan asked.

"You should rest," Jess said, but she shook her head.

"I only wanted to see that you're all right. I'm going back to the doctor's house to stay with Wolfe and Santi."

"I'll walk with you," Jess said. "The more they see us doing normal, unremarkable things, like visiting our sick comrade, the better our chances of doing something remarkable later. We should all go."

He wanted to see Santi for himself, and he wanted to be sure Morgan arrived safely back at Askuwheteau's house.

And a walk in the dark with her, however brief? Irresistible.

There was a minor argument with the two guards who'd been left to secure the prison, and who didn't look too happy to have their *guests* leaving again. They'd only just got settled, and one was halfway through his cold, meager dinner. Diwell, Jess realized. "You're not going anywhere," Diwell said flatly. "Not until we're relieved."

"Which will be when?" Khalila asked. She'd carefully washed the ink stains from her hands. She'd also made Dario mop up the drips from the cone, which might not have been fair, but it had been dead amusing. "Our friend needs to go back to the doctor's home to tend Captain Santi."

"Don't care," Diwell said. He took a bite of stale bread and stared at them as he chewed. The look in his eyes said he personally blamed them for the quality of his meal. "You wait."

"How long?"

For answer, the other guard—older, calmer—simply drew his gun and rested it on his knee. He didn't even get up from his comfortable sitting position.

Jess let out a frustrated sigh. "All right," he said. "We wait."

They did, impatiently. Morgan was looking up, craning her head back, and Jess did the same. It was dizzying. The lights of Philadelphia were thin and weak, and the stars shone so brightly that they seemed to fill the sky. The night had a weight to it, and a pull.

"Beautiful," Morgan said.

Dangerous, he thought, but he didn't say it. She was right. He was just trained to look for the danger in everything. "Morgan, I meant what I said before. Please. Be careful."

"I am," she said. "But there are things only I can do. You know that. Wolfe—"

She broke off, as if she shouldn't have said his name, and Jess looked down at her sharply. She continued to stare at the stars, willfully ignoring the question in his eyes.

"He's got you doing something other than healing Santi," he said.

"That's my own business." She lowered her gaze to meet his, and why, *why* did she have to be so stubborn? But he knew the answer to that . . . because all her life, it had kept her alive. Kept her free.

"I'm asking you to tell me."

It was, he thought, because he asked that she finally said, "I offered Master Beck something to satisfy him when I couldn't reactivate the Translation Chamber. I told him I could increase the yield of their crops."

"Can you do that?"

"Oh yes," she said. "I didn't, but it gave me an excuse to walk through the fields by the wall and find a protected spot in the wall where I could begin to weaken it. The Obscurist who put up the wall generations ago was strong. It takes time and concentration, but—"

"Can you bring it down?" he asked her.

"No. But I can remove the protections that keep it from melting under Greek fire and other kinds of attacks. If I succeed, I can make it vulnerable."

"Enough for Thomas to finish the job." Jess sighed. He felt the beginnings of a headache coming on. He didn't like the moving parts of this plan, didn't like the *ifs* and *maybes*. "Morgan—how hard is this for you?"

"Not bad," she said, and he was almost sure she was lying. That she'd lost weight since he'd seen her in the morning. That the shadows beneath her eyes—in her eyes, too—were darker than they should have been. "Jess. Wolfe's right. We need at least two ways out of here. Three, if we can manage it. But if I can help . . ."

"We can find a way for you to help without destroying yourself."

She reached up a hand, put it on his cheek, and looked into his eyes. A serious, steady regard. "We all take risks," she said. "This one's mine." The coolness of her skin shocked him, and he curled his fingers around her wrist. Her pulse beat fast under the skin, but it seemed to be providing her little warmth.

So he wrapped his arms around her to share some of his own. She sighed, as if it was a major relief, and for just a few moments, there weren't greater issues, or worries, or plans.

Just the two of them, under the stars.

Then the guard change arrived, and Diwell and the older man gladly departed. In their place came Indira, and another man whose ancestry looked drawn from the same part of the world as Dario's. Spaniards had helped colonize the American colonies and still claimed Mexico and beyond. Made sense there'd be some here.

Indira didn't look especially pleased to see them lingering outside. She directed that displeasure at Thomas. "What are you doing here?"

"Taking the air?" Dario said.

She ignored him. "I was talking to you, Schreiber."

"Taking the air," Thomas said, without a flicker of a smile. Dario laughed. "Also wondering . . . what is that?" Thomas asked and jerked his chin toward the wall on their left. Beyond it lay a luminous glow, like sunset . . . but sunset had already passed. For the first time, Jess realized that there was a brighter glow *outside* the city than inside it.

"High Garda camp," Indira said. "Their encampment has grown through the years. All the modern conveniences, including chemical lights. They never let us forget they're out there. Night or day."

Thomas nodded. "We are walking to Dr. Askuwheteau's house, to see Captain Santi."

She nodded back. "Very well. Proceed." She and her fellow guard fell in with them.

Jess realized, as Thomas led them on a course that meandered closer to the wall, that he could actually hear the Library forces. A low, whispering buzz of activity, voices, movement. A sudden, bright spark of laughter. A faint brush of music. Vital, modern life going on just a few hundred feet away, while here, the Burners scrambled for day-to-day crusts of bread and rebuilt their ruined city after every attack. That, too, was an attack. A subtle kind, one that would eat at the spirits of those trapped inside.

"They never shut up," Indira said. She sounded resigned, but there was a tense undercurrent of anger, too. The hatred for the Library that never quite receded, in any of the Burners. And Jess was starting to understand that all too well. "And they never give up."

"Can I tell you a story?" Jess asked her. She said nothing, so he kept going. "Burners read books, so you should appreciate this one. You know of the Serapeum of Pergamum?" Indira nodded. Pergamum was one of the most famous of the original libraries—a Greek establishment, a rival to Alexandria in the early days. "Artemon of Pergamum was the Scholar in charge of that place after it was made a Serapeum, two thousand years ago. He stood in the doors of the building, in front of a crowd of invading Roman soldiers, and told them that his death would come before they touched a single volume. They killed him. When he fell, another librarian stepped into his place. When she was killed, another. And another. One by one, they died to keep the Romans from looting the shelves. The last was a newly christened Scholar, just arrived that day. Her name was Flavia, and she was from the kingdom of Carthage. She stood on top of the bodies of her friends and colleagues, armed with nothing but a knife. She knew she would die, but that didn't stop her."

Indira said nothing. But she was listening.

"The Roman commander himself stepped up to that bloody doorway and commanded her to save herself. She said, 'Better I die than a single book is lost.' Flavia was just fourteen years old. She'd been a full Scholar for less than a week. Her statue stands over the entrance to the Serapeum at Pergamum, because she saved it. The Roman commander said, 'If your love of these books is so great, then they must be worth saving.' And he set his men to guard the building, while the rest of Pergamum was looted and destroyed. It was the beginning of the Library's neutrality."

"You must have a point to this story," Indira said.

"Flavia is the spirit of the Library," Thomas said. "Not the Archivist. Not the Curia. You call us booklovers, and it's true. We are. And so are you, at heart. You believe in the power of them to change the world."

"It's a nice story. I don't believe in fairy tales. It's the Archivist and the Curia who run the Library, not your martyred saint."

"No," Jess said. "They're just running it *now*. If you want to change the world, you don't destroy the entire Library. You put Flavia back in charge."

"As I said, a nice story," Indira said. "We don't tell each other stories. We fight. We take action."

"You huddle behind your walls here and fight a losing battle," Morgan said. "And you're going to lose. What good are you really doing here?"

Indira's lip curled, and her tone was softly mocking when she said, "Being a symbol. Like your Flavia. Are you children really intending to teach us the proper way to rebel?"

"No. We're doing it with you or without you," Thomas said. He sounded certain of himself. No bluster, no pride. Just fact. "I don't see a future here, Indira. I don't see many children, and those I see are starving and frightened. You might be surviving, but I do not think you are winning. Do you?"

Only Thomas, Jess thought, could say that with so much understanding and compassion.

Indira's lips went thin, her gaze flat, and she took a faster pace, striding forward. "The doctor's house is this way."

They silently followed her. Jess had been hoping to drift closer to the wall, see the substance of it and more smugglers' marks, but she was going nowhere near it. Best not to push their luck.

He looked over at Morgan. The descending shadows gave her face smooth, strong lines and hollows. Like the sky, she was fragile and beautiful. Like this city, she could be lost, either in a firestorm or by slow, deliberate ruin, and it hurt him to know that he couldn't stop her. That he had no right to try. He silently offered her his arm, and she slipped hers into it. It felt good. It felt seductively *normal*, two people walking together in the beautiful, fleeting night with the stars burning overhead.

He said nothing at all during the rest of their brisk walk, and neither did she; the parklike grounds in front of city hall were largely deserted, except for a couple in the shadows locked in a passionate kiss—two girls, he realized. He waited for Indira to react to that, but she simply avoided them and moved on with a businesslike stride. The Burners, for all their passionate fanaticism against the Library, had very little prejudice to spare for anything else. He was seized by a desire to pull Morgan into those leafy shadows, to kiss her in just that way, with no thought for tomorrow, no cares for plans and future troubles. He wanted to lose himself in her, while he still could.

He was a little startled when he felt Morgan pull *him* in that direction, into the shadows. When it was *his* back against the rough bark. When it was *her* sweet, urgent lips on his, her hands cool against his cheeks, her body pressing his.

But he didn't question it, and for a moment, nothing else mattered, until he heard Indira say sharply, "You two! Here! Now!"

Morgan pulled back, regretfully, and Jess realized they were both trembling a little. He felt on fire, everywhere she'd touched him, especially his mouth, and he tasted her on his tongue and desperately wanted more, like a starving man given a single drop of honey.

"Morgan," he said. "Please don't let Wolfe push you into doing more than you safely can."

"I could say the same to you," she told him, and smiled. "We both learned Flavia's lesson."

Then she slipped away.

He had no choice but to follow.

The doctor's housekeeper—a tall, strict-looking woman—managed to convey both disapproval and welcome at the same time as she let them in. Thomas had to duck to fit under the low doorway, and his head came perilously close to the ceiling once he was inside the small house. With all of them crowding in—except Indira and the other guard, who took up positions outside—the room felt crushingly tiny.

"Quiet!" the woman whispered at them as they shifted around. "The doctor is exhausted. He needs his rest. I'll take you to your friend."

As they filed after her, Jess got a better look at the place. It felt like a real home—more of a home, he thought, than his own house in London had been, though he'd had a mother, a father, one living brother, and rich enough surroundings to give it all the right appearances. Jess had never felt comfortable there, in the Brightwell family residence. He'd been happier in abandoned places, so long as they were quiet and had enough light to read by.

Books represented home to him, and around every wall, the doctor's shelves were full to bulging, a haphazard organization of varied colors of binding, sizes, shapes. There was a happy disorder about it that made Jess feel something settle inside he hadn't even known was restless. Beside him, Morgan whispered, "So many!" in a tone that was half awe, half horror. Because these weren't Library editions, stamped with the seal and protected in the Archives. They were entirely illegal copies. Ink on paper. Vulnerable. "I didn't know they had so many!" The doctor's house, Jess realized, must be the unofficial library for the town. Nothing so formal as the pretentiously bound editions in Beck's office. Here was the heart of the town. The life that sustained it.

The hallway beyond was also narrowed on either side by shelves and shelves of volumes, and the smell of old paper struck Jess with memories of his father's warehouses, of curling up with a glow and an original volume in the rafters.

He'd never really been safe in his childhood, but the books . . . books had made him feel that way.

Their little group filed silently into the room at the end of the hall, where Santi lay unmoving. His color was some better, if still at least three shades off normal, and his exposed arm looked raw and glistening. Covered in a fresh coating of salve, Jess realized, and the skin beneath looked fragile but healthy. Already healing.

But Santi's face was damp with sweat, and there was a smell in the room that raised the hackles on the back of his neck. Sweetly rotten—the lingering stench of burned flesh and infection.

Wolfe sat in a chair next to Santi's bedside, holding his lover's uninjured hand with his left, and an open book in his right. As Jess stepped in, Wolfe let go of Santi to remove small, square glasses from his nose and stow them in a pocket, then put the book aside after slipping a feather in for a bookmark. The doctor had found new clothes for him, sized well, but he looked disconcertingly small in them. Jess was used to seeing him in the smothering, swirling cloud of a Scholar's robe.

"Close the door," he said, and Dario, the last one in, did so. "Guards?"

"Outside the house," Jess said. "We're alone, for the moment."

Wolfe nodded. He looked weary. "Then we'd best use the time well."

"Sir," Dario said, "is he all right?"

"He's drugged," Wolfe said. "If he wasn't in an opium haze, he'd be screaming. Try not to ask the stupidly obvious, Santiago."

Glain said, "Is he going to lose the arm?"

It was a blunt question, and very like her to say the thing they were all wondering. She put no inflection on it. It was just a request for information.

"It's hard to know yet," Wolfe said. "The next day will be critical. The burns were . . . significant." He cleared his throat. "Any problems?"

"No, sir," Khalila said. As always, she was the opposite of Glain; even that simple response had a wealth of gentleness in it. "No need to worry about us. We're fine. All proceeds well enough."

"And no one has harassed you again about—" He gestured vaguely to his head. She touched her own fingers to her hijab and shook her head. "Good. Not that I worry. I trained you to be sturdier than that." He blinked and looked away. Looked at anything, it seemed, but Captain Santi's still, too-pale face.

"Sir—" Jess tried to think of something to say that was useful, but his mind was as empty as a snowfield. "Have you eaten?"

Wolfe shook his head. "Not hungry," he said. "Thomas. Jess. Update."

"We have most of the parts for the press designed, and we'll start casting tomorrow," Thomas said. "The first mirror will be ready to grind and polish in the morning. That will take most of the day. Jess will be tending to it."

"Oh, will I?" Jess asked.

"Yes," Thomas said, with a flash of a grin. "You will. They watch me, because I'm large and sweaty and working with heavy tools. You'll quietly do the important work."

"The boring, hard, repetitive work of polishing glass?"

"Well, yes."

Wolfe gave them a quelling look. "And the tunnels?"

"Maybe," Jess said. "I'm of the mind that the one they're trying to point us toward is far too obvious. Even Dario noticed the entrance, and no smuggler worth a damn would build a tunnel so exposed." Jess had been turning it over in his mind, and now he looked at Khalila and Dario. "Any chance you can slip away to explore city hall at all?"

"They can't," Morgan said. "But I might, if I claim to be able to build them a new Translation Chamber. He'd let me explore. He'd keep me guarded, of course, but that doesn't matter. Obscurists can see more than the obvious."

"No," Jess said, but at the same time, Wolfe said, "Yes," and when Jess paused, Wolfe kept on speaking. "You're the only one who can make a good search of it besides Jess, and he's otherwise needed. And can you make the Translation Chamber work?"

"Not a chance in the world," she said. "Too long idle. But I did make headway on the other matter."

Jess knew what that meant, but he could see the others didn't; Khalila whispered something to Dario, who shook his head. Wolfe was trying to keep that quiet, then. And if Wolfe wanted it quiet, it was because it was dangerous to Morgan, who was far too willing to risk it.

"Then Morgan will look for any sign of tunnels leading into the city hall building—and I think Brightwell is right: it would be the most secure place for smugglers to bring goods, and for any communications to take place between Beck and those from outside."

"I should be the one to do it," Jess said.

"Mirror," Thomas reminded him. "And Beck will be receiving reports of where each of us is, what we are doing. Just let her do the job."

"I'll be fine," Morgan said quietly. Her fingers brushed his, very lightly. "I've survived the Iron Tower. Willinger Beck doesn't frighten me."

"Still. Don't assume you're safe at any time." Wolfe's smile looked thin, and grim. "I don't assume we're safe here, either."

"He hasn't given you reason to think . . ."

"The doctor's done his best," Wolfe said, and swept a dismissive hand at *best*. "It isn't much. Without Morgan, we'd have lost Nic. Infection carries away many burned with Greek fire, even with modern Medica help. But whatever the doctor's intentions, he can't protect us from Beck."

And Santi had never been as vulnerable as he was right now, Jess thought. Wolfe referred to *us*, but he meant Santi, really. He meant that he would not be separated from him as long as Santi couldn't defend himself.

Morgan had been studying Santi closely, and now she said, quietly, "His fever's still high. I can concentrate the medications in his bloodstream a little more." With that, her fingers moved down a little, to brush the tattoo inked high on Santi's biceps: a lion that snarled in startlingly lifelike blue ink, as if it might leap out of the skin to defend the man. Tattoos were a High Garda tradition. Glain already had three. Jess's first was of a closed book on his chest, over his heart. He felt it described him best.

He felt sick now that he was watching Morgan expend more energy, but he knew he couldn't stop her if he tried.

"The captain will be all right," Jess said, which was an empty promise, and he knew it was a mistake the moment he said it.

Wolfe's gaze snapped to him with a blazing fury, and he said through gritted teeth, "Don't feed me platitudes. I know how bad it is. *He protected me.* He didn't hesitate, the second he knew we'd been hit with Greek fire. He pushed me down and took the burns for me."

That, Jess thought, was pure Santi. And here was Wolfe, with that knowledge shimmering like dull flames in his eyes. Hating himself for the sacrifice.

"He always protects you," Jess said. "He always will. You know that."

Wolfe blinked and looked away, toward his lover's sleeping face. He reached out and put a gentle hand on Santi's sweating brow. "I know. But I'm perfectly free to give him his Christian hell for it, too."

Morgan's face had drawn tense with effort and worry, and Jess could see a faint shimmer at the tips of her fingers where she touched Santi's shoulder. She breathed deep and closed her eyes and stood motionless—gone, in a sense. Lost to the rest of them until she came back of her own will.

"Leave her with us," Wolfe said. He was watching Jess now, as if he knew exactly what Jess was thinking. "I'll make sure she doesn't do too much, and she can have my bed there in the corner. I won't sleep anyway."

"Do you want us to stay?" Khalila asked him. "Would it help?"

He shook his head. "Go," he said. "I need you all alert and strong. We're not even beginning our struggles yet."

"Come on," Dario said quietly—*Dario*, of all of them, suddenly the sensible one. He tapped Thomas on the arm. "Scholar? Is there anything else we can do?"

"Pray," Wolfe said. "You can pray."

Jess was on his way to join the others when his steps slowed. The comfort of these cluttered shelves in the hallway . . . he couldn't quite understand it, but he couldn't deny it. He needed comfort just now, and he stopped to take in a deep breath of the smell of old paper, leather, *books*. A talisman against that fearful sickroom smell.

A volume caught his eye, and he pulled it out to look. The dull red leather was stamped *Rose Red, Sea Blue*. It was, he gathered from skimming the book, a novel . . . one about lovers separated by distance, each pining for the other but thinking the other had abandoned them. The man had been abducted out to sea, to serve on a pirate ship. The woman, thinking herself betrayed, had married another and regretted it. A needlessly dramatic story, no doubt overwritten and dripping with breathless prose, but there was something about it that offered an escape.

"Take it," a sleepy voice said. Jess nearly dropped the book, but his respect for the written word kept his grip firm as he spun around to find the tall, thin doctor standing there, yawning. His hair was out of the braid, spreading in a fine black silk sheet over his shoulders. He was wearing a loose shirt ghosted with old stains, and a pair of trousers that had seen far better decades. Feet thrust into rough leather sandals that looked painful.

"I thought you were asleep, sir."

"I'm not a *sir*. My people don't have royalty. And I never sleep long. Too much to do." The doctor plucked another book from the shelves—a small green one—and smiled at it like an old friend. "You're shocked by my collection?"

"Delighted," Jess said. "I think all houses should be stuffed with books. It makes them—"

"Homes?" the doctor finished. "You are quite the heretic, for someone in a Library uniform."

"Guilty."

"Then take the book. Read it. If it pleases you, keep it. I love for them to find good homes." The doctor studied him with a sharpness at odds with the yawns. "Did that Obscurist girl tell you that Beck asked her to join us?"

"What?" Jess's fingers tightened on the cover of the book.

"He offered her sanctuary here. Freedom, and her own home. A life without fear of being locked into a collar. They're kept as little better than slaves in that tower, you know. No will of their own—"

"I know what the Library does to Obscurists," Jess cut in, and the edge in his voice was too sharp. "They'll lock her up, make her work the rest of her life keeping the Archivist Magister and his cronies in power, and breed her like a prize cow—" He stopped, because that crack in the bedrock of his soul had widened with an almost audible *snap*. "And I'm supposed to believe that the Burners will treat her better? Beck isn't a man who offers things from pure goodness. What kind of slavery will she have here, if he keeps her?"

The doctor watched him in silence, then said, "Why do you think I warned you? The girl deserves better."

Jess gripped the book tightly, and left.

The next day, Jess drowned himself in work. Morgan hadn't come back to her bed in their prison/guesthouse, and it hurt like he'd taken a crippling wound. He spoke little at the workshop, methodically following Thomas's instructions as he crafted more gears. Thomas had removed the stone vessel from the forge first thing, while Diwell fetched his meager breakfast, and quickly poured the thick, honey-colored liquid glass into a set of small frames they'd made ready the night before. Jess set it to cool behind some concealing junk. They both made themselves industrious and busy, and Diwell quickly got bored and took to his chair.

It was hours before the glass had cooled and hardened. Once it had, Jess nodded to Thomas, who took to heating metal and beating it with hammers, a spectacular show of strength and noise, while Jess took up the sandpaper he'd made earlier and began to polish the small mirrors, with a box of gears ready to pull over to conceal his work if needed. Thomas had explained the process to him and warned him it was exhausting and hard, and he was right: polishing, turning, polishing, turning, always in precise patterns. It made Jess's body ache in ways he'd never known it could. But he kept at it. When Diwell paid attention to him, he worked on cast-metal gears and sanded them to perfection; as soon as the man's attention moved on, it was back to the mirrors.

For *hours*, until the glasses were uniform in size, and he'd put in the precisely measured curves that Thomas had asked. Then it was *more* polishing, this time with a much softer-grit cloth. More hours. More grinding pain in his arms and shoulders, neck and chest.

Thomas finally called a halt by shoving a pitcher of water under his nose—said nose was dripping with sweat, Jess realized. And outside the barred windows of the workshop, the day had gone well into sunset.

"Drink," Thomas ordered, and Jess did. The sweet relief of cool water on his parched throat made him realize that he ached in every muscle, and he sank down on a wobbly bench that gave an alarming creak as Thomas sat next to him. Jess gulped half the container and handed it back. Thomas finished it off and put the pewter down. Diwell was snoring in the corner. Loudly.

Jess passed over the mirrors. Six of them laid out on a soft piece of cloth on the tray. "Will they work?" he asked.

"They should," Thomas said quietly. He examined them closely and nodded. "We won't know until it's all mounted. But I think yes. I will put everything together, but only when we're ready."

"We still don't know if it will even work."

"No," Thomas said. He didn't seem worried. Such an engineer. "But that's why we have different plans on how we exit. Yes?"

"Sure." Jess leaned back against the dirty, splinter-prone wall and closed his eyes. "What about the press?"

"I'll have the last pieces cast tomorrow," he said. "Another day to put it together. Then we can set the timing as we like, to let Beck see the fruits of our labor."

"How fast is Santi healing?"

Thomas shook his head. *Not fast enough.* But they had to keep Beck's attention, and there was only one way to do that: show him the goods.

Jess wiped a dirty cloth over his face. It probably did nothing but spread around the dirt and grime, but at least it dried his sweat a little. "Have you done the pieces of type yet?"

"Not yet. What language should we start with, do you think? English or Greek?"

"Both," Jess said. "We want to impress them."

"Casting will take a day. Then it's just assembly."

"And then?"

"Then we show him what he wants to see," Thomas said, and smiled. It was not the same innocent smile he'd had before the cells, before the torments. This one was a cold, confident thing, and it made Jess worry when he saw it. It also made him think, *They should be afraid.*

Jess certainly was, for a moment.

Then the moment passed, and that unsettling smile warmed and shifted, and Thomas stood up. "Come on," he said, and took up the cloth that Jess had used to wipe his sweaty face. He used it to scrub away the charcoal-sketched plans from the wall. "There must be something left to eat. Perhaps Morgan will be back to tell us good news. And if not, you have a book to read and keep your mind off your troubles."

True. The promise of food, Morgan, and words on paper made Jess shake off the last of his weariness as he followed Thomas out of the workshop. They had to wake up Diwell on the way out, and he seemed chagrined about it, but grateful they didn't take the opportunity to lock him in.

It was just after sunset, and Jess saw Khalila in the park across the way; Dario was with her, and she had a small prayer rug that one of the other Muslims in the town must have lent her. She unrolled it on the grass and began her evening prayers. Dario stood silent watch, far enough away that he wasn't a distraction. He nodded to Jess and Thomas as they passed.

Morgan's was the first face he saw inside the prison walls. She looked as worn and tired as he felt, but she smiled as she set a few pieces of dried fruit and an entirely too small chunk of bread and cheese out. "The doctor sent this," she said. "You two look like you can use the first choice."

"You're a kind girl, Morgan," Thomas said, and raised his dirty hands to wiggle his fingers. "But we'd better wash first, I think. Charcoal and metal shavings make poor spices." He studied her carefully, seeing the same things Jess had, most likely, and asked the question they both were afraid to pose. "How is he?"

"Better," she said. "His fever is down, and the skin is healing faster. The infection's gone. He'll be scarred, and it'll be another couple of days before he's strong enough to join us, but he'll be all right."

Thomas closed his eyes. "Thank God. I prayed, as the Scholar asked."

Jess had, too. He normally wasn't much for it, but he'd quietly whispered one himself, last night in the darkness. It seemed to have done some good. "Now the problem is to keep him down until he's really healed."

A stray breeze stirred Morgan's hair and exposed a vulnerable patch of skin just below her ear, where the skin curved sweetly down toward her neck. Jess had kissed that place so recently the memory of it burned. "Well, you know the captain. As soon as he can get up, he will. Wolfe's finally sleeping. He refused to lie down until Santi woke up. His devotion is amazing, though I'm sure he doesn't want anyone to notice. Men. Always so worried about what others think."

Morgan smiled suddenly, looking directly at Jess, and his mind emptied. She gave him what he was almost certain was a wink, so quick he might have imagined it, and then she turned away to talk to Glain.

Jess flinched as Thomas clapped a huge, strong arm over his shoulders. "That girl," Thomas said, "is going to be very good for someone. I hope it's you."

"Oh, get off me, Mountain," Jess groused, but he wasn't angry. He was, in fact, feeling better. "Let's find a bucket and wash."

"And eat."

"If you want to call it that."

Once they'd washed and taken a meager meal, Jess slipped into Morgan's cell. She was sitting cross-legged on her mattress, and it pleased something deep inside to see that she, too, had chosen a book from Dr. Askuwheteau's vast collection. Hers was a biography. She smiled when she saw him, and closed her book.

"Here." He pulled out a blue feather he'd plucked from the grass outside. It was a rare piece of beauty in the dull rust and brown of Philadelphia—bent, but unbroken. The moment he'd spotted it on the walk back, he'd known it was meant for her. "I saw Wolfe using one as a bookmark. It seems appropriate."

The way her tired face lit up in joy felt like standing in sunshine, dazzling and warming. "Thank you." He hated to see the smile go thinner, more tentative. She moved over, he slid in place beside her, and she lifted the book to show it to him. "Askuwheteau said he gave you a book, too."

"Fiction," Jess said. He watched her twirl the small blue feather idly and brush it against her cheek. He imagined the softness of her skin under his fingers and quickly looked away to put a stop to that. Not the time. He had more serious things to discuss. "You didn't tell me Beck made you an offer to stay."

"He made all of us that offer."

"Not like he made to you," Jess said. "Your own home? Askuwheteau told me."

She didn't quite meet his eyes. She concentrated on twirling the feather in her fingers. "Are you afraid that I'll take it?" He didn't answer. She risked a glance at him, and he saw half circles like bruises under her eyes. Darker today than yesterday. "I won't. Even though the idea of a real home is appealing."

"Nothing's safe here."

"I know."

"Did you find anything inside city hall? Any sign of tunnels?"

"Nothing. I'd hoped—but if there's anything there, I couldn't see it. Tell me how you and Thomas are doing."

"We're a day or two from being ready with our work. But we *need* that tunnel."

"The wall is almost ready," Morgan said. "I spent hours at it today." She hesitated, on the verge of saying something; he saw doubt in her eyes.

"What?"

"Nothing."

"It isn't."

"It's just that—" She fell silent, twirling the feather in her fingers. "It's hard, what I'm doing. Exhausting, I admit that. And today it felt . . . different. I couldn't concentrate as well, toward the end."

"That's because you're running yourself too hard," Jess said.

"Says the pot to the kettle. But it has to be ready."

He took her hand and held it. "Morgan. I don't have a smuggling tunnel where I can leave a message out to my family. I can't communicate with anyone outside these walls. There are High Garda camped out there. Even if you do get the wall weakened, even if Thomas's mad invention works, what then? We walk into the arms of the Library?"

"You know, you're both depressing me," said a new voice from the door of the cell. Glain stepped in and leaned against the bars. "Sorry. Hard to have a private conversation in here, since these walls are not just paper-thin, but actual paper." She was right. The thin pages torn from Blanks that Beck had given them to make their cells into proper rooms weren't soundproofing. Weren't even much of a modesty screen. "What are we weeping about now?"

"No way to contact anyone outside these walls," Jess said. "So there's no point in escape, if we just die out there rather than in here."

"It's a fair point," Glain said. "We can pass for Scholars and soldiers."

"The Scholar robes are ashes," Morgan pointed out. "And I'd expect the Archivist would have our likenesses in every Codex by now."

"What about your family?" Glain asked Jess. "Would they help?"

He shrugged. "Honestly? I don't know. Beck was going to write to my da, but he hasn't said anything yet about a reply."

"But your family knows we're here."

"Presumably, if Beck kept his word."

Glain sank down into a comfortable, cross-legged position on the floor. "Then you just need a way to talk to them secretly, right?"

He gave her an exasperated look. "That's what I was saying."

"Thick," she said, and shook her head. "What exactly do you think is pasted up behind me?"

She tapped the papers fixed to the bars of Morgan's cell. Jess glanced at them, then her, and lifted his shoulders. "Paper?"

Glain plucked a sheet free. Then another. Then another. She gathered up a handful and gave them to Morgan. "Now what do you have?"

Morgan's turn to shrug this time. "I don't understand what you're getting at, Glain."

"How exactly does a Codex work?"

It was a ridiculous question on the face of it, but Jess and Morgan put it together at the same jolting moment. Jess looked at her. Morgan stared back. "A script written by an Obscurist," Jess said.

"In the binding!" Morgan finished. "My God, why didn't I think of it?"

"Because you're tired, and I'm smarter than you think," Glain said. "We can stitch together the pages; I'll sacrifice my extra shirt for the thread, if Thomas can forge us a decently thick needle. For the binding . . ."

"Glain," Jess said.

She ignored him, focused entirely on Morgan. "For the binding, we can use the tops of my boots. Good leather. I remember the Turks once destroyed a library for the leather covers to make marching shoes for their troops. Seems fitting to do the opposite."

"*Glain!*" Jess nearly shouted it, and both of them looked at him with identical expressions of surprise and annoyance. "No."

"Why not? It's perfect." Glain swung her look to Morgan, who nodded. Of course she would, Jess thought. He felt sick.

"I can write a touchstone script to narrow the communication, one to one. The Library won't be able to see it."

"And we can send a message to your brother," Glain said to Jess. Her eyebrows rose. "Problem solved, and why are you looking at me like I killed your sainted grandmother?"

He fought not to throw Glain out of the cell and slam the door behind her. "Morgan's done too much already."

"Jess." Morgan put her hand on his. "No one else can do this. Stop. Stop trying to protect me."

"Fine, then we'll do it in the morning," Glain said. She pulled out a set of faded, much-bent playing cards. "That gives you the entire night to rest up. Jess? Care for a game?"

"A game?" Jess repeated. He'd gone from stunned to furious— with Morgan, for volunteering *again* to overextend herself, with Glain, who didn't seem to understand the point at all. "No. I don't." He cast a look at Morgan that begged for her to change her mind, to understand that she was destroying herself, but she held his gaze without flinching. All he could see were the dark circles beneath her eyes. The slight tremble in her hands.

He was right; she'd lost weight these past few days. *If you burn, you'll burn fast.* Askuwheteau's words to her. Was she already on fire, somewhere deep inside? How long before she failed, or something worse happened?

"Jess, please," Morgan said to him. "Please stay."

I'm not going to watch you burn, he thought, and went to his cell. He wrapped himself in blankets on his cot as the others sat down to play. All of them. Even Thomas.

He'd never felt exiled from their circle of friendship before, but it made him remember that if they succeeded, if his brother came through, if their plans worked, if they escaped from Philadelphia . . . then there was far worse to come. And he, Dario, and Morgan would have to lie to everyone to get it done.

This is what it will feel like.

Maybe he needed to get used to it.

EPHEMERA

Excerpt on the subject of theories of printing from a work by Scholar Plato, interdicted and sent to the Black Archives. Restricted to the eyes of the Archivist Magister.

. . . *familiar with the common practice of inscribing notes upon tablets of soft wax, which it seems childishly simple to reproduce upon a fabric surface. A simple application of dye upon the tablet produces, when impressed upon fabric, a reverse of the letters inscribed upon the tablet. I have seen children playing at such games, pressing molds into the mud to make objects of great delight. Surely there is therefore a way to inscribe such letters in reverse, and when dyed and impressed upon the fabric, to create a record that may survive, rather than a tablet that is wiped and reused daily. We copy information to scrolls, yes, but this is still subject to error, and each copy must be made with time and skill.*

We must find a way to save for later generations the knowledge so laboriously written and rewritten. We must find a way to easily and quickly copy, for the more accurate reproductions we make, the better our chances of such knowledge surviving our lifetimes. Scrolls are prone to mold, to ruination by water and fire, by storms . . . and so are the lives of men.

Our words must live after us, if we are to lift ourselves up.

CHAPTER FIVE

Glain woke Jess screamingly early, when dawn was still just an idea on the horizon. She put a finger to her lips and beckoned him up, past the still-sleeping Thomas, and then out. The guards stationed there came to alert, but Glain said, "We're not going anywhere. Just over here, to the corner."

The woman on duty nodded and went back to sewing up a cut in a piece of cloth, but she was no fool; all her attention stayed on the two of them as they walked over a little distance.

"If this is about last night—," he said, but she cut him off with an impatient gesture.

"There. Look." Glain crossed her arms as she stared at the repaired but clearly melted and misshapen corner.

"There, where? What am I supposed to be seeing?"

She didn't bother to answer, only gave him a cool side eye that he knew all too well from their time in training. She expected him to work it out, so he tried, staring until his eyes ached.

And then he got it. "That's . . . not right."

She nodded, clearly pleased she didn't have to bang his head into the melted wall to make him recognize the truth. "Why not?"

"Is this rhetoric class? Who died and made you Scholar Wolfe?"

"Shut up and answer the question. If you can."

"All right," Jess said. "This damage isn't the same. If the Library had launched a bomb from beyond the walls that landed here, the whole prison should have gone up, not just this one corner." *And,* he thought with a chill, *that would have killed everyone inside.* It had been a miracle only Santi was badly hurt, but he'd been so grateful for the miracle, he hadn't really thought about anything else.

Glain handed him a sharp-edged piece of age-clouded glass. When he reached for it, she said, "I took it from the rubble. Careful. There's still residue." She transferred it to him, and he held it by one small corner, lifted it to his nose, and sniffed.

The odor was unmistakable, an oily blend of sweet and rotten. He coughed it out and handed it back, and Glain slipped it into a folded piece of cloth that she concealed in a pocket of those truly un-fashionable trousers she'd acquired. "Greek fire," he confirmed. "But the glass is too thin to have been thrown by any ballista."

"Exactly. It was a bottle of the stuff, tossed by hand from . . ." Glain measured off paces, moving back as she stared at the damage. Nobody, Jess realized, seemed to be paying attention to them, but he was suddenly very aware of what Glain was saying. "About here."

She exchanged a look with him, and he understood her meaning perfectly. Someone had stood within these walls and tossed that bottle. Someone inside Philadelphia had tried to kill them. It hadn't been a ballista on the other side of the wall with blind lucky aim. They'd been targeted, very precisely.

Jess was too angry to speak, so he just nodded, stuck his hands in his pockets—a habit he had, when thinking—and rocked on his heels. "Do you think that was done on Beck's orders? Or by someone acting on impulse against us?"

She sighed, as if he were utterly hopeless. "Jess. Grow a brain. That glass for the bomb must have been at least, oh, this large—" She described it with her hands, and Jess nodded to accept the estimate. "Glass is precious here. So is Greek fire. So who has those things freely available?"

"Beck."

"And it would have been filled with liquid. Heavy, yes? Someone came prepared. And I don't think he'd have done it without authorization."

"Beck *knew* a Library bombardment would come, sooner or later. He must have, if he had someone waiting with the Greek fire." He mimed pitching an imaginary bottle at the prison's roof and, in his mind's eye, saw it tumble and shatter on the corner . . . not in the center of the roof, where it would have done its worst. "Which is why the angle of impact is all wrong for a bombardment bomb. But he knew the Library would be attacking and trusted that to cover his tracks. Trusted no one would look closer."

"You seem proud to have figured it out. That's mildly charming," Glain said. "I don't suppose Wolfe would have given you full credit, so I won't, either. But yes. This was planned, cold-blooded attempted murder."

"Do you think they were specifically after Wolfe? Or Santi? Or both?"

"I don't think Beck much cared," she said. "He thinks that without them, we'll be easier to manipulate. He's probably bloody disappointed that it only resulted in a wounding, which means he could try again. We need Wolfe and Santi back with us. Now." She hesitated, which wasn't like her. "Let's talk about Morgan. Specifically, that you're trying to hold her back."

"Not funny, Glain."

"Stop thinking like a lovestruck idiot; she's a *weapon*. She *can* build us a channel to communicate with your brother. Let her do the job she needs to do, all right?"

He turned toward her. Hands out of his pockets, body set as if he expected her to attack. He saw her shift to match it. It was probably unconscious. Probably. "I'm not willing to break her to serve the rest of us. We do that, we're no better than the Archivist."

Glain's expression didn't shift. It was calm and set and confident. "Flavia chose to pick up the knife."

"Flavia stood on the corpses of everyone who died first *trying to protect her.* So think about that a moment." His tone had gone so hard, cold, and final that he scarcely believed it was his.

"Flavia was a child," Glain said. "And you don't have a moral right to treat Morgan as one!"

It was a poisonous argument, done in whispers, but fierce enough to cut. Jess didn't acknowledge her point. He was already walking away, with long, angry strides—not to the prison, but toward the workshop. As he passed her, the female guard stood and walked after him, tucking away the cloth and needles. When he reached the door, he fumbled for his copy of the key. His fingers felt thick and clumsy, but he finally managed. He was angry, but he knew it was for all the wrong reasons—because he was frightened by what Glain had un-covered, by the fact that Beck was more than willing to kill them for his own purposes. And because she was right about Morgan. Of course she was.

He just didn't want to face it.

When he looked back, Glain had gone inside the prison. Good.

He didn't think he could stomach being next to her another moment. He felt betrayed, and stupid for feeling it. The fact that he was wrong was going to haunt him. *Is there no way that this ends well for Morgan?* She was being used, either by the Library, which at least took utmost care of her, or by him and the rest of her friends, who didn't.

He hated that he couldn't protect her. That, in truth, he didn't have the right.

So he went into the workshop, stripped off his shirt, stoked the fire, and began forging letters for the press instead.

Jess threw himself into the work. Nothing else to do, and it was pure physical labor, blanking his mind and erasing the worry that was never far away now. He hardly noticed time passing. Thomas joined him, and they didn't speak—well, Thomas tried, but Jess was in no mood for it.

It wasn't until half the day was gone before he asked, "Is Morgan making the Codex?"

"Yes," Thomas said. "I made a needle for her earlier. Glain cut the leather for the binding from her boots. It's a good idea—"

"I don't want to talk about it."

"Morgan requires a drop of Brightwell blood to link it to Brendan."

"I'm damn well not doing it."

"Jess," Thomas said. "Look at yourself. Your fingers sliced open getting the glass for us. Burns and bruises on you. You've gone to skin and bones because you're giving me your food, and don't think I haven't noticed. We all have to risk things. All of us. Together."

It's different, Jess wanted to insist, but he couldn't. It sounded hollow, and Thomas, of all people, knew him too well. So he went back to work and tried not to think.

He was so focused that he nearly missed the arrival of their visitor.

"Hard at work, I see," said a voice from the door of the workshop, and Jess, sweating from the constant pulse of heat from the forge, wiped perspiration from his face, blinked to focus.

Captain Santi stood in the doorway. Well, *stood* was an exaggeration. He leaned both on the wooden frame and on Scholar Wolfe's shoulder, and without both of those supports he likely wouldn't have stayed upright for long.

He looked better, though. His arm had been bound up in a sling, and even at this distance, he smelled quite oddly of honey.

Jess helped Wolfe ease Santi down onto the only bench. "Oh, stop hovering like I'm broken," Santi snapped; there was a tight flush to his cheeks from the effort spent making the walk. "I've taken worse than this."

"Liar," Wolfe said, but briskly, as a statement of fact rather than an accusation. "I know all your glorious war wounds. You've never been burned this badly."

"And I've never had honey and moldy bread smeared on my skin, either. It's a week for new things." Santi turned his gaze to Jess. "So. Progress?"

"We're almost done," Thomas said as he left the glow of the forge; he wore a makeshift apron made from an old quilt, and mittens of the same material, and an eye covering he'd made from scavenged pieces of leftover broken glass and bits of cloth. He was glowing with sweat, hair glued tight to his head with it, and his grin looked exultant as he stripped off the extra layers. "Captain. I'm so glad to see you better!"

Santi nodded, acknowledging the good wishes but clearly not wanting to discuss them. "You realize that once you build this for Beck, he could easily reverse engineer it?"

"Yes, we've taken all that into account," Thomas said. "And it won't even be our fault, really."

Santi's smile started small, then grew. "You two," he said, and it sounded like affection. "You have an alarming talent for destruction."

"Learned from the best," Jess said, and grinned back. His whole body ached, but he couldn't deny that seeing Santi alive and relatively well had done wonders for his spirits.

He also didn't miss the worry that Wolfe was trying hard to conceal. As usual, Captain Santi was pushing himself. And Wolfe was trying to hold him back, for his own good. *That sounds familiar.*

Thomas wiped sweat and smoke from his face with a rag that was already well sooted. He looked, Jess thought, like the ancient Greek god Hephaestus, stripped to a bare, ash-streaked chest, with a heavy hammer in his hand.

"Too bad you can't demonstrate it for me," Santi said. "I'd have liked to see it print something."

"I'd have thought Scholar Wolfe would have demonstrated the one he built to you . . . ?" Thomas asked.

"I was away when he was working on it," Santi said. "Training a new High Garda company in Belgium. I knew he had an important project, but not the specifics."

"That ignorance saved your life," Wolfe said. "They'd have killed you if you'd ever laid eyes on it."

"Most likely," Santi replied mildly. "When I returned from my assignment I found Chris gone, with all his work. You know the rest."

The rest: imprisonment, torture, erasure from the records of the Library—for a Scholar of Wolfe's caliber, it was the assassination of immortality, the burning of a life's work, and for what? For being brilliant. For being exactly what the Library stood for in the first place. It gave Jess a hot ache in the back of his chest, like an unvoiced shout. Such a waste. It was all such a waste.

He still couldn't come to terms with the harsh, awful fact that it had been going on this way for *hundreds of years*. The Archivists, generation after generation, eliminating anyone who threatened their hold on power—like Thomas, and Wolfe. Two examples that a thousand years earlier, the Library would have elevated and celebrated.

Santi's calm acceptance of that left Jess chilled, even in the heat of the forge.

"When will you be ready to demonstrate?" Wolfe asked. Thomas exchanged a quick look with Jess and raised his eyebrows.

"I don't know. Two more days?"

"Tomorrow," Wolfe said. "I'd rather you soothe Master Beck's anxiety sooner than later. The more nervous he becomes, the more he'll want to grandstand for his people." That was all true, but Jess thought there was the tiniest hint in Wolfe's expression, in the way he avoided meeting Jess's eyes, that it was more than that. Wolfe was playing his own game. Again.

"We can manage it for tomorrow," Thomas said. "If you're sure of the timing."

"He's sure," Santi said, and gave them a small, determined nod. "I'd best go get some rest now."

They were speaking around the subject, for the benefit of the female guard sitting in the corner. She was, unlike Diwell, all too alert.

"Yes," Wolfe said. "Come, Nic. We'll leave them to work."

Thomas slid his goggles back on and silently returned to the forge, but Jess watched in silence as Wolfe helped Santi up. The captain's weakness was alarming. *Tomorrow's too soon.* But there were reasons that Wolfe wanted the timeline to be set just this way, and Jess felt the sick foreboding inside spiral up into real dread.

Tomorrow, everything was going to change.

They got nothing at all for dinner that night. The guards got nothing either, and said—with barely concealed anger—that as a precaution against inclement weather, rations were being cut. For the present, only the ill, elderly, and very young were to be fed.

It was horribly late when Jess was able to stagger, half-hobbled, back to his bed, but the letters had been carved, the molds made, and the metal poured. Now they had two long, neat rows of letters and numbers in English and in Greek, and his muscles felt as if they were coated in Greek fire. He was unconscious and uncaring for four hours before something—he wasn't quite sure what—brought him groggily back to the world. When he tried to sit up, the muscles that had been hot and painfully tight had hardened into poured concrete, and moving seemed like a terrible idea.

Morgan stood looking down at him, and as he got enough awareness to identify her, he also saw the stark exhaustion on her face. She sank down to a sitting position when he didn't get up, and leaned against the frame of the bed.

"God," he whispered, and sat up. "What's happened?"

"Don't," she whispered back. "Please." Her hands were shaking, even as they rested in her lap. He saw tears glisten faintly in her eyes. It was blushing dawn outside, and the new light should have been kind to her, but it only made her look more broken. "It had to be done. It had to be. But the cost, oh, Jess—"

"Morgan, *what did you do?*" She just shook her head, and he knew she wouldn't answer. Not now. She shivered all over, a convulsive movement that worried him even more. "Have you even been to bed?" he demanded. Her skin felt very cold. Icy. "You're freezing. Come here."

"I need you to finish the Codex with me. We have no more time. *Please.*"

"After you're warm," he said, and moved the blanket. "Morgan, please. Get in."

She hesitated, but then she slipped in beside him. He moved over to give her the room, and she rolled toward him as he adjusted the blankets over her shivering body. "This feels good," she told him quietly. "I'm just so *cold.*"

He put his arms around her and pulled her close—not to kiss, just to hold, and felt the shuddering sigh of relief that came out of her. He could feel bones beneath her skin. She was just too thin. Whatever she was doing, whatever it was that had alarmed her so much . . . it was washing her away, like sand in water.

She was holding something in one hand, and it was trapped between their bodies. He recognized the shape: a book. The Codex she'd sewn together, with her Obscurist's script written and bound inside it. Waiting for the burst of power she'd give it to bring it to life.

"Morgan, you're too weak to do this. You need to *rest.* We'll find another way," he told her. "I'm not going to watch you set yourself on fire for us." He did the only thing he could think of: he kissed her, and tried to tell her without words how much she meant to him.

His existence narrowed to the taste of her mouth, the silky softness of her lips, the gentle tension of her hands on his back. The dark added to her mystery as he slid his palm over her arm, her waist, her hip, to draw her in the shadows. In this predawn silent world, she was the only thing real to him just now—every sense devoted to memorizing the scent of her, the taste, the touch. The sigh of her quiet breath against his skin. Taking away sight made every other sense come alive to him, and it felt like a dangerous kind of magic.

And then she broke free of the kiss and whispered, "I'm sorry, but there's no choice," and then he felt a sharp, stabbing pain in his arm. A red starburst of sensation, and then a glow was forming around Morgan's hands, and in it he saw she had a thick needle in her hand, and from it hung a single drop of his blood.

He watched the crimson drop tremble there in the dawning golden glow of her quintessence, and then it fell through the light, flaring white as it passed. It landed on a page of the book she'd opened to catch it. It splashed into a vivid red blotch and absorbed without a trace into the paper.

He was close enough to feel the cost of what she did. Her whole body shuddered. The little warmth she'd managed to absorb from him rushed out, as if she'd been plunged into icy waters, and her eyes . . . her eyes went dead for a moment, as distant as those of a corpse floating beneath the waves. Then she blinked and dragged herself back, and the golden glimmer around her hand died . . . but not before he saw black threads woven into the glow, pulsing like veins. Like rot.

"Here," she whispered, and put her head wearily on his chest. "Take it. Use it. There's no more time, Jess. Please. You have to get us help, and we *must* get out of here."

The raw desperation in her voice hurt. He drew in a breath and held her close for a second before he sat up and stepped out of bed, and made sure that she was wrapped as warmly as he could manage. She seemed small, lying in his bed. Broken and vulnerable.

Despite the urgency, he had to limp a step before the too-stressed muscles unclenched in his legs enough to allow him to walk. Thomas wasn't in his bed after all; he must have gotten restless in the night and slipped out to the forge. He was probably still there, oblivious to the time and his own exhaustion. This close to the completion of a project, he'd be driven to finish it. No matter what.

Jess sat on Thomas's bunk, cleared his mind, and focused on his brother, his almost-mirror twin, and opened the book. He realized as he did that he had nothing to write with . . . but Morgan had thought of that, too. The blue feather he'd given her for a bookmark lay in the crease between the pages, and he picked it up and pressed it to the page. There was no ink in it, of course, but a dark dot appeared, shimmering around the edges with a faint gold light that made it easy to see even in the dimness. He wrote his first message. *Ta for nothing, brother. You could have tried to get me a message, at least.* The words were light, but he felt ashen inside. Seeing Morgan broken this way shook him in ways nothing else could.

His words faded and left a creamy, empty page behind.

He didn't have to wait long for Brendan's reply to appear, as if an invisible pen wrote in fast, looping letters. *Da says hi. Hopes your limbs are all attached. I did try to get you a message. Intercepted by Beck. We've made offers for your return.* Brendan didn't express anything about his own worries, but then, he wouldn't. That wasn't how things worked between the two of them, identical in looks, far from it in temperament.

Generous of you, Jess wrote. *Where are you?*

Close, Brendan replied. *Assuming no one else can read this?*

Just us.

Good. Because what I'm about to tell you stays quiet, yeah? Santi's company is here. His lieutenant found some Burners in London to question and found out where you'd gone. She got the whole company sent to duty on the wall.

Jess stared at the words for a long, long moment. He didn't quite know how to take that in. *They've joined the High Garda encampments? They're here?*

Just said so, Brendan agreed. *I'm with them. We're hiding in plain sight, brother.*

You said Santi's lieutenant . . . Zara? Jess wrote the name with too much pressure and nearly broke the tip of the quill. *You can't trust Zara. She's loyal to the Library. Nearly killed the captain, before.*

Yeah, she told me. She's dead sorry about it. Changed her mind after the Artifex Magnus decided to execute a few of her soldiers for disloyalty. She's not the only one who's turned on the bastard, plenty of unrest erupting all over these days. Details later. I trust you have bigger questions.

A full High Garda company would be a blessing, no doubt about that, but Zara Cole? Santi's lieutenant hadn't seemed all that trustworthy the last time Jess had seen her. In fact, she'd been willing to shoot down every one of them, and all hail the Archivist.

But beggars couldn't be choosy, if the beggars wanted to live out the day.

We need a tunnel out of here, Jess wrote. And didn't like the delay. It took a solid minute of molasses-slow time before Brendan's answer appeared.

Yeah, well, he said. *Little bit of a problem with the tunnel.*

What problem?

We don't have one.

I know. It belongs to the Comprehensive.

No, there is no tunnel. The Comprehensive destroyed the last one after the High Garda twigged to its location. They haven't finished digging the new one yet. No way out through a tunnel. I'm sorry.

Jess . . . hadn't expected that. At all. We need that exit, brother. We need a way out. They must have something!

You'll find a way, Brendan repeated. *When you do, tell me where. We'll get in position to cover you. If you can wait a few weeks—*

We don't have a few weeks. We'll be dead long before then. Jess paused and then wrote, *I think we have to do it today.*

TODAY?! Brother, this is not making me feel calm.

Jess let out a little huff of a laugh, too quiet to be heard. *Me, neither, Scraps. Me, neither. But have faith.*

He waited for Brendan's usual comeback. It was always the same, with varying degrees of anger: *Don't call me Scraps.*

But instead, when the message appeared, it said, *God be with you, brother. Get me a message when you can.* And then, after a blank line: *Don't go and die on me. I wouldn't know how to tell Da.*

That, Jess thought, was as close as he was ever likely to get to an *I love you* from his own brother.

He put the feather in place and closed the book, and sat for a while, drinking in the stillness, the quiet.

When he was ready, he added Thomas's blanket over Morgan's body. She was deeply asleep. She'd never looked so alone, he thought, and he hated Wolfe, purely and completely, for doing this to her. He wanted to crawl in beside her and hold her, but there wasn't time. *There never is,* he thought bitterly. And for one wild moment, he wanted to just forget it all, close his eyes, and pretend for another hour that it wasn't all moving too fast.

"Jess. With me." Scholar Wolfe was standing in his doorway.

Jess followed him. As he did, he saw that Dario's bunk was empty, and so were Glain's and Khalila's. "Where is everyone?"

"Off on business," Wolfe said. "Inside."

Jess stepped into the cell Wolfe shared with Santi. Despite the repairs, it had a glassy, melted look to the stone, and there was still a faint, cloying smell of Greek fire here that made him want to cough. Santi, seated on his bunk, noticed. "Not so bad once you get used to it," he said. "You've been in touch with your brother?"

Jess looked down at the Codex he still held, with Glain's boot leather binding it, scarred and rough with use. "He says the tunnel's not an option."

That got Santi and Wolfe to exchange a fast, grim look. "Narrows our options to one," Santi said. "The wall. But that means we have to fight our way out of a High Garda camp. I don't like those odds."

"They're better than you think," Jess said. "Brendan says Zara Cole's here. She brought your company. He says we can trust her."

Wolfe said, "The hell we can," just as Captain Santi said, "I think we should." That led to a strange silence, and the two of them staring at each other. Wolfe spoke first. "Zara's loyal to the Library. *She shot you.*"

"She could have killed me, and she didn't," Santi said. "Believe me, Zara chose that shot carefully. It meant she wasn't convinced then. If she's here, she's convinced now."

"Maybe she's convinced that we need to have our heads on pikes; have you thought of that?"

"I know how you feel about her, but—"

"Nic! This isn't some petty jealousy. *I don't trust her!*"

Jess said, quietly, "Doesn't really matter, does it? She's our only real chance. Brendan's with them. If we tell them where to meet us, they can cover our escape if we can get through the wall. If you've got another choice, say so."

Wolfe glared, but he shook his head.

"Tell your brother we're coming out at the eastern end of the wall, just behind the grain storage," Santi said. "Dead-on east. They'll need time to arrange the move, if they need to move camps. A few hours at most."

Jess nodded, but he was looking at Wolfe. "If nothing goes wrong," he said. "But something has, hasn't it? I saw Morgan. What happened?"

"Something that wasn't her fault," Wolfe said. "But it shortens our timeline considerably. Tell your brother we're coming this afternoon. There's a storm moving in. It's better cover than we'd hoped. If you can summon Beck midafternoon, he'll bring his counselors, and many of the guards. While you're about that, we'll be quietly leaving. Once it starts, we can't break off. We're committed. You understand?"

"Yes," Jess said. "Midafternoon."

"Try to spin it out until the storm begins," Santi said. "And have a way out of that workshop besides the door. Understood?"

"Morgan does nothing else," Jess said. "Let her rest as much as you can."

"We all have our parts to play," Wolfe said.

"Really? And what's your part, Scholar? Because from where I sit, you've done nothing but use her."

"Jess," Santi said. He leaned toward him and held back a wince as he straightened his arm to push himself forward. "Believe me, none of us is clean. None of this will be easy. The others already know their jobs. Now we're telling you yours."

"Kind of you to include me."

"You *were* included," Wolfe said, with a sharp whip in his tone. A barbed one. "You and Thomas had to remain focused on the press and that invention of Thomas's. That was imperative." He took a tightly rolled scroll of paper from his pocket and smoothed it out. With a jolt, Jess recognized the map that Khalila had drawn from memory. Wolfe pointed to a building she'd painted black, hugging the eastern wall behind city hall, on the far side of the fields. "This is where we'll rendezvous."

"You realize that we're planning to burn a hole in a wall that's stood for a hundred years," Jess said. "You realize what that's going to do."

Santi said, "It's out of our hands. The wall can be patched, and the city will have to hold on the best it can. Believe me, I don't want more death on my conscience."

"But this won't be bloodless," Wolfe said. "And we have to look out for ourselves now. Agreed?"

Another Brightwell family motto, Jess thought bitterly. He opened the book, sketched the map, and gave Brendan the approximate time, along with the warning to stay well back from the wall.

When he looked out the window, he saw that dawn was coming cold and steel gray, and Wolfe was right: there were black clouds massing on the horizon.

The storm would be on them soon enough.

Jess headed for the workshop. Inside the dark, smoky confines, he found that the forge had been allowed to sink back to coals, and the tiny amount of Greek fire that they'd been given to keep it burning had been carefully stored back in a padded box. Jess started to pocket it. There was no sign of Diwell, oddly enough.

"No, no, don't take that," Thomas called. He was half-hidden under the machine as he connected springs. "It's just water. I colored it with some dye I stole from a clothing shop. The real bottle is over there." He pointed toward a shelf cluttered with scraps of unused metal. Jess felt around and found a tiny glass vial, half-full and carefully stoppered. "Not much left. But good to have in an emergency."

"Where's Diwell?"

"Privy," Thomas said. "Something he ate disagreed with him. I offered him food I'd saved up. It was nicely rotten. It isn't my fault he decided to take it. I gave him a choice. Don't worry, I don't think it will kill him. Just make him wish he was dead."

"And I remember when you were just an innocent farm boy who

wouldn't hurt a fly." Jess's smile quickly faded. "I got in contact with my brother."

"And?" Thomas slid out from beneath the frame of the machine to look at him. "The tunnel?"

"We're not going out the tunnel."

"Then it's good I made the Ray," Thomas said.

"Where is it?"

"I haven't put it together yet."

"Wait. *What?*"

Thomas slid back under the press. "All the component parts are completed. All it needs is assembly. It will work."

"Have you tested it?"

"It will work."

That, Jess thought sickly, wasn't an answer. "Thomas! We recycled old glass and I polished it *by hand*. With terrible supplies! These are not fine manufacturing conditions!"

"I know," he replied calmly, voice muffled by the machine looming over him. "And the great Heron had far less to work with when *he* invented it. So it will work well enough."

Sometimes, Thomas's cheerful optimism could be painful. Jess stepped back and looked at the towering machine that now stood in the middle of the room. It wasn't a pretty sight—no elegance to it at all, in fact—but Thomas had assembled it while Jess was still sleeping, and it was very nearly . . .

"Done!" Thomas said, and slid himself out from under it again. He stood up and shook the frame, but he did it carefully. It didn't look entirely stable; the woods were mismatched, and though carefully braced, the entire structure had the look of everything in Philadelphia: cobbled together. "I think it's ready to test," Thomas said. "Paper?"

Jess found one of the sheets of paper they'd cut carefully out of Blanks and brought it over. He saw that Thomas had already laid in metal lettering, in English and in Greek. Reading it backward in the dim light was difficult, so he said, "What are you printing?"

"Something that will whet Beck's appetite." Thomas wiped dirty sweat from his face with an equally filthy sleeve. "All right. One test only."

Jess reached for the pot of ink that they'd begged from the meager stores, and swabbed the letters in a thick black coating, placed the paper, and stepped back. He looked at Thomas, who placed his hand on the lever.

"Do you want to do it?" Thomas asked.

"No. It's your invention."

"I suppose we should say something important."

"I just hope the damned thing works."

"I guess that will have to do," Thomas said. "Do we risk it?"

Jess looked at his friend's grin, at the sweaty, exalted expression on his face, and threw caution out the door. "What's life without risk?"

Thomas pulled down on the lever, and springs engaged to snap the press down—paper against ink against metal, a sudden and violent collision. Nothing shattered. Both of them stayed quiet for a second, and then Thomas let out a gust of breath that ended in a shaky laugh. "I admit I was not as confident as I seemed. Now, for the second part." He turned a wheel and cranked the plate back up again, revealing the paper adhering to it. Jess peeled it off, and he had to admit, there was a spark of real wonder as he held it up to the light.

"English and Greek," he said. Jess stared at what they'd made from that simple pull of the lever. The ink stood out clear and crisp on the creamy paper, chillingly perfect. They'd done something so world breaking that he couldn't even imagine the waves that would ripple out of this moment, out of something he and Thomas had built from sweat and pain and hope.

It was the start of something. And the end of something else. And in that moment, he couldn't find the thread of what was right, or wrong, in any of it.

Thomas set the catch to hold the plate in place, and came to look. He put a heavy arm around Jess's shoulder, and together they stared at the page they'd printed. The ink still glistened wet, giving the letters an almost supernatural gleam. *We did this,* Jess thought. *We did.*

He couldn't speak, he found, and he looked at Thomas and saw tears in the big German's eyes. He couldn't fully understand what this meant to him, either; it had started as a pure thing, and then it had become the reason he'd been dragged into torture and imprisonment. Was this anger? Joy? Was he crying for what had happened, or what was still to come? Or just from the same wonder that Jess felt pressing inside him?

Jess didn't know, because Thomas didn't speak, either.

They stood together, holding the page until the last of the damp sheen faded from the letters, and Jess finally cleared his throat to say, "Show me the pieces of the Ray. We need to have them on us."

Thomas nodded, put the page down, and moved around the room. From a heap of scraps he pulled out what looked like just another piece of wood—only more shaped and polished than the others. From a tangle of iron, a straight, thick tube. From behind the forge tools, a trigger mechanism. From behind a loose stone in the wall, a small golden ball that he pitched to Jess. "Don't drop that," Thomas said.

"Will it blow up?"

"Of course not," Thomas said. "But you'd crack the casing, and we've only got the one."

"Ah." Jess slipped it in his pocket. It was the power source come from Morgan's little singing bird. He watched as Thomas found the other pieces—small bits that he handed to Jess, while he used a length of cloth to bind the thick tube to his thigh. It came almost to his knee, but at least the heavy canvas trousers he wore helped conceal it. Jess took the other pieces and fashioned them into a necklace on another strip of cloth he tied around his neck, to dangle under his shirt. He had the Codex tied on his chest already, and slipped the trigger mechanism into the binding. "I hope this all fits together."

"It will," Thomas said. "What else?"

"Santi said to make sure we have another way out of this building, if the worst happens."

"Ah," Thomas said, and picked up a crude shovel. He tossed it to Jess, who nearly got knocked down by the weight of it. "So we make one. You start."

Jess couldn't hold back a groan.

He hated digging.

Two hours had passed by the time Diwell, looking terribly unwell, staggered back to his chair by the door. The fact that he hadn't dispatched another guard to cover his shift was, Jess thought, fairly significant; accepting extra food must have been a dire crime for him to avoid mentioning why he was ill. He was afraid Thomas might report him.

We can use that, Jess thought. He checked the time—a crude sundial using the sun from the window—and saw they were approaching the hour. He wished he felt more confident.

He wished he knew that Morgan was all right. *Wolfe will see to her,* he told himself. *Mind your work.* It didn't help.

"Feeling better?" Thomas asked the guard, with a cheerful glee that made Diwell send him a look that wished him burning in hell. "Good. You can take a message to Master Beck for us: we will have his prize ready for him to see within the next hour. I'm sure he will be pleased."

Diwell groaned. It was a faint sound, but raw. He put his head in his hands for a moment, then nodded and stood up. He started to speak, but maybe he realized that threats had no force now, and they watched in silence as he left. It might take him half an hour to limp his way to city hall, at that rate.

"Now we wait," Thomas said. "Here." He tilted back an enormously heavy anvil, and beneath it, Jess saw he'd dug out a small space. Into it he'd thrust two wicked knives, gracefully shaped but deadly at edges and points. He handed one to Jess. "Careful. It will split hairs."

Jess nodded and slipped it carefully into a slot in his boot—one made for a dagger about this size. Something Thomas no doubt had observed, or asked Glain about. Thomas had made a small leather sheath from scraps here in the workshop, and he slipped his own knife into it and strapped it to his forearm, hilt down. He rolled his shirt cuffs down to cover it. "Do you think we're going to die?" Thomas sounded almost academic about it. Remote. "I wish I could write to my parents. In case. But I suppose there's no way to do that, is there?"

Jess silently took out the makeshift Codex that he'd concealed under his shirt, and opened it to the empty page. The blue feather was still there, waiting. "I'll have to write it for you," he said. "But I can ask Brendan to deliver it."

Thomas nodded, eyes fixed on the window. On the storm, still rushing toward them. "It would be a bad omen," he finally said. "No. I will wait. I will write to them when I am free. When this is done. Just—just ask him to tell them that I love them."

Jess quietly wrote his brother the message, and added, *Same from me to anyone who might care. And I suppose from Khalila to her family, and Dario, and Glain. Captain Santi has a brother somewhere. Morgan and Wolfe have no one, so if there are prayers to be done, I suppose it's left to you.*

He wasn't sure his brother would write back at all, and when he finally did, the pen moved slowly, as if Brendan was fighting to write the words. *Don't be such a morose bastard. You'll live to bury me. You're the luckiest ass who ever lived. And the fastest, and the bravest. So live, and do your own praying. We're moving our camp. Zara's made up some excuse. We'll be in place as agreed. You just get yourselves there. Understood?*

Understood, Jess wrote, and closed the book with the feather caught inside the pages. He retied the book across his chest. Not as secure as a smuggling harness, but it would have to do.

Outside, the air grew charged and heavy, and the clouds massed higher and darker to the west like an approaching army. As Jess watched, lightning laced a bright line through the black, and a rumble of thunder rolled in the distance. *Coming on fast,* he thought. All of it. Too fast.

Diwell returned nearly an hour after that, limping and looking miserable; he collapsed into his chair and glared at Thomas. "You've poisoned me, you Library bastard."

"I did not!" Thomas protested. "If I had, you'd be dead by now. But some of the food might have spoiled, I suppose. My apologies."

Diwell muttered something, took a deep breath, and suddenly bolted again for the door. Retching.

"I really am sorry," Thomas said, not to Diwell exactly. Just in general. "For all of it."

"I didn't think Protestant Germans went to confession," Jess said.

"We don't," Thomas said. "But sometimes, confession is good for the soul. And I think before this is over, our souls will need a little cleansing, don't you?"

He was probably right about that.

EPHEMERA

Text of a letter from Scholar Johannes Gutenberg to
the Archivist Magister, interdicted to the Black
Archives. Not indexed in the Codex.

With the greatest respect and admiration I have always borne for you,
great Archivist, I must ask why you have ordered the High Garda to
remove the model of the device I described to you, a device I believe to be of
eminent importance that will only add to the great reach of the Library.

I must also ask why soldiers have taken from me all papers, drawings, and journals that refer to this device, and warned my family, in
the safety of their own home, to say nothing of this, on pain of death.

I cannot believe this is done with your approval, or if it has been,
that you have been properly apprised of all the wondrous possibilities
of my device for the greater glory of the Library.

If I may pay a personal visit to you, I may put your mind at rest
upon this matter.

Text of a notation in the margins of the letter, from the
Archivist Magister of the time to the Artifex Magnus.
Not indexed in the Codex.

Arrange for him to come to you. I have no stomach for the bloody
work to be done here. His family, too, must be silenced, and you must
see it done. Make sure no one else knows of this device. I want every
tongue stilled, and every eye made blind that ever beheld the thing.

I despise the necessity of such things, but the safety of the Library
comes above all else. Gods help us all if this knowledge should ever escape.

CHAPTER SIX

The storm hadn't yet arrived when Beck entered the workshop another hour later, surrounded by a small mob of guards and followers. "I hope you haven't summoned me for nothing—" He fell silent. The light from the windows and a single oil lamp glimmered on gears, metal springs, and the tall wooden frame. At the very least, Jess thought, what they'd built looked imposing, and Beck seemed momentarily impressed. Momentarily. He slowed and walked around the machine, then gestured to Thomas.

"Interesting," he said at last. "Explain it to me."

"Best to show you," Thomas said. "Jess? Ink and paper."

Jess sponged the ink on the letters and fixed the paper in place.

"Now, Master Beck, step back. All the way back, please."

Beck made a cautious retreat, and so did his men, as Thomas pulled down the lever. Beck let out a surprised yelp at the resulting crash, and several of the guards drew weapons. Luckily, they seemed unsure what exactly they should shoot or stab.

"It isn't dangerous," Thomas said, perfectly calmly. "Now you will see."

"See *what*?" Indira barked. "All right, all of you. Relax. Fire only on my orders!" Thank God, there was a professional in the fanatical ranks.

Thomas had managed to ignore their peril completely. Which was . . . very Thomas. "This machine is the future of the Burners," he said. "And the Library. Jess?"

While Thomas cranked the lever up and secured it, Jess stepped forward to retrieve the printed page. He carried the sheet to Willinger Beck, who took it, still looking doubtful . . . until he examined it in the light of the window.

"A life is worth more than a book," he read aloud, and the astonishment in his voice rang clear. "This is in both English and Greek. Our motto. The motto of *this city*." He stared hard at the paper, then turned it to face Jess and Thomas. "What kind of Obscurist trick is this?"

"It's not magic," Thomas said. "No Obscurists involved. It's pure machinery. Anyone can build it. Anyone can operate it. All you need is the machine, ink, and paper to print as many copies as you like, of anything you please."

"But . . . this is only a page," Beck said. "You said I could have books. A book made of the same words, over and over? What use is it?"

"This is all movable. Each letter is a separate piece. They can be removed and replaced, like a child's spelling blocks. You can write out anything you like, in any language known . . . we used English and Greek, but you could as easily use French and German, or Arabic and Chinese. You can mirror the text of any book and produce a thousand copies, one page at a time. All you have to do in the end is bind those pages together."

Beck slowly turned the page around again, and his lips moved silently as he read what they'd printed once more. When he looked up this time, his eyes were shining. At first, Jess thought it was with lust for power, and then . . . and then he realized he was seeing tears, as they broke free and spilled down the man's stubbled cheeks.

Beck said, "My God . . . my God," and fell into wrenching sobs. He sank down on his knees, still clutching the page in trembling hands, while his soldiers looked on. Some of them clearly understood what had brought him low; as Jess looked around, he saw the comprehension on their faces. Some looked elated. Some, like Beck, seemed overwhelmed.

Only Indira seemed unmoved. She watched them with cold focus.

Beck managed to regain control of his emotions and roughly swiped a handkerchief across his face and eyes. He cleared his throat with a sound like gravel turning over in a bucket. "I am sorry. I just realized . . . that the words on this page exist by themselves. They can't be erased from existence. They are both original and copy." His eyes had taken on a faraway look. He was seeing the future, Jess thought. "The Library does not control this page. It can't even *see* this page." He looked around at the others he'd brought with him. "Do you understand what this means? What we have?"

"What you have is dangerous," Thomas said. "I give you fair warning: the Library will do anything to see this machine destroyed, any trace of it wiped away. When I sketched plans for it in my journal, I was taken. My machine was destroyed. I was put in prison. I would have died there without—" Thomas's steady, calm voice hitched just a little, and Jess felt him flinch. "Without the devotion of my friends. You *must* not let them know what you have."

Thomas was blunt but honest; Jess wouldn't have warned Beck about consequences. He didn't think the man deserved the courtesy.

Beck hardly paid attention at all. His whole attention was on the inked letters in front of him. "Brilliant," he said, and it was clear he hadn't heard a word Thomas had said. "This is *brilliant*. We will print our messages on this machine! We will post hundreds of them in every city, every town in the world where the Library lays its hand! We will shove them down the throats of every High Garda bastard we kill. We will shape the world at last in *our* image, not the Archivist's. It will be our calling card, these very words, printed on this wonder." Jess felt his stomach lurch at that, picturing Glain lying dead, a grinning Burner stuffing her mouth with paper he and Thomas had printed. He imagined Santi defiled like that, and Wolfe lying broken beside him. He opened his mouth to speak, but Beck rushed right over him. "How quickly can you print more?"

Thomas's face had gone entirely blank, but Jess had never seen his clear blue eyes so dark. "We can begin now. Would you like to operate the machine yourself?"

Beck looked stunned, as if someone had offered him the chance to sit in the Archivist Magister's throne. "Yes, yes, I would!" Beck said, and rushed to stand uncertainly next to the cobbled-together press. "What do I do? Show me, boy! Quickly!"

Without comment, Jess brushed ink over the metal lettering and placed another blank sheet of paper over them. He stepped back. Beck stared expectantly, as if he was waiting for some magical process to begin.

"Pull the lever," Thomas said. Beck looked down, took hold, and pulled. He jumped and gasped when the weights snapped down, pressing the paper, and Thomas showed him how to crank the lever back until it caught on the ratchet. Then Jess demonstrated how to carefully peel away the still-wet paper.

"It has to dry," he said. "Touch it when it's wet and it'll smear."

"Yes, yes, fine, we'll build drying lines to hang the pages on," Beck said, and flapped a dismissive hand. "Counselor Lindsay? You may keep the first page from the press."

One of the group who'd been standing in the shadows stepped forward and took the page almost reverently, and held it as carefully as she would something liable to break apart at a touch. "Amazing," the woman said to Jess, and then bowed to Thomas. "Astonishing. You have shown us a miracle. It will change the world."

"Yes. Yes it will, under our direction, of course," Beck said. "Valin, you saw how the young men placed the ink and paper. This time, you do it. I want everyone proficient in the use of this machine."

Thunder boomed again. It sounded closer. Jess looked out toward the window. The clouds were rushing in on them, and as he watched, shadows began to strangle the light.

The storm was no longer coming. It was here.

Jess stepped back as the Burners crowded closer around the press. So did Thomas, and as he did, he took hold of Jess's arm and moved him farther away, all the way to the corner. It was done casually, as if giving the Burners possession of the device, and in truth, Beck hardly noticed. His attention was all on a small older man—Valin, must have been—who stepped forward at Beck's impatient gesture. He was clearly terrified of the machine, and he trembled as he slopped too much ink on the metal letters, and wasted a page when he placed it crookedly and tried to adjust it. He murmured a nervous apology and tried again, this time clipping the paper in the right spot before stepping back.

Beck hardly waited for the man to get clear before he yanked hard on the lever, and the weights slammed down. When he cranked it open again, he nodded to Valin, who peeled the paper free. Smudged, but readable. "It's the same!" Valin said. "Sir, the same exactly!" He sounded overwhelmed.

Beck's face was florid with pleasure. "Again!" he ordered. "I want a full hundred of these pages before we're done!"

"Will this work?" Jess whispered to Thomas.

"It had better," he whispered back. "It would be tragic if we built it *too* well."

The springs failed spectacularly on the fifth pull of the lever.

Jess heard the difference as the springs engaged; there was a distinct, flat *snap* to it, and the weights crashed down . . . and collapsed straight through. The wood frame shattered under the strain. Parts spun off in all directions, broken springs flying, gears smashing and breaking and rolling.

It was as magnificent a failure as they might have wished, and it was all Jess could do to keep from grinning. He nudged Thomas without looking at him, and thought, *You brilliant, crazy fool,* as Beck shouted in horror and alarm and his men—those who hadn't been struck by flying pieces of shrapnel—ran uselessly around trying to salvage the rolling gears and broken parts.

Beck's shock lasted only a few seconds before his gaze turned on Jess and Thomas.

And Thomas, bless him, shrugged with what looked like absolute innocence. "My apologies, Master Beck, but this was never meant to be a permanent version of the machine. You gave us pot metals and castoffs to build your future. We did the best we could with what was available. We can do better, of course. We just need better materials. Perhaps you can acquire those for us?" He picked up a piece of paper from the table to his left. "Here's a list of the items that are necessary."

Beck didn't take the list. He was staring at them with angry, bitter eyes, but it had *looked* like an accident, all right, and there was no denying that Thomas had worked a miracle from scraps, however long it had worked. Beck suspected he'd been tricked, but he couldn't work out how, or why.

But one thing was certain: he now felt he *needed* them. He lusted after this machine with a passion that was going to drive him for the rest of his life.

Beck was still clutching the last page that had come off the machine, and from the way he held it, it seemed he didn't intend to ever let it go. He stooped and, with his other hand, picked up a broken, misshapen spring and ran his thumb over the coils while he stared at them both.

"Draw the plans," he said.

"The plans are no help to you without a working prototype, given your resources," Thomas said, in his most reasonable voice. "Let us build you another, Master Beck. And we will do it in full cooperation with your picked craftspeople and provide detailed plans at every stage."

Beck's friendly face took on new lines, new hard angles that made him look completely different from the man who'd been on his knees just a few moments before, weeping in joy . . . This one, Jess was sure, was the *real* Beck, the one who'd ruthlessly held power and kept a city together in the face of constant Library attacks. Not a man who would take no for an answer.

Thomas's ploy was not going to work, and Jess felt himself go a little cold inside.

"Indira," Beck said. "Shoot the Brightwell boy in both knees. We'll cripple all of them to make sure they have no plans to cheat us."

She drew her gun. Jess threw himself backward and to the side, diving behind a pile of scrap metal. She cursed and moved forward to try for a better shot.

Thomas roared and moved. *Fast.* As Jess fumbled in the pile of broken metal for something of use, Thomas crossed the space to where Beck stood, put one enormous hand around his throat, and jerked the man off the ground and held him there to choke.

"Thomas, *no!*" Jess shouted. Indira turned her gun on his friend, and at this range, she couldn't miss. Jess rose, grabbing the first thing he could reach—the broken, twisted remains of a gear—and flung it at her head. Poor throw, but he hit her shoulder and knocked her back a step. The gun went flying. Jess flung himself over the pile of metal and grabbed one of Thomas's massive hammers; adrenaline gave him strength to heft it easily. He rushed at Indira, and she dodged away, trying for her gun. He cut her off.

Her other guards were starting to react now, shaking off shock and going for their weapons. *This will be a massacre.*

"Thomas! Don't!" This was not the plan.

Thomas wasn't bloody well listening.

Beck's toes thrashed the air, and he dropped the paper and the spring to slap at Thomas's arms, which did absolutely nothing. Thomas's face was bone white, his blue eyes wide and merciless in the dim light. He said something in German, and then switched to English. "Drop your weapons, all of you, or I'll crush his throat."

Jess shot him a disbelieving glance—*Who are you? What have you done with my friend?*—then quickly returned his attention to the soldiers, who seemed torn between saving Beck and avenging him. Jess kept the hammer ready to deliver a blow if he had to, but there was something in the silky, even inflection of Thomas's voice that made even the most militant of the guards believe him. One by one, they dropped guns and knives.

All except Indira, who retrieved her gun and aimed it at Jess's head. "Kill him, and I kill your friend, Schreiber."

Thomas lowered Beck back to the ground but didn't let him go. He did loosen the grip enough that Beck drew in a raw, whooping breath and coughed it out again.

"Tell her to put down her gun," Thomas said, "or I'll follow your example. I'll cripple you for life. You know I can, as easily as closing my hand."

Definitely not the Thomas Jess knew. *This* Thomas had been born from pain and despair down in the depths of Rome's prison. *This* version of his friend was feral and angry and dangerous, and most of all, he was very, very strong.

"Indira! Put it down! For God's sake, put it down!" Beck wheezed. She didn't seem inclined to obey, but his angry hysteria got to her at last. She crouched and put her weapon on the ground. She rose with both hands in the air. Thomas still didn't let go. He looked as if he was considering, very strongly considering, separating the man's head from his neck with a pull and a twist.

"Thomas," Jess said, in as calm a voice as he could manage while threatening men with a hammer. "He's agreed. Let him go now or they're going to kill us. *Including our friends.*"

Thomas still held his position, but he must have comprehended sense, because he released Beck with a sudden, dismissive push. Beck sprawled on the dirt floor, gagging and coughing as his soldiers quickly grabbed him and dragged him behind them to safety.

Now was the moment of real danger, Jess thought, and adjusted his sweaty grip on the hammer. If Beck ordered their deaths . . . and Thomas, alarmingly, didn't seem to care. He stooped down and began picking up broken machine parts as if the men and women threatening the two of them didn't even exist. Jess felt faintly stupid, and very alone, brandishing a household tool.

"You've seen what we can do for you. You know you can use us. Leave us alone now," Thomas said, and wrenched half a broken cog from a bent iron rod. "You're in our way. Go and get us decent wood, metal, and materials."

"You're mad!" Beck said. He could only manage it as a croak. "He's mad!"

"He's a genius," Jess said. "Master Beck, give us better materials and you'll get what you want. Threaten us, or any of our friends, and I don't think Thomas will stop next time at bruising you. You'll never reconstruct this machine without us. Do we have an understanding?"

"You cocky little *bastard*," Beck grated. He sounded like he'd been gargling the leftover broken glass. "You think you hold any kind of power?"

"I just saw you weeping for joy, didn't I? You want this. We have it. That's the definition of negotiating, and if you contact my father, you know he'll give you a very fine deal on the things you need to make your dream a reality. Now, *go*."

Beck didn't respond to that at all, but Jess knew he'd scored the point. He waited until the last of Beck's entourage disappeared out the workshop door, then slammed it and shut the bolt from inside before he turned back to Thomas.

Thomas stopped picking up the shattered pieces to look at him, and slowly, very slowly, a grin the likes of which Jess had never seen spread across his friend's face.

"So," he said. "That was glorious."

"It was." Jess didn't want to spoil the moment, which had a kind of demented joy, but he also had to know. "Why did you attack him?"

Thomas's smile dimmed to a curl at the corners of his mouth. "If I hadn't played the German berserker, he'd have done it. It was a good strategy: hobble you, cripple the rest one by one, and we're not likely to be able to flee, even if we've worked out how. Now he knows I'm half-mad, and he thinks he needs me. He will be more careful."

It was part of the truth, Jess thought. Not all. He studied his friend a moment before he said, "Thank you."

Thomas's fingers were restlessly exploring the metal parts in his hands, and he lifted one shoulder in a shrug. "You are my best friend," he said. "And I will always fight for you."

As simple as that. Jess's throat closed up, as if Thomas's hand had taken hold, but it was only a rush of gratitude that left him weak.

"Check to make sure we have everything," Thomas said. "All the parts of the Ray. They'll be waiting for us." He was still picking up parts and gears, and Jess didn't really understand why.

"You're not seriously going to make them another press, are you?" he said. Thomas raised his brows and opened the forge. He dumped the entire bucket of metal parts and pieces inside and slammed the forge closed again. It would take only a few minutes to reduce all their work to a metal sludge.

"Absolutely not," he said. "Let's go."

Despite his dislike for digging, Jess was very glad he'd made the effort as they wormed through the newly excavated tunnel under the back wall and out into the rapidly darkening afternoon. The guards were still watching the closed, locked workshop door.

A single drop of rain hit his face as he scrambled out. He couldn't judge the time accurately now.

But it was definitely time to go.

Wolfe, Santi, and Morgan were no longer in the prison. It was deserted—except for the dead bodies of two guards, lying in the bunks that Wolfe and Santi had occupied. They'd been covered up to look like they were sleeping.

Jess remembered what the men had said, in the dim early morning. *No going back.* They'd meant it.

"Where are we to meet them, then?" Thomas asked.

"Didn't Wolfe tell you?"

"Only to stay with you. Which I will."

"Good. I'd hate to think I was on my own right now," Jess said. He took one last look at the prison, all the cell doors opened. *If all the world's a lock, be a key.* His father had been right. "We're to head for the grain storage across the fields, far side of city hall. And we'd best do it quickly and quietly."

They were halfway across the park when the rain hit in earnest, and it went from fat, cold drops to a heavy, silvery curtain in moments. The storm was all to the good now, though Jess could see people out moving in the rain. Running here and there. No one could see well enough to recognize them and sound an alarm.

And then he realized that the people were coming *out* of their houses and buildings. That they were not running for shelter, as would be sensible. The people of Philadelphia were pouring out of the buildings, into the streets, and they all seemed to be heading toward city hall . . . the very place Jess and Thomas, also, had to go.

The rain soaked Jess's clothes and hammered them close to his skin; the force of the drops was truly shocking, and overhead, lightning flashed in heavy, constant explosions. Thunder hit hard enough to echo in Jess's chest. This was very different from a London rain shower; it was violent, full of wind and fury, and the trees in the park—including the one half-burned by the last Library attack—were whipping their branches angrily, as if they intended to rip themselves from the ground and walk.

Thomas leaned close as they broke into a run to shout, "What is it? What's happening? Is this part of the plan?"

"I don't know!" Jess shouted back.

He was sickly certain that it wasn't.

The crowd grew thicker around them, condensing as they drew near city hall, and in the flash of lightning, Jess saw that it numbered in the hundreds now. Nearly all of the city, it seemed, had come out in this storm, which was the opposite of what they needed.

And then he saw the figures starkly illuminated at the top of the city hall steps. Even at this distance, he recognized them: Santi. Wolfe. Morgan. Khalila.

And every one of them was being held by a guard.

"God, no," he said, and pulled Thomas to a halt in the mud. "Stop!" He dragged his friend off to the side, under the dark shelter of thrashing branches, and quickly dug from his pockets and bindings everything that Thomas had given him for the Ray of Apollo. "Make your way around through the side streets. If the mob's gathering here, you should be able to make it around that way, to the fields. Get to the barn near the wall. Wait for us, but don't wait too long. Understand? Brendan knows where we'll be coming through. Make a hole behind that building. Morgan's weakened the wall for you. It should work, but when we come, we'll be coming fast. Start as soon as you can."

"I can't just leave," Thomas said. He sounded reasonable. Jess wasn't in the mood for reasonable. He grabbed Thomas and shoved him in the direction he wanted him to go. It was like pushing one of the trees. "Jess. I can help you!"

"No. You're the only one who can open up our way out, and I can't risk you. I need you to do that. Go. *Go!*"

Thomas gave him one last, silent look, and then turned and went the way Jess had pointed. Away from trouble, for once.

Jess ran toward it.

Willinger Beck had come out from shelter now, and took his place on the landing next to the captives. He raised his hands and shouted, but Jess couldn't hear what he was saying over the roar of the rain and the crowd. And couldn't bother to care. His attention was on his friends. *Think.* Dario and Glain weren't with them. Wherever they were, whatever they were doing, they'd slipped this trap, and that was good.

What was bad was that Jess saw no chance at all to free the rest of them, and he was all too aware that at any moment, one of the men or women in the crowd might glance at him and recognize him, and then he'd be up there, too, pinned and helpless.

You should go, Wolfe's imaginary, sour voice lectured him. *Staying to witness our deaths is less than useless. Get out while you can. That was always the plan.*

Imaginary Wolfe's advice was still crap, and he wasn't going to abandon them, any more than he'd abandoned Thomas back in Alexandria—and he'd thought Thomas might be *dead.*

The crowd was shouting, anger and fear smeared into a fog he could almost taste. He didn't know why they were so angry, but it didn't matter now. He cast a fast look around and fixed on one of Beck's guards lingering near the edge of the crowd. Jess faded back, and as he did, he picked up a fallen branch from one of the trees. Heavy wood. The guard was *just* in the shadow of a tree, and Jess circled around the trunk and came up behind him. He hit him hard in the back of the head and dragged him backward in the same instant, then hit him again to be sure he was unconscious before he stripped off the man's hooded coat and put it on. He relieved the man of two pistols and a knife. The coat smelled foul, but he hardly noticed; the hood kept his face in shadow and kept the rain off.

A bolt of lightning sizzled from the clouds to strike the statue of Benjamin Franklin on top of city hall, and a cry went up from the crowd. They took it as a sign, he supposed.

So did he. He pushed through the crowd as if he had the right.

He was wearing the guns, the coat, the attitude of one of Beck's security men. No one stopped him.

He went right up the steps.

Khalila saw him first, and her eyes went wide; she was soaking wet and shivering, and her dress was clinging to her in ways that would probably make her blush, but she managed a very slight nod. He wanted to go to Morgan, but Morgan was next to Beck, and Khalila was at the end, easy to reach. He stepped up next to the guard who held her, pulled his hood lower, and thought about relieving the other guard . . . but that wouldn't work. The town was small. He'd be instantly recognized.

So he stood silently, tensely, and waited for his chance.

Beck's voice was still hoarse from Thomas's hold, but he managed a full-throated shout to carry over the booms of thunder. A trick of acoustics on the steps amplified him, though how many of the crowd could hear was anyone's guess.

"I hear your anger!" Beck shouted, and lifted his hands for quiet. Rain bedraggled him, like it did the rest of them, and gave him less of an imposing presence. He had mud on his shoes and trousers, and his glasses were beaded and blind with water. "My people! I hear it and I understand it! We knew better than to trust the Library, or any of their creatures, and that was my mistake! But it is a mistake we will rectify, *now*! Come with me and see for yourself!"

That . . . didn't bode well at all. Jess flexed his fingers and eased one of the guns out and to his side. Beck pointed—bafflingly—off to the side, and his guards began hustling the prisoners in that direction.

Khalila was still last in that line. Beck and his attendants were striding down the steps, leading the movement wherever they were heading, and Jess took the chance, as lightning struck again, to slam the butt of his pistol into the neck of the guard who held Khalila. He staggered and turned and started to draw his gun.

Thunder shook the world and drowned out the sound of Jess shooting.

The man went down, and Jess quickly rolled him to the side and off the steps behind a row of bushes. He grabbed hold of Khalila and held her as if he were hustling a prisoner, but at an angle to the others. "Make way!" he shouted, and the crowd surging off to follow Beck parted for him. Some cast filthy looks on Khalila. One tried to slap her, but Jess reached out and shoved the other woman away.

He got Khalila down to the grass and moved her into the shelter of a shadowed corner, where they crouched together. He took the coat off and put it around her.

"No! Jess, keep it!" She was trembling, but it was cold, not fear. "You'll need it to get the others!"

"What is all this?" he asked her. "What happened?"

"Food riot," she said. "We were getting the books. I gave everything to Dario and Glain and told them to go. The mob went to the prison and took Morgan, and Wolfe and Santi tried to stop them. I couldn't get them free. I tried. These people are frightened and angry, and they blame us for the crops rotting in the fields."

"Crops rotting in the fields," Jess repeated. They'd cut the rations days ago. But he remembered something Morgan had said. And something Wolfe had said, too. *Unintended consequences.* The way that suddenly, everything had accelerated.

"We have to go behind city hall, through the fields," he told Khalila. "If we get separated, find your way to the building at the far end, near the eastern wall. Thomas and the others should be there. I'll fetch Morgan, Wolfe, and Santi."

She grabbed his collar as he started to rise. Her dark eyes were wide and worried. "Can you?" she asked him.

"I have to try."

She flung herself into his arms and kissed his cheek. "Allah guide and keep you, my brother. We'll wait for you."

"Don't," he told her, and held on just a moment more. "Promise me you won't. I need to know you'll be safe."

She shook her head as she stepped away, and gave him that beautiful smile he loved. "I will never promise to abandon you," she said, and turned and ran into the rain. It was still heavy enough to hide her in seconds.

Jess looked up at the sky, the flickers of lightning, and rain stung cold against his skin. He let it wash him for a few brief heartbeats, and then he went up the steps to city hall, kicked the door open, and drew his guns.

There was no one inside city hall, which didn't much surprise him; he ran straight across the marble entry hall, the crudely done Burner seal, and kicked open another set of doors just beyond. It led to what must have been offices, but these held only a few startled clerk types, who cried out and dived for cover as he ran past. Through the far glass windows, he could see the back stairs of the building, and a broad swath of grass . . . and the fields. It was the first time he'd set eyes on them, and even though they were obscured by the rain, it was clear that Philadelphia was in real trouble. The plants looked black. Wheat, corn, all of it.

No wonder there were no rations. No wonder Beck was looking to place the blame. And no wonder the people were in a rage. *Beck asked Morgan to increase their crop yields,* Jess thought. And they'd seen her in the fields. It wouldn't have taken but one or two voices to start the outcry that Morgan was to blame for it.

Jess skidded to a halt and looked for doors, but all he saw were windows, and he had no time to bother with niceties. He picked up a handy sculpture—a bust of one of the Burner leaders, he presumed—and hurled it through the nearest plate of glass, which shattered with a gratifying crash that sprayed sharp points out to be lost in the rain. He dived through and nearly slipped on the wet landing, but he gained his feet again, made sure the guns were in place, and jumped off the edge of the steps to take shelter. The mob, led by Beck, was coming around the corner now, marching toward him. He knew Beck. He knew he'd want to make a production of their justice.

The wind shifted and blew toward him, and Jess gagged on the unmistakable smell of decay. It was coming from the fields. This was far worse than he'd imagined. There was something dark and awful about seeing these crops corrupted in the soil, battered and broken by the rain. A stand of apple trees not far from him held nothing but balls of black rot, and the trees themselves looked pale and diseased.

Morgan had done this without meaning to. And they were shoving her, Santi, and Wolfe up the steps just as he'd expected, while the mob filled in the space between the steps and the fields. The rain was starting to slow a little, but the fields were a stinking mass of rotten plants and mud, and no one seeing it could fail to understand that they were going to starve this winter.

Beck needed a scapegoat, or it would be his head on the chopping block.

The Burner leader took Morgan by the arm and marched her to the edge of the stairs, showing her to the crowd. It was easier to hear him now, and his voice seemed to have come back to full strength again. "*This creature* is the traitor who destroyed our crops—an Obscurist, sent by the Library to poison our food and force us to submit! We trusted her! We allowed her safety and shelter and *our good welcome.* I ask you, good people of Philadelphia: what punishment do you demand?"

The answer roared back from a hundred throats: *death.* They were going to kill Morgan. They'd tear her apart.

Jess tried to breathe against the weight of suffocating fear. *Think. Find a way out.* He didn't see one.

Beck moved on to Wolfe. "*This one* is her master and her protector, a full Scholar of the Great Library! A Stormcrow, sent to us to destroy us! What punishment, good people?"

Death. They took it up as a chant this time, and the power and fury of it chilled harder than the rain.

Santi was next. *Sworn enemy of our city. Captain of the High Garda. Murderer of our children.*

And the sentence was obvious.

Beck turned to the three of them, and Jess saw him smile. It was a terrible, cynical thing, and it made him tighten his grip on the two pistols he'd drawn. "Make her bring back our crops," Beck told Wolfe, "And I'll let her live."

"I will," Morgan cried out. "I'll fix this if you let them go!"

"She can't fix it," Wolfe said with ruthless precision. "Nothing can bring back the dead. You believe in the Christian teachings, Master Beck? Well. You reap what you sow."

Beck hit him. Backhand, a viciously fast blow that rocked Wolfe's head to one side and left him spitting blood. Santi snarled and tried to pull free, but he was too weak.

"*You* reap what *you* sow, you filthy crow," Beck said. He swung around to glare at Morgan. "Last chance, girl. Save our crops, and save their lives." Beck pulled out a pistol and leveled it at Santi's head. The captain looked at the weapon, then past it to meet Beck's eyes.

"I will not say it again, girl," Beck said. "*Bring back our crops.* Or I'll kill this man right now, and his blood will be on your hands. I'll save the Scholar to burn alive and screaming. Do you hear?"

Santi said, in a deceptively calm and unbothered voice, "None of this is your fault, Morgan. No matter what happens. *In bocca al lupo,* Christopher."

Wolfe took a sharp, sudden breath, and whispered, "*Crepi il lupo,* dear Nic."

It meant good-bye.

Jess stood up, but he had no shot, no clear one; he could see a sliver of Beck, but not enough to aim for, not enough to do any good, but he *had to shoot* . . .

And that was the moment when sirens began to wail beyond the walls.

The tone was different. Louder, higher, more dissonant than before. And an amplified voice with an Alexandrian accent spoke first in English, and then repeated the same phrase in German, Spanish, more languages that Jess didn't even recognize.

But the phrase would be the same in all of them.

The Great Library declares no quarter will be given.

Philadelphia was about to die.

EPHEMERA

Urgent directive from the Archivist Magister to
commanders of all High Garda surrounding
Philadelphia

You are ordered to disregard previous instructions on the preservation
of the city, its occupants, and the capture of the Burner leaders. For the
safety and preservation of the Library, you must bombard the city
immediately with all speed and all strength, with no regard for casualties or for damage.

Let the city of the Burners be reduced to ashes. Let no living thing
remain.

Let it burn.

Text of a letter from the Spartan poet Tyrtaeus to his
son. Available in the Codex.

My son, these are the ways of brothers: you must reach the outer lim-
its of virtue before you die. You must trust the man at your back and
to your side. You must joyously run to the fight, and never from it. Do
these things, and you will be both a good man, and a brave man.

And the brave never die. Mark this well: the brave never die, for
we remember.

CHAPTER SEVEN

Jess took his finger off the trigger, and thank God he did, because he knew he would have killed someone he didn't intend to hit, his hand was shaking so badly. The mob had gone from rabid to panicked in a breath, and now they were starting to scatter. Now to run, slipping on the slick grass and in the mud. Desperate to get to a shelter.

Jess lunged forward, got Beck square in his sights, and very nearly killed him. Would have, if the guard Indira hadn't fired on Jess first. Her bullet hissed close enough that he felt the heat of its passage, and the shot intended to put Beck down went wide.

Beck still had a gun of his own, and now he realized he was under attack. He turned and sighted on Jess.

Santi hit the man with his uninjured shoulder, hard enough to lift Beck clear off his footing. Santi slammed him down on the steps. Beck landed with a bone-cracking thud, screaming.

Now Indira had two enemies, Santi and Jess, and a hesitation of which to target cost her dear. Neither of them was quick enough to get her.

Wolfe was.

He turned, slipping out of his guard's hold with a grace that would have been unexpected to anyone who didn't know him, and just as easily plucked a knife from the man's belt. As he spun, he threw with an accuracy Jess knew he'd never equal, and the knife tumbled in a perfectly stable arc, end over end, to bury itself in Indira's chest.

She shot anyway, but shock disrupted her aim, and the one directed at Santi went wide, to pock a hole in the marble wall. She looked down in disbelief and then took hold of the knife and started to pull it free. She didn't manage more than a fraction of it before she was folding at the knees, and then down.

Beck was screaming where he lay on the stairs, one leg at a drastic angle, but he had no weapon and was no threat now, and Jess, Santi, and Wolfe all turned on the guard holding Morgan.

He let go and ran. Morgan lurched forward, nearly falling, into Jess's arms.

"What is this?" she shouted over the awful keening of the sirens. "What's happening?"

He didn't have time to explain. Even thinking of it made him sick. Santi tried to reach for Wolfe, but the Scholar shook him off and rushed down the steps, past Beck, to kneel next to Indira.

The woman was still alive, Jess saw. Wolfe bent and said something to her, and put his hand on her forehead. Her lips moved, and her eyes closed, and he jerked the knife free with one fast motion.

She died quickly, then. Fast and clean, as she probably deserved. Indira wasn't their enemy. Beck was, perhaps. But most of these people . . . They were just frightened and desperate, and it had all gone so suddenly, devastatingly *wrong*.

"What can we do?" Jess shouted to Santi. Santi shook his head without taking his gaze from Wolfe, who was wearily rising. "Sir!"

"We go," Santi said. "There's nothing else to be done."

Morgan wasn't strong enough to run, even with Jess's help; he picked her up and carried her as they moved through the muddy, stinking, dead fields toward the outbuilding near the wall. Halfway across, Jess had the feeling that someone was following, and looked behind them.

It was the doctor. Askuwheteau. He was approaching at a slipping, stumbling run, and he was leading a small column of people, including the woman Jess had met at the doctor's home. His housekeeper. "Wait!" Askuwheteau called. A young child tripped and fell, and the doctor, without pausing, scooped him up and carried him. "Do you have a way out? Please!"

Jess looked at them. People of Askuwheteau's native blood, he thought, and a number of others who must have put their faith in him. *This is mad. It'll get us all caught.* "Yes," he said. "Come with us. Hurry."

Wolfe and Santi were ahead of them, and though Wolfe gave Jess a stern look when he saw the stragglers trailing in his wake, he didn't say anything. Santi opened the door of the building—a barn, made for the storage of grain—and gestured them all in. He clapped the door shut behind them.

A lamp came alive with a soft hiss of flame, and it cast a smooth golden light over Khalila Seif's face. She took in a deep breath of relief at the sight of them. "How did you get free? I thought—"

"Doesn't matter now," Wolfe said. "Go. *Go.* Once the sirens stop—"

And as if he'd commanded it, the wailing came to an abrupt end. Echoes shattered back from distant walls, and then it was ominously silent. Not even thunder broke the stillness. They looked up, though all they could see was the dark roof overhead.

The paralysis broke when Jess heard the first thin, high whistle of a ballista bomb. He remembered that hellish sound all too well. He'd heard it in Oxford, in England, and he'd seen what a no-quarter bombardment by the High Garda really meant. "Go!" Jess shouted, and they were all moving for the back of the building, where Khalila slid aside a door wide enough for a hay cart. They were only a short distance from the wall.

And the wall was unbroken.

Thomas wasn't there.

"Where are they?" Jess turned on Khalila.

"They aren't with *you*?" she demanded in turn. "Thomas and Glain never arrived! Dario went to fetch them, I thought—" She pulled in a sudden, agonized breath. "Does Beck have them?"

"No," Jess said. "He'd have shoved them in our faces if he did." *Thomas, you fool, what are you doing?* "Glain and Dario went to get the books?"

"Yes! They're here!" She pointed to a stack of bags and packs near the door. Familiar ones. They'd carried them from Alexandria to London to here. "Glain went to get something else, and Dario went after her. I never saw Thomas!"

But Thomas, Jess thought, had seen the others and decided they needed help. Without Thomas, without that device to melt a hole in this wall . . .

"I've got to go find them," he said, and ignored the protests that burst out of Morgan, Santi, Wolfe. Khalila said nothing, and he kept his gaze on her. "If the building goes, stay near the wall. Ballista bombs don't drop straight down; you should be safe there."

She nodded, though they both knew that if the Library had declared no quarter in the battle, the volume of Greek fire that would shortly be descending on this city would leave nothing alive. Nothing safe.

"Which way did they go?" he asked her, and she pointed back to city hall.

"Jess!" Wolfe shouted, but he wasn't listening.

He was running.

Jess felt the waves of the explosion shudder through his body, and he nearly lost his footing; he watched one of the buildings in the street across from the fields shatter apart, wood and metal spinning in strangely beautiful arcs into the air, glittering end over end . . . and then the Greek fire contained inside the projectile caught fire. It was an awful, beautiful fountain of raw green liquid that breathed and spread, falling on other buildings, coating the street.

Everything, burning.

He ran faster, heart pounding as he heard more high, keening screams overhead. More bombs coming, from every direction now. *This is suicide!* But he didn't know what else to do. He couldn't leave them. Better to die honest.

He'd just reached the strip of mud and grass where the mob had been when two bombs hit city hall. One shattered right through the tower, like a rock through an eggshell.

The other descended on the broad, white landing where Beck had threatened the prisoners. Right in front of him. He had just enough time to see Willinger Beck, with his badly broken leg, roll over and put his hands over his head in a futile attempt at protection, and thought, *I'm sorry,* and then the bomb went off.

He didn't realize he was falling. It was like a black stutter in the world, and with no transition at all he was lying on his back. A strange, hissing whine buzzed his ears, and he batted at it like a wasp, but it was *in* his ears, inside his head, and as he rolled slowly onto his side he remembered the ballista, the explosion. The thin, screaming sound of death approaching from the sky.

Then he saw the fire.

It lived, breathed, roared like a beast, greenish at the edges, raw, bleeding red at the center as it melted the stone steps. The building itself was burning, the tower collapsing in on itself. He saw Benjamin Franklin's golden statue tumbling down in an arc, melting into golden streamers as it fell.

The grass around him exploded in poison green patches, spreading, crisping the soil beneath into brittle glass. A tree near the corner became a burning matchstick weeping lacy, lazy curls of flame.

The air swirled with ashes and bitter smoke so thick he could bite it, chew it, swallow it whole. The acrid taste made him retch uncontrollably. He wiped thick, colorless spit away from his lips and levered himself up on shaking legs. The burning tree began to hiss and screech like a human strapped to a pyre; it was only the sap boiling and cracking through the bark with thick pops, but it sounded so alive.

He could hear more bombs exploding, and the high, thin shrieking now wasn't the bombs falling; it was people with no way out, nowhere to run. *Am I burning?* It occurred to him only then, in a blind panic, that he might be, that if he looked down, he might see his skin crisping and curling off of muscle, and fear nearly sent him reeling until he got ahold of himself. *I'm not. I'm not burning.*

A window at the far corner of the building suddenly exploded outward in a white shower of glass, and a large tufted chair crashed to the ground.

Glain was the first through in a leap and a roll. Dario clambered out and made the jump, awkwardly.

Thomas came last. He was holding a thick, crude weapon clutched in one hand, and he had a large, bulky sack over one shoulder. He jumped and landed to his ankles in the thick mud, and doubled over coughing. All three of them were stained with smoke, retching out thin drools of phlegm.

Jess heard the whistling of incoming missiles—more of them now. The keening of angry ghosts, made even more chilling by the thick clouds of smoke already spreading across the sky. Philadelphia—a defiant, crumbling wreck of a town—was burning, and burning as it never had before.

Jess stumbled to his friends and shouted, "Run!" He wanted to ask what had been so damned important that they'd risked everything, even the chance of life, but he had no breath to spare and neither did they. The air around them had grown hot, and every breath came painful and thick with smoke. He could taste the Greek fire now, as more and more containers shattered and the stuff spread into a fine, hazy mist. *Flashover is coming.* When Greek fire reached a dense enough fog in the air, it would ignite, and then there'd be nothing to breathe at all.

They ran through the rotten, dead fields. The plants were still too wet to burn, but mist rose off the mud like phantoms as the heat increased. Thomas had the advantage of extra-long legs; Dario and Glain struggled to keep up with the two of them. Jess ran like his life depended on every step, because it did.

He slowed as they approached the barn, and turned to look back. It was like looking back on hell. Philadelphia was a seething lake of flame, and still the ballistae keened, still the bombs exploded. The park where he'd kissed Morgan burned, every tree a candle. No building remained standing. None would.

"Jess!" Thomas shouted, and tackled him into the mud, just as a ballista bomb shattered through the roof of the barn in front of them. *We're dead. We're all bloody dead,* Jess thought, because the explosion would catch them, catch those crouching near the wall . . .

But nothing happened. Thomas rolled off, and Jess ran to the door of the barn. The glass container of Greek fire had fallen on a pile of hay, and it hadn't broken . . . but the fuse still burned, and when it ignited the contents . . .

Jess didn't think. He moved. He hardly felt the shock of the burn on his fingers when he grabbed the fuse and pulled, because it didn't matter; all that mattered was that this bomb *could not* explode.

He dropped the hissing fuse to the ground and crushed it into ash with his boot, then allowed himself to stagger back outside, lean against the wall, and scream. It came out raw with terror, fury, horror . . . a sound as agonized as all those sounds in the town, all those voices crying out.

He couldn't *do anything*.

"Jess," Thomas said, and Jess looked up at him. The German's face was smudged and filthy, but tears made clear tracks through the soot. "Come. Come now."

They followed Glain and Dario to the other side of the barn, where the rest of their friends crouched with Askuwheteau's fragile group of survivors near the wall. Wolfe shot to his feet when he saw them, and the anguish and relief on his face made Jess want to weep himself. This was too much, too much for anyone.

Thomas said, "Everyone, get away from the wall now," and they did, though they still crouched low, looking up at the swirling black clouds, the bombs shrieking through the air somewhere above, an unseen terror.

Thomas had found the time to put the Ray of Apollo together

from the components. It was bulky, crude, the ugliest thing Jess had ever seen Thomas craft; the long barrel flared out into a wide curve toward the end of it. *We didn't test it,* Jess thought with a horrible sense of fatality. *We didn't test it, and now there's no time.*

But Thomas was right. Heron had built this device back in the dim mists of antiquity. He'd made something that wouldn't be seen again until Archimedes, with his giant array of mirrors built to burn ships at sea. As Thomas had said, Heron's tools had been little better than what they'd had in Beck's workshop.

Thomas pressed the button, and a thick red light erupted from the barrel of the thing, spreading out but staying somehow *solid* in the air. *The mirror,* Jess thought, and remembered all those painful hours of grinding and polishing. *It's working.* The light hit the metal of the wall, and the wall began to hiss and glow and melt off in liquid layers. Concentrated light, burning its way through the surface of a wall softened by Morgan's efforts.

It was why she was so weak. She'd created this chance at life.

It took a long, torturous minute to burn completely through, and when Thomas switched off the gun, there was a hole in the wall just large enough to crawl through. The edges glowed sullenly, but they were already cooling.

Thomas groaned, dropped the weapon, and staggered backward—and Jess realized, in the next instant, that his friend's palms were burned bright red. "I didn't have time to put in shielding," Thomas said when Jess came toward him. "I didn't think— No, no, I'm fine. Go, Jess, *get them out!* We don't have long!"

"He's right," Santi said. He was already pushing Wolfe toward the escape. "It's going to flash over soon. Move!"

"The books!" Dario shouted, and grabbed packs. They all grabbed for them, and the rest Jess shoved quickly through the hole and let Wolfe, on the other side now, drag away. *Librarians to the end,* Jess thought, and it should have been funny. Nothing was funny now.

Santi went next, then Morgan. Khalila pushed Askuwheteau and his refugees ahead of her when her turn came, and no one argued, though Jess kept a nervous watch on the gathering mist. It had begun as a reeking, pale thing, but now it had taken on a definite tinge of green. The flames burning at city hall and in the town hadn't died at all. They'd grown into twisting, green, violent furies. He could feel the heat from here. Anyone closer would be dead from it.

The last of the Philadelphians went through, and then Khalila. Dario. Glain.

It was just Thomas, and Jess.

"Go," Jess said, and Thomas gave him a strange little smile.

"No," he said. "You go first."

That was the moment when Jess, to his shock, realized that the hole just wasn't big enough. Thomas had dropped the weapon before he'd burned a hole big enough to accommodate his broad shoulders.

That smile meant that he knew he was about to die. That he'd worked it out and accepted it.

"No," Jess said. He meant it to the bottom of his soul.

He bent and picked up the still-hot gun, flipped the switch, and began to widen the hole.

It was hard to know how Thomas had managed to hold the weapon at all; Jess's hands began to sting and scream in the first few seconds of use, and he felt his whole body tense against the rising red pain. *It won't take much. Thirty seconds. Maybe a little more. You can do this.* He counted it off under his breath. Started strongly, then ran out of air. Couldn't even gasp against the agony. *Hold on.* Somehow, he did, even though the pain had built to an exquisite, vile pressure like nothing he'd ever felt. It felt like being boiled alive. He was dimly aware that Thomas was shouting at him to stop. But he couldn't. The hole wasn't big enough for Thomas yet.

And then he felt something shudder inside the weapon, and the Ray of Apollo went dead. He tried the switch. Nothing. His hands were clumsy, and the metal slick, and he dropped it into the mud as he tried to get it working again; it had to work, *had to.*

But it would never work again. Pieces of it had melted. More of it glowed a dull red. The mirrors inside had shattered.

"You have to go," Thomas said to him.

Jess took a deep breath and said, "Not until you do."

Don't look at your hands, he told himself. He knew how badly they were burned, but he thrust his right into his pocket anyway. It felt like plunging it into molten glass, and he nearly screamed, but he managed not to, somehow, and when he pulled his hand out again, he was holding the small glass vial of the leftover Greek fire. He uncorked it and threw the liquid in a green, hissing arc to splash against the edge of the hole they'd burned.

It wasn't much, and it widened it by only an inch or so.

But it was enough.

Thomas picked Jess up and bodily *threw* him into the hole, and a pair of strong hands grabbed hold of him and pulled him to the other side. He hardly cared, but a glance up told him it was Dario Santiago who'd just saved his life.

Jess dragged in a sickly cool breath of air and bent over to retch out the poisonous stuff he'd been choking on. He didn't bother to see if they were under attack. He didn't care. He just crawled away to the side, gasping and shaking with pain.

And then he thought, *Thomas.*

His friend made it just in time. He only just squeezed through, even with the widening of the hole, and as he emerged, Jess saw his clothes were giving off wisps of smoke and flickers of Greek fire. Someone shouted, and a fire blanket was thrown on him to smother the flames.

Scholar Wolfe grabbed Thomas's reaching hand and pulled him—and the sack that Thomas wouldn't leave behind—well away from the hole.

Jess had only just begun to realize they'd made it, actually *made it*, when someone cried, "Watch out!" and the wall beside them boomed with a sudden pressure. It creaked and groaned, and an explosion of brilliant green light boiled upward within it. Curls of fire lashed the low black clouds. A tongue of green flame blasted through the hole in the wall, burned for long seconds, and then vanished in a reeking, rotten puff of smoke.

The aerosolized Greek fire mist had just burned off and cooked everything inside the walls. If they'd still been in there . . .

Jess froze, thinking of what they'd just escaped. He was shocked to be alive. He wanted to be glad his friends were with him. But all he could think was, *This is our fault.*

"Jess." He looked up. For a second, nothing made sense to him, not even the face of his own twin . . . and then he flung himself up and embraced Brendan with trembling strength. Which Brendan returned. "You gave me a fright, idiot!"

Jess managed to say, "What else am I for, then?" and tried to wipe at his eyes. His hands felt clumsy, and Brendan drew in a sharp breath when he saw the damage and yelled for a Medica.

"What did they do to you?" Brendan demanded, and his voice shook a little.

"I did it to myself."

"Shoveled burning coals with your hands?"

"I'm all right."

"You're not!" Brendan half snarled. "*Medica!* Damn you, get your arse over here!"

Medica, not doctor. Back to civilization through the small span of a metal wall. It seemed impossible. He'd started to see Philadelphia as a world in itself. And now it was gone. The Library had ordered it gone, and it was like it had never been there at all.

"Jess?" Brendan was in front of him now, eye level. Frowning in real worry. "Jess! Are you with me?"

"Yes," he said, though he wasn't sure. But things were starting to make some sense again. The tents arrayed around them in a protective huddle seemed familiar. The Library sigil fluttered in gold embroidery on the flags. The company symbol—a cobra coiled around a book—flew just below it to identify whom the tents belonged to. Santi's company. So Jess and the rest had managed to come out among friends—or, more accurately, the friends had managed to position themselves to meet the escape. He should thank Brendan for that. And for many other things. He just couldn't find the energy.

Jess caught sight of a tall woman striding toward them in her crisp uniform, with a shining black cap of hair hugging her face. Startling eyes. He knew the look she threw at Captain Santi, at Wolfe, and at each of them in turn. Not friendly, exactly. Assessing.

"Zara," Santi said, and struggled up to his feet. "Thank you."

She ignored that and focused on the knot of refugees who were still huddled together, Askuwheteau in the center of them. "You asked me to rescue Library personnel," she said. "And you bring *them* with you? Burners?"

"Innocents," Santi said. "You know they didn't deserve that!"

"All I know is Burners have spat on us and tried to kill us my entire life." Zara's dark eyes were utterly unreadable as she glanced at him, and then she said, "But we can save that particular discussion for later. I thank the gods you're still with us, Captain. And still causing trouble."

"I'm still the captain?"

"Until you say you're not, sir."

He nodded. "Then I'm grateful, Lieutenant. For many things."

Zara transferred her stare back to the refugees. "And what are we supposed to do with them?"

"Can't leave them," he said. "Find them uniforms. I assume you have something appropriate for the rest of us."

"Scholar robes and uniforms," she said. "Though finding anything in the German giant's size will be a challenge."

"He'll make do. He always does."

Jess was watching the exchange for any hint that Zara was about to turn on them, shoot Santi where he stood and announce that the rest of them were facing Library trial. He didn't trust her. Never had, really. But Santi did, and she seemed to be completely loyal again. However improbably.

When he looked away, there was a Medica next to him, an older woman with a strong, walnut brown face and easy smile who said, "I understand you've been— Oh, son. That must sting."

He glanced down at the swollen mess of his hands and said, "Some." Better to sound tough than to give way to the emotion boiling inside him. He didn't even know what it was, only that the pressure of it made his eyes water and his breath come short. The relief as the Medica sprayed an anesthetic foam on the skin made him go a little weak, and he felt his brother gripping his shoulder from behind him. Holding him upright, it seemed, and Jess wasn't quite sure when he'd lost balance. "Is everyone all right? Everyone else?"

"No," Brendan said. "Your big friend over there's having his hands treated, too. Santi's moving like he's wounded—"

"He is."

"And your girlfriend isn't in the best shape I've ever seen. Not a one of you looks healthy, by the way." Brendan paused. His voice went quieter. "I've never seen you this thin."

"You try finding a solid meal in a city that's been under siege for a hundred years." Jess cut his brother a look. "Worried about me?"

Brendan snorted. "Hell freezes and the devil skates before that happens. You can survive anything." But despite the tone, the words, his hand was tight on Jess's shoulder, and there was a dark shadow in his eyes. Not for Jess's sake, purely. None of them could remain unaffected by what had just happened. There was no screaming from Philadelphia now. It was a city of dead bones and ash, and they all knew it. For the first time, Jess was glad the smell of Greek fire was so overpowering.

He didn't want to think about what that hot, searing wind would bring otherwise.

"I don't know why they did it," Jess said. He felt dull now that the pain was passing away. The Medica hadn't spoken again; she was covering his hands in a thick salve, and he expected the next step would be bandages. "A hundred years, the Library let Philadelphia stand. Why would they declare no quarter now? Why—"

"Doesn't matter," Brendan said, and this time, Jess heard the false note in his voice. Saw the telltale hitch. His brother was lying to him. "Lucky they did, though. They were about to kill you, I understand. Without that distraction, you'd never have made it out."

Jess's stomach turned cold. "We had a plan."

"Yeah. How'd your plan go, then?"

"We made it out!"

"Would you have, if the bombs hadn't started falling?" Brendan's face was fixed now. Masklike, and reflecting green from the flames beyond the wall. "Serves them right. Beck thought he could take on everyone. The Library. Their own allies. Us."

Us. It was hard to know if *us* meant the brothers, the Brightwells, the smugglers. Jess turned and stared at him, and Brendan looked away, into the middle distance—but not in the direction of the dead town. For no reason at all, Jess remembered the woman in the glass shop, worn and tired and poor, desperately living as best she could.

"What did you do, Brendan?" he asked quietly. His brother shook his head. *"Brendan."*

His brother squeezed his shoulder, painfully tight, and then said, "Look after him for me," to the Medica, who nodded without looking up. She was fully fixed on her work. Jess watched his brother walk away with a disconnected, drifting sense of horror and loss, and closed his eyes when it all swept over him again. *Flames. Screams. Beck, lying helpless as the bomb exploded. Indira, falling with the knife in her chest. What happened to sour Diwell? The woman in the glass shop? The counselors who'd been so captivated by the press?*

What did our survival just cost?

He sat, unmoving, locked inside that private hell, until the Medica finished and said, with a gentleness not usual for her type, "Rest if you can."

Jess shook his head. He didn't know if he'd ever rest again. But he was thinking one thing now, over and over: *There's no going back. We have to make this mean something.*

No matter the cost to him.

He did rest, because the Medica gave him some kind of injection to knock him out. At least it kept him from nightmares . . . from any he remembered, anyway.

Jess woke to a rush of nausea so intense it made his whole body burn with it, and immediately turned on his side and threw up thick black bile. Then he coughed up more.

Someone, he vaguely realized, was holding a bucket for him, and as he finished and collapsed back to the ground—no, to a *cot*, a real one—he realized that the person holding the bucket was Scholar Wolfe.

He was truly a Scholar again, washed clean, wearing a black robe and a severe expression of distaste as he set the bucket on the ground beside Jess's bed. "Don't do that again," he said, and gave Jess a clinical stare. "Can you breathe?"

He could. Not easily; his lungs felt scorched and fragile, but each breath he took in felt cleaner than the last. The ceiling overhead waved and rippled, and he finally realized he wasn't imagining it. He was in a tent. A High Garda tent. He struggled to remember, because all he had in that moment were disorienting flashes . . . Beck, screaming, his leg bent wrong. Ben Franklin's golden statue tumbling and melting into green flames as the tower collapsed.

When he blinked, he realized his heart was racing and cold sweat had broken out on his face and arms. He felt filthy and, despite the sleep, dully exhausted. "We're safe?" he asked. It seemed important to ask. His voice sounded appalling—a toad's croak, barely understandable even to his own ears. Wolfe silently offered him a cup of water—clean, fresh water that washed the grit out of his throat and went down wonderfully cool. Jess closed his eyes a moment to enjoy that, and then repeated what he'd tried to say.

"For the moment," Wolfe said. "We'll leave soon. But we have some choices to make, and I want everyone healthy enough to make them intelligently." He paused a moment and then said, "We were lucky, Jess. We won't be lucky again. From now on, once the Library knows we've survived, it will do everything in its power to wipe us from the earth. Us, our families, our friends. Everyone who has ever known our names. It's the only way the Archivist can win now."

Jess swallowed. "No quarter," he said.

"That's why we must decide, once and for all, what each of us wants to do. There's a chance that if we hide, we could live out our lives in peace and obscurity. If we fight . . . if we fight, the Library will wage total war on us, wherever we go. There will be no safety. No rest. Win, or die."

"You make it sound so appealing."

"I mean to. Each one of you deserves the truth and is strong enough to stand up under the weight. I have known many Scholars and students. I have never met a more unruly, unteachable lot, and I thank the gods for forcing you all into my life." Wolfe's words were severe, but the look in his eyes, the quiet smile—those were anything but. They said, *I am proud of you.* "You came into this for me, in the beginning, and for Thomas. But this is your chance to walk away. Here, in the ashes, you can start new."

"You think that's what I want?" Jess asked. "To give up?"

"I think we'll all discuss it more," Wolfe said, and stood up. He indicated the bucket with one dismissive wave. "Empty that yourself; I'm not your nursemaid. And your brother wants to see you."

Jess said nothing to that. He didn't think he could stomach seeing Brendan just now. So, of course, his brother immediately threw back the tent flap and strolled right in.

Jess hadn't had much leisure to examine him before, so he did now, and it was like looking in a flawed mirror. His twin had lost the soft padding he'd acquired while lounging in Alexandria and falling in love with a Library girl; he looked more like the half-wild London urchin Jess had once been, and Brendan was dressed in an entirely wrong High Garda uniform and grinning like the devil on a drinking spree. Jess sat up, which served to remind him how incredibly sore he was, to lessen the height difference between them.

There was a terrible truth between them. It wasn't clear, and it wasn't spoken aloud, not yet, but Jess knew it all the same. His brother had arranged for the bombing of Philadelphia . . . how, he had no idea. But it had been horribly effective, both in securing them the chance at escape and in showing the Burners that double-crossing smugglers was bad, bad business.

Brendan didn't want to talk about it any more than Jess did, it seemed, because he noisily dragged over a camp chair, made a face at the bucket Wolfe had abandoned, and edged it away with one booted foot. "I came to tell you how your girl is doing. Thought that would be the first question you'd ask."

He was right, of course. Jess had been forming the question even as his brother spoke. He gave in. "How is she?"

"Morgan is receiving the best possible care from Library-trained Medicas," Brendan said. It sounded like an official, rehearsed answer that he'd been told to deliver.

"I said, how is she?" His brother looked down at his hands and rubbed his thumbs together. Another tell, but a new one, and Jess didn't know what it meant. It put him on edge. "Saint's sakes, just tell me!"

"Weak," Brendan said. "Burning up with some kind of fever that your Scholar Wolfe says has to do with her overusing her talents. He and that American doctor are doing their best, along with the Medica. Wolfe told me not to tell you. He thought you'd come rushing in."

"Exactly what I'm doing," Jess said, and sat up. The world melted and swirled around him, and he felt Brendan's strong hands holding him back from collapse. He tried to take in a deep breath, but his lungs weren't having it, and he heard a thick, noxious rattle of liquid in them. He coughed, and once he'd started he couldn't stop.

Brendan eased him back down again, and he wasn't in any shape to say no to it. The bunk felt safe, even if everything inside him was screaming to *get up*. "Nothing you can do but hover and look murderous," his twin said. "The rest of them are doing that on your behalf, I promise. You and Thomas got the worst of the smoke. You'll be coughing through the night. I'm to sit and make sure you don't choke on it or stop breathing. If you stop breathing, by the way, I'll beat you until you start."

"I don't think that's a valid Medica technique."

Brendan shrugged. "Seems fine to me."

"And why are you dressed in a High Garda uniform?"

"I was planning to kill you, dispose of the body, and take your place. After all, isn't that what twins do?"

"Stop."

Brendan cocked his head, a familiar gesture that made Jess want to cuff him on the ear. "Wouldn't do to be some civilian in the middle of this camp. Did you trade your brains for tasty pudding? The Library's swarming like a hive; they're dismantling the walls and sending troops in to search the city. Zara's securing us a transport and sending us on our way as soon as night falls. And I can't wait to be out of this damned uniform, because it makes me itch."

Jess looked down at himself and, for the first time, realized he was no longer wearing the filthy, half-seared rags he'd had on; instead, he wore a silky shirt and trousers, the sort provided to patients by Medica hospitals. And nothing else beneath. He was grateful for the blanket, suddenly, and yanked it up. His hands were expertly bandaged, and the burns twinged. Not nearly as bad as they ought to have done. It occurred to him to wonder if, in addition to the Medica's sprays and ointments, Morgan had poured some of her healing ability into him and further damaged herself in the process. He prayed that hadn't happened. He had to hope that Wolfe would have had the good sense to prevent it, if Morgan tried.

The bandages were aggravating, and before Brendan could stop him—if he was inclined to—Jess grabbed the end of the one swaddling his right hand in his teeth and yanked until it came loose. He clumsily unwrapped it and surveyed his fingers and palm. Blistered, tender, but not nearly as bad as he'd expected. He stripped off the left hand's covering and flexed both. Winced. Then he tried to sit up again and was slightly more successful this time. His lungs heaved and protested with bubbling gurgles, but he managed an upright position without help. "Are we safe here?" he asked.

"Of course not; stupid question. But turns out Captain Santi has a significant number of friends, even here. Out of the other three captains here, two of them aren't well pleased with the Archivist removing the High Garda commander or demanding loyalty tests of his soldiers. And they're friends of Captain Santi. So they'll turn a blind eye and cover for us. The last one is going to be kept in the dark."

"So . . . we're leaving in a transport, but Santi's company is staying?"

"No real choice. If Zara pulled out, there'd be no mistaking that she'd turned her loyalty. Santi says they stay and do everything asked of them until it's time to do something important. He's gambling that they will, of course. I'm not sure I'd take that chance."

So, they were going it alone. They didn't have much choice. As Wolfe had said: they'd have to decide to hide and play dead, or rise and fight. Brendan, ironically, was the one who'd liked the shadows. Avoiding duty and playing his own game.

Jess tried to stand up. His brother held him down. Jess snapped, "I'm all right! Hands off, Scraps!"

"You'd walk on severed legs and claim you were all right, but fine. Suit yourself; fall on your face and spit your lungs up while you're at it. I have things to do. You haven't asked, but I'll tell you anyway: we've got a ship waiting on the coast, and we'll be sailing home."

"Home? Meaning where?"

"To our new fortress. You're going to love it. Da wants you with us. And he's generously agreed to give all your friends shelter, too." Brendan started for the tent's exit, then turned back. "Don't call me Scraps. I'd beat you blue for it, but seems redundant."

Looking at him was disorienting, like seeing himself at a distance. *Am I really that annoying?* Too late to ask. His brother was already gone.

It was significant, what he'd said, and the way he'd said it, dropping it at the last, casual moment. Jess's head hurt too much to decipher that message, but he knew it would come to him. Eventually. Meanwhile, he had somewhere to be.

Jess took a deep breath, reached for the support of the bunk's frame, and managed to stand. Didn't manage much more than that, for a long few moments, then spotted a uniform neatly folded on a chest nearby. *That's not so far.*

It was miles, and he was sweating and coughing up a red-tinged liquid by the time he got there. He spat mouthfuls of the sickening stuff into the bucket and, when he felt more steady, stripped off the loose, soft shirt and trousers. His skin, most places, was blotched and reddened. His hair felt dry, and singed at the ends, and it smelled like burning death.

Dressing seemed a lot of effort, and after he'd drawn on under-clothes, fastened the trousers, pulled on the shirt and jacket and boots, he felt tired enough to lie back down again . . . but he wouldn't, for fear Brendan would come back and laugh. Instead, he got up, coughed again, and proceeded with slow care outside. The hand-made Codex and the book he'd carried out of Philadelphia both lay bound together with dirty strips of cloth. He put them in the pock-ets of his coat.

Niccolo Santi wasn't resting. He was sitting in a folding camp chair, but he was engaged in earnest conversation with his extremely capable and dangerous lieutenant. Too busy to notice Jess at all.

Somehow, he wasn't surprised to find yet another person stand-ing just behind him, off to the side, as if waiting to catch him when he inevitably collapsed. He made damn sure he was steady, and then turned his head. It was Dario, who attempted to look like total ac-cident had placed him there.

"Really?" Jess asked. Dario shrugged without commenting. "Who put you up to it?"

"Who's the one person I will unquestionably obey?"

Khalila, of course. That went without saying. "So why did she turn on the Library, really?" Jess asked, and jerked his head toward Zara. Not very hard, so as not to lose his balance. He could take a lot. He wasn't sure he could stomach Dario Santiago having to come to his rescue.

"I think she really did miss the captain," Dario said. "And his sol-diers didn't have the heart to turn against him. He's well liked, and she isn't, so it's in her best interests to stay loyal to him. Always an on or off with that one. Loyal, or not. I never know what to make of her, but Santi does. I suppose that's all that matters."

"So . . . ," Jess said slowly. "We have . . . an army?"

"Two companies' worth, possibly three, but they won't be of any use to us until it comes to a real fight," Dario said. "Still. That's . . . not insignificant." He was right about that. That was stunning. Defections from the High Garda were rare, and defections of entire *companies*? Unheard of. Jess imagined the Archivist's face turning a shade somewhere between crimson and eggplant when those companies turned on him. Maybe he'd burst his heart in fury. That would be most welcome.

"Chess," Jess said quietly. "Three moves ahead."

"And now would be the time to plan it," Dario agreed. "We'll have troops moving into position in Alexandria that we can count on. I assume your brother's arranged for passage for us?"

"Not to Alexandria," Jess said. "My father wants us with him."

"Why? Because, no offense to your family, but I never quite trusted any of you." He hesitated a long beat before he said, "Present company excepted, of course."

And that was the moment when Jess's head cleared, and he saw very plainly what his brother had tried to tell him without telling him at all. *Da wants you with us. Fortress. Generously agreed to give all your friends shelter.*

Dario was talking to him, but he ignored him and shut his eyes to think. He knew his brother. He knew his father.

And he knew exactly what was coming for them in England.

"Shut up," he said to Dario, in the middle of what was probably an elaborate non-apology. "You're always bragging about your family connections. Just how important are they, exactly? And no exaggerations. Facts."

Dario went silent for a long moment, then said, "My cousin Jaume is the Spanish ambassador to the Great Library. My aunt Xijema is the speaker of the Cortes Generales, the Spanish congress. She's also the Duchess of Badajoz. And my second cousin twice removed is

Ramón Alfonse, His Royal Highness, the king of Spain." Jess opened his mouth to reply but couldn't think of anything to say for a moment. He just shook his head. Dario gave him a shrug. "That's why I didn't tell you."

"You're . . . actual royalty."

"No. Not really. There are plenty of those scampering around, anyway. But you asked."

"And you never thought to mention this? *It might have saved your life.*"

"I know that. I also know that the first thing Beck would have done would be to demand a ransom, and I know that my family wouldn't pay it." Dario spread his hands. "They stopped paying for me a long time ago. So it sounds impressive; that's all."

"Apart from money, would they extend you any other kind of help? Diplomatic help?"

"If there was something in it for them. Jaume would be the one I'd count on. He's clever, and he likes me well enough."

"Can he offer us sanctuary at his embassy? If we need it?"

That made Dario turn and look at him with a blank expression. "What are you thinking, Jess?" *Jess,* not *scrubber,* or one of the even less attractive nicknames he generally used.

"I'm thinking," Jess said, "that I agree with you. I don't trust my family, either. But I think I know how we can make that of some real use." He took in a breath. He had a plan. It made his stomach twist and his head hurt, but Dario had been right: chess was not about playing your opponent, but knowing him. And clearly seeing everyone, and everything, in your path.

For the first time, he was really seeing clearly. It wasn't pleasant.

"I'm going to see Morgan," he said. "And I'm going to take a shower. I smell like death."

"You do," Dario agreed. "Really quite repulsively."

Dario wore a black Scholar's robe now, and a gold band, though Jess imagined it had been fiddled with to remove any chance of tracking it. He'd bathed already, obviously. He looked every inch the part of a respectable young man of the Library. And he gave Jess a sudden frown. "You're not asking me to go with you, are you?"

"No." Jess turned to go and almost faltered. Dario's hand slid under his elbow and steadied him.

"Fine, since you're begging, I'll walk you there. But I'm not washing your back."

"Gods defend us both from that terrible fate."

Dario saw him into the shower tent and left him safely deposited on a bench. Jess quickly washed the worst of the dirt and smell off himself in the small cubicle, and came out to find two things.

First, Dario had abandoned him. Fair enough.

Second, Tom Rolleson and three other members of the Blue Dogs squad—the one that Jess and Glain had belonged to, in their brief career with Santi's company—were waiting for him when he stepped out of the shower cubicle, dressed in a towel and feeling especially vulnerable. They were all in uniforms and boots and identically harsh expressions, and Jess set himself mentally for the fight. *Won't go well,* some part of him said, which was not a help. *Probably undo all the good work the Medica put in.*

There was a sick irony to surviving the Burners, only to end up dying at the hands of his friends. But he wasn't going easily, if that was the direction they intended to take it.

"Troll," he said to the squad leader. Tom's nickname, and it usually brought out a brash grin. Not this time. The young man just stared at him. He'd acquired a new scar since the last time Jess had seen him: a long, jagged one that ran along the edge of his jaw. Still pink, with a faint red line in the middle. "So what's this, then?"

"What do you think it is?" Troll asked him. The three soldiers flanking him—one a Chinese recruit named Wu Xiang, one a Greek named Phoena, and the last he didn't know even faintly—gave him identical blank faces. "Look like a welcome home to you, Brightwell? You think you deserve one?"

"I wasn't looking for it." Jess decided to move to the bench where he'd folded his clothes. When no one stopped him, he sat and, with the typical High Garda lack of modesty, took off the towel and put on underclothes while they stared at him. With each bit of the uniform going on, he felt better. "What do you want?"

"What were they like?" Phoena asked suddenly. Jess froze in the act of doing up the crisp black fabric of his trousers.

"Who?"

"The Burners."

He was suddenly, acutely aware of the humidity in the little enclosure, the ever-present faint smell of mold, the painful scrape of stiff cloth over his burns. For a second the memory rolled over him of watching the first ballista bomb hit, of seeing that first building explode into looping curls of pure death.

He didn't want to think about the Burners. He was short of breath, and when he tried to slow down and breathe deeper, his lungs gurgled again. He nearly coughed but managed not to. Not yet.

"Why?" he asked without looking up. He found himself staring at his still-reddened hands. He could see the faint scars of the glass cuts on his fingertips, and for an instant he saw the shy smile of that woman in the shop. His hands curled into fists. They hurt. Throbbed.

"Because you were in there," Tom said. "You met them. We wanted to know. Were they all—"

"Fanatics?" Jess looked up then and met Troll's eyes. His squad leader didn't flinch. "I don't know. Does it matter? I didn't sit down and have long, meaningful conversations with them. I was busy trying to figure out a way *out*. Why?"

Wu said, "Because we were in charge of loading ballistae. We need to know—"

That trailed off into silence. Jess couldn't think of anything to say to that, to the painful quiet between them, and finally, shook his head. "I don't have an answer to that question. You did what you had to do. We all did. We have to accept what we can't change."

There was a short silence, and then Tom offered his hand. No change in expression. Jess looked at it for a second, then took it and let Troll help him up. "Glad you're alive," Tom said. It wasn't a warm welcome, but it was something. "Glain said to tell you they're in the command tent, when you're ready to join them."

"I'm going to find Morgan first."

"She's in the Medica tent, but you'd best go to Glain first. Morgan's asleep, and you'll want to stay with her."

Jess leaned closer and said, "I thought you came to kick my skull in."

"Honestly?" Tom said. "Hadn't decided." He suddenly dragged Jess in and clapped him on the back, which hurt intensely, but Jess managed not to wince. Much. "You have a spot with us, Blue Dog. Always."

Tom's advice was sound; Jess knew that once he saw Morgan, he'd want to stay with her. So he went to the command tent and found Khalila and Dario arguing.

Or rather, *Dario* was arguing and Khalila was ignoring him when Jess pushed open the flap of the command tent, and all of that skidded to a halt as Khalila rushed to Jess and examined him with intense, toe-to-head scrutiny. "Does it hurt?" she asked. Under stress, her accent grew stronger. "The burns?"

"Not as much as it ought," he said. He was out of breath and, yes, aching all over, but determined not to show it.

"Good." She embraced him then. Gently. When she drew back, he saw his damp hair had left little dark patches on the sky blue cloth of her hijab. Her eyes were very bright with tears, but she blinked them away. "We made Thomas go back to bed. He looked terrible, and he was coughing constantly."

Which, of course, made Jess's throat tickle uncomfortably. When he swallowed, he could still taste bittersweet ashes. Imaginary, most likely, but very real to him. He blinked and saw a flash of green flames, falling buildings, screaming faces trapped and helpless. Pressure formed in his chest, dangerous and sickening, and he felt a terrible urge to *run*. But there was no running away from what he'd left behind. It would be with him, always. And he had to learn to stand it.

"Are you all right?" she asked him quietly, and he nodded. "When you didn't follow us through at first, I was so afraid—but you came through; of course you did. I knew we couldn't lose you. You, of all of us, are a survivor."

She underestimated herself, he thought, and almost said it, but he knew she wouldn't like to have it pointed out. He and Khalila sat down on camp chairs a little distance away from the others in the tent, with the whispering, billowing fabric at their backs. Dario watched, arms folded, but didn't try to join them; Jess was dimly glad of that.

Khalila looked exactly right once again, perfectly elegant in a long dress of thick, nubby silk that some other Muslim woman in the High Garda must have unearthed from a chest. She had the matching head scarf, and a full, black Scholar's robe over the dress. The only jarring detail was her hands—treated with a Medica's skill, but still showing signs of burns. She'd cleaned her nails with scrupulous care, but the rest gave her away.

Jess nodded at them, where they were folded in her lap. "What happened there?"

Khalila looked as if she had the impulse to hide her hands in the folds of her gown, but she didn't. She looked down to consider the scratched, burned fingers, and then said, "After you collapsed, there was—there was another young man, alone. A survivor. He crawled out the gap. He was—he was on fire."

Jess's whole body registered the meaning of that in a horrific rush. "You pulled him out."

She nodded. Her eyes were dark and distant, and he hoped never to see that look in her again. "Dario and I, yes. We tried to—to help him. But he died." She smiled, but it looked forced, and painful. "We had to try." The smile faded, and her eyes suddenly filled with tears. "Oh, Jess. There were so many—so *many*—"

"I know," he said, and held her hand while she wept almost silently, but painfully. He had the same grief, but it seemed to be trapped behind a wall, seething and angry and bitter, and he didn't know how to let it out.

But he was glad she did.

Dario had turned his head away, but Jess couldn't miss the stiff line of his shoulders. *He* wanted to be the one Khalila turned to. And most of the time, Jess thought, he would get his wish. But not now.

The storm passed within half a minute, and she carefully dried her eyes and gave Jess a small, apologetic smile as she pulled away. When she started to speak, he shook his head. "No apologies," he said. "Not for being more human than the rest of us."

"We all deal with things in our own way," Scholar Wolfe said as he took a seat on Jess's other side. "No shame in any of it. Even despair." He almost sounded . . . kind. Surely that couldn't be right.

Jess preferred a safe, solid world where Scholar Wolfe didn't have a kind bone in his body, and to preserve that, he moved back to watching Santi and Zara, who stood together at a long table, with maps.

Zara reached down and took a book from her pack. She opened it and flipped pages, and as Jess watched, she picked up a stylus and wrote in it.

A Codex. She's writing in a Codex? He felt a chill, then a rush of heat, and fear. Easy for Zara to betray them doing that, and when he stood up, he meant to put a stop to it. But Wolfe grabbed his sleeve and said, "Sit down before you fall, boy. You look wretched and you shouldn't be upright."

"I heard the captain wanted me to come here, and *why are they writing in a Codex?*"

"Because it's important that Zara be seen as a loyal High Garda commander. Misdirection. Confusion. If we can't take the company with us, we have to protect them from suspicion. That means creating false reports and trails." Wolfe watched the two of them silently for a few seconds, and Jess had the feeling that he, too, was uncomfortable with the closeness between Santi and his lieutenant. Not quite jealousy, Jess thought, but there was a wariness to the way Wolfe held himself. Still, his voice sounded confident. "Zara is meticulously documenting everything that she should, including the receipt of sealed secret orders from the Artifex."

"Are there sealed secret orders from the Artifex?"

"No. But if we can sow a little distrust between the Archivist and his chief lackey, all the better. The other two commanders who've pledged to us will also be recording receipt of the same orders, and noting that they've been instructed to burn them on receipt, so there'll be no copies or records to disprove it. That's bound to cause conflict and confusion." Wolfe glanced at him. "What would you give to see that another city never dies like that again?"

It was the question he'd been asking himself so relentlessly. And he had his answer ready. "Everything."

"Your life?"

"Yes."

Wolfe sighed. "So say we all, then. Are you with us? To fight?"

"Of course I am," Jess said. "Did you really doubt it?"

"I didn't," Santi said from the table. "Dario's decision rather surprised me, though."

Dario made a mock bow. "Happy to fail that test, Captain. But I've never really been afraid to die for a good cause."

Santi brushed that aside. "Dying is the easy part," he said. "Fanatics do it every day. I need to know—*we* need to know—if you'll be ready to fight without the rest of us. You have to be ready to *win*. Not just die in a blaze of glory. Sometimes, what you have to do might not be glorious. Just dirty, and necessary."

One by one, they nodded. But of all of them, Jess thought, he was the only one who clearly, fully understood what that might really mean.

EPHEMERA

Text of a letter from High Garda Captain Wellington, found on his body in the field near Philadelphia, sent to the attention of the Archivist Magister by Acting Captain Zara Cole. Burned upon receipt.

It is with great sadness and loathing that I report to you the total victory of High Garda forces at Philadelphia.

Hardly a stone remains fixed to another, and in walking that wretched hell, I have seen not one living thing . . . not bird, dog, blade of grass, or human. What I have seen are carpets of bones, mounds of them from victims huddled together for protection that never came.

Damn you. Damn you for forcing us to be your murderers. May the gods curse you forever.

Text of a report from High Garda Acting Captain Zara Cole, in the field near Philadelphia, sent to the attention of the Commander of the High Garda. Available on the Codex.

It is with deep regret that I inform you of the death of High Garda Captain Wellington, who served the Great Library with selfless devotion for more than thirty years. His death came at his own hand, out of despair and overwhelming grief for what has been done in the name of the power we all serve so faithfully. May the gods have mercy on us all.

CHAPTER EIGHT

Morgan lay perfectly still. Her color was like porcelain, drained of all the warmth and vitality Jess loved in her.

She looked like a dead girl waiting for her coffin.

Dr. Askuwheteau was busy checking a supply of Medica vials and compounds in a brand-new case, but when he saw Jess standing in the tent doorway, frozen, he said, "Come in, close the flap. We need to keep her warm."

It was, Jess thought, suffocatingly hot in the tent already, and they'd layered blankets on Morgan's motionless body as well. "Has she been awake?" he asked. Askuwheteau shook his head silently. "Not at all?"

"I don't want her awake just now," he said. "This is necessary. An Obscurist who uses power too wildly . . . Well, you saw the fields in Philadelphia. She couldn't control the scope of what she did. She had to stop before it was too late. She was coming to pieces when she came out of that hell. She'll hurt herself, or someone else, if she doesn't allow herself to heal."

There was something in the phrasing of that, and Jess put the pieces together almost instantly. "*You* did this. You've drugged her."

The doctor shrugged. "For her protection. And ours. She would say the same."

"How long do you intend to keep her out?"

"A day, maybe two," Askuwheteau said. "I was trained for this, Mr. Brightwell, back when the Library thought me worth saving. Even the Iron Tower needs Medica. As someone with a trace of the talent, they thought I was . . . worthy." He drenched that word in a rich sauce of irony. "The treatment is sound. Certain specific compounds to help her quintessence heal properly. Certain others to keep her conscious mind from interfering with that process."

"But she'll come out of it fine," Jess said. He made it a statement. The doctor said nothing either for or against it. "She'll be all right." The silence stretched on. "This is where you agree with me."

Askuwheteau dragged a chair over and put it beside Morgan's bed. "Sit," he said, "before you fall. I can hear the state of your lungs from here. You realize that breathing in the vapors ruptures the lining of the lungs?"

"Stop avoiding the question." Jess realized his voice had grown edges, despite the faint wheeze in it. "We saved your life!"

"And I've saved hers," Askuwheteau snapped back. "If I hadn't kept her in this coma, she'd insist on trying to help you and your big friend."

"Did—" Jess didn't want to ask, but he forced himself. "Did anyone else make it out?"

"None that lived," the doctor said. His voice sounded tight and angry, but his eyes were flat and distant. Unfeeling. "There's only so much to be done, by doctor or Medica or even Obscurist. Greek fire takes most who are touched by it even in passing." He finished his inventory of the bag and snapped it closed. "They tell me we will be leaving just after dark. Your party and mine. I've asked for us to travel with you for a while, and then we will leave on our own for Boston, where we have tribal relations who will take us in."

"I thought—I thought you'd stay with the Medica."

"Why? So I can treat the soldiers who destroyed my people?" Askuwheteau looked down at the coat he wore, with the Library's symbol on it. "It's like wearing someone else's skin."

Jess understood that. He didn't quite know how to reconcile himself to wearing a Library uniform now, either. He remembered the blank silence of Troll and his soldiers in the shower tent, the quiet suffering in their eyes.

Maybe none of them knew how to do that anymore.

"Can I stay with her awhile?" Jess asked, and took Morgan's cold, entirely limp hand in his scarred, burned one.

"Please yourself," Askuwheteau said. "I need to go sit with my people and offer prayers for my friends."

Then he was off, long strides, his long black braid bouncing against the new Medica robe he wore. He'd abandoned his battered old hat. He now looked like any Medica professional, though one badly in need of solid meals. He didn't fit here. Maybe he didn't fit anywhere.

He will, though. We all find our place, Jess thought, and brushed his thumb across Morgan's knuckles. *And if we can't find one, we make one. We find our way through what's done to us, and come out the other side.*

We heal.

He raised her limp fingers to his lips and whispered, "Please come back."

Three hours passed, and Jess watched the color of the light washing the west side of the tent. It had gone from pale gold to the color of honey to a rich orange, and then dark. He could almost pretend—almost—that it was a normal day, normal sunset, that the air didn't reek of smoke and ash and death.

That the flickering, ominous glow to the west wasn't the simmering remains of a city that would take weeks to finish burning.

He hadn't been able to sleep, though he'd been very tired; he kept running things through his mind in obsessive detail, looking for the risks, the tricks. The biggest risk, he thought, was that Brendan wouldn't help him . . . But somehow, he knew that his brother would. It had been there, in the inflection of his voice, in the way he wouldn't meet Jess's eyes as he lied for their father.

Santi had asked what they would be willing to do. Jess doubted he had any idea that *this* would be the price of that question.

"Jess?" The whisper was soft, but it went right through him—not a sharp intrusion, but a wave of relief, and he looked down to see that Morgan's eyes were open, her dry lips parted. Her fingers tightened on his. "Jess?"

"I'm here," he said. One part of him hoped this was good, her waking this early. Askuwheteau seemed to believe that she'd sleep for the rest of the day and through the night, but the doctor was gone now, and the important thing was, *she was awake.* "How do you feel?"

"Tired," she whispered. Her voice was just a thread of sound, and her eyes seemed dull. "Thirsty."

He quickly poured her a cup of water and boosted her up to sip at it. Not too much. He wasn't sure what would be good for her, and there was no one to ask. "Better?"

She nodded a little, and shivered. He tucked the blankets around her, and her grip on his hand suddenly tightened. Tingled.

Burned.

"Morgan?"

He looked up, and she was staring at him with that fixed, unfocused stare he recognized as her accessing her Obscurist talents. She was still shivering; he could feel the convulsions of it through her fingers.

He suddenly felt a cough explode in his lungs, and turned aside to let it out. The coughing didn't stop. It got worse, doubling him over, and the liquid in his lungs that had been receding seemed to come out of nowhere, flooding up, suffocating, and he spat out one mouthful, two, three, each one redder than the last, and he *couldn't get his breath*, and Morgan's hand was holding his so tightly that he couldn't shake her loose . . .

And then Askuwheteau burst through the tent flap, took one look at them, and stepped forward to grab Morgan's arm and twist it, breaking her hold on him. She cried out, and Jess nearly fell trying to turn to defend her, but he wasn't hurting her, she was saying *I'm sorry, I'm sorry,* and Askuwheteau, his face a grim mask, injected her with a solution of bluish liquid and held her down until she quieted again.

Once she was still, eyes closed, breathing steadily, he turned to Jess, who was still fighting to catch his breath. The dirt on the floor by his chair was soaked with liquid, and the liquid looked terribly like blood.

"What's wrong with her?"

"She's trying to heal you. That's what her instincts tell her she must do. It will kill you both if she tries just now," Askuwheteau said. He rummaged in his bag and came up with another small glass vial. He pitched it to Jess. "Drink this."

"What is it?"

"Drink it or I'll hold you down and inject you with it."

Jess tipped it up and swallowed. It tasted faintly of berries, and something bitter beneath, and he felt the constriction and pressure in his chest begin to ease. "That's not half-bad—"

The darkness was already descending when he heard the doctor say, from a great distance, "Better than the alternatives."

Waking up came with a fierce, walnut-sized headache buried deep in his skull, a surging feeling of dizziness, and . . . no cough. Jess took in two or three breaths before he recognized that he was breathing easily and normally again. His memory seemed cheerily out of focus, and it took time for it all to trickle back to him . . . Philadelphia, burning. Morgan, coming awake, and the burning tingle in his hand where she gripped it. The helpless coughing fit.

Askuwheteau's potion. *Bloody man tricked me.* But he had to admit, though his chest and throat still ached a bit, he felt *much* better. Except for the headache, and even that was starting to slowly unwind and vanish as he opened his eyes and sat up.

Well, tried to. He couldn't. He was tied down. The most he could do was lift his head, and he did, straining to see, but it was very dark. He was in some kind of room, and it smelled of oil, metal, sweat. A hint of blood. The ground under him shuddered and rattled, and as he jerked against the restraints, he heard someone in the shadows say, "Sleeping Beauty's up. Might want to cut him loose before he bruises." Dario's voice, dryly amused.

"Jess, I'm going to let you loose," said Glain's voice close to his ear. "And if you try to take my knife away, I will punch you so hard you'll never wake up. Understand?"

"Glain?" The fog was lifting. The close, stinking room wasn't a room. The ground wasn't shaking. He was in a High Garda transport, and they were moving at a good rate of speed over rough ground, and he was safe. "Why the *hell* am I tied up?"

"Because nobody wanted to cradle you like an oversized baby while you slept," Dario said. "Surprisingly enough."

"You'd have cracked your head open bouncing around, as rough as the travel is," Glain observed, and he felt his left wrist come loose, then the warmth of her body as she bent over him. "I wasn't going to be the one washing your brains off the floor. There. Sit up and do the rest yourself."

His eyes were adjusting now to the very low lights. It was just enough of a pale glow to see shadows, hints of faces, and the glint on the edge of the knife she was holding out to him.

Jess sat up, took it, and cut through the restraints around his ankles. He'd been lying on a stretcher, taking up space in the middle of the floor. As he tried to get up, the transport lurched and nearly sent him pitching at the wall; hands from either side steadied him. "Thanks," he muttered, and sank down into an empty seat along the side. He passed Glain's knife back to her, then snapped the restraints in place for the seat. It didn't make the ride more comfortable, but it did make it safer. "How long was I out?"

"Two years," Dario said.

"Shut up," Glain said. "All night and half the day." As if it were taking her cue, the dull hissing of the transport's engine suddenly changed gear to a lower, more throbbing speed. "We're stopping to let Askuwheteau's people off from the second transport."

Thomas was in this vehicle; Jess could see him curled uncomfortably in the small space. Dario. Glain. His twin brother, who wasn't saying a single word. Khalila was close, and she offered her hand to him silently. He took it and squeezed. Santi was driving the transport, and Wolfe sat beside him.

There was no sign of Morgan. There was an empty seat where she should have been.

"Before you ask," Khalila said, "the doctor felt it was good to keep her in the other vehicle. But she will be moved here now. How do you feel?"

"Better," he said. It was true; he did feel better. He could draw a breath without coughing, and some of the feeling had come back to his burned hands.

"That's good, because the doctor wasn't going to let the two of you in the same cabin until you were," Dario said. "No idea why. Care to share?"

"No." Jess knew. He remembered the burn of Morgan's touch. The explosion of fluid in his lungs. She'd tried to help, and nearly killed him. "I'm all right."

"We're stopping," Glain said. She climbed past Jess, slid open the door of the transport, and hopped down before Santi had brought it to a complete halt. Jess had to blink against a sudden blast of daylight, and tried his balance once the vehicle had rolled to a stop with a hiss of steam. Not too bad. He jumped down and walked after Glain. Behind him, the others were coming out, too. Thomas was last, looking relieved to be released from confinement.

There was another transport directly behind them, and as Jess watched, Dr. Askuwheteau descended from the driver's position and slid open the side. One by one, his people came out. They'd all changed clothes, sometime since Jess had succumbed to the drugs . . . Most wore a mixture of plain cloth and soft leather. Askuwheteau wore the same patchwork coat he'd had in Philadelphia. He'd unbraided his hair to fall loose over his shoulders.

Seven survivors of a dead city. Three were children, but Jess couldn't judge how old they were. They were too thin, small for their ages. None of them said a word, not even Askuwheteau's housekeeper.

Askuwheteau tossed something to Captain Santi, who caught it out of sheer reflex. It unfurled in his hands. The Medica robe. "You saved us," the doctor said. "We don't forget. But we'll never wear the colors of our enemies again."

"Where will you go?" Khalila asked him.

"To our people in Boston," he said. "And we will tell what we know. What we saw. Within a week, there will be no safety for any of the Library here in this country. If the Archivist believed he could stop us by that slaughter, he doesn't know us at all. We will fight."

"We'll all fight," Khalila said. She took another step forward. She was wearing her black Scholar's robe, and it rippled like shadows in the breeze. "When you go to Boston, you will carry the word of what happened. You will become symbols of what the Burners will become—for better, or for worse. I beg you to think of that legacy, and the future we will share, because one day, we will be friends again, Dr. Askuwheteau. One day, the Library will meet with you in peace, and we will bury our dead together. We are not your enemies. The people in the Serapeums are not your enemies. Please remember, when you tell your stories, when you start your fires, that we saw your home, we saw the love you had for books. Remember that for each of us, that love is why we are here. Why we exist. And remember that we see you, and we grieve for you."

There was something mesmerizing about her in that moment, Jess thought; she seemed taller. Stronger. More *real* than ever before. It was impossible to look at Khalila Seif and not believe her, not feel the compassion that flowed out of her.

She bowed to the survivors of Philadelphia.

Askuwheteau stood there for a long, silent moment, staring at her. "You are my enemy," he said to Khalila at last. "But you have my respect. I will think on what you say." He picked up a small leather pack from the grass by his feet. "But you should go. Because if any of us find those wearing the sign of the Library here past tomorrow, I may not want to protect you. Anger is like the fires that still burn in my city. It will take time to die."

They watched them walk away in silence, until the Lenape and his small band of survivors were lost from sight, and then Khalila sighed.

"I think he means it," she said. "We should go. As fast as we can."

"You know what you did?" Santi asked her. "That man is going to become the new leader of the Burners."

"I know," Khalila said. "And someday, we will have to sit in a room with him and make our reparations for what the Archivist has done. Better we start that now, before more blood flows."

Wolfe said nothing. He watched her walk back to the transport with Dario before he said, "Our children are growing up very well."

Santi laughed softly. "And I said you'd never make a good father. Come help me get the girl."

"I'll do it," Jess said. "You're still half-healed, Captain. Thomas?"

"*Ja,*" his friend said. He was still staring after Khalila. Jess couldn't really tell what he was thinking. "I'm coming."

Morgan was asleep, but as they drove on, she woke up. Khalila had taken the seat beside her, displacing Dario, to Dario's annoyance. "Better I talk to her," she told Jess. "The doctor said to keep you away from her, for now."

"Why?" Dario asked, suddenly and irritatingly interested.

"None of your business. Khalila, I'm fine. I'm better." And surely, the reason that Morgan's talents had turned on him had been because of his damage. Not hers. He didn't want to believe that.

She seemed all right, he was relieved to find. Exhausted, despite the drugs, or because of them, and she dozed for the next two hours, until Brendan got up from his place near the rear of the vehicle and pushed forward to lean over Santi's shoulder. "We're coming to the coast," he said. "You've followed the map?"

"He's a High Garda captain," Wolfe said. "Of course he followed the map. Probably better than you could."

Brendan shrugged. "Just checking. All right. You should see the cliffs coming up soon. There'll be some thick brush blocking the way. We'll need to clear it. It covers a switchback path down to the shore."

"And you're certain there's a boat."

"Oh, I'm very certain."

It didn't take long for Santi to ease the transport to a halt, and Brendan was out the side door, with Glain hot on his heels. Thomas went, too.

Jess stayed where he was, watching Morgan. She'd opened her eyes, and in the quiet, as Khalila and Dario got out, and Wolfe and Santi left the cab, they didn't say anything at first. Then she reached out her hand to him. When he didn't take it, she slowly let it fall. "I suppose I deserved that."

"It isn't because I don't want to," he said. "Morgan—until you're fully in control again—"

"I know. Best I don't touch you. Or anyone else." She looked down at her hands, loose in her lap. "I didn't mean it, you know. Killing the fields. I was so tired, and I had to find the energy, the power, to keep going. I didn't know I was taking it from living things. Does that make me a monster?"

"No," Jess said. "It makes you powerful. You saved our lives, weakening that wall. If you hadn't, we'd never have left that city. We'd be ash and bone."

She nodded wearily. "I don't want to hurt anything else. Anyone else." Her smile didn't warm her eyes. "I don't ever want to hurt you."

He wanted to cup her face in his hands and kiss the doubt and anguish from her, and for a moment he thought he might, until

Thomas leaned the door in and said, "You'd better come. Now." His friend had a tense look on his face, and that drove everything else out of Jess's mind. He forgot and offered his hand to Morgan to help her down, and the momentary press of their skin made her take in a sharp breath and quickly withdraw. She pulled well away after they hopped out of the transport.

"What?" he asked Thomas, who jerked his head toward the trees to the south of where they were standing.

A tall, handsome man stood there dressed in a flowing black Scholar's robe, with white Arabic garments on beneath. He had one hand on a large, gilded pole, and at the top fluttered a gold-fringed flag.

The flag of the Great Library. The all-seeing eye. Next to him, sitting on its haunches in the whispering tall grass, was a large bronze automaton lion.

Khalila said, "Cousin Rafa." Glain and Santi had drawn weapons. Jess did, too, but none of them were pointing them. Not yet.

"Khalila." He nodded. "Captain Santi. Scholar Wolfe. I come in peace."

"Guns back in your holsters," Santi said, and put his away. Brendan swore softly. "I mean it. Shoot a Scholar under a Library banner, and I'll be the one shooting you. Understood?"

"Fools," Brendan said to Jess. "Your friends are fools, you realize that?" He lowered his voice to a fierce whisper. "Get to the transport. We can't outrun the thing, but it'll have a harder time gutting us before we can kill it."

It was good advice, but Jess didn't take it. He stood where he was, watching Santi. Watching Khalila, who looked stricken. Her cousin, for all his pronouncement of peace, looked like a man who could handle himself in a fight if it came to it. He had a High Garda–issue gun on one hip and a fairly impressive sword on the other. Not quite *completely* peaceful, then.

"Peace is given when peace is received," Santi said. "Hello, Rafa."

"Niccolo." The Scholar nodded. He planted the banner in the ground with one decisive thrust and left it there to sway and snap in the wind as he crossed his arms. His black silk robes fluttered and spread in the breeze, too, giving him an almost unnatural air, as if he were half made of smoke. "It's been a long time since you guarded me on my journeys, but I hope we're still friends."

"I hope so, too," Santi said. "It depends on why you're here."

"I'm here to beg my cousin to come home," Rafa said, and looked at Khalila. "You had such promise, little one. Such a bright, bright future. And you've thrown it away, for what? For friendship? For some false ideal? We want to bring you home. Me, your uncle, your father. You need to come with me. Now."

"How did you find us?" Jess asked. The Scholar's black eyes shifted to him, then dismissed the question. "Who sent you here?"

"You know who sent me," Rafa said. "The Artifex Magnus, whom I serve. Whom you all serve. I'm not the only one who was dispatched, if that eases your mind. There are messengers at the seaports, and I bribed smugglers to tell me the most likely place a ship loyal to the Brightwells would dock. He thought you would have survived, you see. And he wanted to be sure you understood that you have a choice. You can come home. All of you. Before you bring more disgrace down on yourselves and your families."

Khalila said, "I don't think you're one to speak of disgrace, Cousin Rafa. I remember that my uncle had to buy you a pardon from prison. Twice."

"You're very young," Rafa said. "And the young are often stupid.

If you live through this, it's possible you might come back to find a place in the Library once more. I did."

She shook her head. "Not while the Archivist Magister sits in that chair."

Rafa sighed and moved his attention back to Santi. "And you? Have you really betrayed everything you've been loyal to all your life?"

"When it betrays me first? Sometimes one has to take a stand."

"Ah, but is it really *your* stand?" Rafa's gaze moved toward Wolfe. "I know you're doing it for love, but it borders on obsession, the way you come running. Is he really so wonderful, to make you betray everything you believed in?"

Jess recognized the perfectly friendly, chilling smile that came on Santi's lips, and the tone that went with it. "Well, since you're asking," he said, "he is. Why? Jealous?"

That volley hit. Rafa's face went tight.

"Enough," Wolfe said. "If you have something useful to say, get on with it. If you're trying to bait us into a fight, it won't work."

"I think it might, with a little encouragement. But you're correct; we should move to business." The Scholar reached into his robes and came out with a scroll case. It was made of finely tooled leather, and he opened it, reached in, and then smiled even wider as Glain and Jess drew their sidearms at the same moment. "Peace, peace. I am no Burner," he said. "Though that seems to be company you prefer these days. It's only paper. Nothing more dangerous than that."

It was an official Library document, that much was clear, heavy with ornate braids as well as seals, and the Scholar offered it with a certain formal respect. Santi accepted with both hands, just as respectful, and then both retreated a few steps—the Scholar to stand under his flapping banner, and Santi to snap the seals on the document and unroll it.

He said nothing. An alarming lot of nothing. He read it completely through and then let it snap shut. Rafa waited, and when Santi didn't speak, he crossed his arms. "You surprise me. I've rarely seen you silent."

"You don't know what it says, do you?" Santi turned and held the document out to Khalila. "I'm sorry. I truly am."

It was the gentleness in the way he said it that made Jess go still, and he watched as Khalila unrolled the document and read. She made it only halfway, he thought, before she seemed to lose her balance, and immediately Dario moved forward, his shoulder a solid wall for her back to lean against and to keep her on her feet. She didn't make a sound as she let the scroll snap shut again.

"I told you—I'm to accept your surrender, and you're to return with me to the New York Serapeum and then be Translated to Alexandria." Rafa still seemed unbearably smug. "I'm told what the Archivist wrote will explain the uselessness of your continued defiance."

Nothing for Morgan, Jess, or Wolfe. Jess scrambled to understand what was going on here. Something big enough to rock Khalila on her heels.

But she was back on balance again now, and when she spoke, her voice was tight with suppressed fury. "A question, for my friends," she said. "Who else has family in Library service now?"

"Now?" Dario asked. "I've had dozens, but none at the moment."

"Same," said Thomas.

Glain nodded. "First and only in this generation."

"I had one," Santi said. "A brother. He's retired."

"No wonder he only meant this for me, then," Khalila said. She flung the scroll into her cousin's chest. "Death sentences," she said. "For our *family*! That is a sentence of death for my father, my brother, and *your own father*! All of them loyal to the Library without question, their entire lives. All arrested! He didn't even bother to tell you!"

Rafa froze, then unrolled the scroll and scanned it enough to know that she wasn't lying. "But—"

"They've already been arrested. They're in prison, under sentence of treason," she said. "Your name would have been here, too, only he must not have such respect for you. Instead, he uses you as his errand boy."

"I—" Rafa stared at her for a few seconds, then licked his lips as though they had gone suddenly very dry. He let the scroll drop again. "I didn't know. I swear it."

"Then now you know why we're fighting," Santi said. "Rafa. Come toward us."

"Why?"

"Just try."

Rafa frowned, but he took a step out into the open space.

Next to him, the automaton lion gave a little shake, as if it was waking up. They all stopped and looked toward it, but it subsided without more movement. But Jess could feel it watching. Waiting. *What was it here to do?* Rafa must have thought it was simply for his protection. Jess knew better. *This is wrong,* he thought.

Khalila slowly drew the sword that she'd belted on at her side before they'd left. "Rafa," she said. "Pick up the scroll. It might believe that you're presenting it to me again. I don't think it can understand what we're saying."

"It's just an escort," Rafa said. "It won't attack me."

"You're wrong," Santi said. "Listen to her. She's trying to save you."

"From what?"

"From your own stupidity," Khalila said. "Rafa, do what I ask! *Now,* for the love of Allah, I beg you, while you still have a chance—"

Rafa didn't move. He stayed under the fluttering, fragile protection of his banner, next to the lion, and stared at her with a grim frown. "I'm going nowhere with you. I'm loyal to the Library! The Archivist understands that I'm his servant, that I am trustworthy, and my loyalty will save our family from what *you* have done—"

He broke off suddenly, because the automaton lion rose from its comfortable sitting position. Standing, its head was level with Rafa's chest. It was massive and beautiful and terrifying, and it turned toward the Scholar and bared sharp metallic fangs.

He backed away, suddenly realizing that he was not in control of this situation. That he never had been.

That was the moment when, in utter silence, another lion eased up to a standing position from the grass directly behind him. Not bronze, this one. A dull matte pattern that blended perfectly with the grass, like High Garda camouflage.

This was what the Artifex had really planned. Not parlay. Not negotiation.

Death.

Jess couldn't shout, couldn't *move* for the shock of it . . . until the camouflaged lion lunged, sank teeth into Rafa's shoulder and cruel claws into his back, and dragged him screaming into the grass.

"No!" Khalila shrieked, and would have lunged forward except that Glain caught her and held her back. It was a cruel choice, but wise; Rafa was dead already. A spray of ruby red blood clouded the air, and it seemed to Jess that he could see each and every drop with perfect, individual clarity . . . the way they rose, fell, spun, caught the light, splashed, dripped. The way the Scholar's heels flailed at the ground before they, too, vanished into the green hell of grass.

Gone.

Jess couldn't think about that, couldn't think about the sounds of flesh rending; he looked out, instead, at the large open field around them. Sunset was coming on fast, but the last gilding of light on the grass showed some of it shifting the wrong way. *Seven of them,* he thought. *Seven at least, plus that damned bronze one meant to draw our attention.* Another irrational fact stuck in his mind: the lion that had taken Rafa had no showy, flowing mane. That lion had been constructed to resemble a female.

Female lions, he remembered, hunted in packs. They cooperated.

"Circle!" he shouted, almost at the same time as Niccolo Santi, and they all drew together, arms nearly touching. It wouldn't save them, but it would be the best they could do. Jess had his sidearm out, still, and struggled to think where to shoot the creatures.

It was Thomas who said, in a very cool, calm voice, "If you shoot, aim for their foreheads. There is a nexus of cables there that will disable their front legs if you hit it squarely. If you can't, try for the right flank. The script that powers it is the only other vulnerable point."

"Off switch under the jaw, near the throat," Jess added, almost as an afterthought. His hand felt slippery and sweaty on the grip of his weapon. Zara might send reinforcements up to help; already, he could see one of the scouts racing away in the distance on his cycle. Still. Eight lions would kill them all quite efficiently before rescue could arrive, if they didn't do this on their own. "Go for the off switch only if there's no choice. You can do it if you're fast and don't hesitate."

Dario let out a bitter bark of something halfway between a shout and a laugh. "Just shut up and let me die in peace, for the love of God."

"We're not dying," Santi said. "Not here." There was something so solid, so certain, in his voice that Jess sent him a sidelong look, half-shocked . . . and then it was too late, because the sleek, grass-clouded shape of an automaton lion rose from a crouch and sprang right for Jess's throat.

It was instinct, what he did then—instinct and repetition. Running was useless; so was dodging—she was too close. He lifted his arms and jammed his weapon sideways into her open jaws even as her weight slammed into him and carried him helplessly backward into the middle of the circle. Everything went razor clear again: the vividly red shimmer of her eyes, the way her metallic skin stretched as cables tightened, the way she bit down on the metal of the weapon with a bone-chilling *crunch*.

Without his even directing it, his hand slipped under her jaw and felt for the switch. *Please be there, please . . .*

By that time, he'd hit the grass, which was curiously like hitting a mattress; it might have even felt good, if the weight of the lion's cruel paw hadn't landed on his left arm, pinning it down. Her right raked down his chest, and he felt cloth and leather tear, but the chain armor built into the High Garda jacket blunted the attack enough that he got only bloody scratches, not fatal wounds. He didn't even feel them.

He was too focused on the switch, and the switch *wasn't there, it wasn't bloody there,* and he tasted a horrible flood of nausea and terror as he realized that this time, this time he wasn't getting out of it, that Santi was wrong, that they would all end here, bloody rags in the grass . . .

And then he found it. Not on the jaw, but on the neck, set farther back. A slight bump beneath the hot, flexible skin.

He looked the lion in the eyes as she opened her jaws wider and the mangled remains of his weapon dropped away, and pushed the switch.

The lion froze, and the open jaws cranked down to a snarl, but it was too late for her. The light faded from her eyes, and in the next breath, she was still—a horrible weight on his chest and arm, and he struggled to free himself. That wasn't as difficult as it might have been, since the slick grass helped, and he was able to slither to one side enough to overbalance her and send her crashing over like a felled monument.

Jess rolled to his feet, staggered a little from the dizzy bite of adrenaline, and found the next lion. It was on top of Dario, who'd likewise sacrificed his weapon and was frantically slapping at the creature's throat as it snarled and clawed at him. Jess slid in place and hit the proper spot just as the automaton's claws ripped Dario's shredded jacket away, exposing his equally tattered shirt and a bloody chest. One more swipe, and blocked jaws or not, he'd have been dead.

Dario was mumbling in Spanish, and Jess didn't wait for a translation; he moved on, looking for anyone else in trouble.

Wolfe was still on his feet. So were Khalila, Santi, Thomas, and Morgan. Glain had somehow—the great inventor Heron only knew how—managed to get on *top* of her lion and was actually riding the thing as it twisted, snarled, and tried unsuccessfully to claw her off. She poured one shot after another into its head until it suddenly collapsed in a heap, sending her into a roll that she somehow made look graceful as it brought her back to her feet.

Thomas had turned his lion off and must have done for Morgan's, too, because she stood close to him. Dead pale, his girl, but intently studying for the next target. *No,* Jess thought. *Don't use your power.* But he couldn't spare the breath, or time, to say it.

Santi twisted loose from the lion that had come for him and ripped a glass vial from a loop on his belt. He threw it in the creature's face, and the distinctive, sickening odor of Greek fire blew into Jess's face and nearly made him retch. Where the liquid touched and clung, the lion burst into green fire and began to melt, but it was still moving. Santi fired into the thing's head but slipped and had to roll away as it leaped.

It kept coming for him until all that was left of the automaton was a metal skeleton and rage, and as Jess watched, the cables melted through and the whole thing collapsed in a melting inferno. The grass, Jess thought in alarm; they were in the middle of the stuff, and if the fire spread, it would go up like tinder. Santi must have had the same thought, because he took out a pouch of powder and threw it into the center of the fire. It guttered away into a surly, smoking ruin.

Wolfe's lion had one bullet hole in its head. Just one. And it was as still as the others, incredibly. Jess looked from it to Wolfe, who shook his head. "Nic shot it for me," he said. "I'm not that good. He took mine before he tried to take his. Stupid."

"Incredible," Thomas murmured, but he wasn't talking about Santi's accuracy. He was running his hands over the statue of a lion in front of him. "A new version, so strong; you see how the cables are attached? That's new. Pack hunters, just incredible. And stealthy. Very dangerous. The artistry it takes to create these—"

Khalila collapsed into a sudden sitting position, and Jess went to her, but she wasn't bleeding. Wasn't wounded. She was staring at the frozen lion in front of her, and her color had gone far too pale, her eyes too dead. She wasn't seeing the death she'd avoided, he thought. She was seeing that paper her cousin had brought.

Jess crouched next to her and said, "It was a diversion; you know that. Rafa was only meant to keep us occupied while the lions closed in."

Her lightless eyes shifted to lock on his face, but he didn't think she was actually *looking*. "Not just a diversion, though. None of the rest of us have family in service. He's taken them, Jess. He'll kill them."

"We don't know that," he said. It sounded hollow, and it felt like a lie. "Khalila—"

"I know. No quarter. I'm the first one to feel that bite. But I won't be the last. He'll come after everyone we love now. We'll have to get word to our families. Send them to safety." She finally looked up. "You're bleeding."

"Scratches," he said. "Dario's got worse." He silently offered her a hand up, and she took it and walked to the young Spaniard. Jess thought he'd never seen a look so vulnerable—and so relieved—as the one that flashed over Dario's face at the sight of Khalila, alive and safe.

Jess looked away and left them to it, whatever it was, because Morgan was rushing toward him.

"Are you all right?"

"Yes," he told her. "All right." And he put his arms around her, just for a moment. He was afraid for her and afraid *of* her, too; that made him feel weak and exposed. But then again, risk made the safe harbor of her embrace all the sweeter. Standing here, with these people, with *her*, was like coming to something that was better, and more dangerous, than any home he'd ever known.

It hit him in a rush that he *did* have family at risk here, too. "Brendan?" He pulled away and turned in a fast circle, looking for his brother. He'd been standing—where? There, near Glain and Morgan. "Brendan!"

His brother rose out of the grass almost as quietly as an automaton. "I thought it was best to hide, since all of you seemed to know what you were doing." He looked over the scene: the destroyed or defeated lions, the blackened, melted skeleton of the one that Santi had burned. The look Brendan turned on Jess was purely and completely impressed. "That," his brother said, "is the most flash thing I ever saw. I thought for certain you'd all be stew meat. *One* lion is bad enough. This . . . this is . . ."

"This is the Archivist coming after us," Jess said. "No more prison, no more captives. He just wants us all dead now. Even Thomas. Maybe especially Thomas."

"Then they shouldn't send these poor creatures to do it," Thomas said. "Morgan? Do you feel able to help me with rewriting a script?"

"No," Jess said instantly, but at the same time she said, "Of course."

Thomas looked from one of them to the other. "Which is it?"

"You need to save your strength," Jess told her in a fast whisper.

"I can rest on the ship," she said. "And he's right. We can't leave these automata here for the Library to retrieve. We can use them." She gave him a smile. Forced, but it was a credible effort. "I'm all right. This is easy. I can do this."

She went off to join Thomas where he crouched by one of the turned-off lions, expertly pressing panels to open the skin and expose the interior.

Brendan looked far too fascinated by what Thomas was doing, so Jess turned him to look in the direction of the bloody grass where Khalila's cousin had died. "That's what we're fighting," he said. "They sent him to die just to keep us distracted while they set us up for the kill. This isn't a skirmish. It's the opening battle of the war."

Brendan looked without expression on Rafa's corpse and said, "You didn't count them. You're one beast short."

"What?" Jess asked, an instant before he realized what his brother meant.

The lion that had ambushed Rafa rose out of the grass and lunged.

Jess shoved Brendan one way, and he dived another; it never would have worked had there not been two of them, two nearly identical . . . The lion was confused, conflicted, trying to decide which of the two to kill first. As Brendan sprawled and slid, fighting to get back to his feet in the slick grass, Jess took a page from Glain's book. The lion turned toward his twin, and Jess leaped on its back.

This is a mistake, he thought instantly, because the sense of power in the thing was eerie and horrifying, and all he could do for the next few seconds was wrap his legs under the belly and his arms around its neck and hold on, hold on for dear life as the lion thrashed, writhed, ran, tried to claw him loose. It ripped its own flexible metal skin in the effort. Jess heard shouting, screaming, heard someone—Santi?— ordering someone else to *stop shooting for God's sake*, and he heard Glain's deep-throated shout of encouragement as he hung on, tenacious and now desperate to make this hell ride stop at any price. She seemed to think it was fun. It was not fun.

Switch, he told himself, and even though it went against every possible instinct to release his hands from their death grip, he forced himself to do it and nearly got flung off in the next stomach-lifting gyration the lion made. He had to grab hold again, and keep holding, as the automaton suddenly flipped itself end over end through the air in a vicious, athletic circle, landing hard on all four paws and then rolling on its side. It was only the softness of the grass that kept Jess from being crushed and broken. As it was, the pain was lightning hot and too big to think about, and then just as quickly gone as the lion sprang again to its feet.

Now.

He moved his nearly numb fingers, found the switch, and pressed it home just as the lion sprang forward, straight for his twin brother's throat.

"Down!" Jess screamed at him, and Brendan threw himself forward, and flat, which was intelligent, because the lion landed just after him, took a wobbling step forward, and then froze.

Jess felt the cables trembling beneath the lion's metal casing. It felt like fury, like thwarted rage, but he knew he was reading into it; the lion didn't *feel.* Couldn't. But he still thought he could sense the bloodlust pulsing just under that skin, in the unbeating heart of the thing—and it reflected the bloodlust of the man who'd set these automata after them.

He slipped off and nearly toppled over; his knees barely held, and his balance spun wildly until he felt a firm hand grip his shoulder and hold him steady. He thought it was Thomas, but a glance backward showed him it was Glain, grinning from ear to ear. "Well done, Jess," she said. "What possessed you to do that?"

"You did it!" he half gasped.

"Don't be stupid. I broke horses as a child. How many have you been bucked off of, you blazing fool?"

"None," he admitted.

"Stupid." She tousled his hair, which hardly needed it after all that, and he shook it back out of his eyes. "Brave, but still stupid as a bag of stones." She stepped forward and offered a hand to Brendan, who was still facedown in the grass. "Well? Are you dead?"

"Damn well ought to be," his brother said, and rolled over to look at her. "God, that was close."

"You realized it before I did, or it'd have been a damn sight worse," Jess said. "Get up. You're not broken."

"Only in spirit," Brendan said, and groaned when he clambered up. "Is this what you lot do all the time? Because I'm reconsidering my decisions very quickly."

"Oh, you get used to it," Thomas said. He sounded maniacally cheerful, and of course he was; he had the skin loose from one of the lions and was poking around inside, moving cables and parts and fumbling in the bag at his side for tools.

"What's he doing?" Brendan asked. Jess turned him away again. "Jess, enough with his tinkering. We need to go. Now. They'll be following up with worse; you know that. That Scholar must have reported in. High Garda will be on the way here. The lions, they sent on ahead."

"If they're coming out of New York, they have a long way to go," Jess said. "And Boston's a hotbed of trouble. They haven't dispatched High Garda out of there in a year. We've got time to get aboard. Assuming your ship's still there."

"It's there," Brendan said. "Already checked."

"Then we wait until Thomas is done," Jess said. He plucked the gun from his brother's holster, ignored his objection, and walked over to Captain Santi. "Sir. Show me how you dropped that lion. If we're going to do this more often, we'll need to know how to hit them from a distance."

They buried the Scholar's body before they left, and planted the banner as a marker. Wolfe wrote something on the back of the message and shoved it into the snarling open mouth of the bronze lion.

Jess checked. The message said, *We will see you in Alexandria.*

Thomas finished the last of the camouflaged lions and closed the skin back up. He activated them, one by one, and Jess waited with a sense of creeping horror to see if Thomas had made a mistake—or worse, if Morgan had.

But the lions gave a soft mechanical purr when Thomas stroked their heads, and followed him placidly when he walked.

"Quickly," Morgan said. "Jess, say, 'I am your friend.' The rest of you, do it in turn."

It felt stupid, but Jess said it, and as he did, he saw the lions turn as one to look at him. Remembering him, he realized, for later. All of them did it, even Brendan. His twin looked like he didn't half believe it, and Jess didn't blame him, but the lions ignored them all as Thomas sent them coursing out in a box formation around them.

Their own nearly invisible metal army, to escort them back to the coast. Broken and reprogrammed.

They had a pack of their own now.

As he passed close, Dario said, "The Archivist is right, you know. We are dangerous."

"We'd damn well better be," Jess said. "Or we're all dead."

Somehow, he wasn't surprised to find that the ship moored in the secluded cove flew a familiar flag: that of the Great Library of Alexandria. The golden eye of Horus flapped and hissed in the strong breeze, and it seemed to blaze even in the cloudy light.

But it wasn't a Library ship. Jess knew that, because he recognized the girl standing on the beach, surrounded by a small army of hard men and women of no particular uniform. "Cousin Anit," Brendan called brightly, and swept her into a twirling hug. "Good to see you!"

"Put me down." She was stiff in his arms, and her voice was chilly, and Brendan let her go and stepped back. Well back. "I'll pretend you didn't do that." She ignored him and shifted her gaze. "Cousin Jess."

The girl was Egyptian to the bone, and of no blood relation to him; she was a cousin in business, though, and those ties counted for nearly as much. Her father—implied, he thought, by those red stripes on the ships—was Red Ibrahim, one of the most powerful smugglers in the world . . . and *the* book smuggler of Alexandria, which was precisely the most perilous and impossible place to practice such a craft. Not one to be underestimated, her father . . . and young Anit, for all her demure prettiness, was just as dangerous and clever. She was apprenticing in the trade and was well on the way to mastery, all as barely more than a child.

"You're joking," Jess said to his brother. "You got *her* to help us. All the way from Alexandria?"

"I wasn't in Alexandria," Anit said. "I delivered a shipment of goods from Egypt to a port in Mexico and retrieved some new things. Diverting here was little trouble. But it will cost you." She smiled—at Jess, not Brendan. "My father does nothing for free."

No mistaking it—she didn't care for Brendan much. She looked older, Jess thought . . . taller, and rounder beneath her practical trousers and jacket. Armed with both a gun and a knife, though the knife looked almost ornamental. She wore her dark hair up in a no-nonsense twist, and as she bowed slightly to Jess, he mirrored it, just a little lower.

"Didn't you make the deal?" he asked his brother. Brendan raised his eyebrows. A familiar gesture. An irritating one.

"With what? You're lucky I arrived here, trading on favors, in time to save your sorry skin. Da didn't pour his fortune in my pockets. You want passage, *you* make the deal."

"I'm sorry," Anit said, and it sounded genuine enough. "You understand this is business, not friendship."

"I do."

"And have you anything to offer? I would hate to leave you here, at the mercy of—well—enemies."

Jess turned toward Thomas, who was holding out a leather document case. He'd spent his time on the trip drawing plans and writing detailed instructions, and Jess held up the case with both hands. Anit raised both eyebrows and shifted her weight a little but didn't reach for it. "Unless that is full of the handwritten papers of Archimedes, I don't think that is enough," she said.

"It will make you a fortune," Thomas said. "It will change the world. And you can be part of it."

Anit took the case. She opened it and looked at the plans for a good long time, then put everything back inside and said, "And if we don't want the world changing? My father has built an empire on scarcity. So has yours, Jess. You want to destroy that?"

"Yes," Jess said. "And so do you. The world is going to change with or without us, Anit. Now, or next year, or ten years from now. The Library's desperate hold on the future is slipping. We change now, we stay in front of that. We profit. Cling to the past, and you go the way of the Archivist."

"It's just paper," she said. "You're paying me with an idea."

"You trade in ideas," Brendan said. "And paper. And so do the Brightwells. We stick together, don't we? Cousin?"

Anit didn't answer. She lifted a hand to her neck and played with a necklace chain there; the pendant ring on it was concealed under her shirt, but Jess remembered it well. It had belonged to a brother she'd lost to an automaton, when they'd been trying to puzzle out how to turn them off. Jess had been the first to manage it and live, and she—and Red Ibrahim—owed him much for that discovery.

Brendan shifted minutely. Making ready to fight. Anit, he noticed, saw it as well. She exchanged a lightning-quick glance with the man who stood on her right, and then made a tiny, almost imperceptible motion with her hand. Since no one died in the next few seconds, Jess assumed she'd told him to be calm.

"Do you accept this offer?" Jess asked her, very quietly. Respectfully. He could see the calculation in the look she was giving him. She was very aware of both her youth and her responsibility. The decision she was making could destroy her family or seal its future wealth. A heavy weight for someone even younger than he was.

"Yes," she said then, as if it was not a hard decision at all, and smiled. It looked easy. His respect for her ability to lie grew. "Of course, that is speaking cousin to cousin. If it proves not to be enough in the eyes of my father, well. We'll have talks, family to family. No doubt my father might speak directly with yours." That was a veiled threat of war, and from the corner of his eye, he saw Brendan start to speak.

"Fine," he said quickly and casually, and turned to his brother. "Fine, yes?"

Brendan's eyes had gone dark, but his smile came as easily as Anit's. And just as falsely. "Of course. But let's not make a mistake: you hurt one Brightwell, you hurt all of them. Right?"

"Your father has two sons," Anit said. "My father has only me. Red Ibrahim will also give blood for blood. But we are not talking about blood, my cousins. We talk gold. Rivers of it, if Jess and his friend are right."

"Rivers of gold," Brendan repeated. "Enough for everyone."

Jess had to fight back a vision of the tower of the Philadelphia town hall crashing in, and the golden statue of Ben Franklin melting in ribbons. *Rivers of gold.* It must have run through the ashes of the dead and covered up bones. Gilded skeletons.

He closed his eyes for a moment and smelled the stench of Greek fire again, and gulped in a deep breath of sea air, then another.

"Actually," Thomas said, "I did bring something else I thought might come in useful. Perhaps it would be of use to you, miss."

He had a sack over his shoulder, one with burned patches on the fabric, and Jess remembered the one he'd dragged out of Philadelphia. Refused to leave behind. He handed it to her, and Anit opened it, just a little tentatively.

It was full of books bound in matching red leather.

"What is this?" She opened the first volume and gave Thomas a wide-eyed glance. "Journals."

"The records of Philadelphia," he said. "A hundred years of them, handwritten by the Burners. I . . . I didn't think their history should die with them."

That was what he'd gone back for, when he'd realized that the Library would destroy everything. History. The history of a city now in ashes.

They were all silent for a moment, and then Anit bowed to him. Deeply. "I accept this as payment in full for your passage," she said. "My father will treat this gift with the respect that it deserves. Thank you."

Anit boarded the ship, but she paused at the rail to say, "The lions must be kept below. And turned off. You understand."

"Of course," Thomas said.

"And I might like to keep one, perhaps."

"Our gift to you," Wolfe said. "With thanks."

Anit practically grinned this time. She was, Jess thought, coming out of this *far* better than she'd ever expected.

They all boarded quickly, and Jess helped Thomas get the lions stowed and turned off in the cramped hold. Morgan had already been shown to a cabin, and so had Wolfe and Santi. Dario stood at the railing, watching as the ship pushed away from the dock.

Next to him, Khalila didn't seem to be watching anything, but there was something in her face that made Jess pause beside her and ask, quietly, "Are you all right?"

"I'm thinking of my cousin," she said. "All wars have casualties. Rafa was dead the moment the Archivist handed him the letter. I pray we can get everyone else's family safe."

"We will. My family's been hiding from the Library for five generations of criminal success. We'll make sure they're put where the High Garda won't find them."

"If he dispatches them to Wales, Glain's family will send them packing," Dario said. "Wales has already nearly broken away from the Library's control. My family is too royal for the Archivist to threaten. So that just leaves Thomas's to worry about, in Germany."

"I'll see to it," Brendan said. "Least I can do, since I didn't pay a copper penny for our passage." He strolled off to speak with Anit. Dario followed him.

Khalila swallowed hard, and for a moment there was a shine of tears in her eyes, but then it was gone, as if it had evaporated under the intense heat of the anger she was banking inside. She hesitated for a moment, then said, very quietly, "Jess? It's past sunset. I have prayers. I can't think of a time I've needed them so much."

"Do you mind if I wait with you?" he asked. She gave him a smile that nearly broke his heart. Brave and painful.

"Your God and mine are listening," she said. "Perhaps you might talk to yours, as well."

"I might try. How do you say *amen*?"

"Amen," she said, though it sounded slightly different from the English version, and laughed.

He repeated that, and she said the word with his pronunciation, and for a moment, it felt like . . . peace.

As Khalila prayed, facing toward Mecca, he stood and did his own kind of prayer. More of a bargain. *Let me find the strength to do this,* he said. *And let me be strong enough to protect them from what's coming.*

The ship's engines set up a low, steady thrum and raced them into the teeth of a howling, cold wind.

Toward England.

EPHEMERA

Alert sent out to all coastal ports in which the Library has presence

ATTENTION

The Archivist Magister commands that you mark, record, and investigate every vessel that arrives or leaves your seaports. We are seeking a dangerous group of rebels who may be attempting to move through your area.

Our best information is that they are aboard a vessel recently departed from America, but we have been unable to locate this ship, which may be traveling under different names and flags. You are directed to make all possible efforts, even to the disruption of normal trade and the inconvenience of passengers, to locate these individuals. Likenesses and descriptions are attached. These renegades may be traveling under the guises of High Garda uniforms and Scholar robes.

They are the enemy of the Archivist and the Library. They must be stopped at all costs.

A handwritten note appended to the order by the vice chancellor for the king of Wales and sent to all ports in Wales and England controlled by his forces

In the name of our king, you are to ignore this and any other demands from the Great Library. Let them come do their own dirty work, and they can pay for docking privilege just like anyone else. We don't do their job for them in finding their runaways. Let them come search and see how far they get.

EPHEMERA

A handwritten declaration sent under diplomatic seal to the Archivist Magister of the Great Library, signed by the reigning rulers of Wales, England, Portugal, Turkey, Russia, and Japan, as well as the queen in exile of the Library Territory of France, and the United Colonies of America

Comes before you now the will of the free people to withdraw from the Treaty of Pergamum, by which the Great Library in all its forms is held apart and above the laws of kingdoms in which it provides its service. Knowledge is a greater good, there is no dissent upon this fact, but we can no longer ignore the abuses of power pursued by generations of Archivists, and the use of High Garda not to protect knowledge, but to destroy it.

The lessons of the past must guide us to the future, and as the Library once stood brave and alone against the dark, now we must stand together against the greater injustice that same Library now represents. We will not fight you, but we will no longer provide free passage within our territories, and we will no longer acknowledge any claims of Library neutrality. You have taken sides, Great Archivist. Proof has been offered that you have suppressed and destroyed the same knowledge you claim to hold sacred. We will no longer support, or allow, the Library's vendettas.

Librarians may remain and operate the Serapeums within our borders, but be warned: if High Garda are sent by any method, whether land, sea, or Translation, we will act upon this as a declaration of open war. You are warned by the queen in exile that she reclaims France for its people, and so may choose to pursue war within those borders.

May the ancient gods of Egypt, in whose shadow you still stand, guide you back to the path of wisdom and light.

To this, we set our hands.

[signatures and seals]

Text of an addendum written by the Archivist Magister, to the Artifex Magnus. Not indexed in the Codex.

They think they can defy us. They aren't the first, but they will be the last. If they want war, we'll wage it on every front. If we allow these insignificant kings and queens and leaders to dictate to us, we lose everything. There is talk of interdicted mechanical presses. We must stop this before it's too late. Under my seal, you are to order the High Garda immediately from our borders to the attack on any country that opposes us in this document.

Text of a handwritten message from the newly appointed High Garda commander to the Artifex Magnus

You may send all the orders you like, sir. But I refuse to start wars I cannot win for the sake of an old man's desperation and vanity. I expect he will kill me for it, but it is my duty as a sworn soldier not of the Archivist, but of the Great Library, to tell you that he has become a danger to everything we hold dear.

Text of a handwritten message from the Artifex Magnus to the Archivist

If you want to keep your throne, you must make examples. And you must do it soon.

CHAPTER NINE

The north of England, Castle Raby

Setting foot on a rocky English beach felt familiar to Jess—cold, windy, damp. At the same time, it felt entirely alien to him, because England, for him, meant London, and London was gone. Not destroyed, not by half, but war torn, looted, scorched, and beaten. And in the hands, at least for now, of the Welsh, who were busy installing their own government in Parliament.

They'd put Anit's ship—now repainted, with false windows and a brand-new figurehead, plus a different set of flags—in at a smugglers' cove on the north coast, far enough from York to be safe and near enough to the Scottish border to be dangerous. Coming ashore brought with it weak, uncertain legs that had gotten used to the rolling seas, and a conviction that the horizon would never stop moving on him, but leaving the ship was a huge relief. Jess was not a good sailor.

Thomas was. His big friend clapped him on the shoulder as he tilted, and pulled him straight again. "Good to be home?" Thomas asked.

"This isn't my home," Jess said. "I'm from London."

"Which is in England, yes? Isn't that the same?"

Jess didn't bother to answer that. His stomach was cramping, his legs ached, and the stones turning under his boots didn't make walking uphill any easier . . . but he forgot his discomfort when he arrived at the top and was confronted by two men with drawn weapons.

Jess held up his hands and said, "Stormcrow," which was the phrase he'd arranged with Brendan during the voyage. "And don't try to fire that thing, Grainger; you've always been a terrible shot."

"Aye, that's true enough," said the taller of the two men, who had a cadaverous face, hollow eyes, and a strangely lush crop of black hair and whiskers. "And you're a small enough target these days, Master Jess. What did they feed you on your travels, vinegar and air?" Grainger put the weapon away, and so did his smaller, silent companion. "Welcome home, sir. I expect your brother will be along?"

"Sooner than either of us want." *And it isn't home,* Jess thought, but didn't say. He glanced behind him. "Captain Santi, Scholar Wolfe, this is Mr. Grainger. My father's trusted secretary and man of all work." He politely ignored the other man, because Grainger did, too. New, since Jess had been off to Alexandria. "Will we be walking?"

"Thank God, no," Grainger said. "We have cabs for you. Can only take four in each; how many do you have, then?"

"Nine," Jess said, but Brendan stuck his head over Jess's shoulder and said, "Ten," at the same time. As Jess shoved him back, Brendan grinned. "Anit's coming, too. She says a night off the ship would do her good."

"Ten," Jess said, and turned back to Grainger. "Is our father here?"

"Waiting at the house for you. Said you were to take my word for his until then."

"Meaning I can ignore it altogether?" Brendan said. "Excellent.

Good work, Grainger." He turned and politely bowed Khalila up the path to the road. "Ladies first."

"Shut up," Glain said, and kicked him soundly on the backside. "We don't need your smarmy consideration. Just shift yourself and get out of the way."

"I'm starting to like you," Brendan called after her. The hand gesture she gave him was not encouraging. Brendan threw an arm around his brother's neck. "Come on, Jess. Smile. We're safe. We're home!"

This isn't home, Jess thought again. But he was starting to realize that maybe he didn't really have a home, except with the people he loved. And they were piling into the three steam carriages lined up on the road.

Back in London, his da had always favored modest transportation; he'd had his town house luxurious enough, but since he'd been pretending all his life to upper-merchant class, he'd never indulged in excesses.

That was clearly not the case anymore. The steam carriages were gleaming wonders of black lacquer and shining brasses, with the clockworks and hydraulics of the engines visible through transparent panes of thick, no doubt unbreakable, glass. *Fit for kings and Archivists,* Jess thought. He wondered how many rare books his father had sold to ink-lickers, to be eaten like so many delicious forbidden treats, to pay for them.

Dario had pushed on past Brendan to help Khalila into the carriage. The journey hadn't done well for her, either; she had a hungry, hollow look to her just now, and as Dario sank down beside her and took her hand, Jess was glad she had someone who cared so much. They'd had no word of her father, brother, or uncle, except that they were still in the Archivist's prison inside the Serapeum. Glain's family was safe. Thomas's had been moved, over their protests, to a remote mountain village, with considerable manpower protecting them, thanks to Santi's brother, and retired soldiers who still owed him debts.

Khalila was bearing her weight of fear and grief alone, and they all could see the strain of it on her.

Morgan stopped at Jess's shoulder and pushed her hair back from her face. The wind blew it in wild, shimmering strands. It had grown longer, and the heavy air had sent it into even thicker curls. He liked it. "I wish there was more we could do for Khalila," Morgan said. "It breaks my heart to see her so—withdrawn."

"I know," he said. "Me, too." Morgan had prospered at sea, as if she was drawing energy and strength from the vastness of it; she'd spent endless hours at the rail, watching the waves and the dolphins that raced ahead of the bow. She'd even put on some of the weight she'd lost in Philadelphia, regained curves beneath her clothes.

He offered her his elbow, and she took it with a crooked little smile. She'd tanned, sailing under the sun. It suited her.

She even let him boost her up into the carriage with his hands on her waist. It was the most contact she'd allowed since they'd boarded the ship. It had frightened her, what she'd nearly done to him outside Philadelphia. She'd wanted to be certain she was stronger, and more in control, before risking it again.

He'd hated every moment of that long, solitary voyage, and not only for the miserable hours he'd spent seasick.

Brendan piled in behind him and took the seat facing him, then reached out a hand to pull in Anit. Red Ibrahim's daughter shut the carriage door and tapped the roof as if she were born to the practice, as at home here as she was in the streets of Alexandria and the smugglers' markets below them. "Thank you for the hospitality."

"Surprised you're not staying with your ship and on your way," Jess said. "I'd think this diversion put you off schedule."

"A small delay. I am to pay your father my sincere respects," she said. "As you would if visiting my father's home."

Jess would have, of course; there was nothing to it but business courtesy. But it still set him on guard, and he saw the brief flash in Brendan's eyes before he turned to look out the carriage's window at the rough, rocky coast. Anit wasn't here just to smile prettily and offer family greetings, and his brother well knew that.

"You seem at home away from home," Jess said.

"You mean, considering my age?" Anit said coolly. "I have traveled with my father since I was old enough to remember. But this trip to Mexico is the first I've taken alone on his behalf."

"And we landed you in it, didn't we?"

She looked away and lifted her shoulders in a very small shrug. "I think none of us have ever been out of it."

Morgan laughed. It had a bitter little edge to it. "You and I already have much in common, Anit. It isn't just the smugglers who spend their lives hunted."

"No doubt." Anit glanced back at Jess. "Thank you for the lions. I will hold them in trust for you, as I promised."

"We'll be along to get them. Sometime."

"Of course," she said. "You may count on me, Jess."

She sounded all right when she said it, but she was still young, and he sensed that hint of falseness in it. Lying was as easy to smugglers as respiration, normally, but not among family. She wasn't quite comfortable with it yet.

Morgan sighed and leaned her head on Jess's shoulder. "I need a bath. A hot bath, with rose soap. And a meal that isn't military rations."

"I think that can be arranged," he said. "One thing I know about my da: he won't be living in a tent and eating beans from a metal can if it can be helped."

"I think I'll like it, then."

"Oh, you won't," Brendan said. "But I don't think he'll care."

There was a certain relaxing quality to the ride, the sway of the carrier, the hiss of the tires . . . at least until they hit a bump that lifted everyone in the vehicle six inches into the air, and slammed them down hard. They'd all been through enough to take it in stride, but even Brendan had to wince. The driver's cheerful cry of "Sorry!" didn't seem very sincere.

Nearly an hour later, and (by Jess's count) more than twenty similar bounces, they finally squealed to a halt, and the back doors flapped open to admit gray daylight. No rain, and though Jess had expected to step out onto mud, he found himself standing on clean, ancient flagstones. The sight of the brooding old walls that rose thirty feet into the air made the breath in his lungs turn sick and tainted. He turned, staring. The walls circled the court in which the carriage had parked. Another carriage had already come to a halt beside theirs, and a third rattled over a wide wooden bridge and in through an enormous arched door.

And then, as the bridge cranked up with a hiss of powerful hydraulics and a clank of iron chains as thick as his legs, as it sealed shut with a *boom* and inner doors were pulled closed, Jess realized that his brother hadn't been exaggerating.

His father was living in a castle. And the sight of the walls made him feel sick and hot and short of breath, and he didn't know why, until he thought he smelled a phantom whiff of rotting plants and Greek fire.

I'm past Philadelphia. I'm over it.

But it left him shaking and sweating, with a sick taste in the back of his throat, and he flinched as Morgan put her arm in his. "Sorry," he murmured.

"This is your home?"

"I've never seen it before," he said. The fortress proper consisted of gigantic, brooding buildings and towers. The London town house he'd grown up in could have fit within the entry hall, he imagined. The place was large enough to hold an entire High Garda company. Pity they'd had to leave theirs behind. "I thought Brendan was exaggerating."

"Not a bit," his brother said, and lifted Anit down from the carriage. "Da's owned this place for twenty years, give or take. Never in his own name, of course. And this is the first time he's felt threatened enough to make use of it."

"Jess! Oh, my dear boy!"

He turned toward the voice, and his mother came rushing down the narrow stone steps of the castle's main door and threw her arms around him. He froze for a long second, staring in blank panic at Brendan, who'd crossed his arms, and then tentatively hugged her back. Celia Brightwell had always been a distant presence in his life; Callum had married her for position and money, not love, and though she'd been a dutiful enough mother, she'd never been a warm one. She'd certainly never embraced him like this before. If it weren't for her familiar features and the expensive cut of her dress, he'd have thought it was someone playing her.

"I was afraid you'd never come back," she told him, and put him at arm's length to stare at him. He realized, maybe for the first time, that he'd inherited the color of his eyes from her, as had Brendan. He couldn't remember what color their dead brother Liam's had been. More like his father's, he thought. "Callum hasn't told me much, you know, but I know you've been in terrible danger. Oh, Jess!"

"I'm all right," he said, and it sounded awkward; he cleared his throat and tried to make it sound warmer. "I've missed you, Mother."

She'd always been *Mother*, never anything more affectionate. Then again, Callum had always been *Da*, and there was little enough affection there, either . . .

"I've missed you so," she said, and kissed his cheek, which was shocking. "Welcome home, my dear."

She went to greet Brendan with the same outpouring of emotion, which must have surprised his twin just as much, but Jess didn't have a chance to observe it. His father was coming down the steps at a much more sedate, lordly pace, and he was using an ebony cane that he probably didn't need. Knowing his da, there'd be a poisoned blade inside it.

"Jess," his father said, when they were face-to-face.

"Da," he replied, and was unprepared for his father—like his mother—to sweep him into a strong, crushing embrace. It was confusing, and at the same time, he felt some war that had been waging inside him go silent, too. Had he needed this? God help him if he had, because it was very likely that it wasn't real at all. His da was perfectly capable of putting on a show for those he wanted to impress . . . which would be who, exactly?

Ah, of course. *Anit.*

Callum let Jess go and gave Brendan the same greeting, and then gave Anit a decorous, formal bow. "Your father always said you were as beautiful as the dawn," Callum said. "I see that for once his genius for poetry failed him, because you're far lovelier than that, my dear."

She bowed, too, and stepped forward to offer him the kiss of greeting between friends—one on each cheek, then one lightly on the lips. "My father sends you warm greetings, my uncle. I am honored to be welcome in your house."

"Ever welcome, my dear. You're part of the family, after all." Callum—still bluff and strong and barrel-chested, still expensively togged out, only a little thinner and a little grayer than Jess remembered him—offered Anit his crooked elbow, and she took it with the calm assurance of a princess. "And I see the lovely young Morgan is with us again." He bowed to her—shallowly—and she gave him a little nod back. "Have all your friends survived your journey? That's a credit to your skills. A considerable achievement."

This smarmy flow of compliments, Jess gathered, was all for Anit's benefit. He glanced at Brendan and saw the answering glint in his brother's eyes. Cynical, but weirdly reassuring. His memories of the chilly distance with his mother weren't wrong. And neither were his recollections of the slaps his father dealt out to teach him the proper way to run a smuggled book through London.

Their parents moved on to greet the others with a good deal more restraint, and then led the way up into the castle.

"Quite the show," Brendan said, falling into step beside his brother, and Jess made a throwing-up sound in the back of his throat. "What? Are you saying it isn't good to be back in the bosom of the old family?"

"I feel welcome as ever," Jess said. "Do you actually live in this great pile of rocks, or is it just a stage for whatever play they're putting on?"

"Oh, I live here. For now, anyway." Brendan shook his head with a crooked smile on his lips. "Come on, brother. I'll help get everyone sorted for sleeping quarters. There are twenty extra bedrooms in the place that can sleep three in a pinch, and ten more in the guesthouse—"

"*Guesthouse?*"

"And you don't need to worry about our safety. Besides these castle walls, the entire grounds stretch on for miles in every direction. The borders are surrounded by walls and sentries. Plus, we're remote here, and we have spies on every road and approach who'll send word immediately if anyone starts our way. Unless the damned Library has learned how to fly, they won't be able to get here without ample warning, and a hell of a fight."

"You have troops."

"We have . . . hired men. And a great deal to defend. You know how it goes."

What Brendan was really telling him, in so many words, was that this was a prison, and every escape route was guarded.

Dario came up the steps, where Brendan and Jess were locked in communication, and said, "You never told me you lived like a real grandee, scrubber. I'm impressed."

"Yes," Jess said, "you would be."

The warm welcome lasted through a receiving line of uniformed servants—all armed, Jess noted, even the maids and cooks—and stepping inside the hall was like taking a trip a thousand years into the past. The place was obviously well maintained, but ancient, from the enormous carved beams that rose far into the shadows, to the three huge fireplaces big enough to burn half a tree at a time. There were giant feasting tables that could seat at least a hundred, and tattered old battle flags hanging from the walls.

Best of all, the hall was lined with bookshelves, double Jess's height, that stretched the length of the room on both sides. A dizzying archive, and everything in it original. Callum Brightwell's warehouse, right out in public view.

That, for the first time, made him feel less trapped.

"Mr. Grainger will show you all to your rooms," Jess's father announced, and then beckoned to Jess. "Not you, boy. I'll need reports. And I'll need to speak with you and your big friend Thomas. Oh, and I understand you have books you've rescued from the Black Archives of Alexandria. I'll be needing those as well."

"There's my father," Jess murmured to Thomas. "I was afraid someone had taken his place."

"Do you trust him?" Thomas asked, just as quietly.

"Do you?"

"I trust everyone. Until I see I shouldn't. But you know him."

"Yeah," Jess agreed. "I do."

That wasn't an answer, but Thomas didn't push for one; they walked together after Callum, through the great hall. A grand stone staircase big enough to march five across up it lay beyond, and split to the left and right. Callum went right, and Jess had been correct: he didn't need the cane at all.

The top of the stairs led to another grand hallway lined with tapestries and paintings, and at the end of it, with a fine lord's view of the deer park and gardens beyond the walls, lay his father's office. It was surprisingly familiar. Jess remembered the desk, with its carved crouching lions. Da must have had it rescued out of London. More shelves of books, expensive warm rugs, and a smell of leather and old paper.

This was like coming home.

"Sit," his da said, and took his own advice. His winged desk chair was new, and quite like a throne. Jess took one of the three matching seats that faced the desk. The one Thomas chose was almost big enough for him. "Books?"

"They're coming," Jess said. "Dario and Khalila will deliver them."

"Good." His father sat back and studied them. Warm smile, but his eyes were like cold pebbles at the bottom of a frozen lake. "I understand that you built the unfortunate Philadelphians your press. And it worked."

"We did," Thomas said. "And it did." He had his bag with him, and now he pulled out a copy of the blueprints that he'd sketched aboard the ship. "Here is what we built. Of course, we can improve on it."

Brightwell picked up the paper and peered at it closely. Jess knew that frown. It was mostly for show, done to get the best deal in any negotiation. It was so ingrained that he doubted his father even noticed he was doing it. "Doesn't look like much, to be changing the world. That's what you're promising?"

"Yes," Thomas said. "If you give me the tools, Jess and I will build one for you. We'll need supplies. I can make you a list."

"Then, do that." Somehow, Callum made it sound like a failure that Thomas hadn't done so already. "You find my son an adequate assistant, or do you need someone better trained?"

Thomas looked up, and for the first time, his smile flattened and his blue eyes seemed darker. "I don't take your meaning, Mr. Brightwell. Do you not think your son is good enough for such a job?"

"I suppose he's bright enough, but—"

"He is bright enough," Thomas said. "And I don't need anyone else."

For the first time that Jess could remember, his da didn't have a ready response. He parted his lips and looked at Thomas curiously, then shook his head. "If you're satisfied," he said. "Of course."

Thomas stood up and took the plans back, to Callum's astonishment—and, if he had to admit it, to Jess's own surprise, too. It was a bold move. One that Callum debated challenging, and then clearly decided to let pass. "When can you start building this wonder?"

"As soon as we come to an arrangement," Thomas said. "You are a negotiator, I understand. So what do you offer?"

"You don't think saving your hides from the High Garda and the Archivist is payment enough? You do set a high price on yourself, Scholar."

Thomas gave him a pure, and purely alarming, smile. "Not on myself, sir. But on the knowledge I have to share, yes. On the lives of my friends, yes. On the future of the Library . . . yes. That, I put a high price on."

Callum shot a glance at Jess. "Last I met this one, he was a featherheaded optimist. You've had a bad influence on him."

"He's right," Jess said. "What he has is valuable. Anit sold us passage here. What are you selling?"

"Safety and shelter! A place to conduct whatever inventing you plan to do, at my cost, so long as I share in these discoveries! Isn't that enough?"

Thomas didn't answer. He left it to Jess, which was wise. "We're going to need a way back to Alexandria," he said. "Something secure and secret. That's part of the deal, when we want to go."

"For how many of you?"

"All of us."

"That's a stupid waste," his father said. "Dragging your friends right back into the hands of executioners. Unless you have some larger plan . . . ?"

"We can discuss it later," Jess said. "Thomas and I will build the press for you, to pay for the cost of our protection here. Thomas gets to build anything else he wants, and you pay for the costs of that. We'll discuss payment for the plans."

"Payment!"

"I know exactly how much money you're going to be making from this." Jess smiled slowly. "Did you really expect us to give things away for free, Da?"

Callum glared at him for a long, red moment, and then, quite suddenly, laughed. Slapped the surface of his desk so hard a sheet of paper curled into the air in surprise and floated back down. "My son," he said. "I used to think you'd never be good for much in our trade. I might have been wrong about that."

From the corner of his eye, Jess saw Thomas flinch a little at the casual insult; he'd come from a different sort of family, and that had stung him, on Jess's behalf. But it hardly even registered, really. Growing up in the Brightwell household had meant being coldly judged, measured, trained, slapped, and corrected. Not encouraged.

By Callum's standards, that had been a real compliment.

"Do we have an accord?" Jess asked.

His father reached for a piece of paper, pulled it over, and wrote rapidly. Signed with a flourish. Handed it to him with the pen. "Sign," he said.

Jess scanned the text of what his father had written down. Flawlessly phrased in his own favor, of course, but it didn't much matter; Jess nodded and signed his name. His father took pen and paper back, sealed the document with wax, and filed it in a drawer that probably held a hundred similar agreements, some going back decades.

"Now," Callum said, and sat back in his chair. "I expect you'll want to get yourselves off to a decent bed. Dinner's served at eight in the small reception room; they'll fetch you for it. Clothes in your rooms. Had to guess at sizes, but I think our tailors did well enough. Go on with you. I have other business."

Callum had already pulled a stack of paper onto his desk and was rifling through it, ignoring them completely. Jess shrugged when Thomas sent him a baffled look.

This was the kind of welcome he'd been expecting all along.

They walked out together and closed his father's office door behind them, and Jess said nothing. Felt nothing, really, until he glanced at his friend's face and saw the anger there.

"I don't mean to offend, Jess, but your father is a fool if he thinks so little of you. Is that how he always treats you?"

It was an odd question, and Jess shrugged. "He's had his moments of fondness, I suppose. Swings between that, benign indifference, and from time to time, the back of his hand when he felt he needed to make a point."

Thomas was staring at him with the oddest expression. "It's wrong, you know. For a father to be so cold."

"I know," Jess said. He forced out a grin and wondered if it looked as false as it felt. "Whatever doesn't kill you, isn't that the saying?"

Thomas shook his head. "You are strong in spite of him. Not because of him."

It was, Jess thought, the kindest thing anyone had said to him, and for a moment he didn't say anything at all. Didn't quite know how. Then he said, "Come on. If I don't find a bath and a bed, I might not live until dinner."

With the help of one of the maids, Jess was shown to his bedroom—a cavernous, ornate thing with a bed larger than the cell he and Thomas had shared in Philadelphia. There was a bathroom attached, and Jess made good use of the shower until he was certain he was finally clean of every trace left of his time in Philadelphia. His burns had healed, but the scars still showed, and beneath them, like shadows, he could still see the faint lines of the cuts from the glass he'd gathered up. Good. That was like a badge of honor, those cuts. He wouldn't like to see them disappear, because they reminded him of what was lost.

The closet yielded too many choices, so he grabbed something at random that proved to be plain black trousers and an equally plain shirt in white, with red stripes on the edges of the collar and cuffs. He put it aside and tried the bed, but the softness of it felt wrong to him. He was drowning in it, after all the deprivations. The bare accommodations on the ship had seemed luxurious. This felt overwhelming.

So he dressed, found that his father had provided a new pair of soft leather boots, and went to wander the castle. One thing he'd learned not from his da, but from Wolfe and Santi: landing in a new place represented an entirely new set of challenges, and knowing the terrain might mean the difference between life and death. He'd rather make his map than sleep.

Not that he thought he could sleep, anyway.

His circuit made it through only six rooms on the ground floor, because that was where he opened a set of doors and found a small old library, and Morgan curled in a chair, reading. She didn't hear him come in.

The soft light of late afternoon fell gently over her as she turned pages, and for a moment he just looked at her. He'd seen paintings that weren't as beautiful; the glow of her hair, the curve of her cheek, the drape of the simple dress she wore, all demanded study. The dress was the blue of a perfect sky, and perfectly flattering to her.

"I see you found my father's rarest books," Jess said, and startled her into a flinch, which he regretted. Seeing her peaceful was a gift. She marked her place with a ribbon and closed the volume. "And did you find that bath?"

"I did. Rose soap and all," she said. "And I think you did, too."

She put the book down and came toward him. He ended up with his back to the shelves, and her warm lips on his. The dark floral scent of her rolled over his senses and blotted out everything else but the feel of her skin, the taste of her mouth. It was a long, sweet, burning kiss. They'd been so careful, since Philadelphia; they'd barely touched on the ship. She hadn't trusted herself not to hurt him, and he hadn't trusted himself to push her away, if he had to.

They parted with a shared gasp for air, and he pressed his forehead to hers as she let out a breathless giggle. "Like champagne on an empty stomach," she said. "Ah, I've missed you."

He curled his fingers in with hers and pulled her tight against him, as if they were prepared to dance. "You seem much better."

"I am stronger," she said. "Better is a different subject altogether. Being at sea was . . . good for me. All that energy, all that possibility. But . . ." She took her fingers from his and lifted her hand. A thick glimmer of power formed around it, but it was shot through with dark, shifting stars, like a handful of black glitter. "I'll never be what I was. Dr. Askuwheteau said as much. It's not a matter of strength as much as it is . . . a change of instinct."

It was dangerous, he knew that, but he reached for her hand again. The buzz of power felt like bees against his skin, and when he threaded his fingers through hers and pressed their palms together, he felt the sting. And then it cooled. Vanished.

But he still felt a little wave of weariness ripple through him. Just a little.

Her smile seemed sad. "I can control it. To a point. But what you saw—the black spots—they may lessen over time, but they'll never quite go away. I'm stronger, and I'm more dangerous. But we knew that would happen."

"And it might be needed," Jess said. He hated himself for saying it, but it was true. "You know what we discussed? On the ship?"

She seemed to stop breathing for a moment, and he hated the flutter of panic he saw pass across her face. Then it was gone, and she seemed entirely calm. "We're not safe here."

"I don't know that for certain, but—" It was an instinct he couldn't fully explain, built out of history and hints, memories and feelings. "If we aren't, I need you to be on your guard. Ready for whatever we have to do. All right?"

"Yes." Her fingers curled in the collar of his jacket, and her smile seemed sweet and unreadable. "Not all Brightwells are as honest as you?"

"No."

"And you're an unrepentant criminal."

"Exactly." He wondered whether the doors locked properly, and if that curved divan across the room was sturdy enough to hold them both . . . until Morgan stiffened and stepped back out of the embrace.

"Should have known I'd find you where the best books are kept, Jess," said a voice from the door, and Jess realized with a savage pulse of fury that Dario stood there, arms folded. Enjoying the show, no doubt. "Though I admit, finding you doing something other than reading them is a new experience. This must be the most excitement this room's ever seen."

"Oh, *shut up*. What do you want?" This was one of the moments, Jess thought, when punching Dario until his hand got tired seemed very, very tempting.

Dario's lurid delight slid away, and he stepped in and closed the door behind him. Bolted it. Jess moved away from Morgan and in front of her—protecting her, though he didn't know why, or from what. But Dario only walked to the divan that Jess had been so recently considering, and sat down. He must have had a closet full of clothing waiting, too, and he'd chosen the most opulent thing he could: a rich black velvet coat with gold buttons, thick cuffs, and a wine red silk shirt beneath it. Boots so shiny they seemed coated in glass. He'd had his hair cut and his beard trimmed back to a precise goatee, and somewhere, he'd found a single ruby stud to wear in his left earlobe. Somewhere—possibly from Jess's father's collection— he'd found an ebony walking stick with a golden lion's head.

He looked like he belonged in a castle. Like he owned at least two.

"Jess. Sit down," he said. "We need to talk."

"Get up," Jess said, "and walk out."

They stared at each other for a long moment, and then Dario crossed his legs and sat back, clearly refusing. "I know you're not stupid enough to think we're safe," he said. "And this might be exactly why we started our discussions back in—back there." The little hesitation, the way he avoided the name *Philadelphia*, told Jess that Dario wasn't over it, either. He just hid it better. "So sit down."

"I'll go," Morgan said. "I should rest." Jess turned to face her, and she positioned him so that she could kiss him with his back to Dario, and Dario wouldn't see her whisper, "Careful, whatever it is you're plotting. I still don't trust him."

He nodded, just slightly, and let her go.

Once she'd gone out the door, he locked it behind her and turned, leaning against it, arms folded. "This isn't the time."

"It's the only time there is. Anit received word while I was loitering near her—close enough to hear her captain deliver the message. I credit you with spying skills, but I grew up eavesdropping."

"Get to the point, if you have one."

"The Archivist has announced the closure of the city of Alexandria."

"What?"

"A defensive measure against Burner attacks. So he says. But the Welsh-run newspapers—your father keeps quite a good collection of them, by the way—say differently. There's been a defection of treaty countries—more than the Archivist can safely try to punish at once. America's in open rebellion, and the New York Serapeum fell to the Burners yesterday." Dario inspected his fingernails. Manicured, Jess noticed. "Your rescued doctor seems to be their new spokesman. Better than the last *cabrón*. But the important thing is that it's starting. Even without Thomas's press working yet, there are *rumors* of it. The Welsh and the English only agree on one thing, and that is that they both want the Library to stay out of their affairs. The French queen may be in exile, but Portugal agrees to shelter and help her. Add America to that boiling pot, and the Archivist will be wanting to crush resistance quickly."

Jess, without really meaning to, found himself sitting in a chair across from Dario, elbows on his knees. Leaning forward and thinking hard. "He'll purge any dissenters from inside Alexandria. Go after anyone who opposes him in any way."

"He's already started. There was an announcement in the Alexandrian paper—your father gets that, too—that they will celebrate a Feast of Greater Burning at the statue of Horus in thirty days. Pomp, circumstance, and sacrifice."

Jess slowly raised his head and met Dario's dark gaze. Neither of them blinked. "They'll be killing prisoners at the Feast of Greater Burning. And Khalila's family—"

"Is in cells at the Serapeum," Dario finished. "We have thirty days to find a way to stop it. And we can't do it from here."

"And do we tell the others?"

For answer, Dario reached in his coat pocket and took out a rolled sheet of thin paper. He let it fall open. It was the Alexandrian newspaper—a Library-linked document that refreshed itself with new words and illustrations every few hours. "I took the liberty of lifting it," he said. "Until we decide, you and I, what we will do. Because we know what our beloved friends will do, don't we?"

"Run straight into a trap," Jess said. "Like heroes."

"And you and I, we are not heroes." Dario gave a small, ironic smile, mostly to himself. "Much as I hate to admit that. But what we are might save all of us, and I think we have to settle for that."

"All right," Jess said, and leaned forward. "Then let's find out just how much of villains we're going to have to be."

Jess had no taste for it, but dinner wasn't optional; he'd tried to beg off, but the servant had been calmly insistent, and in the end, he'd followed her off to find the rest already gathered. The small reception room was still vast, and ornately decorated. The table could seat twenty, and only half that many took chairs.

His parents put on a good show of graciousness, but the strain was evident in every forced interaction. Wolfe maintained a chilly silence and left it to the more socially eloquent Santi to oil the conversational wheels; Jess elected to be seen and not heard, except for murmured comments to Morgan, who'd been seated to his right next to Brendan, and Khalila, on his left. Glain and Thomas seemed quiet, though in Thomas's case, it was because he was eating everything in sight.

Jess seemed to be the only one with a lack of appetite, but he forced himself to eat. Roast beef, mushy peas, mash. A solid meal, uncomplicated, but that was probably by design. In this, at least, he could thank his mother, who seemed to understand that they were still recovering.

It was toward the end of the meal that Callum Brightwell tapped his crystal wineglass with a knife and brought all the conversation to a halt as he rose to his feet. "I know this isn't a comfortable partnership," he said. "I don't like Library folk any more than some of you like me and mine. But we have enemies in common, and friends as well." He nodded to Anit, and then to Jess. "My son is more one of you than one of mine, and though that isn't a comfortable thing for a father to say, I'm proud of the company he's chosen. Tough and smart, all of you." He lifted his glass. "To our rebels. Confusion to our foes."

They all drank—Khalila, her water, and the rest, the free-flowing Brightwell wine. Some even echoed his toast. Not Jess. And, he noted, not Santi or Wolfe. Maybe they didn't like to see themselves as rebels. Or foes.

And, Jess thought, maybe they'd realized that it was entirely out of character for his father to be so grandly supportive.

"Thank you for the most generous welcome," Wolfe said, once silence had fallen again. For once, he sounded less than mocking. A little less. "But we won't impose on you for long. Our place isn't here, hiding. It's in Alexandria, fighting for what we love."

"Don't be daft—you'll be slaughtered two steps inside the city, if you can even get there," Callum said. "You lot, always thinking of a fight as a gentleman's duel instead of a proper throat cutting. Must be the Library training, eh? Makes you convinced you're invulnerable."

Jess drew in a breath to say something, but he wasn't needed. Santi took another sip of his wine and beat him to it. "Some battles you have to fight face-to-face. Not in a dark alley."

"Knifing your enemy in a dark alley's how you avoid the fight in the first place," Callum replied. "Which is something those of us who have to scrape a living outside the Library's generosity know."

"Yes, we can all see the shocking poverty in which you live," Santi said. "Our fight is to free the Library to follow its real mission, not destroy it wholesale. That's for the Burners. And people like you."

"Oh, it's in my good interest to keep the Library alive, too. At least until it's no longer necessary, which will be several lifetimes from now, I'd imagine. So you needn't insult me by lumping me in with bloody Burners."

"He doesn't mean to insult you, sir," Khalila said. "But he's right. We have to bring light back to the temple where it's gone out. We can't kindle that fire from here."

"And you can't go *there*," Callum said, "or anywhere else, until it's safe. But not to worry, you're well protected, and we'll provide you with everything you need. Jess and Scholar Schreiber have seen to that. They'll be paying for your keep with a few jobs for me."

"Building the press," Wolfe said.

"Among other things. So have no fear—all the plans are under way for your safe departure. Until then, enjoy the hospitality." Callum picked up a small bell next to his plate and rang it. "Ah. Dessert."

Khalila left the table first, pleading weariness, and she took Thomas, Glain, and Morgan with her. Jess stayed, even though he longed to see Morgan to her room; he wanted to watch Santi and Wolfe and his father. Besides, his twin had stayed, gleefully tucking into the sweet pudding that had been served, and though Jess could barely manage a mouthful, Brendan gestured meaningfully at it. "Go on," he said. "You need some cushion back on those bones. You look half-dead."

Felt it, too, Jess realized; he was aching in every muscle. He forced down three more bites, until Brendan finally sighed and took the rest of it from him to finish.

Wolfe and Santi exchanged a few more words with the elder Brightwells, but not many, before they rose to leave. Jess intended to follow, but Brendan got up with him and said, "We're off to bed, then. Good night."

Callum mumbled the same back, concentrating on his pudding. Their mother looked at them both with distant sadness and nodded.

They hadn't gotten to the stairs before Jess pulled Brendan off into a side room. A dark one, until he dialed the glows up a little. It was cold and damp and was lined with shelves and neatly ordered crates and boxes. Storage, Jess thought. There was a lingering smell of spices, so likely it was for the kitchens.

"What are you not telling me?" Jess asked him. "Come on, Scraps. I know it when you're hiding something."

Brendan tried to look innocent. He failed miserably. "The usual Brightwell intrigue, old son. Nothing out of the ordinary, is it?"

"*Brendan.*"

His twin went quiet, staring at him, and then turned away. Picked at a rough spot on a shelf, winced as he gained a splinter. And finally said, "You know our da. One profit isn't enough. Neither is two. He wants it all, and you've handed it to him on a silver platter, with a gift note."

"We're not guests," Jess said.

"Well, *you're* not a guest; you belong here."

"You know what I mean! *They're* not guests!"

His brother's shoulders rose and fell in a faint shrug. "They're fugitives. What exactly do they expect, that everyone will be rushing to join their army? Even us? Come on, Jess. When has Da ever done anything for anyone who isn't family?"

"They're *my* family."

"They're prisoners," his brother said. "And when they leave, it'll be because Da's made a better deal. You know it. We both know it."

It wasn't anything but confirmation of what Jess had already suspected, but he still felt the trap closing with an almost audible *snap*. Another set of walls. Another set of cells. Luxurious ones, with soft feather beds and plenty of food to distract them, but Callum Brightwell was no different from Willinger Beck, and never had been, really. For all that he was their father.

"And you're going along with it," Jess said.

Brendan looked at him for a long, telling moment, and then dropped his gaze to his finger. A red dot of blood welled there, and he wiped it away. "I haven't decided," he said. "But I'll let you know. Go on, Jess. Nothing will happen tonight. Da wants that bloody machine of yours. Maybe you can convince him the lot of you are assets worth keeping, not selling."

Jess didn't try to argue with him. He wasn't sure he could even speak. All of the darkness had rolled up inside him, all the rage he'd felt since Philadelphia, all the fury of being trapped and hounded and threatened and *helpless*.

But he wasn't helpless here. And there was another, darker game to play.

He silently left and went up the stairs to the hall where they all had rooms, intending to knock on Morgan's door, but changed his mind when he heard soft voices and realized that the room at the end of the hall still had its door open. Not fully open, as if inviting others in, but cracked, as if it hadn't been fully latched.

Men's voices. Wolfe and Santi. Jess knocked lightly and pushed the door open.

He wasn't surprised to find them standing close, as if they'd been arguing fiercely. There was a strong sense of emotion in the air, something that immediately made Jess wish he'd kept on to his own door, but it was too late now. Without looking at him, Wolfe said, "Well? What?"

He told them about what Brendan had said. Neither of them seemed surprised by the news that Callum Brightwell had plans for them. That they'd escaped Philadelphia only to land in yet another net.

"We have time," Wolfe said, and it sounded as if he was continuing the argument that Jess had walked in on. "Your father wants this

press as much as Willinger Beck ever did. We made it out of Philadelphia. We'll leave this place on our own terms."

"Maybe we don't want to leave," Santi said. "This castle is strong and
defensible, well situated to withstand any kind of attack. Brightwell was
right about one thing: running into the Archivist's city like brave heroes
of old will get us cut down. I don't want to see that. Neither do you."

Wolfe glared at him, and Jess saw the rage simmering in him,
barely contained. Jess knew that feeling, because he'd just felt the
helpless shudder of it, the desire to lash out. He'd walked away from
his brother because of it.

"So we stay here, in this—overstuffed prison, waiting for the Archivist to turn the High Garda on us? I won't. *I can't!*"

"Chris—"

"No!" The word came out of Wolfe in a barely checked snarl.

Santi threw up his hands and stalked away to stare out the mul-
lioned window at the darkness beyond. They were all raw, Jess thought.
Too raw, too angry, and still too far from right.

On impulse, Jess said, "Do you still smell it, too?"

Wolfe frowned at him. "Smell what?"

"The smoke." Jess's throat convulsed as if a finger had brushed the
back of it, and the nausea broke cold sweat onto his brow. "Sweet and
rotten. Every time I think about being trapped, I smell it. Feels like
I'll never cough it all up."

The silence after he said it was profound and painful, and Wolfe
dragged in a breath and then shook his head without speaking.

Santi opened the window, and a blast of pure, cold air rushed into
the room. It felt . . . clean. He turned and looked at Wolfe and said,
"I'm sorry. I didn't understand."

Wolfe managed a sick little laugh. "No. Neither did I. The things we think we put behind us . . ." He gazed down at his feet. "We don't ever put it behind us. I should know that by now. I never meant to take it out on you, Nic. I'm sorry."

Santi walked over to stand facing him and held out his hand. Without looking up, Wolfe took it.

"This isn't a time to make choices, sir. We'll make bad ones," Jess said, which was three-quarters of a lie; he was making choices, wasn't he? But he needed to keep Wolfe and Santi from anything more . . . aggressive.

"You're likely right," Wolfe said. "You'll be working with Thomas on the press, I presume?"

"I will."

"Then you need to pay attention for the same from him. Thomas has exceeded what anyone could have thought he could do. But . . . I know how the Library's cells can break a person, and sometimes they don't even know they're broken. Anger is as poisonous as arsenic, and it rots you from the bones out." He looked up at Jess, and it felt like the old days, like being pinned under the Scholar's gaze like a butterfly to a board. "If he falls, you must be the one to catch him."

Santi, Jess noticed, was standing close to Wolfe, standing as if *he* expected to have to catch his lover. The press was pure tragedy for Wolfe; it was the physical expression of an idea that had destroyed his life and sentenced him to unimaginable pain. The symbol of all his hopes and dreams, and all his despair, too. And now Jess could hear the echoes of it in his voice.

"I'm all right, Nic," Wolfe said, and finally looked at him. "We walked through the dungeons under Rome, survived Philadelphia, and this perfumed cage won't bring us to our knees. We're all stronger than that."

"All right," Santi said. "But don't ask me to stop standing next to you. Because you know I will, however much you shout about it."

"I know." For the first time, Wolfe smiled. It was such a kind, unguarded sort of thing, it didn't seem to fit on him. "That's what makes me live when the alternative seems so peaceful."

Without answering, Santi placed a quiet kiss on his lover's lips. It began quietly, at least. They'd never been prone to public displays, but *that* kiss . . . that was more intimate than most Jess had seen, and clearly, neither cared who was watching.

Santi laughed softly when it ended and said, a little regretfully, "Now, that's a proper hello. Haven't had one for a while. And you haven't talked to me about Philadelphia."

"True for you, too."

"I'm a soldier."

"That just means you hide it better, not that it didn't leave marks on you."

The two of them weren't paying Jess any mind now, and he wasn't wanted here, or needed. He silently turned to go.

"Jess." The two men were still close, still with their arms around each other, but Wolfe had turned to look at him. No rage in those dark eyes now. Just something like concern. "You'll stop tasting that smoke. You never leave it behind you, but even that fades with distance. Even that. All right?"

Jess nodded and kept walking. He was swinging the door shut when he said, "Make sure you lock the door. I don't trust my father any more than you do."

He waited until he heard the *thunk* of the lock being turned, and then leaned against the wood, heaved a great sigh, and wished he could push away the plan that was forming in his head. Because it was starting to come clear to him exactly what his father had planned for them, and why his brother still wasn't being honest about the whole of it.

And it was horribly clear that the wild idea that had come to him at dinner, watching his brother, represented the best chance any of them would ever have to accomplish the impossible . . . but it would cost them dearly.

It would cost him *everything*. But if he was right . . . it had to be done.

EPHEMERA

Text of a letter from Callimachus, first Archivist of the Great Library, near the end of his service. Interdicted from the Codex to the personal records of the Archivists.

I look back on this road we have together paved, stone by stone. I have served my pharaoh faithfully, but my gods more faithfully still, and the Library itself most of all. I have put it ahead of my own happiness, my own achievement. This is not a sorrow for me, and here is where I depart from this road, into the setting sun.

But I warn you, my successors: even now, in such a short space as my single lifetime, I come to understand that knowledge is like any other treasure: it can be hoarded. It can be stolen. It can be scattered to the winds. And worst of all, it can inspire greed of a particularly poisonous kind.

For who am I to say who should know a thing? Who am I to say to you, a farmer, that you may not read of a mason's work, or to you, a mason, that you may not read of a priest's duties? Who am I to say this is too dangerous, and that is not? Some say that women should not read, for they may be led astray into impurity, as if our women are not fit guardians of their own worthiness. Some of my fellow Scholars, to my eternal shame, say those of different skins and faces and nations are too backward to learn, and when that false belief is proven wrong, they claim such examples as prodigies, as exemptions, instead of realizing their own grave errors of evil pride.

It is a terrible arrogance to think that there are any of humankind who are better or worse, or worthy or not. It comes of a pitiful need to believe in one's own worth when one is hollow within. We are all worthy. And none of us are, all at once. Once that is acknowledged, that hollow, howling space may be filled with understanding.

But so many cling to their emptiness, and I fear that they may yet prevail.

I worry, you who come after me, that we will stray from this barely begun path of truth, and instead set our stones toward . . . more. More wealth. More power. More authority. Away from a path up, and toward one that seems easier, and leads down.

Never forget that we, too, are mortal. And the greed that the Library has already felt to possess, to control, to judge . . . and if it continues, all will end in fire.

CHAPTER TEN

H e couldn't sleep.

Jess prowled the halls of the castle, which were mostly deserted; he ached and felt a terrible drag of weariness, but the bed held no real comfort for him. Neither did dreams, because he knew, without question, that they would turn to nightmares.

When he tapped quietly on Morgan's door, he heard nothing from within, but her door wasn't locked, and after hesitating only a few breaths, he eased in, closed the door, and whispered her name.

She touched a glow beside the bed, and the warmth of it spread over her, shimmering in her skin, her eyes, the fall of her tousled hair. It took him a second to realize that she was fully dressed, still. Wearing the same thing she'd worn down to dinner.

"Can't sleep," Jess said. "You?"

She sat up and shook her head. "I keep waiting—waiting for something. The moment I close my eyes, it's there. Coming in the dark."

It perfectly described his restlessness. "Walk with me?"

She nodded and slipped off the bed. *Stupid,* he shouted at himself, because he wanted to be in that bed with her, the way that Wolfe and Santi were no doubt already in theirs, and put everything else away for a time. But it wasn't right now. He could feel it.

It was freezing outside, and Jess fetched coats and blankets. The drawbridge was up. There was little inside the walls except the smooth, paved courtyard, but they walked down the steps into the cold, heavy moonlight.

"There," Morgan said, and pointed. To the south side of the fortress wall, part of the grounds had been tamed into a garden. Hedges and an arched iron gate, and beyond that, a beautiful little oasis. A fountain bubbled softly, though the water ran thick, on the verge of icing over as it dribbled from the edge into a bowl below. The cold had already stripped the trees bare, but the hedges were still full, with sharp, waxed leaves. A few winter-blooming flowers struggled on. The grass had gone a pale yellow.

And it was still oddly peaceful.

Jess spread the blanket, and they sat on it, with another wrapping the two of them together. Cold, clean air cut hard into his lungs and plumed out as he exhaled, and somehow, Jess imagined that vapor was cleansing him of everything still left of toxins and terrors. They looked up at the stars in silence for a few moments. Then Jess turned his head and saw her watching him.

"Can it stay like this?" she asked. "Just like this?"

He leaned close and kissed her. Gently this time, but a kiss that lingered. Her lips were cold, but so soft. "I wish it could."

She took his hand in hers and held it to her cheek—his fingers warm, her face chilled. Contrasts with her, as always. "It's beautiful here, you know."

"It's nearly winter."

"No, really. Look." Her grip on his hand tightened, and he felt something strange twinge inside him, almost a pain, and then his head began to ache as well . . .

And he *saw*. Exactly what he was seeing was hard to fathom; the world around him took on form and space, colors, shifting lines. None of it made sense, but all of it had a shimmering, breathtaking, living sort of beauty. He watched the leaves of a hedge across from them blur and shake and shift colors, saw the sap rising red through the trunk and branches, saw the *life* of it, muted by the cold . . . and then the pain in his head took on the sharp edge of an axe cleaving his skull, and he cried out and closed his eyes.

Suddenly, it was all gone. The headache drained away like water from a broken glass. Morgan's hands touched his forehead, smoothed the last of the pain away, and she whispered, "I'm sorry, I didn't know that would hurt you."

"Is that—" He could barely speak, and his throat felt strangely dry. "Was that what you see? What Obscurists see?"

"I have a gift for it; at least Wolfe's mother said I did. The colors you see, that's the quintessence, the element of life. It exists in everything, living or not. The difference between living things and non-living things . . . it's smaller than you might think. It's only a matter of . . . activation. Or removal. We are all made of the same eternal material."

"Did they ever teach you this in the Iron Tower?"

"No. They taught us just the opposite, but as usual, they lied. Layers and ages of lies, until nobody recognized the truth anymore. They warned us we'd all go mad, we'd become Gilles de Rais if we questioned their rules, but it isn't true. Quintessence isn't good. It isn't evil. It's just a force, like fire. And they never intended us to really use it for what it was." She hesitated a moment. "I need to show you. Come with me."

He followed her to a stone bench under the tree. He sat, but she didn't.

"Stay there. No matter what. Understand?"

"Why? Morgan, what are you doing?"

"You remember the fields?"

The memory grabbed him deep. The smell of dying things, rotten crops. The despair and anger of the people. "That was a mistake," he said. "You're better now."

"It was a mistake then. I spent my time on the ship learning. I won't hurt anyone by accident anymore." She walked to the center of the clearing. "Stay there, Jess. It's important."

Morgan held out her hands. There didn't seem to be any effect at first, and then he saw a mouse creep from the shadows. It was a field mouse, a small one, and it hesitantly made its way across the dried grass toward her. It stopped a few feet away and rose on its hind legs, nose twitching.

A larger movement. A rabbit, hopping out into the clear space and stopping around the same distance. Then another mouse.

"That's enough," Morgan whispered. "Forgive me."

Suddenly, the mouse on its hind legs twitched, rolled, spasmed, and fell flat on the grass. It went still. Jess shot to his feet, heart pounding, and he didn't know where to run—toward her. Away. He only knew that there was something powerful and dark happening in front of him.

"Jess, stop! Stay there!" Morgan's urgency froze him in place, and the rabbit slumped and rolled over. It shivered and went limp. Then the other mouse. Something plummeted out of the air above her: a night-flying bird, graceless as it landed broken on the grass.

Dead.

Insects were not exempt, either. Beetles struggled to the surface and died. Worms thrashed and went still. He could see the glimmer of tiny bodies like jewels thrown across the grass.

Morgan opened her eyes and breathed in sharply. Her eyes seemed flat and lifeless for a moment. He didn't dare move, and she didn't speak. It was only when he saw a moth flap past her, unharmed, that he rushed forward past the invisible boundary in which the dead things lay.

He grabbed her. She felt solid and rigid, like a statue. Cold. "Morgan? What did you do? *Morgan!*"

"I'm here," she whispered, and blinked. Some life came back into those eyes, but not nearly enough to settle his fears. "Here." She suddenly sagged, and he had to catch her. "Now you see." She took a deep breath.

His own throat felt tight, his stomach roiling. "For Heron's sake, Morgan—what—what *is this*?" He already knew, but he needed her to explain it in a way that made sense to him.

"Practice. I started small," she said. "Flies. Spiders. A sparrow. A mouse. Rats. The rabbit . . ." She swallowed and blinked, and tears welled in her eyes. "The rabbit was the largest I've done so far. Oh, Jess. I felt how afraid it was . . . but he didn't feel pain. None of them do; I make sure of that. But anything near me, in that circle . . . even the grass . . . I took the life from it. Just as easily as dousing a candle. I used it to make myself stronger."

He held her closer, though he had no real comfort for her. What she'd just said dried up his mouth and locked any capacity to speak. He just held her as she shivered and wept, in a circle of dead things.

Finally, he asked, "How long have you been at this?"

"Since we boarded the ship," she said. "Doctor Askuwheteau told me it was a corruption of my ability, that once I healed, once I rested, it would go away. But it didn't. I killed a fly that had gotten in the cabin on the ship—I saw the spark of it, and . . . I turned it off. It was gone before it fell out of the air. Then a rat I found creeping in the corner. After that, I was afraid—I was afraid to touch anyone. Afraid I couldn't control it, but the more time I spent out looking at the water, *seeing* the life out there, taking bits of it . . . the more I knew I could control it. And that was actually more frightening. This *isn't* a corruption. It's a talent, and we'll need it. Dr. Askuwheteau's a good man. I don't think he would ever understand what I'm saying."

What she was saying, Jess thought, was that she was not as good. And maybe she was right. Maybe a lifetime of fear, of hiding, of knowing her future held slavery . . . maybe being wholly good was something that had never been in her, any more than it was in him.

It was a hard truth that right now, they didn't need to be purely good. They needed to be capable of *anything*.

Her hands fisted in his shirt, as if she never wanted to let him go. "Say something," she said. "Please."

"Morgan—" He rested his cheek against her hair and ran a soothing hand down her back. "It's all right."

"Do I frighten you?"

"No," he said. He wanted to believe that. Morgan was *Morgan*. Fearing what she could do was as bad as fearing what Santi could do with a gun. What Thomas could invent in his workshop.

Fear turned minds, and he would *not* be afraid of Morgan.

But he was now afraid, *very* afraid, that he knew exactly how best to use her.

By the time he finally found his bed, it was well on toward morning, and the thick, soft mattress let him doze, but not really rest. Between the High Garda, the deprivations of running from the Library, and a prison house in Philadelphia, his body had grown used to hard, lumpy beds and—as he discovered when he lacked appetite for the rich breakfast—unaccustomed to the greasy sausages and eggs that his family preferred. Buttered toast seemed like an indulgence, but he allowed himself that much, along with coffee that seemed weak, after Alexandria's.

Strange, he'd been away from home for such a short time and had changed so much. Like Morgan, he'd grown into something new. He had no idea if it was something better, but he knew one thing: this Jess Brightwell was far, far stronger than the green, innocent one who'd boarded a train to the Great Library, hoping to find his place.

"Good night, elder brother?" Brendan clapped him on the shoulder and squeezed, then left off when Jess didn't wince. "The guards saw you go out into the garden with your girl last night. Must have been freezing out there, but I suppose you found a way to keep warm."

Morgan wasn't here, but Glain was, and she missed absolutely nothing from where she sat contemplating a single poached egg and toast. Apart from her, the dining room was deserted, save for a servant putting more hot sausages in the warming tray, and so Jess put his plate down, met Glain's eyes, and then turned and grabbed Brendan hard by both arms. He shoved him up against the fine wood paneling and pressed very close, close enough that Brendan couldn't miss the seriousness in his eyes.

"Enough," he said. "Taunt me about anything else. Not her. Understand?"

Brendan lost his cocky edge, and there was a flare of anger in his face, quickly damped. He nodded. "Maybe I'm just out of sorts, you having got a girl to comfort you, and me having nothing but mocking you for it," he finally said. "You remember what I left behind in Alexandria, don't you?"

Jess *had* forgotten, but Brendan had spent months there, wooing a young woman who worked for the Archivist . . . a lovely, intelligent woman whom he'd professed not to care about. But there was something he recognized, twin to twin: heartbreak. When his brother had left Alexandria, he'd left his chance of happiness behind, too.

"When all this is over, go and find her," Jess said. "I imagine she'll forgive you. Everyone does, for some insane reason."

"Even you?"

"Even me, Scraps." Jess patted him on the cheek, none too gently; it was half a slap, and then a scuffle when Brendan retaliated, and soon he had his slightly younger twin in a headlock. He marched him to the breakfast room door and sent him packing with a boot in his ass, and when he turned back, he saw Glain still placidly eating her egg.

"Brothers," she said, and shook her head. He grinned and slid into the seat across from her with his toast and coffee. "Unbearable creatures. Though at least mine were straightforward. It must be close to hell, having one nearly as clever as you. Like watching an angel struggle with a demon."

"I'm no angel."

"I didn't say which of you was which, did I? Shut up and eat, Brightwell."

"You seem uncommonly cheery."

"I'm not. All this"—Glain gestured at the hall, the tapestries, everything—"makes me itch. How long before you and Thomas have that press built and working?"

"We'll start today," he said.

"Good. Because I don't half trust all this. Or you."

Jess sat back and stared at her, because he hadn't expected that. It was blunt, and utterly serious. "Why?"

"I can see you thinking. And I know that look, Jess. It's not a good thing. You and Dario, whispering together—that isn't good, either."

Jess ate his toast and tasted none of it. She was waiting for an answer. He didn't have one to give.

Glain didn't take that well. She stood up, pushed her plate away, and came to loom over him, one hand on the back of his chair, one pressed flat against the table. "Don't," she said. "Don't lock me out. You *can't trust Dario*."

"I don't," he said. "I don't trust anyone." He sat back and looked up into her face. He could see the look that came into her eyes. "Disappointed?"

"Angry." She almost growled the word. "Furious that after everything we've been through, you're this *stupid*. And you're not doing this."

"No?" It hurt, looking into her eyes this way. Seeing everything he liked about her. Everything he knew wasn't going to agree with him. "What exactly am I doing, Glain?"

"I'll be watching you," she said. Her voice had gone low and calm, and it reminded him of how Santi got still and strangely happy when things were the worst. "And if it comes to it, I'll break your bones to convince you not to be ridiculous. Because that's how much I like you, Jess: I'll hurt you to save you. Count on it."

She shoved his chair forward, bruisingly hard, and then she was gone, abandoning her breakfast to stride out with hard thuds of boots against wood. Jess pushed himself back from the table, rubbed his sore ribs, and finished his toast.

He'd hoped that it wouldn't come to this, but he wasn't much surprised. Glain was observant and decisive, and he was going to have to take that into account. She expected no better from him, though she hoped for it.

The only one he was absolutely certain he could fool, when it came down to it, was Khalila, and only because of all of them, she was the one who trusted without reservations. He remembered her in the cell in Philadelphia, claiming them as family. For her, trust, once given, was unbreakable without real proof of betrayal.

He wished he didn't have to break that trust so completely.

But you must. So let it begin.

He drained his coffee and went in search of Thomas.

The workshop they'd been given was set up in the vast old carriage house, where a blacksmith's forge had been replaced with a more modern furnace, something capable of producing high-tempered metals. Jess found his friend hard at work already, which didn't surprise him at all.

"How long have you been up, if you've chopped down half the forest?" Jess asked as Thomas swung the furnace door closed with a heavy *clang* and spun the wheel to dog it shut. He was already sweating in the cool air, and the light shirt he wore clung to him; he wiped his forehead and gave Jess a full, unhindered smile.

"Long enough to tell you hardly had enough sleep at all," he said. "Here. Your father had a gift for us. Look."

In the place where the horses, in older days, would have been stabled, the area had been cleared to a large open space, and along one wall a long trestle table held a row of wooden crates. Jess grabbed a pry bar and opened the first one, uncovering a supply of small, finely made gears. The next box held larger ones, and the next still larger. Another box held bars of lead, for casting movable letters. Jess checked off each one against the list in his memory. There was nothing lacking. His father had given them everything they needed, even strong oak boards to build the frame. How he'd done it in the space of less than a day was something Jess didn't care to think about.

He watched Thomas pick up gears, fit them together, run admiring hands over the fine craftsmanship like a miser who'd found a cache of gold. "Perfect," Thomas murmured. "Well. To start, anyway. Nothing is ever quite perfect once you start to build, yes? And we'll need a good watch. As small a one as you can find. Can you get one?"

"A clock? Why?"

"Because I have something to repair," Thomas said. "Go find one. Two watches would be even better. And ask Captain Santi for as many extra power capsules as he can spare from his weapons."

"You want me to run errands."

"Well. Someone has to. And I can be at work, constructing—" Thomas suddenly fell silent, looking past Jess. When he spoke again, his voice had changed. Gone quiet. "Scholar Wolfe."

"Schreiber," Wolfe said. He stood in the doorway of the workshop, looking at them in a distant kind of way that Jess found unsettling. The Scholar had left off his robe today and wore plain clothes, suitable for work, just as Thomas and Jess wore. "I was thinking that I might help you."

"I—" Thomas glanced at Jess. "Of course, sir. If you wish."

Wolfe nodded and moved to look over the boxes. The gears. Ran his fingers over a board, testing its straightness. "I need something to do," he said. "You understand. Rooms grow small. Silence gets heavy."

Thomas nodded slowly. "I know. And you are welcome here. You created this, too."

"My version was crude. You improved on it," Wolfe said. "But I'm not unskilled. Between us, I think we might do very well."

"Yes," Thomas said. "I would be glad of your assistance and knowledge."

"Don't butter me, Schreiber; I'm not a piece of bread. You're a rare kind of genius. I'm not your equal and never will be in this particular area. Tell me what to do. Show me plans. I'll do the rest, without complaint."

It was a new idea, thinking of Wolfe as someone who *wasn't* in charge. But as Jess watched him pick up a thick leather apron and put it on, he found himself smiling. It didn't altogether lift the heavy cold inside him, but for a moment, for this moment, he saw the delight in Thomas's expression, the answering spark in Wolfe's eyes, and warmed just a fraction.

"Then, here," Thomas said, and unrolled a huge drawing over the trestle table, while Jess and Wolfe shifted boxes to make room. "Get started. And you." He leveled a finger as Jess put his heavy box on the floor. "Go and find me those parts."

Jess saluted crisply. "Yes, sir."

He'd already been forgotten by the time he reached the door, and when he looked back, Wolfe and Schreiber were bent together, pointing and talking and already starting to make notes on the paper.

Scholars, doing what Scholars did.

Jess wasn't a Scholar and realized that he'd accepted somewhere along the line that it wasn't what he really was suited to, after all. So he went to do what thieves did.

He went to acquire what was needed—and not necessarily ask permission.

When he arrived back with two clocks and a couple of pocket watches he knew wouldn't be missed, Thomas and Wolfe had already constructed the frame of the machine. Wolfe was working with a grinder that spat huge red sparks across a stone wall, and he didn't stop for Jess's arrival.

"Watch your step," Thomas called out to Jess without looking up from his work. "No, no, little Frauke, friend Jess is allowed. You may let him be."

Jess almost dropped the loot when he realized that one of the shadows behind Thomas was *moving*. It was nearly invisible where it crouched, but as he watched, he saw the outlines of it. "Thomas," he said. "You built an automaton? *When?*"

. "I didn't build it. Anit sent one along for me. To keep me company. And, I think, to keep us safe." Thomas seemed distracted but amused. He nailed a crossbar together with a single fast blow of his hammer and sat back on his haunches. "Beautiful, isn't she?"

It was one of the camouflage automata from America, and as Jess watched, it stretched, yawned to show bright, sharp metal teeth, and stretched out in a lazy sprawl by the furnace. It hadn't stopped watching him. "I thought you named the one we had in Rome *Frauke*."

"I did."

"And that one was male."

"No, it was a machine. She is a machine. I may call them as I like. And her name is still Frauke. Did you get the watches?"

Jess put the clocks down and pulled the watches from his coat, and Thomas stopped what he was doing to open the backs and examine the works.

"Yes," he said. "Yes, this is exactly what I need. Good quality. Thank you." He stood back and stared down at the clocks with his big hands stuffed in the pockets of his trousers. "I never expected to have to make anything but things of peace, you know. Things to better the lives of others. But that is not what I am doing, is it? Even this, the press . . . it's a weapon of war. A different kind of war, perhaps, but people will die for it. They already have."

That was a hard thing to acknowledge. Jess changed the subject. "What did you want the clocks and watches for?"

"I'm building another Ray of Apollo," he said. "And a few other things that require delicate parts. If I have enough time, I might repair Morgan's bird for her. I know she prized it." Thomas put the watches on the workbench. "Take those apart. Sort the parts into sizes. That should keep you too busy to frown at me. You are frowning at me, aren't you?"

"No," Jess lied. He was, of course. "You don't want me working on the press?"

"The press is the least of what we need to do. With these tools, with Wolfe's help, with a little time . . . I think we can do a great deal. And we'll need to, if we're planning to take on the Archivist. We need a different kind of genius to do that, I think."

That sounded eerily like things that were taking shape in Jess's head. He thought he could fool Thomas, with a little work. A little luck. But he wasn't sure.

So instead of trying, he sat down, took the set of delicate tools that Thomas set out, and began dismantling watches. "So is there anything else you might need?" he asked, slipping on magnifying glasses to better navigate the inner workings.

"Yes, when you have time," Thomas said. "I don't suppose your mother would part willingly with the three largest of her gemstones?" He drove home four more nails with sharp, perfectly aimed blows.

Jess unscrewed a gear from the watch assembly, picked it free with tweezers, and put it aside. "Let's just say that it's a good thing you have a thief for a best friend."

Stealing from his mother was a line Jess found himself unwilling to cross. He wouldn't have thought himself capable of such squeamishness, but he finally had to admit, after arguing with his worse angels for a few hours while breaking down the clocks and watches, that he didn't want to do it. Not alone.

So he asked Dario.

"No!" Dario exclaimed, far too loudly. "Who do you think I am, scrubber?"

Jess had brought him to the old library at the farthest end of the castle from his parents' quarters, and he'd hoped to find it deserted. He hadn't quite succeeded there, because Khalila was curled up on the lush old divan, book in her hands, and of course she'd heard that indignant outburst and looked up, and there was no use in pretending otherwise.

"I thought you were someone who might be able to exercise some discretion, but I see I was wrong," Jess shot back. "Never mind."

"No, just a minute, what is it you want me to, ah . . ."

"Steal," Khalila supplied. She set her book aside, stood, and came toward them. "Oh, don't bother—I heard it quite clearly, and I know you're aware of the word. For all your protests, you're probably the second-best thief in our circle; don't pretend otherwise for my benefit. So what exactly is it you wish for us to steal?"

"Us?" Dario said, at the same time Jess blurted out, *"You?"* They were, in that moment, identically shocked.

Her eyebrows formed perfect little arcs to frame the amusement in her gaze. "I admit I don't have much experience, but it seems to me that I could help. Somehow."

"You," Dario said, "have been around our pale little smuggler far too long. What would your father say about—" He caught himself, but too late, and Jess saw the amusement drain out of Khalila's expression, and her light turn to ashes. Dario reached out and took her hand and, in a very genuine motion of apology, pressed it to his lips. "Forgive me, my rose. I wasn't thinking."

"No more than I was," she said, and swallowed, and raised her chin as she reclaimed her hand. "From the cell where my father sits now, I imagine he would understand the necessity of doing whatever must be done. What are we stealing, then?"

She put him to shame, Jess thought; he was wincing like a child at the thought of losing his mother's affection, and Khalila was enduring so much worse, and still willing to go on. "My mother has a walnut jewel box in her room. Last I remember, she had a very large ruby in a necklace, an equally large emerald, and a diamond pendant big enough to choke on. Those are the three I'll need."

"From your mother?" She seemed less comfortable with that. "But—"

"It's only three pieces," he assured her. "And believe me, she has more. Many more."

"I'm happy enough to do it," Dario said. "I think your whole family should be behind bars, but as they're not, I'm happy to lift from the pockets of your father."

Khalila gave him an exasperated glance. "It's his *mother*!"

"And I very much doubt Jess's father allows her to own anything outright. I know the type; he's very much like my own father. Except my father is an arrogant, blue-blooded noble, of course, and not some jumped-up housebreaker."

"Is this you trying to say we're friends?" Jess asked. "Because I wonder how you think that sounds."

Khalila put a finger to Dario's lips to shush his reply. "Stealing is wrong, of course. A sin. And your mother has been quite kind to me," Khalila said, and then took in a deep breath, as if ready to plunge into deep waters. "But I'll take care of keeping her occupied in conversation. You and Dario can, I hope, carry off this daring adventure by yourselves?"

"Of course," Dario said instantly.

"If he doesn't arse it up," Jess said at the same time, and almost laughed at the glare Dario gave him. That was vintage, straight out of the Ptolemy House, in their more innocent postulant days. "We'll meet after lunch. Once Khalila draws my mother off, we'll do this quickly. Right?"

"Right," Dario said.

"Wrong." They all turned. Wolfe stood in the doorway. He was sweaty and disheveled, straight from the workshop. "I was on my way to clean up for lunch. I met your mother in the halls."

He pitched something toward them. Jess effortlessly caught it out of the air with sheer reflex before Dario even raised a hand to intercept. When he opened his palm, he was looking at a leather pouch, snugged tight with a drawstring. Jess opened it and spilled out three loose stones: two diamonds the size of pigeon eggs, and a ruby as dark as claret that blazed bright in a stray ray of sun. He looked up at the Scholar, not quite sure how to even phrase the question.

"I overheard Thomas asking you for these. Not everything needs to be a crime," Wolfe said. "As Khalila said, your mother's been kind enough. I don't know what troubles you have in your household, but one thing I do know: mothers love their sons, however flawed that love might be. And a few gems is a small price to pay."

"She *gave* them to you."

He shrugged. "She'd have given them to you, if you'd asked. But I knew you wouldn't."

Jess felt a wave of shame so strong he nearly gagged on it, and felt his face go hot, then cold, as a flush took hold and receded. He clenched the stones so hard in his fist that they cut. When he tipped them back into the pouch and tossed everything to Wolfe, his blood was still on them. "She gave these to you for reasons you don't understand," he said. "And it isn't out of generosity. Don't presume to know my family. *Sir.*"

Wolfe caught the pouch without even looking at it. Nimble and focused. "I know you," he said. "Don't forget that, Jess. It might save you, in the end."

Khalila and Dario were watching in silence, and it continued while

Wolfe walked away, leaving Jess with that flush again rising in his face and a nasty feeling in the pit of his stomach. *My mother doesn't just give things. He's wrong.*

"Are you all right?" Khalila asked him. "Jess?"

"Fine," he said, and smiled at her. Offered her his elbow. "May I have the honor of escorting you to lunch, desert flower?"

"That," Dario said, "is *not* fair."

Khalila slipped her arm into Jess's. "The honor is mine, dear thief. But only because you didn't actually have to steal."

As they walked away, Dario followed and muttered, "I didn't steal anything, either, you know."

"I know," Khalila said. "And now you won't."

"Is it finished?"

Glain leaned over Thomas's shoulder to stare at the small, elegant-looking weapon that lay on the workbench, under the merciless glare of a light almost as bright as the sun. Jess stared, too. He'd been watching the thing come together for three days now, piece by carefully crafted piece. Thomas had cut the three stones into shapes his mother would never have recognized—taking away any flaws, he'd told Jess, who'd winced at seeing so much smashed away—and built the rest of it around those three focal points.

The casing was made of walnut and brass, and now that it was all completed, the weapon looked to Jess's eyes much like a country squire's version of a High Garda rifle. It was a bit longer and thinner, and altogether simpler. There was a sight, and a trigger to pull, and a small knob to adjust. That was all.

It wasn't the same as what Thomas had built in Philadelphia, but there were undeniable similarities to it. And refinements. This had the fatal elegance of one of the Library's automata.

"Yes, it's done," Thomas said, and took off the magnifying spectacles he'd been wearing. He put them on the trestle table, stood up, and stretched. "Just now done."

"You haven't tested it yet?" Glain asked, looking the thing over. He shook his head. "Want to do it now?" Thomas gave her a strange smile and quirked his shoulders, and she smiled in return. "You're afraid it won't work."

"It will work."

"I'd rather not stake my life, no matter how bright you are, you great cabbage. We're not playing games anymore, you know."

Something dark flitted through Thomas's eyes as he cut them toward the Welsh girl. "I should know if anyone does," he said. "Step back, please. I don't like to be crowded."

Glain did, immediately. A generous step, at that. "We still should test it," she said. "Jess? Don't you agree? An untested weapon is no kind of weapon at all."

"May we not take a moment to admire what it is that he's done?" Khalila stood on the other side of the table, and the light's glow made her look almost ethereally lovely as she raised her gaze to fix it on Thomas. "It's an amazing attempt, whatever happens. I don't think anyone else on earth could have built the earlier version in Philadelphia. And *this* . . . it's beautiful in itself."

"It's not a work of art," Glain said. "And even if it was, I'd still insist on seeing what it *does*."

"Same," Dario nodded. "How do we know how to use it if we don't know what it can do?"

"Morgan?" Thomas asked. Morgan sat on a chair a little apart from them, staring not at Thomas's invention but at her clasped hands. "You seem very quiet."

"It seems like a deadly thing," she said. "The one you made in Philadelphia, you made to set us free. This one . . . I think you made it for another purpose. Don't we have enough things meant to kill?"

Maybe no one else heard it, but Jess did: a broken emptiness in the words, a haunted quality that made him want to hold her in his arms.

"Jess?"

Now Thomas was calling *his* name, which he'd been dreading, because it meant he had to agree with Glain and Dario. "I'd rather never see it used," he said. "But . . . it's true, we should know."

"And if the stones inside fail and shatter, and we've wasted the chance?" Thomas asked. "What then?"

"My mother has other jewels." Jess managed a grin. "You don't keep me around for my wit and charm. I'll find you what you need, when you need it. Count on it."

"How . . . noisy is this likely to be?" Dario asked. "Given we're in the middle of an armed encampment."

"The peacock has a point," Glain said. "But still. You know my vote."

"If it works, there shouldn't be any sound at all," said Wolfe. He and Santi stood a little apart, together. Santi looked fascinated, and quite like he was itching to pick the thing up. "Light doesn't make sound."

Thomas put his hand on the stock of the weapon that lay on the table. He seemed to hesitate for a moment, then picked it up. It looked small in his grasp, and then he held it out to Jess with an abrupt move. "You do it," he said. "I don't think I can bear it if it breaks. Dial it to the lowest setting, aim, and fire. Keep the trigger down as long as you want the beam to burn, yes? Simple. If it works."

Jess took the gun and was surprised at the weight of it—it had looked like a toy in Thomas's hand, but this had substance. Finely balanced, though. The weapon felt heavy and hot in his sweaty hands, and he looked carefully at the dial to be sure it was turned as far down as it could go.

It was.

"No point in waiting, English, unless you're worried it'll blow your hands off," Dario said.

"Want to try it first?"

"No, by all means. Your privilege. I wouldn't dream of taking the honor."

"That's exactly what I thought." Jess was stalling, and he knew it. There was a moment of truth coming, and it frightened him, just as Morgan must have been terrified of her ability to kill so easily. It wasn't the same, but he knew that pulling this trigger would change his world, too.

But there was no way around that. The world was shifting faster than he'd ever imagined it could.

Jess silently stepped away—far enough, he hoped, that any catastrophic disaster would spare the others—and raised the weapon to his shoulder. He braced it, as if it might kick (would it?) and took aim at the far wall.

He took in a slow breath and pressed the trigger.

There was no kick. There was a hum, something that he felt more than heard, and the brass fittings of the gun went from cold to skin warm . . . but no hotter, thankfully. He actually *saw* the beam that came from the barrel of the weapon, a pure reddish line pointing straight to the wall, and then . . .

And then nothing. There was no explosion. No devastating surprise. Jess let go of the trigger and lowered the weapon slowly, staring.

"Is that it?" Dario asked. "Disappointing."

"It's glowing," Morgan said, and Jess realized she was right. Santi moved toward the wall and held his hand about two feet from it.

"It's very hot," he said, and jumped back half his body length when the wall suddenly let out a sharp, percussive sound and a crack raced from the center of the wall from top to bottom. The entire workshop structure groaned, and for an insane moment Jess wondered if he'd just dropped the roof onto their heads . . . but then nothing else happened. The glowing point in the center of the wall began to fade. There was, he realized, a black scorch mark where he'd aimed the beam, and the wall had cracked in half at exactly that spot.

"¡Joder!" Dario came rushing up and stopped with his hand feeling the heat, just like Santi had. "That was the *lowest* setting?"

"Yes," Jess said, and checked it a third time. "Lowest." He looked at Thomas, who had no particular expression on his face at all. Certainly no triumph. "What happens if it goes higher?"

"I expect it will destroy things quite easily," Thomas said. "You remember the wall, in Philadelphia?"

Hard to forget. "Yes."

"This would have burned through it in seconds, even at half power. It is much stronger. And you might notice, I have shielded the heat."

"I did notice," Jess said. The casing was cool now, not even a trace of warmth remaining.

"Do it again," Santi said. "On a higher setting."

"No. One test, Captain. We agreed." Thomas looked stern. And a little worried.

For answer, Santi walked to the end of the hall, picked up an empty wooden crate, and set it on top of the long trestle table. "That will do," he said. "Shoot it."

Jess, for answer, held out the weapon to him. Santi came back and took it, and Thomas silently shook his head, but didn't object, as Santi turned the dial up. It was, Jess saw, almost halfway.

"Niccolo," Wolfe said. "I don't think—"

"Weapons are my part of the world. Not yours." Santi put the stock to his shoulder, sighted, and fired.

The crate . . . It didn't *melt*, exactly. It . . . dissolved, in a flutter of black ash. The only sound was a kind of sinister *hiss*, like steam escaping, and as Jess went forward to look, he saw liquid metal simmering and scarring the top of the thick wooden table. *The nails,* he realized. The crate's nails had melted.

The table began to smoke where the molten metal touched, and Jess grabbed a leather apron and flung it down over the top. Black scorched patches appeared on the thick material but didn't burn through. When he cautiously moved it, he saw the metal was cooling into sharp-edged smears.

"Dios santo," Dario whispered. He sounded shaken.

"It's what Archimedes used, to burn the Roman ships at sea," Khalila said. "But stronger, and held in one hand. He called it the Forge of the Gods."

"The Romans probably called it something less flattering," Glain said. "Imagine what it would do to a human body."

Jess did, all too vividly, and his stomach clenched. He looked back at Captain Santi. The tall Italian stood there, staring at the destruction with a cold calculus. The weapon in his hands no longer seemed so beautiful.

"It's demonic," he said. "But this demon's out of hell now, and in our hands. And there's no going back from that now." He handed the weapon back to Thomas, who took it with the same solemnity. "Can you hide it? Make sure the Brightwells don't find it?" He cast a lightning-fast glance at Jess. "The other Brightwells."

"Yes," Thomas said. "Frauke will guard it for me."

"Can you make more?"

"Not like this," Thomas said. "Not without more gemstones. But smaller ones, with mirrors, yes."

"Then, do it. We may need them." Santi had stopped being their friend again and was now a High Garda commander; it was all in the way he stood, the way he looked at them. "No one talks about this. No one, for any reason. Understand?"

One by one, they nodded.

Wolfe said, "Tomorrow, we show Callum Brightwell the press."

"And then?" Thomas asked. "What will happen then?"

No one answered, but Jess had his suspicions.

And in the morning, after Callum Brightwell had been shown the miracle of Thomas's press, Jess saw the look that passed between his father and his brother, and he knew he was right.

Their usefulness to the Brightwells was fast coming to an end. It was time to make sure, as Dario had said back in Philadelphia, that they take command of the chessboard.

And that, Jess knew, meant sacrifices.

He waited until the deepest, darkest part of the night and slipped out of his room, down the long corridors. He checked Brendan's room first, but it was empty, the bed still neatly made.

He found Brendan and Anit in the one place he supposed he should have expected to find them . . . playing chess in the library where he'd last found Morgan reading. He had a vision of his girl bathed in sunlight, there in the chair, and wished with aching sincerity that he could go to her, be with her, avoid this moment forever.

But he silently walked in, sat down, and pulled up another chair.

Brendan and Anit played in silence for a few more moments. Anit took two pawns. Brendan took a rook. Then Anit froze, studied the board, and sighed. She tipped over her king. "Third time," she said. "I do not understand how you distract me. I'm very good at this."

"I'm better," Brendan said. "But Jess? Better still. Anyone outplay you these days, brother?"

"A few," Jess said. "Khalila, for one. Dario, occasionally." He glanced at Anit, then back at Brendan. Silently asking, *Are we doing this in front of her?* Brendan nodded, just a little.

Jess turned to the girl and said, "I thought you'd left."

"You knew better," she said. "Because you understand the game. You were born for it, even though you wish you were not."

"She says you remind her of her brother," Brendan said. "Ironic, because I don't, apparently. And if you're thinking what I believe you are, you're still underweight, you know."

"I know," Jess said. "But not enough to matter." He leaned forward and rested his elbows on his knees. "When will he do it?"

Anit raised her eyebrows and exchanged a quick glance with Brendan. His twin wasn't surprised. Anit was. "You told him?"

Brendan shook his head. "He was born to this, like you said. And he knows my da as well as I do. Maybe better, in some ways. He understands people in ways I don't." He began resetting the chessboard—not so much, Jess thought, to play a new game as to give his hands something to do. Restless, where Jess was suddenly and unexpectedly calm. "Da's sent out summonses to the family, those who can arrive in time. Three days. There'll be a trick pony show that you'll all be expected to attend, and then . . ." He didn't seem willing to say it. So Jess said it for him.

"Then the guards move in. My friends are taken prisoner, and Da ransoms them off. Some—Thomas, Wolfe, and Santi, at a guess—he's selling off to Red Ibrahim, who'll use them as bargaining chips with the Archivist. That's why Anit is still here."

Neither of the other two said anything. Jess caught the slight hitch in his brother's movements in placing the rook, and then the knight.

"Almost correct," Anit said. "I'm to take Khalila, Thomas, and Santi. Dario, your father plans to ransom back to Spain; he wants to build goodwill with the queen."

"And Morgan?" Jess asked. He sounded calm, as if it were all of academic interest. It wasn't. "Scholar Wolfe? Glain?"

"Glain has no use to anyone," Brendan said. "I convinced Da to offer her a post with us. She won't take it—I know that—but I had to try."

"And when she doesn't accept?" For answer, Brendan tipped the knight over. "Does Da really believe I'll ever forgive him for any of this? *Ever?*"

"No, not really. But he'll keep you locked up until it's over. He thinks that once they're all gone, once the thing's settled, you'll—and I'm quoting him, you understand, so don't take a fist to me—you'll come to your senses."

"He's the one who's out of his mind. And you haven't told me about Morgan and Wolfe. What's he planning to do with them?"

Brendan set the knight upright again and finished putting the rest of the pieces on the board. He was playing black, Jess realized. Somehow, he wasn't at all surprised that his brother had let Anit have the advantage.

"This is where it gets interesting," Brendan said, and sat back to look directly at Jess. "I'm taking them to Alexandria, the two most valuable prizes, as a gesture of good faith directly to the Archivist. We're making a deal to sell ten thousand original volumes to him at an extortionate price. They're the sweetener."

"Why?" The question tore out of him, bloody and raw. He meant *why* to everything . . . *why* was he born into this family, *why* would his father betray him so badly. His brother.

Brendan deliberately mistook the meaning of it. "Because these are ten thousand obscure texts no one is going to want anyway, and it buys us time to print up the real treasures with your miracle machine. Once we start selling those, we'll need the warehouse space to store our profits. And it keeps the Archivist pointed away from us, until we're ready."

"I mean, why is he sending you, you idiot. You're his *heir.*" That was half a lie, but Jess knew the rest of it had no answers. Or rather, the answers had always been right in front of him.

"No," Brendan replied quietly. "*You* are his heir. His firstborn. I'm just his manager. His assistant. His bullyboy he sends in to solve a problem. You're the one he's always wanted. And now he can have you, because sooner or later, the lure of those books coming off the press will draw you. We both know that. *That's* the business you're inheriting."

It struck Jess with a sick little thrust that Brendan was saying that he was being sent to negotiate with the Archivist because *it didn't matter if he lived to return.* The old saying he'd once heard his father say, so jovially, came back in a rush. *I still have an heir and a spare.* And the other men around him had laughed.

Brendan was the spare.

Anit silently got up from her seat and offered it to Jess. He hardly knew what he was doing when he sat down across from his brother and began to move the pieces. Playing from instinct, and with foreknowledge of what his brother liked to do.

He won in six moves.

"You need to eat hearty," Brendan said as he tipped his black king forward on its face. He looked up, and their gazes locked, and Jess, on impulse, extended his hand. They were, on occasion, capable of this kind of communication, silent and instinctive; for all they were different, they were made of the same body, two halves of the whole. And Brendan knew exactly what he intended to do. Maybe he had from the beginning.

His brother took his hand and shook. They both stood and embraced. Jess understood precisely what Brendan had just said. He understood the magnitude of the sacrifice.

Anit looked from one of them to the other, mystified by the fact that they were both smiling. "What? What are you going to do?"

"Nothing," Jess said. "We're going to do nothing at all. It's the only way to win."

When he left them, Anit had departed for her ship, and Brendan had stretched out on the divan and fallen soundly, immediately asleep—a skill Jess had once had and wished he could recapture. *I have to sleep,* he thought. His body had a weight and drag and ache to it that only rest could cure, but there was so much to think of, and so much to dread.

He slipped into his room and locked the door behind him and was stripping off his shirt in the dark when he heard a small rustle of cloth and froze. He reached for a knife he'd concealed in his boot, and for the control of the glow by the door, and was already moving forward to engage the enemy when the light's glow rose like false dawn and spread over the young woman lying asleep in his bed.

He stopped, staring at her. Knife still in his hand. Mind gone entirely still, for the first time in what felt like an age. She had that effect on him, he realized; she created silence in the noise. Peace in the storm.

He put the knife down on the bed table with a soft *clink,* and her eyes opened. Morgan sat up and brushed her hair from her face. She was, he noticed, wearing a soft nightgown, something that showed the blush of her skin underneath it, and he had to drag his gaze away from that, back to her face. And the smile—warm, sleepy, welcoming . . . and then changing into something else as she came fully awake.

He sank down wearily on the edge of the bed, watching her.

"You've been waiting here," he said. She nodded without saying anything at all. "I'm sorry."

She studied him so closely that he felt strangely uncomfortable, as if her power allowed her to reach too far into him. Maybe it did, because she said, "I'm not a fool. You and Dario, you've been whispering together for days. You and your brother, too. Every day, I see the shadows get stronger in you. What are you *doing*?"

"Is that why you're here?"

She put the back of her hand to his cheek, and he held it there as he closed his eyes. Soft and warm. "No, you fool, that's not why I'm here, but maybe it's why I ought to be here. Where were you?"

He shook his head. *I have two more days before I need to tell her,* he thought. *Two more days of her seeing me this way, as the Jess she likes.* But that would require lying to her in a way he didn't think he could do. Not anymore. He moved her hand away from his face and captured it in both his hands. Rough hands, hard used lately in the workshop.

"My father's selling you and Wolfe to the Archivist," he told her, and watched the fragile peace in her break like dropped glass. "He's got some way to send you there. That's not all; he's planning on selling the rest off to Red Ibrahim, so our business partners can use them for leverage inside Alexandria, to save their own operations. Khalila's family is going to be executed in twenty-one days. It's all falling apart, Morgan."

Saying it out loud felt like relief, but it was just transferring the burden, not getting rid of it; he saw the shock in her, the anguish, then the resolution. "All right," she said, and the grip of her fingers on his was almost painful in its strength. "Then we fight. I can do that, Jess, I can—"

"You don't understand. We *can't* fight. My father's ready for that, and we've nowhere to go. No friends. No allies to magically swoop in to our rescue."

"What—what are you saying?" Morgan's voice had gone soft now, and unsteady. "We can't *give up*."

"You don't fight a battle you can't win," he said. He didn't sound strong now, either. But he did sound certain. "You take a loss to set your pieces where you need them. The Archivist won't hurt you, Morgan. He wants you in the Tower. And—we need you there, too. If we're going to get to him at all, in Alexandria, it can't be done if he still controls the Obscurists."

She took in a sharp breath, ready to argue with him, and he saw the anger flash in her eyes, and burn away. "You want me to take it from the inside for you."

"Because you can," he said. "You're stronger than Gregory. And you want what the rest of the Obscurists want: to be free. Once you're Obscurist Magnus—"

But Morgan was shaking her head now. "Not me," she said. "I can win the fight. I can't lead them, Jess; they don't trust me. They'll never trust me, and I can't blame them for that; I never made any secret of the damage I'd do if I had the chance. But . . ." She pulled in a breath and let it slowly out. "You understand what you're asking me to do? Go *back* in there? And if this fails . . ."

If it failed, he was sentencing her to a lifetime of slavery inside a prison. Alone. And he couldn't bring himself to admit that to her, out loud, so he only nodded.

"There might be someone else," she said. "Eskander."

"I don't know who that is."

"Some say he's more powerful than Gregory," she said. "But he locked himself away. Refuses to work or to speak with anyone. The only person he ever spoke to, as far as I know, was Wolfe's mother, when she was Obscurist. I've never seen him, not in person. But if I can convince him to help me, there might be a chance. A small one, but—" Her smile was beautiful, and shattered. "But you've been thinking this all along, haven't you? This was never about finding shelter. It was about planning the war. You're using your father as much as he thinks he's using you."

"Not from the beginning," he said. "But . . . yes. In a way, I suppose you're right."

"And Scholar Wolfe?" Her eyes searched his, looking for something he wasn't sure she'd ever find. "You know sending him there means sending him back to his death. And Santi will *kill* you."

"I'm sure he'll try," Jess said. "But I won't be the one taking you. That will be my brother."

Her lips parted, and then closed again, and it was strange: just as with Brendan, he didn't need to explain it to her. She knew. He saw the flash of it in her eyes, and the horror, and the understanding. She knew what was coming. And now he *did* feel lighter. A burden shared, at least. Neither of them worrying what would come next, because for this moment, at least, they had no more secrets.

"You can't tell the others," he said. "Not even Wolfe. He'd never be able to hide it from Santi, and . . ."

"And Santi would never accept it," she finished. "Agreed. Dario knows?"

"Yes. We'll need him." He didn't explain why, or how; it didn't matter just now. "But nobody else. The fewer of us, the better. I didn't even want to tell you, but—"

"But you knew I'd kill too many fighting," she whispered. "Of course." There were tears in her eyes, brief and bright, and then she blinked them away.

"I would have waited to tell you, but—"

"No. No, this is better. It gives us time. I knew—I knew you were keeping something from me. And now this is right again. We're right again."

"For as long as it lasts," he said. "Morgan—"

She put her hands on his chest, slipping beneath the fabric of his half-open shirt, and stopped his words, and thoughts, completely. All he could think of in that moment was the warm trail of her fingers moving on his skin, and then the tug as they released another button, and then the last, and eased the fabric off his shoulders. She leaned forward and kissed his bare skin, and his arms went around her and held her close.

"For as long as it lasts," she said, "let's make it something to remember."

And then she was kissing him, and it was all whispers and silence and heat, and no thought at all, and for the first time, when he fell asleep in this soft bed, it felt like heaven, and heaven included the young woman curled against him as if they would never again be apart.

EPHEMERA

An excerpt from a historical letter on the importance
of chess as a guide to war in the reign of King
Noshirvan of Iran

*Even as the wise have said, victory must be attained through wisdom
and forethought upon the field of battle. In this, we look to chess, for
the play of chess is that one must not wait for, or react upon, the movements of the other player, but rather comprehend one's opponent in
his person, and thus shape a game to his defeat.*

*As in war, chess requires one should preserve what one can, and
sacrifice what one cannot.*

Even to the sacrifice of the most valuable of pieces to win the game.

CHAPTER ELEVEN

"I think we've made a terrible mistake," Thomas said. He looked awful, Jess thought—pallid, sweating hard enough to paste little tendrils of blond hair flat to the sides of his face. His hands were steady, though. That was a good sign.

The bad sign was that he was using those steady hands to pluck at the knot of his silk tie. He looked very elegant—the Brightwell tailors being what they were—and the sober dark blue velvet of the jacket suited him well, but he seemed to *really* hate the tie. He couldn't leave the thing alone, and he'd already jerked it nearly out of position.

Glain slapped his hand away from his collar and stepped closer to pull the knot back into the right position. "Stop yanking at that, you baboon," she said. "Even my brothers aren't this bad at looking good."

"Easy for you to say. You get to wear what you like!" Thomas's gesture took in the thick leather jacket that poured sleekly around her in graceful, dangerous lines to her thighs. Beneath that, she wore a loose dark shirt, fitted dark pants, and heavy boots, and in her own way, she looked elegant. Deadly, but elegant. "Maybe if I put on the robe—"

"No Scholars' robes today," she reminded him. "This isn't a time to remind anyone about the Library, now, is it? Even the captain is out of uniform. You need to be, too."

Her brisk, matter-of-fact sureness settled Thomas, finally, and he took in a deep breath and nodded. He took out a handkerchief and wiped sweat from his face and attempted a vague smile. "I hate speaking in public," he said. "Jess, would you—"

"No," Jess said. He was dressed, like Thomas, in elegantly cut clothes; his tie was a dark purple to Thomas's wine red, and his jacket was black instead of navy blue, but they looked quite a bit alike. He hated the tie, too, but knew to keep his hands off it. "Pretend it's your first lecture. You'll do fine."

"Lecture," Thomas repeated, and paced a little. It was the sign of very well-done tailoring, Jess thought, when someone of Thomas's size could clasp hands behind his back and not create a wrinkle in the coat. "Lecture, yes, that's better than speech. Much better. And it is a lecture, you're right. I'm simply—"

"Explaining the principles and demonstrating the function," Jess said. "You have it. You'll be all right." He kept smiling. He'd split himself into two halves over the past few days: one half had wolfed down double portions of every dinner and kept them down. Had coldly calculated every aspect of this night and made all the arrangements. That half was howling with rage and anguish, silently. It was more than a little insane.

The other half—the half that smiled and talked and laughed and pretended that everything was all right—that half was a liar. A good one. Maybe the best that Jess had ever been at deceiving everyone, even himself. The only person he'd been able to become real with had been Morgan, and only in secret, in the darkness. Magic and regret and fear, and a longing that only grew stronger with the knowledge that it was all coming to an end.

"Just remember that these are murderous criminals who won't hesitate to kill us and dump our bodies down a well. Talk in small words," Dario said, and shook him out of memory. If Jess and Thomas looked elegant enough, Dario looked . . . well, like Dario, only intensified. He wore a black-and-gold brocade coat that swept from neck to ankles, and beneath that, like Glain, he'd favored a dark shirt and trousers, but he'd added a brocade vest in a black-on-black design that was both decadent and subtle.

Good enough to be buried in, Jess thought, and choked off the thought. The emotion. He needed to be silent inside. And empty.

"He doesn't mean that," Khalila said with an apologetic smile directed at him. *Don't; don't smile at me. Of all of them, I can't stand it from you.* She looked especially vivid tonight; the beautiful fine silk of her dress—wine red this evening, with a matching hijab with gold embroidery—was far better than what she'd been wearing for at least the past six months. She looked . . . happy. "And he certainly doesn't mean to insult you or your family, Jess."

He felt his lips stretch. He could see from the look in her eyes that it was right, that this empty mannequin was still convincing. "I'm sorry, did Dario say something? I never notice," Jess said. Dario grinned with bared teeth. Friendly, with an edge, as ever. There was a wild light in his eyes, a suppressed panic. And for a terrible moment, Jess was afraid that he was going to say something to upset everything.

He couldn't forget how Dario had looked this morning. For all his talk of chess moves and strategy, cold-blooded calculation and hard choices . . . when Jess had put the final plan to him, he'd flinched. Hard. *There's got to be another way.*

He'd convinced Dario there wasn't, and he could see the horror of it in his friend's face. He had to believe that Dario was steady enough to do this. He was the only one Jess could trust with it.

The only one, except for the other, vital piece of the puzzle.

"Is Morgan coming?" Khalila asked. "I expected her—"

"Now, I hope," Morgan said, and swept in the doorway. She looked *magnificent*—dressed in a long, fitted dress in dark gold velvet, with a black velvet jacket that hugged her in soft curves. Her hair spilled down in shimmering curls, and he remembered how it felt, having her hair in his fingers, her lips pressed to his. He didn't want to remember it, but there were some things, sharp things, that cut even through the darkness.

Her smile shattered him into a million pieces, and he had to turn away, to pretend to pick up a book he deliberately knocked from the table, because the reality of this was closing in around him and stealing the oxygen from his lungs. He wanted to scream. Seeing the strength in her eyes, the acceptance, even though she *knew* what was coming . . . it was harder to take than he'd thought.

Morgan knew. Dario knew. Brendan and Anit knew. But that was all. Everyone else, everyone, would smash into this at speed, and the results would be . . . unimaginable.

Jess swallowed and tasted the smoke of Philadelphia again. Walls closing in. Saw the tower collapsing.

Steady, said the other part of him, the mannequin with the smile and the straight back and the lies. *It's almost done.*

They stood in the huge, brooding, dark-paneled expanse of the great hall, waiting for the others. For Wolfe and Santi, Brendan and Callum Brightwell.

Wolfe and Santi arrived together. Both were dressed, as the orders from Callum had specified, in formal clothing; Wolfe, in utter defiance of the spirit of things, wore his Scholar's robe over his black velvet coat. Except for the coat, he looked much as he always did.

Santi, like Dario, wore a brocade jacket. His was a mix of navy and black, subtle enough, but just a little flash, with silver buttons that winked down the front and on the cuffs.

"You look very fine, Captain," Glain said.

"I've worn my share of dress uniforms. It isn't so different." Santi seemed on edge, Jess thought, as if he scented something in the wind. Jess faded back a step, put himself next to Morgan and at an angle. If Santi was searching for signs of trouble, he didn't want the captain reading his blank expression, any more than he wanted Glain to study him closely.

He was going to break, and it might just be for an instant, but if either of them saw it—

"Jess." He looked at Morgan, and she put both hands on his face and pulled him to her for a kiss. The shock of it stilled all the turmoil for a long, sweet moment, and when the kiss ended, she stayed close, lips touching his, to whisper, "We can do this."

He nodded, took her hands in his, and held them. Breathed in and out and found his balance again.

At the far end of the hall, wide double doors opened, and Brendan stepped inside. He was dressed formally, too, only his jacket was a dark gray, and he wore a bright blue silk vest beneath it. No tie; he'd substituted a loose cravat instead. "Ladies and gentlemen," Brendan said, and his voice rolled and echoed through the cavernous space, over the bookshelves and the ornate couches and chairs and walls. "Dinner is served. Follow me."

"Pretentious prat," Jess muttered, and offered his elbow to Morgan. She took it, and the light touch of her hand on his arm, even through the coat, seemed to tingle against his skin.

"I heard that," Brendan told him as they passed.

"Meant it," Jess replied. The backs of their hands brushed, and when Jess glanced at him, he saw that his brother's face was pale but calm. He'd carry this through.

The dining hall's formal table was set for forty, and almost all of the chairs were already filled with Callum Brightwell's guests, save for the ones reserved for Jess and his friends, and Brendan. No Anit; she was waiting at her ship.

As Jess led them in, with Thomas and Glain, Dario and Khalila following, the men and women at the table stood silently, waiting. Once they'd all reached their chairs, and Brendan had gone to Callum Brightwell's right hand at the top end of the table, Jess's da said, "Welcome, all of you," and took his seat. There was a great rush of scuffling and rustling, and then they were all seated, and the meal was under way. Jess found himself next to a scruffy old man in a suit that had seen better days; he vaguely remembered him. Another smuggler, named Argent. Morgan, across the table from him, was next to a younger, scarred man called Patel, who seemed completely at ease in his very fine evening dress. Dinner proceeded with perfect elegance, course by course, and Jess couldn't force himself to do more than pretend to take bites. He made small talk as best he could. Morgan fared better.

They were halfway through the main course—lamb, though Patel had received a vegetarian option—when the old salt next to Jess said, too loudly, "It's said you were at Philadelphia when it was destroyed. Likely they meant *before* it was destroyed, eh? Couldn't have been there when the bombs fell, could you?"

It was probably meant for casual conversation, but it hit their end of the table like, well, a globe of Greek fire. They all froze in place, knives and forks stilled. Everyone looked at Jess, who slowly put his utensils down and reached for the wineglass. He took a generous gulp, didn't taste it, and said, "We were there." It was just three words, said softly enough, and he was proud that they didn't signify any emotion at all. Morgan was looking at him with wide, worried eyes. "When the bombs started falling." He picked up his knife and fork and began cutting meat again. He chewed and swallowed, and that was a mistake, because the sweetish taste of rank smoke came back to him, and he nearly coughed. He reached for the wine again.

"Well, young lads and ladies, that is a truly remarkable thing," said the old man at his left elbow. "The cleverness of smugglers, eh? Come out by one of the cousins' tunnels, did you?"

Patel was more sensitive to their stillness, their silence, and he leaned forward and said, "Perhaps not the time, Mr. Argent."

"We didn't have any help from smugglers," Dario said. He had his wineglass in his hand, too, and fire in his dark eyes. "We got ourselves out. Together."

Not entirely accurate; Brendan *had* helped, but Brendan was twenty chairs away and couldn't hear, and Jess didn't feel the need to defend him.

"You were prisoners of the Burners?" Patel asked, very politely indeed. Jess fervently wished he'd abandon the topic. They all did. But Khalila nodded, equally polite.

"For a time," she said. "And while we don't like what they stand for, the destruction was—" Khalila, of all people, was suddenly at a loss for words. She glanced at Jess, but he had nothing to say. Even Dario stayed silent.

It was Morgan who said, very quietly, "It was inhuman. And none of us wish to remember it. I'm sorry. We're lucky to be alive, and we know that."

Patel said, "Of course. I'm sorry." When Argent began to ask something else, Patel shook his head so sharply that the old man, too, fell silent, and the next comment was some grumble about the cold northern weather, which they could all agree to.

After dinner, it was time for the show.

They, of course, were the show.

Argent was right about the weather; even swathed in coats at the door, crossing the open space to the carriage house workshop was a reminder of just how unfriendly England could be; tonight, it was icy rain and fog, and they moved quickly into the warmth of the workshop. Thomas had tidied it up a bit, but even so, there was just barely enough space for everyone to crowd in out of the cold . . . but unlike Philadelphia, there was no expectation of destruction to come.

Thomas mounted the small, improvised steps and stood there uncomfortably next to his machine. He cleared his throat, opened his mouth, and then closed it again without speaking. He gestured to Jess, who sighed and came up to join him.

"You talk!" Thomas whispered fiercely.

"No," Jess whispered back, and took the spot at the controls of the machine. Not a simple lever anymore. This was a small stand of levers and switches, and Thomas threw him a look of hurt betrayal . . . and then, with a deep breath, the German started speaking. He started out a little uncertainly, but before long, just as Jess had thought, he was well into the details and comfortable with them. Talk of *ink density* and *valve pressure* and *tensile strength*. The audience looked intrigued but still not impressed, and when Thomas's explanation came to a halt, Jess flicked the first switch.

The only thing that happened was that the large copper boiler in the corner began to hiss as it built up pressure. It was decidedly *not* impressive.

"Is this all?" Old Man Argent asked, and ostentatiously checked his pocket watch. "I didn't come to the hinterlands for an oversized kettle and vague promises—"

The hiss in the boiler reached a high-pitched whine; Jess flicked another switch. The machine lurched into motion. A roller spread ink over letters set in a metal plate. The watching crowd fell silent and craned forward to watch.

"Step one," said Thomas. "The master plate is inked." He nodded, and Jess turned the next lever, which pulled a thick roll of paper into place and stretched it over the plate—not close enough to touch. "Now, the paper. You notice that it is in rolls, not in sheets, for speed." Thomas looked at Jess, who nodded. "And now, the printing."

Jess flipped the final two switches together, and the paper was pressed down, lifted up, measured out, and cut with a sharp blade. It settled in the tray, and already, the next page was in place, the ink ready, the process repeating.

"We can print copies of the page at the rate of almost a hundred per minute, when we turn the speed higher," Thomas said over the steady thrumming of the machine. "And as you will see, we print two pages at once—the first and the last of the folio."

Thomas plucked the first sheet from the drying pile, and in the bright lights of the workshop, Jess felt a strange, exhilarating chill run through him. There, in block letters on the paper, were two full pages of text in Greek that had never been seen before by anyone but them. There was so much wrong with what would happen tonight.

But this . . . this was right. And important.

Thomas held the page up for all to see. "The first and last pages of *Hermocrates*, by Plato," he said. "Suppressed by the Great Library since Scholar Plato's death. Careful. The ink needs time to dry. This is one of the books we rescued from the Black Archives." The murmurs started then, and built. Thomas raised his voice again to be heard. "These are words that few living people have read. *This* is what the Library has kept from us. This, and so much more. But with this machine, they no longer have that power."

One of the guests stepped forward—a tall woman, severe in a long black gown. Jess vaguely remembered her from his childhood—a refugee Frenchwoman who had built up a business in smuggled originals out of Sardinia. "If none of us have ever read it, you could have made up the words, no? We're not blind fools. We've seen false miracle machines before that turn lead to gold, or glass into steel."

Jess reached for a leather case that lay on the table near him, opened it, and took out the scroll. He handed it to her. "The original's here. You can compare it for yourself."

They had to almost shout now to be heard over the press, which continued to print page after page, slotting them into racks for drying. The thick smell of hot metal and ink made some of the visitors hold their noses, but they weren't leaving. They were crowding forward, experts all, to examine the original and then the copy.

"Word for word!" one man exclaimed. "And you can print the rest? Page by page?"

"Yes. We can print anything. We have letters and symbols cast for seven languages already, and more to follow. It's as simple as putting the letters and symbols together in the tray," Thomas said.

"It's not that simple," Jess said in a quieter tone, but just to him.

"No point in disillusioning them with details," Thomas whispered, then went back to a near shout. "We will turn off the press now, and you may inspect it for yourselves!"

Jess shut it all down, reversing the order, and with a last, hissing sigh, the press went idle again. There were enough copies drying in the rack for every single one of Callum Brightwell's visitors to go home with a souvenir.

And now Callum was taking the stage, as Thomas gratefully descended. Jess stayed where he was, not from any desire to be there, but his father was blocking his way out. "You see the beginnings of this," his da said. "Yes, it's a loud, noisy, smelly process. Yes, it takes an investment of time and ink and paper, bindings and skill. But *you can print books*. Any books. Sell copies of whatever you'd like. The Great Library doesn't control this machine. It can't even see it, or the pages that come off this press. This machine renders the all-seeing eye of Horus blind." He looked at the machine with something, Jess thought, like real reverence. "It's freedom."

There was a roar of suddenly competing questions, protests, all vying for attention. Some people pressed forward to demand detail from Thomas, who immediately started providing them. Some were hanging back, arguing with one another.

And one stepped forward to say, "Freedom, you say? Freedom to what? Destroy our own businesses? Get us all killed?" The man was speaking so precisely his words could have been printed on the press in sharp edges and ink. "You'll destroy our family with this— abomination. And what do you think the Library will do? They'll kill us for just *seeing* this!"

"It's a temporary loss and risk for a vast long-term gain, Cormac. With this machine, *we* become our own library. We sell endless copies of every book, to every set of hands eager to hold one . . ." The glitter in Callum Brightwell's eyes was as much greed as hope. "Imagine the possibilities. Hand-tooled bindings, engraved with the name of the printer, or the owner. Gilded titles. Mass production of forbidden classics! There's nothing people want more. Even the Burners would pay good money to get their hands on those books. And the plans for this machine. *Which we now own*."

"I still say it's a leap," said Cormac, but he seemed less against it now. In fact, most of those talking seemed to be discussing possibilities now, not penalties. "And how long does it take to build one of these things? We'd need an Artifex to do it, and they're all Library sworn—"

"It's not that difficult," Thomas said. "We can show you. And there are many Library-trained mechanics who can easily build, run, and repair these machines."

"Ink and paper, though," mused one elderly man, who leaned on his cane. "They must be secured in large quantities. Might draw suspicion."

"Not if you buy the company that makes them," Callum said. "And I've already acquired one of each right here in England. They'll supply what we need to our own specifications. My son Jess will be in charge of the business of the presses, while I continue to oversee our rare books." He glanced at Jess and, for the first time, smiled at him. Really, warmly smiled. Knowing what he did, Jess felt a tide of dizziness come over him in a shuddering wave. He couldn't bring himself to smile back. "And my son, who's also participated in the building of this press, will answer any questions you may have on the workings of the machine. Along with inventor Thomas Schreiber, of course. The credit for this engine of change goes to them."

"No," Jess said, and held up his hands. "No." He met Thomas's gaze and got the nod he expected. "Not to us. You have to understand: this machine has existed for hundreds of years. Discovered by Scholar after Scholar, who died for their daring to imagine it. We aren't the first. We're just the ones who survived to tell you, and show you, what the world can be. If you want to give credit, give it to Scholar Gutenberg, who was murdered for this idea. And to Scholar Christopher Wolfe, who suffered for it in prison, at the hands of the Archivist." Wolfe deserved the recognition, tonight of all nights. He saw Santi and Wolfe turn, saw Wolfe's face, blank for a moment, and then full of some storm of emotion Jess couldn't properly read. Didn't want to know.

People turned toward Wolfe in silence, and for a long moment, no one seemed to quite know what to do. Then someone applauded, a lone clap of hands. A scatter joined in, and then a wave, then a roar. Jess watched as Wolfe bowed slightly, accepting the applause. Santi squeezed a hand on Wolfe's shoulder. All of his friends were smiling now, applauding . . . all except Glain.

Glain was watching Jess, with a sharp intelligence that alarmed him. He turned away to talk to an imperious old man who wanted to inspect the type pieces in the tray, and felt her continuing to watch him.

He'd known his false face couldn't hold with her. Not for long.

His da was suddenly at his shoulder, and slapped his back and whispered, "Well done, son. Though I'd rather have *not* drawn attention to the bloody Scholar." And then he was gone down the steps to press palms.

As Jess stepped to the floor, Brendan blocked his way. For a moment, they just looked at each other, and then his twin threw his arms around him in a quick, fierce embrace. "Now I'll never catch up to you. Always seconds and steps ahead, you are. Why did you have to make it more difficult than it has to be?"

"Shut up, Scraps," Jess whispered, and the little broken pieces inside him healed a bit—crooked, perhaps. A touch brittle. But better. "You run your own race. You always have." He shoved his brother away. "Doesn't mean I can't still beat you if I have to."

"Right. And now I'm going to pretend to be you and tell people absolute bollocks about how this thing runs. Meet me in ten minutes." Brendan slipped away into the crowd.

When he turned, he found Morgan next to him. The room was full of noise, and it seemed too loud, suddenly, too warm, and he grabbed her hand and pulled her through the crowd, nodding at those who wanted to congratulate him, answering a few questions about power and capacity, and then they were through and out into the icy, whispering fog. The rain had stopped, though it glittered like diamonds on the branches of the old trees in the forecourt. The heavy bulk of the fortress loomed over them, stone and steel. No stars showing, just some dim, cloud-veiled moonlight.

Enough for him to see her, even in the shadows by the carriage house. Enough for him to kiss her. The dark floral scent of her rolled over his senses and blotted out everything else but the feel of her skin, the taste of her mouth. It was a long, sweet kiss, and when they finally parted, she just held him tight. "I know," she whispered. "I know."

"I can't do it," he said. He wanted to scream. He wanted to gather her up and take her somewhere, *anywhere*, to hide with her and pretend none of it was happening, none of it would ever happen. He wondered if some part of her wanted that, too. He didn't think so. She wasn't the coward he was. "I was wrong. I can't see this happen to them. To you. Morgan—"

She took hold of his tie to pull him even closer. He wondered rather wildly just how secluded this spot truly was, and whether they could find deeper shadows . . . and then she broke the kiss with a gasp and pulled back, lips damp and parted, eyes shining with tears. He hadn't meant to make her cry. Never that. "I'm not the one in danger," she said. "But Wolfe—"

"He's a survivor," Jess said. "We know that. I'm more worried about what the captain and Thomas will do tonight when they realize what's happening. Do what you can to protect them. Please."

She nodded and said, "I've got to go back in."

"Make sure that Dario does his part when you do," Jess said. "Make it look good."

He heard the distant bells from the clock tower and pulled out a pocket watch to check the time. He needed to go, but something in him wouldn't let go of her hand, as if he knew this might be the last time he held it.

Some of his father's guests were spilling out of the carriage house now, still talking, arguing, every one of them clutching one of the printed pages. Some had wrapped them into tubes, like scrolls; some had carefully folded them in half, to read later. All of them cradled them as if they were sacred, valuable objects. As usual, Callum Brightwell was going to get his way. And make a profit.

Jess saw that Callum was working his way toward a particular spot as well. He could see the Brightwell guards changing positions. Moving to plan.

"Go," he said, and lifted Morgan's hand to his lips. He kissed the back of it and saw her lips part. She said something, but it was lost in the noise of the crowd around them as the guests spread out.

Then she turned and was gone, walking through the crowd to stand close to Santi. He felt cold. Alone. Separated from them now, the last tie cut, the last chain broken. Already, some of Da's guests were calling for their vehicles. Da had one of his trusted men taking payments—discreetly, of course—at a gilt-edged table set up near the exit. Even the toughs were dressed in real finery this evening, though most looked uncomfortable about it.

Thomas came barreling at him and wrapped him in a smothering embrace. "Thank God I won't have to lecture again." He lowered his voice to a rough whisper. "Where are you going?"

"To piss," Jess said, and shoved him back. "And the joke's on you, Mountain. You'll have to lecture all over Europe before long, once your press becomes famous."

"*Ach*, you're no fun," Thomas said. "Come back here. Dario's promised to steal one of your father's prized wines."

"I will," Jess said. Thomas started to turn away, and on impulse, Jess held out his hand. Thomas frowned at it. "Congratulations. You've done the impossible, you know. You've made Callum Brightwell believe in something."

"I've made your father believe in money," Thomas said archly, but he took Jess's hand and shook it anyway. He didn't let go. "You don't look well, Jess. Is something wrong?"

"Tired," Jess said, and smiled. "Go on with you. I'll see you soon."

"All right."

He watched Thomas walk away and had to close his eyes and take deep breaths against the pain.

He needed to get to Brendan. He avoided the last few questions with an apologetic smile and jogged up the steps and into the castle hall. Crossed the vast open space with long strides, short of breath, his heart pounding like he'd run a marathon.

He'd almost gotten to the stairs when an arm like an iron bar closed around his throat and pulled him sharply backward, and he felt the sharp sting of a knife under his chin.

"Stay still," Glain said. "And explain to me what the *hell* you're planning to do."

"Let go!"

"Not going to happen, Jess. You haven't been right all day. I saw it when you looked at Wolfe. You looked like you were giving a damned eulogy at his grave, and you're going to tell me *why*!"

"*Let me go!*"

"If I have to slice you a new smile, Brightwell, I'll—"

Something hit her. Hard. Jess felt the impact of it throw her forward, and he was slammed into the hard stone of the banister. He twisted and grabbed her as she turned toward her attacker, and yanked her around to face him again. He couldn't let her see who had just hit her, and he moved faster than he would have believed possible, and with as much force as he could. With Glain, there was no possibility of pulling a punch.

He hit her square in the right side of the jaw, and felt a bone in his hand give with a bright red slash of pain. Her head snapped to the side, and she went down. He eased her to the floor and checked her pulse. It was there, slow and steady. She was out but wouldn't stay that way for long.

"*Dios*, is she dead?" Dario asked. He stood there looking as pale as Jess had ever seen him, with a small marble bust clutched in a death grip in his right hand. His voice was shaking. *He* was shaking.

"What are you doing here? You're supposed to be out there, with Morgan!"

"I saw her following you; I had to—"

"Go!" Jess grabbed the bust away, and Dario turned and ran for the castle entrance.

Glain was already starting to rouse—vague movements, eyes rolling behind the closed lids. Jess left the bust there, kicked the knife off into the shadows, and ran to meet his brother.

He found him waiting in the chapel, just where they'd agreed. The peace of the place, the ancient weight of it, felt suffocating, and when Jess came to a halt, he saw the compassion in his brother's face.

"You look as bad as I've ever seen you," Brendan said. "You can still change your mind."

"No. I know what I'm doing."

"It'll be easier for me. You know that."

"Shut up, Scraps."

"Call me that again and I'll knock you over the head and hide you in a corner."

"You thought about doing that already."

"Of course I did." Brendan gave him a broken little smile as he untied his cravat. "And I might yet, if you don't hurry up."

Brendan removed his gray jacket and cravat and handed them over. Jess gave him the tie and black coat, and the two of them dressed in silence. Brendan swept his hair back. "Scar," Jess reminded him.

"Already gone. Your girl fixed it for me. I'm going to miss it, a bit. Just make damned sure your friend hits you in the right place to make it stick." Brendan took a breath and straightened his back. "There. Do I look like enough of a sad, bookish arse?"

"Do I look enough like a cutthroat thief?"

"You'll do," Brendan said, and stuck out his hand. "*In bocca al lupo,* brother."

"*Crepi il lupo,*" Jess replied. He ignored the hand and embraced him, fast and hard, before he turned on his heel and walked out of the chapel. He had to be right now. Focused. Utterly right. *I'm Brendan Brightwell. Shining son of this castle and this fortune. And I walk like I know it.* He lengthened his stride, took on the easy, swinging gait of his brother, and as he did, he stuck his hands in his coat pockets. The clips Brendan had gotten from Da were there. Three of them. Two in the right pocket, one in the left. They felt cool and inert.

Glain was coming up the stairs as he was going down. He flashed her Brendan's wild grin, and she ignored him, gaze sweeping up. Her eyes were a little unfocused, and she was holding on to the banister with one white-knuckled hand. "Where's your brother?" she asked.

"Not his keeper," he said. "I think he just went out the front. Why?"

She turned and ran down the steps. Stumbled and nearly fell, and Jess saw blood on the back of her head, matted in her hair. He resisted the urge to run after her. He followed at a deliberate walk, testing himself. Slowing his pulse. Stilling his thoughts.

The guests had cleared the courtyard. Brightwell guards had

shown them all politely out, and as Jess, no, *Brendan, I'm Brendan,* came out the castle entrance, the drawbridge chains clattered, and the only exit from this place shut with a loud, final *boom.*

Callum Brightwell gave him a narrow look. "Where is he?"

"Upstairs, in the chapel," Jess said. He kept his face turned away, so the lack of a scar that distinguished him easily from his brother couldn't be spotted. "Did the other one come out?"

"The Welsh girl? Yes." Callum nodded off to the side, and when Jess turned that way, he saw that Glain was down on her face, with three guards kneeling on her as they chained her at the neck, wrists, and ankles. She was unconscious again. He remembered the blood in her hair and hoped desperately that they hadn't hit her too hard.

"My advice? Send her off with Anit," Jess said. He kept it light, almost casual. "From what Jess let slip, she might have some money to her name, and besides, we'll be dealing with the Welsh king soon enough. Bad form to be slaughtering his subjects when we don't need to."

His father grunted but didn't give any sign whether he'd take that advice or not. Jess couldn't force it, not without making things worse.

"Santiago, Wolfe, Seif, Santi, and Hault are together," Callum said. "Santiago bribed Grainger to bring them a bottle of my best. When he goes in with it, Grainger will pull Santiago and Seif off with him. Taking them will be easy enough, I think. It's the other three who concern me. We need Wolfe and Hault alive and undamaged. You're certain you can manage that on your own?"

"Yes," Jess said. "I think so. They trust me well enough."

"Pity you couldn't pretend to be your brother. We'd have had them all, quick as lightning."

Jess forced a laugh and moved off, because if he hadn't, he would have dragged his father's gun from his belt and damned himself to hell for murder. He kept moving, past where Glain had fallen, and into the lights outside the carriage house. It came to him with sudden, violent conviction. *Dario's going to crack. He's going to forget where to hit me, and this will all come apart. If Grainger gets sight of me without a scar . . .*

Jess paused and picked up a stray, sharp piece of stone from a pile beside the entrance, and without thinking about it, sliced it in exactly the spot where he knew his brother's scar would be. Blood jetted out, and the pain blinded him; he fought for a breath, then two, then three, and then found a handkerchief in his brother's pocket and clamped it to the wound. No disguising it, of course. But that was the plan.

He dropped the stone and walked into the workshop. No sign of Thomas in here; Jess wondered where he'd gone and realized his father hadn't spoken of him. They'd drawn him off, somehow. That was probably wise. Taking Thomas in close quarters would be dangerous, if not impossible.

He tried not to think about that, and sailed in as if he were Brendan, as if he hadn't a care in the world except for the bloody wound in his head.

Khalila leaped to her feet in an instant and rushed to him. "Brendan! What happened?"

"Nothing," he said, and pushed past her. "Family squabble. I'm fine." Rudeness was the only defense against her right now, when he wanted so badly to look at her, apologize, beg for her forgiveness. Dario was coming now, and he gave Jess a horrified look, and then it turned to relief.

"Let me guess," he said, shifting back to the Dario Jess had always known and loathed. "You pushed your brother once too often? He's got a bite, that one."

"Tell me about it," Jess said. "He gave me the scar in the first place—did you know that? Trust him to hit me in the same spot again. Grainger's coming with your wine. Any moment now. Relax, you won't die of thirst."

Dario understood that perfectly, and he drew Khalila away with him, out of Jess's path. When she started to follow, Dario held her hand. "No, wait, flower. I need to tell you something." Jess almost, *almost* hesitated. If Dario lost his nerve now . . . but then he heard Dario continue, in a fierce, fast whisper, "I love you. I've always loved you. I will always love you. And I am entirely the wrong man for you, I know this. But I have to ask: will you do me the honor of marrying me? If you don't wish that, Khalila, tell me, and I will leave you—"

Silence.

Jess risked a glance back and saw she was kissing him. Dario broke the kiss with a gasp and put his arms around her.

Khalila said, in a voice that was full of heartbreaking happiness, "I do wish it. And don't you dare leave me, Dario Santiago."

Dario held her close and stared at Jess with a terrible joy in his eyes. *I had to,* it said. *I had to know.*

And maybe he was right to do it. They might never have another chance to be happy.

Jess was five steps from Morgan, Wolfe, and Santi. Then three steps. And then he stopped and managed to wink his good eye at Morgan. "Nothing fatal," he assured her. "Not that you'd care, I suppose."

She said nothing, but she stepped forward and pulled his arm down, and the handkerchief away from the open wound. Before he could take a breath, she'd drawn her fingers across it, and he felt the hot twinge of her power washing over him. Saw gold and black stars, and then blinked them away. When he reached up to touch the spot, he found it closed. Healed shut.

"It'll leave a scar," she said, "but then, you already had one anyway. Where's Jess?"

Her voice was steady, and her eyes bright on his. *Don't look at me like that. Like I'm still Jess.* But she wasn't, he realized. She was just afraid, and he saw her gaze shift behind him.

"Ah, the wine," Dario said, too loudly, and let go of Khalila as he turned to face Grainger, who held up the bottle. Jess dropped the bloody handkerchief to the floor, and at the last moment, he looked to the corner, where Frauke lay.

She was entirely still. No sign of life at all.

Morgan had been tasked to turn the automaton off, and she'd remembered, thank God, because in the next instant, it all became suddenly, crashingly real.

All the pieces moved, and adrenaline slowed to a precise, clockwork crawl. Jess stepped forward, one hand diving into his pocket. He came out with a Translation tag, one of three his father had procured for Brendan. He heard the first indrawn breath behind him, as the wine bottle hit the flagstones and shattered, as Grainger grabbed Dario from behind.

Two more guards rushed in. He heard the commotion, didn't bother to look, because he was staring at Wolfe now. The older man was looking past him, at Dario and Khalila, starting to react to their danger.

He didn't realize his own. Not yet.

And then Wolfe's gaze skimmed across him, and those dark eyes widened, and Jess saw the exact instant when he knew what was going to happen. Wolfe was quick and strong, and Jess knew that he had to be faster, stronger, and entirely ruthless.

He threw himself forward and slammed the Scholar back against the wall. He smelled something burning, thought it was the smoke of Philadelphia, but it was the stench of a burn mark on the wall, and Wolfe's head was against that crack, and he was bracing himself to push forward. His hands were coming up to punch, and he was already twisting and trying to pull free.

Jess took the blow that Wolfe landed on the side of his head. It staggered him, but he didn't let it stop his motion. His right arm slammed hard against Wolfe's throat and pinned him in place.

His left clipped the Translation tag to Wolfe's collar, and in that last instant, as their eyes locked, Jess saw the hell of despair in the man's eyes, and something else. Resignation. Acceptance of an end of things. *I'm sorry,* Jess wanted to say, but Brendan wouldn't.

Brendan wouldn't be sorry for any of it.

Santi was coming for him, he felt it like the heat before a fire, and he knew he was out of time. Only two seconds had really passed since he'd lunged, but that was all the grace period he was going to get.

Jess tapped the Translation tag and felt the wash of energy rush out of him and into the tag, and Wolfe opened his mouth and let out a scream of despair and pain as the alchemical energy contained in the clip ripped through him and tore him out of the world, and into it somewhere half a world away.

Off to Alexandria.

There was another scream, one right next to him, loud enough to deafen him, but it wasn't pain. It was *rage*, pure, unbridled rage, and Jess ducked and twisted out of the way just as Santi grabbed for him.

Wolfe was gone. He was *gone*. And Santi was going to rip his head off.

He dodged and rolled over the trestle table, and as he did he saw a whirling kaleidoscope of violence: Dario, down on the floor and screaming Spanish curses while his chains were clapped on. Khalila Seif armed with an iron bar that she'd pulled from next to the furnace, weaving and dodging the guards who were closing in on her. She lunged and stabbed one through the heart, but the iron bar caught in the man's ribs, and as he fell, she was disarmed.

She screamed something in Arabic and lunged at them anyway, a beautiful, defiant, graceful whirl of silk and power.

There was nowhere for her to run, but she wouldn't give up, and he loved her fiercely for that.

Jess rolled off the table, landed on his feet, grabbed Morgan by the throat. He backed into the corner and used her as a shield against Santi—a different Santi than he'd ever seen, a wild tiger that checked his spring at only the last second when he realized that he'd have to go through Morgan to reach his enemy.

"In bocca al lupo," he whispered against Morgan's ear, and pressed his lips there, just for an instant. Then he slipped the second tag onto the collar of her dress and activated it, too. She didn't have a chance to reply to him, if she'd intended to. *Kill the wolf, Morgan. Kill it for me.*

As her body dissolved in a tormented whirl, Jess braced himself and kicked out, hard. He caught the captain with both feet in the chest and sent him flying back, into the arms of two guards, and before Santi could break free they slammed him down on the table, and the chains were going on.

Jess stood there breathing hard, gagging on the knowledge of what he'd done. Khalila was still free. She'd killed two men now, but as he watched, he saw one slip behind her and pin her, and then it was over; she was finished, too. Dario was begging her to stop, stop fighting. He was nearly in tears.

Where's Thomas? He wanted to throw up, suddenly, to weep, to scream, but he couldn't allow himself to do any of that.

Because his father was walking into the room, taking a quick and efficient count of the damage and the gain.

His gaze stopped on Jess—no, on Brendan. Took in the blood on his face, but Jess knew he wouldn't mention it.

He didn't. He said, "Are they away?"

"Gone," Jess said. He kept the answer short, because he was afraid of what he'd say otherwise. "And where's Thomas?"

That was the moment when the wall behind him, the cracked wall, suddenly and catastrophically collapsed, and Jess fell backward into a pair of enormous, grasping hands that closed around his throat and dragged him painfully over the rubble.

Thomas. Oh God, it was *Thomas.*

His friend was bloodied, but he wasn't down. There were four guards around him, but he was tossing them around like children, and his whole focus was on the Brightwell son he held.

Whom he yanked into the air and held there, dangling and choking.

Jess remembered Willinger Beck in Philadelphia, and the way Thomas had dismissed his violence toward the man. *If I hadn't played the German berserker . . .* But Thomas wasn't playing this time. There was nothing but rage burning in those huge blue eyes. Red veins had spread around the irises, and Jess knew that the only thing keeping him alive, the *only* thing, was that Thomas could see the other three behind him in chains. Dario. Khalila. Santi.

Thomas's lips drew back from his teeth. Jess had never realized how *big* they were, those teeth. How straight and white and utterly terrifying, with the inhuman fury burning above them.

"Let them go!" Thomas roared. His mild German friend hardly ever shouted, and he'd never unleashed this particular volume before, not that Jess had ever heard. "Or this one's dead!"

"Back away!" Jess heard his father shouting, but it was harder to hear now; between Thomas's enormous bellow, and the fast, loud beating in his eyes, nothing quite seemed right. He was fighting, he could feel that; his hands scrabbled at Thomas's fingers, trying to pry them away.

It wasn't going to work. Thomas was going to kill him, and they were going to kill *Thomas*, because Callum would lose a valuable hostage rather than his younger son. Besides, Thomas had already built his press. Drawn his plans. In Callum Brightwell's calculus, Thomas's value had already fallen below Brendan's.

There was only one chance, and Jess was just barely clear minded enough to realize it. He stopped fighting, dropped his right hand to his pocket, and fumbled inside. Found the tag.

He clipped it to his coat and slapped at it in the same motion. Couldn't tell at first if it worked, because the only sensations left to him were the black, panicked struggling of his lungs, and the cold, because it was getting so cold . . .

He didn't think he screamed, but if he did, it wouldn't have mattered. He caught one last glimpse of Thomas's fury shattering, and Thomas's hands opened to let him drop.

As the wolf took him midfall, Jess saw his friend's lips move. Saw the recognition slip into Thomas's face like a strike of lightning.

Jess?

And then he was gone, into the rushing darkness, where he would have to kill the wolf to survive.

EPHEMERA

**A contingency-of-death letter filed with the Scholar's
Archives, from Scholar Christopher Wolfe to High
Garda Captain Niccolo Santi. Interdicted to the Black
Archives. Not delivered.**

Nic,

*If you're reading this, my ghost is speaking to you. Ink and paper,
and a memory, because I'm gone. I hope I died well. I hope I died for
something, as I lived for it. But even if I didn't, if accident took me, or
illness, or a thousand meaningless happenstances, then it doesn't matter anymore.*

*The only thing that matters now is that you loved me. You never
should have, you know; I was, and remain as I write this, an unlov-
able man, full of flaws and cracks and terrible habits. From the
moment I saw you, I felt drunk on possibilities, but I knew I would
never deserve you. And I never have, through all of it. But still, you
remained.*

*I know you will be angry. I know you will want to drive out
your grief with action. Don't. For my sake, don't throw yourself into
battles, or pick fights with giants, or whatever mad thing comes into
your head. Live. Because when next we meet in your Christian heaven
or my pagan afterlife, or some shadowy, hidden corner where those
two may touch, I want to hear that you lived a long and happy life
after me. That you did as you liked, and loved as you liked, and left
the world shattered and empty in your wake.*

*Because that is the Niccolo Santi I know, and if a ghost can speak
of love, then know I adore you still. You are my beloved, and I will be*

waiting, and you must not take offense when people speak of me harshly, as I surely deserve. We never cared for their opinions, and we shouldn't now.

And if, with the help of the gods, you find I'm not dead, I will expect a proper good welcome, a bottle of wine, and to find the heaven I spoke of in your arms, because after being away from you, I will never want to be parted again.

Wolfe

CHAPTER TWELVE

When Jess came back in the world, he was on his back on a cool stone floor, and all he knew for a second or two was that he was going to be horribly, violently ill. He rolled on his side, but the spasms passed, and when he opened his eyes, he saw a blurry smear of color and light, heard shouts and voices. Saw running feet go past him, and then there was a hand holding him flat and a gun in his face.

The man kneeling over him wasn't familiar, but the uniform was: High Garda. Jess took in a slow breath and felt the familiar air of Alexandria fill up the empty ruins inside him.

Home.

"Who are you?" the soldier snarled. Jess coughed. Tried to get his breath. Tasted blood and that rotten smoke, and thought, *Who am I?*

But he knew who he had to be.

"Brendan Brightwell," he managed to croak. "I'm the one with gifts for the Archivist Magister; you know I'm coming. Get off me, you bloody fool; I'm expected!" His throat hurt like he'd gargled broken glass, and his head throbbed where Wolfe's fist had connected. He felt cuts and scrapes down his back, where Thomas had pulled him through the broken wall.

All in all, it was a miracle he was still breathing. But he'd have to resist the urge to collapse and enjoy it, because he'd hardly even begun this dangerous night.

The soldier looked up and over to someone else. "Who have you got there?"

"Sir, this is the rebel Scholar! Christopher Wolfe!"

"This one's the missing Obscurist," said another, farther away.

"Alive?"

"Both alive, sir."

Jess tried to swallow the wave of relief. He waited. His heart was pounding itself to bits against his ribs, and he wanted desperately to wage a fight he knew he would lose, but he did nothing. Seconds ticked by, and then the High Garda straddling him stepped off to the side and said, "Get up, you. Slowly."

Jess kept his hands raised and struggled to his knees, then—as instructed—slowly to his feet. "I'm here to make a deal," he croaked. "I've brought you two of the traitors in good faith. Shoot me, and you can explain to the Archivist how you lost ten thousand original books."

He finally risked a look at the others. Wolfe was flat on his stomach, and a High Garda woman knelt on him as she put his hands behind his back in restraints. Morgan looked barely conscious. He kept his face still, body loose, as he watched her being flipped over and cuffed, too.

Wolfe had raised his head at a painful angle to look at him. "You fool," he said. "What do you think you're doing? Your own brother's going to slaughter you. If Santi doesn't get you first!"

"I don't think my fate's your problem, Scholar," Jess said, in a croaking approximation of Brendan's careless, chilly tones. "Seems to me you've got bigger things to worry about. Like prison bars."

"And her? You think Jess is going to thank you for putting her back in the Iron Tower? You know what's going to happen to her, you cold bastard?"

"I don't know and don't care, because I'm not my weak-livered brother. She's not my concern." Jess wanted to take the fear from Morgan's eyes, the pallor from her face, but he had to play this out, *had to*. He looked at the soldier who faced him, and slowly lowered his hands and put them behind his back. "Take me to the Archivist, if you want to live to see the morning."

"Whatever you think you're doing, it won't work!" Wolfe shouted. The soldier with him dragged him up to his knees, and loose graying hair fell around his face. It didn't disguise the urgent fire in his eyes. *"Brightwell! It won't work!"*

For an eerie moment, it felt like Wolfe was talking to *him*. To Jess, not to Brendan. But Wolfe didn't know. They'd taken great care to leave him out of all of this. Wolfe, Dario had argued, could break. *Would* break. But in that second, Jess wondered if Wolfe knew. Had maybe known the entire time.

"Sorry, Scholar," he managed to whisper. Brendan's smile on his lips. Brendan's voice. But inside, his soul was tearing itself apart. "There's no turning back now."

And that was the moment when the door of the entry hall of the Archive of the Great Library opened and the Archivist Magister walked in. Oh, not alone. Not by half. He had a dozen High

Garda elite guards around him. He wore a rich, thickly embroidered robe of midnight blue, and a crown with the eye of Horus rising like the sun from his forehead. Gold and rubies, and worth a king's ransom.

He had an old man's face, worn and seamed and burned by years in the hot Egyptian sun, but his eyes were young. They missed nothing. Not the state that Jess was in, or the relatively undamaged captives.

"I met another Brightwell, once," the Archivist said. "He looked a great deal like you."

Jess spat blood onto the marble floor and grinned. He knew he looked half-savage. Didn't care.

"Yeah, well, I'm nothing like my fool brother," he said. "And you're going to want to keep me close, Archivist. Because I'm bringing you everything you ever wanted. Brendan Brightwell, at your service." He managed a mocking bow.

The silence rang for a long moment. Thomas, Jess thought, had done him a favor damaging his voice. Nothing about him would seem familiar now, not even that.

The Archivist considered all of it for what seemed far too long, and then nodded.

"We'll see," he said. "Take Scholar Wolfe to the cells. The girl goes back to the Iron Tower. And you, Brendan Brightwell . . ." The Archivist paused for so long that Jess had to ready himself for the end, for the sound of High Garda guns to be the last thing he heard. "You come with me."

They walked out of the vast hall of the Great Archives, into the heat of an Alexandrian day, and the smell of the only place he'd ever felt at home, and Jess thought, *Now all we have to do is play the game.*

But he had the eerie feeling that this game was barely even begun . . . and that it wasn't chess at all.

From here on out, it was war.

Continued in Volume 4 of

THE GREAT LIBRARY

SOUND TRACK

As always, music led me through all the dark corners and twisting paths this book took, and I hope you'll enjoy listening to the amazing talents of these artists along with me. Please purchase their music if you can; it keeps them able to create and bring us all more joy.

"Conrad"	SOHN
"Your Future Is Not Mine"	Daisy (feat. Joseph of Mercury, Illangelo Remix)
"Wild Horses"	Bishop Briggs
"River"	Bishop Briggs
"The Ballad of Mona Lisa"	Panic! At the Disco
"Genghis Khan"	Miike Snow
"Kissin' and Cussin'"	Carolina Chocolate Drops
"Emperor's New Clothes"	Panic! At the Disco

"Irresistible"	Fall Out Boy (feat. Demi Lovato)
"Shades of Otherworld"	Dagda
"Ophelia"	The Lumineers
"Daughter's Lament"	Carolina Chocolate Drops
"Way We Go Down"	Kaleo
"Moonshiner's Daughter"	Rhiannon Giddens
"Castle"	Halsey
"The Gifted People"	Dagda
"Reels 113"	Ellery Klein & Ryan Lacey
"I'm Born to Run"	American Authors
"Victorious"	Panic! At the Disco
"Good Die Young"	Molly Kate Kestner
"Empty Gold"	Halsey
"Home"	morgxn
"Pray (Empty Gun)"	Bishop Briggs
"Train"	Brick + Mortar
"Unsteady"	X Ambassadors
"Be Your Love"	Bishop Briggs
"Adventure of a Lifetime"	Coldplay
"Fire"	Barns Courtney

"Unbound"   Robbie Robertson

"The Way I Do"   Bishop Briggs

"Fire"   PVRIS

"Notorious"   morgxn

RACHEL CAINE

ASH AND QUILL

QUESTIONS FOR DISCUSSION

1. In the world of the Great Library, books are seen as valuable and revered objects. Are there any books you can think of that our current world sees in the same way?

2. Why do you think the Burners have been allowed to remain in possession of the City of Philadelphia for so long? What might have held the Library back from destroying it earlier?

3. Were you surprised that Jess and Dario had a plan to get the team safely out of England, in anticipation of Jess's family's betrayal? Why or why not?

4. When Jess trades places with his brother, what do you think his ultimate plan is? Did you expect him to do that?

5. Ultimately, who would you guess becomes the new Archivist in Alexandria? It could be any of our main characters. Who would be the best?

Read on for a preview
of the next Great Library novel,

SMOKE AND IRON

Available July 2018 from Berkley

EPHEMERA

Text of a letter from Red Ibrahim in Alexandria to
Callum Brightwell in England, delivered via secure
messenger

My most honored cousin in trade,

    I am advised by my daughter, Anit, that you have engaged in a
dangerous game with the Archivist Magister of the Great Library.

    I do not think, given your history and your legendary cunning,
that I need to remind you of the danger this brings, not just to you
but to all of us. While we sometimes use the Library in the pursuit of
our trade, we must never allow ourselves to be used in turn. An ant
cannot direct a giant.

    You have placed your son in the gravest danger.

    As one loving father to another, I beg you: call off this plan. Bring
your son home. Withdraw from any further engagement with the
Archivist. I will likewise have Anit deliver her captives back into your
custody, and you may do as you like with them, but pray do not continue to involve my family in this foolhardy venture.

    The Archivist may talk most pleasantly with you. A viper may
learn to talk, but it is still full of poison.

    Blessings of the gods to you, old friend.

Reply from Callum Brightwell to Red Ibrahim,
delivered via secure messenger

My son Brendan can well care for himself, but I thank you for your
concern. Should the worst occur, I still have his twin, Jess. He's not

presently pleased with me for sending his brother in his place, but I expect that will pass.

If you plan to lecture me, you might have taken greater care with your own sons—both lost to you now, advancing the cause of your own business. Don't lecture me on how to protect my own. As to your daughter, she entered into this arrangement on your behalf, and with your full authority; you may take up any misgivings you have with her, not me.

I expect you to uphold the agreement as she has made it. Anit and I are of like minds in this, and as she is the heir to your vast empire of commerce, you should listen to her. She's clever, and as ruthless as you, in many ways.

And you wouldn't like to make enemies of our families.

I think upon calm reflection you will see the wisdom of gathering the Library's favor as chaos gathers around us. The world is more unsafe now than it ever has been in living memory. Being allies with the Archivist means that their guard will be lower when we decide to turn these tables to our advantage, as we might at any time.

Peace be upon you, my friend. Let's see how this plays out.

CHAPTER ONE

JESS

It had all started as an exercise to fight the unending boredom of being locked in this Alexandrian prison cell.

When Jess Brightwell woke up, he realized that he'd lost track of time. Days blurred, and he knew it was important to remember how long he'd been trapped, waiting for the axe to fall—or not. So he diligently scratched out a record on the wall using a button from his shirt.

Five days. Five days since he'd arrived back in Alexandria, bringing with him Scholar Wolfe and Morgan Hault as his prisoners. They'd been taken off in different directions, and he'd been dumped here to—as they'd said—await the Archivist's pleasure.

The Archivist, it seemed, was a very busy man.

Once he had the days logged, Jess did the mental exercise of calculating the date, from pure boredom. It took him long, uneasy moments to realize why that date—today—seemed important.

And then he remembered and was ashamed it had taken him so long.

Today was the anniversary of his brother Liam's death. His elder brother.

And today meant that Jess was now older than Liam had lived to be.

He couldn't remember exactly *how* Liam had died. Could hardly remember his brother at all these days, other than a vague impression of a sharp nose and shaggy blondish hair. He must have watched Liam walk up the stairs of the scaffold and stand as the rope was fixed around his neck.

But he couldn't remember that, or watching the drop. Just Liam, hanging. It seemed like a painting viewed at a distance, not a memory.

Wish I could remember, he thought. If Liam had held his head high on the way to his death, if he'd gone up the steps firmly and stood without fear, then maybe Jess would be able to do it, too. Because that was likely to be in his future.

He closed his eyes and tried to picture it: the cell door opening. Soldiers in High Garda uniforms, the army of the Great Library, waiting stone-faced in the hall. A Scholar to read the text of his choice to him on the way to execution. Perhaps a priest, if he asked for one.

But there his mind went blank. He didn't know how the Archivist would end his life. Would it be a quiet death? Private? A shot in the back? Burial without a marker? Maybe nobody would ever know what had become of him.

Or maybe he'd end up facing the noose after all, and the steps up. If he could picture himself walking without flinching to his execution, perhaps he could actually *do* it.

He knew he ought to be focusing on what he would say to the

Archivist if he was called, but at this moment, death seemed so close he could touch it, and besides, it was easier to accept failure now than to dare to predict success. He'd never been especially superstitious, but imagining triumph now seemed like drawing a target on his back. No reason to offend the Egyptian gods. Not so early.

He stood up and walked the cell. Cold, barren, with bars and a flat stone shelf that pretended at being a bed. A bare toilet that needed cleaning, and the sharp smell of it was starting to squirm against his skin.

If I had something to read . . . The thought crept in without warning, and he felt it like a personal loss. Not having a book to hand was worse punishment than most. He was trying not to think about his death, and he was too afraid to think about the fate of Morgan or Scholar Wolfe or anything else . . . except that he could almost hear Scholar Wolfe's dry, acerbic voice telling him, *If only you had a brain up to the task, Brightwell, you'd never lack for something to read.*

Jess settled on the stone ledge, closed his eyes, and tried to clearly imagine the first page of one of his favorite books. Nothing came at his command. Just words, jumbled and frantic, that wouldn't sort themselves in order. Better if he imagined writing a letter.

Dear Morgan, he thought. *I'm trapped in a holding cell inside the Serapeum, and all I can think of is that I should have done better by you, and all of us. I'm afraid all this is for nothing. And I'm sorry. I'm sorry for being stupid enough to think I could outwit the Archivist. I love you. Please don't hate me.*

That was selfish. She should hate him. He'd sent her back into the Iron Tower, a life sentence of servitude and an unbreakable collar fastened tight around her neck. He'd deceived Scholar Wolfe into a prison far worse than this one, and an inevitable death sentence. He'd betrayed everyone who'd ever trusted him, and for what?

For cleverness and a probably foolish idea that he could somehow, *somehow*, pull off a miracle. What gave him the right to even think it?

Clank.

That was the sound of a key turning in a heavy lock.

Jess stood, the chill on his back left by the ledge still lingering like a ghost, and then came to the bars as the door at the end of the hall opened. He could see the hinges move and the iron door swinging in. It wasn't locked again when it closed. *Careless.*

He listened to the decisive thud of footsteps, growing louder, against the floor, and then three High Garda soldiers in black with golden emblems were in front of his cell. They stopped and faced him. The oldest—his close-cut hair a stiff silver brush around his head— barked in common Greek, "Step back from the bars and turn around."

Jess's skin felt flushed, then cold; he swallowed back a rush of fear and felt his pulse race in a futile attempt to outrun the inevitable. He followed the instructions. *They didn't lock the outer door. That's a chance, if I can get by them.* He could. He could sweep the legs out from under the first, use that off-balance body to knock back the other two, pull a sidearm free from one of them, shoot at least one, maybe two of them. Luck would dictate whether he'd die in the attempt, but at least he'd die fighting.

I don't want to die, something in him that sounded like a child whispered. *Not like Liam. Not on the same day.*

And suddenly, he remembered.

The London sky, iron gray. Light rain had been falling on his child's face. He'd been too short to see his brother ascend anything but the top two steps of the scaffold. Liam had stumbled on the last one, and a guard had steadied him. His brother had been shivering and slow, and he hadn't been brave after all. He'd looked out into the crowd of those gathered, and Jess remembered the searing second of eye contact with his brother before Liam transferred that stare to their father.

Jess had looked, too. Callum Brightwell had stared back without a flicker of change in his expression, as if his eldest son were a stranger.

They'd tied Liam's hands. And put a hood over his head.

A voice in the here and now snapped him out of the memory. "Against the wall. Hands behind your back."

Jess slowly moved to comply, trying to assess where the other man was . . . and froze when the barrel of a gun pressed against the back of his neck. "I know what you're thinking, son. Don't try it. I'd rather not shoot you for stupidity."

The guard had a familiar accent—raised near Manchester, most likely. His time in Alexandria had covered his English roots a bit, but it was odd, Jess thought, that he might be killed by one of his countrymen so far from home. Killed by the English, just like Liam.

Once a set of Library restraints settled around his wrists and tightened, he felt strangely less shaken. Opportunity was gone now. All his choices had been narrowed to one course. All he had to do now was play it out.

Jess turned to look at the High Garda soldier. A man with roots from another garden, maybe one closer to Alexandria; the man had a darker complexion, dark eyes, a neat beard, and a compassionate but firm expression on his face. "Am I coming back?" Jess asked, and wished he hadn't.

"Likely not," the soldier said. "Wherever you go next, you won't be back here."

Jess nodded. He closed his eyes for a second and then opened them. Liam had faltered on the stairs. Had trembled. But at the end his elder brother had stood firm in his bonds and hood and waited for the end without showing any fear.

He could do the same.

"Then, let's go," he said, and forced a grin he hoped looked careless. "I could do with a change of scenery."

Photo © 2013 Robert W. Hart

Rachel Caine is the *New York Times, USA Today,* and international bestselling author of more than fifty novels, including the Great Library series, *Prince of Shadows,* the Weather Warden series, the Outcast Season series, the Revivalist series, and the Morganville Vampires series.